I0719168

REVELATION

OLIVER EADE

THIRD BOOK OF THE
BEAST TO GOD TRILOGY

'Where there is no vision, the people perish...'

Proverbs, 29:18

Dedicated to Yvonne

Acknowledgements:
I wish to thank my family in Texas from where inspiration for this trilogy came, particularly our son, Jeremy, for taking us south over the border into Mexico, and north to the magnificent mesas of Colorado. As always, I am indebted to my unbelievably-patient wife, Yvonne, for coping with my ups and downs. Last, but by no means least, I must thank Iona McGregor, Pamela Gordon-Hoad and Wendy Leighton-Porter in Silver Quill Publishing for helpful support and advice and proofreading.

Story to date...
In _Golden Jaguar of Sun..._
Studiously shy, white Texan schoolboy, Adam, can't believe his luck when his vivacious Mexican classmate, María, dumps her bully of a boyfriend for him. He accompanies the girl, a musical prodigy, to record her first album in New York where unfounded jealousy takes hold after he sees her laughing and joking with a bunch of designer-stubbled media guys. Stupidity, spawned by jealousy, pushes him into the clutches of a teenage siren, Chrissy, who lures the naïve nerd, without María, to a party in Brooklyn. Here, hitherto-hidden bravery urges him to attempt to save an African-American boy, Lee, from drug pushers. On hearing Adam's been stabbed, presumed dead, María loses consciousness.

Adam, wearing a mysterious ancient Mexican golden jaguar bracelet given to him by María on the flight to New York, comes to in Ancient Mexico where María's double, Princess Arima, is to be sacrificed by the Aztecs to bring on the rain. He seeks out a second bracelet, in the knowledge that with two he might overcome the Golden Jaguar who guards the Temple of the Sun on the altar of which the girl is to have her beating heart ripped out. Feeling the love between the girl and the boy, the beast switches allegiance and rescues her, then, sensing who the girl really is, becomes her protector.

On learning that Arima is also María in a parallel universe, Adam vows his love for her, and they're married in that other dimension by a priest identical to his old Mexican friend, Papa Pedro, who runs an antiques shop in Houston.

The teens from Houston wake up at the same time in a New York Hospital. Adam, his survival considered to be a miracle, becomes a national hero for tackling the drugs dealers in Brooklyn.

Back at school in Houston, Adam is befriended by Álvaro, a Hispanic boy who helps him to deal with a rival in love, Fernando. Meanwhile, Papa Pedro's unexpected death triggers an unnatural fear of dying in the young singer, but María's morbid thoughts vanish after she's asked to record a second album in Mexico. She insists that Adam should accompany her.

Álavaro's Mexican cousin, Alejandro, plays host in Mexico City, and all goes well until María is kidnapped. A two-million-dollar ransom is demanded by the drug gangsters. Alejandro's friendship proves invaluable. With help from the Golden Jaguar bracelets and the mysterious 'Old Woman of the Hills', the boy and Alejandro learn that María is being held in the remote Chiapas jungle. As they approach the kidnappers' Mayan temple hideout, Alejandro, cousin of both Álvaro and a Columbian drug baron, Ramón, switches allegiance and takes Adam prisoner. Ramón, it transpires, plans to deflower María, a virgin, in front of Adam, for breaking up his New York syndicate, and threatens to kill the boy afterwards 'for her amusement'.

When Ramón arrives by plane, Adam uses the bracelets to call for the Golden Jaguar from the *Forest Without Time*. Alejandro escapes but the other gangsters, apart from Ramón, are killed. The Golden Jaguar leads the teenagers, together with their injured captive, Ramón, to a Mayan village. Here they're befriended as they await the return of a man called Plácido who is away with the only village truck selling hand-crafted goods to tourists in coastal towns.

Whilst playing soccer with Adam and some village boys, María gets bitten by a spider and dies. Unable to believe she's dead, Adam snatches up her body and takes her to the Golden Jaguar then on into the *Forest Without Time* where María is again 'alive'. They meet up with Papa Pedro and the Old Woman of the Hills and are told that to prevent María from dying they must go to the Mayan Place of Fear, Xibalba. If Adam can extract venom from the Great Spider Goddess, the old woman will make anti-venom. By returning María to the world of the living to relive the spider bite, he might prevent her death. In the netherworld of the forest, Adam also discovers from the deceased Papa Pedro that María is 'special', and should not have died, though he is not told why.

In Xibalba, Adam is helped by the legendary Mayan Hero Twins who appear as Art and Jeannie, his and María's friends from Iowa whom they'd first met at a singing contest in San Antonio, Texas, at which the girl was spotted by a talent scout. After Adam extracts venom from the giant spider, Art and Jeannie must fight off the evil Lords of Xibalba who, having seen María's beauty, now want her for themselves. Adam manages to escape with the girl to the *Forest Without Time* where the Golden Jaguar is waiting for them. The venom is delivered to the Old Woman of the Hills, and, with the anti-venom that she makes, they return to the Mayan village at a point in time moments before María gets bitten. Her death is prevented.

Plácido returns and drives them to the nearest town, Comitán, encountering Alejandro and the remaining drug gangsters *en route*. The Golden Jaguar re-emerges from the forest and kills Alejandro whilst the other gangsters, including Ramón, are taken prisoner. The beast informs Adam that there's another girl who is also 'special', but Adam knows that for him there'll only ever be María.

The youngsters from Texas return to their families after Ramón and his partners in crime are handed over to the police. One of the Mayan village girls, Anna, taken by Ramón, is returned to Mexico. On hearing that her husband committed suicide, she cannot face going back home and, befriended by María's family, goes with them to America. Now pregnant, she marries María's gentle cousin, Jorge.

In Houston, Adam discovers from a picture painted by his clairvoyant little sister, Chloe, that the child was aware of every detail of his and María's untold story, including her death and resurrection. Adam reckons Chloe must be that 'other girl' of whom the Golden Jaguar spoke. Perhaps, he wonders, she might hold the key to his future with the enigmatic María.

Continuing in ***The Merging***...
One night, Chloe awakens her brother to tell him about a 'real dream' girl who is in terrible danger. She appears to be Native American and is begging for help from Leaping Jaguar and White Deer who, Chloe is convinced, are also Adam and María. According to an ancient prophecy, the love between these two spirit animals saves the Native girl's people from destruction. Chloe has no idea who or where this child is. During the summer vacation, she and her brother accompany María to New York when the older girl records her next album, in the hope that their Aunt Jac, a New York lawyer who provides legal support for Native American communities across the country, will solve the mystery of the 'real dream girl with markings on her face'.

Chloe, irritated by lack of progress, reluctantly joins them for a meal with the African-American family of Lee, the teenage boy whom Adam saved from drug pushers the previous summer. Her avowed 'feminist' stance falls apart when she meets the boy. With Chloe being an accomplished artist, and Lee both kind and a keen photographer, they are immediately drawn to each other. Lee shows the blonde girl his photos, including some taken in the Ancient Puebloan ruins of the Mesa Verde in Colorado. In one of these, Chloe recognises the place where she meets her 'real dream' friend: a stone kiva in the Cliff Palace.

After María's album is recorded, Aunt Jac agrees to take them to Colorado. Chloe cannot be persuaded that the Native child whom she wants so much to help won't be living somewhere in the ancient Puebloan ruins. Once there, she runs off. Adam and María chase after her, but she vanishes in a kiva. By chance, Adam is wearing his golden jaguar bracelets and discovers, after one of the bracelets is rubbed, that something happens to a hole in the kiva's centre that connects the world of Man with Earth Mother. It changes. By standing over this hole, wearing and rubbing the bracelets, María and Adam are transported to the thirteenth century and reunited with Chloe.

The 'real dream girl' turns out to be Earth Child, the same age as Chloe, whose father is Chief Eagle Foot. The tribe has suffered a devastating drought for five years. Coyote Spirit, a brave and strong young warrior, who was lured south by a mysterious hooded trader from the land of the *Mexica* people to learn about their gods who might possibly save them all, has returned with a band of warriors. He challenges Eagle Foot's right to remain chief. Thrown out of the village, he starts to build a new city on the plain, frequently attacking the cliff face pueblos, making off with the women and gaining support from village men.

One morning, the scalp of Earth Child's mother is left on the ground outside the chief's house. Using her sixth sense, Chloe locates the woman's body for the chief. After burying his wife, the devastated husband is given an ultimatum by Coyote Spirit: either he yields himself up to the younger man or kidnapped women will be sacrificed to the gods on the temple that Coyote Spirit is building in his city.

Their father is taken away and Earth Child, believes, because of the ancient prophecy, that only Adam and María can now save the tribe from the terror of Coyote Spirit. She enlists help from the village shaman, Crouching Puma. He feels that Adam, also Leaping Jaguar, isn't yet ready to face Coyote Spirit; nevertheless, in a bid to save their father, the chief's daughter, together with her simple sixteen-year-old elder sister Swimming Beaver, María, Chloe and Adam, sets off to get help from her tribal plains cousins under the chieftainship of Running Buffalo. From here, Adam enters Coyote Spirit's city as a trader, hoping to discover where Eagle Foot is being held captive. A Native child leads him to her father from whom the boy learns that the chief is being held prisoner in his own pueblo back in the mesas.

Before leaving the city, Adam sees the Old Woman of the Hills heading for the unfinished temple. Against the Native child's better judgement, they follow her into the temple, emerging in a futuristic city where María, as Mariatli, is publicly made love to by a gigantic Coyote Spirit. Afterwards, he ignores the child's pleas to leave the city and goes to the palace to win María back. He finds her almost naked on a bed, teasing him about his feeble virility. Only after the Native girl concusses him with a blow to the head, and he comes to in the thirteenth century, is it apparent that Mariatli and that futuristic city came from his mind, created through the jealousy which plagued him ever since María dumped her previous boyfriend in middle school.

Adam returns to Running Buffalo's tepee community to learn that Swimming Beaver, still distraught over her mother's death, had disappeared for the day and won't say where she went. That evening, a ceremony is held in the Great Kiva to call upon the spirits and ancestors to help in the struggle against Coyote Spirit. During the ceremony, at which Adam is given a special drink by Swimming Beaver, the boy from Houston acts strangely, as if drunk and deluded. When Coyote Spirit enters the kiva with several warriors and demands María is given to him in exchange for Eagle Foot, Adam is too spaced out to prevent the huge Native leader from carrying the girl away in his arms.

All along, Adam feels a force inside him that seems to be trapped. When he calls for the Golden Jaguar, as he did in Mexico, nothing happens. Instead, jealousy plays havoc with his mind, and he truly believes his girlfriend gave herself willingly to Coyote Spirit. When he learns, because of Chloe's sixth sense, that María has been taken to the chief's house in the mesas, he decides to at least get María back for her family in Houston. Haunted by visions of Mariatli, he believes she has cheated on him. The power inside him, straining to be released, feels more trapped than ever before.

Using his karate, Adam easily overcomes Coyote Spirit's warriors and finds María in Eagle Foot's house. Her joy at seeing him is not reciprocated. Now treated like *his* captive, she is taken, with Chloe, to a secret cave in the valley to keep her away from Coyote Spirit. When Adam refuses to believe that she is still a virgin and calls her a whore, she tries to stab herself using a knife with which Coyote Spirit had intended she should kill Eagle Foot. Chloe intervenes and saves her life. Adam suddenly realises what a fool he's been and that María truly loves him. The Golden Jaguar, now merged with Adam, is released, and they make love twice inside the cave whilst Chloe waits patiently outside.

Empowered by the strength of the Golden Jaguar and the release of his love from the shackles of jealousy, Adam challenges Coyote Spirit and easily overcomes and kills the man. Eagle Foot is set free and reunited with his daughters. It transpires that Swimming Beaver, who had gone that day to the coyote's city with the intention of avenging her mother's death by killing Coyote Spirit, had been seduced and deflowered by the rival leader and is now pregnant by him. Following Coyote Spirit's instructions, she had poisoned Adam's drink with hallucinogenic Datura leaves before the ceremony in the Great Kiva. Eagle Foot forgives her and tells his people they must now leave the mesas for their ancestral land has become defiled by the evil of Coyote Spirit. Adam reckons this must explain the well-known North American mystery of the sudden disappearance in the late thirteenth century of the Anasazi from the cliff-face pueblos in Colorado.

When the world around them begins to turn transparent, Adam, his sister and María know that their time in ancient Colorado is running out now that the prophecy has been fulfilled. They return to the twenty-first century as they entered the thirteenth century, via Earth Mother's hole in the centre of a kiva. When met by Aunt Jac, it seems only minutes had passed since all three youngsters vanished. Adam and María discover they have no underclothes, having left them in the cave after making love, confirming that something really did happen beyond the kiva.

When Aunt Jac learns the truth, her deep understanding of Native spirituality allows her to believe everything without question. But Chloe is irrationally upset to have lost 'real dream' contact with Earth Child, and begs her Aunt to let her contact modern Native Americans, descended from the ancient Anasazi, who might know what happened to Earth Child and her family after they left the mesas. They find an old Hopi medicine man in Arizona who knows all about the prophecy of which Adam and María were a vital part. She is devastated to learn that her friend died from fever only five days after they left the ancient pueblos, as, apparently, also foretold in the prophecy.

Chloe, together with her long-suffering friend Lee, vows to track down Eagle Foot's descendants across America using a combination of sixth sense plus Lee's photographic skills and her own artistic ability to look for facial features that might resemble those of her dead Anasazi friend's family from six hundred years ago…

Characters:
Adam Winters, a Texan high school geek changed forever by the Golden Jaguar, also **Leaping Jaguar**.
María López, Adam's singer-songwriter Mexican wife, also **White Deer** of a Native American prophecy, **Princess Arima** and temptress **Mariatli** in a parallel world as imagined by Adam.
Pepe and **Carla,** children of above.
Chloe Winters, Adam's younger sister, also **Living Water**.
Lee, Chloe's African-American photographer husband.
Kurt and **Jimmy,** twin sons of Chloe and Lee.
Aunt Jac, Adam's and Chloe's New Yorker aunt, a lawyer.
Uncle Jason, Aunt Jac's lawyer lover.
Earth Child, Chloe's 'real dream' ancient Anasazi friend, also **Mountain Flower** in Xibalba and **Bella** in present-day Houston.
Swimming Beaver, Earth Child's elder sister.
Eagle Foot, Earth Child's father and the tribal chief.
Moon Water, Earth Child's murdered mother.
Crouching Puma, Ancient Anasazi village shaman.
Coyote Spirit, Eagle Foot's rival for power.
Papa Pedro, deceased illegal Mexican immigrant antiques dealer, now in another dimension.
The Old Woman of the Hills, a mystical woman who lives in a Mexican mountain cave accessible from different dimensions.
Hunahpu and **Xbalanque,** the Hero Twins of Xibalba, also **Art** and **Jeannie Weissenbach**, María's guardian angels.
Jorge López, María's gentle Mexican cousin.
Anna, a young Mayan woman, rescued from Mexican drug gangsters, who married Jorge.
Sam Royal, Adam's African-American mentor and karate instructor.

Chapter 1: Doubt and Death

"Who's she?" asked the deceased priest. From nowhere, a frail, white-haired old lady had appeared. She walked towards a bench covered with scientific paraphernalia, including a large binocular microscope.

"Isn't that obvious? She's a scientist." The one-time Mexican antiques dealer felt pleased to have new company. As the old lady approached the bench, a swivel-seated laboratory chair emerged out of the mist. She sat on this.

"Was," stressed the ex-priest. "What's she doing here, anyway?"

"At a guess, minding her own business."

"Hmm!"

"I bet no one back there listened to her either, huh?"

"Either? What do you mean? My church was always full for every mass. Folk loved my homilies. Standing room only before Christmas."

"There's listen like in 'hear' and listen as in actually doing something."

The other man shrugged his shoulders then glowered at the scientist who was now peering into the microscope.

"What is the point of looking down one of those things here, huh?"

"She's hoping to find an answer, I suppose. Like you and me."

***

"It's Aunt Chloe and Uncle Lee!" the little boy exclaimed. He jumped down from his chair, in the middle of breakfast, and ran to the phone. It rang just before he picked it up.

"Pepe's so like your sister, Adam," María remarked, glancing up at her husband. Something in that glance unnerved him. "There's something special between him and Chloe, don't you think? Not just telepathy. It's like...

like they have a kind of—" María's forehead furrowed as she sought a word that would best describe the relationship between their son and his beloved aunt.

"Understanding?" suggested Adam.

María smiled. She reached across and rested her hand on her husband's arm.

"You've got it! But you know what? He gets his brains from his Dad," she added.

His wife's tone and behaviour of late informed Adam Winters that she was seeking reassurance about something. María had seemed so distant, so preoccupied before spelling out to her husband that she knew she had once died and, through events beyond the understanding of any sane person, had been brought back to life. Adam inwardly prayed that this had been the sole cause, and that her sadness would lift after they had shared his secret, but it didn't. It had been getting worse of late, and yet, for some reason, she wouldn't—or couldn't—talk about what was troubling her.

Adam raised his wife's right hand, once fatally bitten by a spider, and kissed it. Her impossibly-beautiful face looked tired and worn. If only he knew what was on her mind. Whenever he asked what it was, she would only say, "Nothing!" Which meant it was too awful to talk about.

He wanted to ask again but instead allowed his lips to journey up her bare arm to her shoulder, lightly stroking her smooth, light brown Mexican skin. After he'd brushed aside her long, jet black hair, they travelled on to the side of her neck and planted a lingering kiss. María giggled and for a few moments seemed her old self again.

"Why are you trying to eat Mama?" asked the young girl seated across the breakfast table, her serious brown eyes wide and questioning. Adam laughed.

"Because I love her, Carla," he replied. "And she tastes yummy too." María playfully slapped his wrist.

"Don't confuse the child!" she admonished. "It's called affection, sweetie. And your Daddy has a lot of it!"

"Can I have some too, Daddy?" Adam held his arms wide and his daughter ran into his embrace. Stroking the child's hair, he turned to María,

"Thank God Carla gets her looks from you, darling."

"Your sister, Chloe, *she's* not bad-looking!"

"Which means?" Adam grinned at his wife.

"Which means you're not allowed to have another slice of toast, Mr Adam Winters! You were the handsomest guy at middle school when I first set eyes on you, you know. And the nicest. But that tummy of yours isn't so nice now!" Carla slipped off her daddy's lap to examine and pat his tummy.

"Not my fault!"

"How come, honey?"

"Married to the best cook in Houston, aren't I? Anyways, since I gave up karate after Sam and his family moved to Dallas, I've not had much exercise."

María chuckled.

"You made up for that in bed last night."

"What did Daddy make up in bed, Mama?"

María clapped her hand to her mouth to hide her embarrassment. Adam blushed.

"Did some Mama-loving exercise!" he explained.

"Can I do some Mama-loving exercise?"

"Sure thing! Give her a big hug too." Carla climbed up onto her mother's lap and cuddled her.

"I love you, I love you, I *love* you!" she repeated.

"And some kisses, Carla. That's part of the exercise!"

Carla kissed María many times all over her face.

"Is that enough, Papa?" the girl asked.

"Enough? Oh, no amount of kissing can ever be enough for a mommy like yours!"

María laughed again, and for Adam her laugh was music from heaven.

"Honey, I'm gonna need a towel to dry my face now!"

Pepe, three years older than eight-year-old Carla, handed his father the phone.

"They're coming tomorrow," he told his mother whilst his dad spoke into the phone. "With the twins. About that documentary thing on global warming they're shooting. There's a bit in it about hurricanes. That means they'll have to spend a long time here, I guess."

"Is that what Aunt Chloe said?" María asked her son.

"Oh no, Mama. I just know it. She didn't have to tell me."

María frowned again. Of late, she'd done a lot of frowning.

The following morning, before lunch, Pepe burst indoors from the yard. He and Carla had been playing soccer. His little sister, to her delight, had been allowed to score all the goals.

"They're here!" he exclaimed, bouncing up and down like an excited puppy.

María, who stood preparing lunch, looked out of the kitchen window at the dusty driveway and the empty road beyond. Not a car in sight. But she knew her son was right as she wiped her hands, removed her Mexican-patterned pinafore, smoothed down her skirt, patted her hair then called out,

"They'll be here any minute, Adam!"

Adam abandoned his computer and hurried downstairs. As soon as the family had reached the top of the driveway of their large Texan ranch house, a rusting, late-twentieth century Oldsmobile appeared from around the bend in the road. They'd heard the splutter of its struggling engine for a while before seeing the vehicle. Pepe and Carla, giggling, had been counting the number of seconds it took for the sound of the car to precede its appearance from around the corner.

"Nine!" the children shouted in unison when the familiar mud-covered headlights swung into view and juddered towards them.

"Pepe, no!" María shrieked when her son, with his little sister skipping after him, took off towards the beat-up old car.

"It's okay, María. They'll be all right."

Adam put an arm across his wife's shoulders. The accident had affected her even more deeply than him, even though it had been his parents who had died. It was approaching the anniversary of their death, and perhaps that, in part, explained her edginess of late—he hoped.

He understood only too well why she had been so upset at the time. Ever since she'd been killed by a poisonous spider in the Mexican jungle, rescued from the haunting terror of Xibalba, the Mayan Place of Fear, and brought back to life by Adam, death must have reminded her that happiness with those whom she loved was little more than a delicate dream that might fade and vanish like early morning mist over the bayou in the harsh Houston sun. A while back, she'd told Adam that she remembered everything about the *Forest Without Time*, the Old Woman of the Hills, Xibalba and the role of the Golden Jaguar of the Sun in her rescue from eternal torment in the Place of Fear as a plaything of the Lords of Xibalba, One Death and Seven Death. Until then, Adam had tried to keep this from his wife, fearing that her life would suddenly come to an end if she were to learn that she'd once been brought back from the dead. But this didn't happen. María had defied all predictions, and now Adam couldn't help wondering whether this was because there was something about her that not even those who had warned him knew; something not just to do with being a wife and a mother, but a reality that concerned the future of the world. Was this yet another impossible burden for her to bear? A burden that she was hiding from him?

As far as the revelation of the knowledge of her dance with death was concerned, for years María had believed that she'd been protecting Adam from his own fear. Fear that he would lose her for good, and that talking about it would have forced him to relive the nightmare. When she sensed his fear grow so out of proportion that it threatened to engulf her, she told him. The man had wept for joy that this knowledge hadn't ended her life as he had previously been told it might.

María, too, wept, but for a different reason.

Chloe had predicted the accident, before it happened, because of the sixth sense she now shared with Pepe. Also because of this, Adam's own life had been saved...

It was a Friday towards the end of Adam's and María's final year at Senior High School. The whole family were to have a celebration meal at a Brazilian restaurant downtown. Adam, as expected, had excelled in all subjects and had won a University of Albuquerque scholarship to study social anthropology. He accepted only on condition that María be offered a place to study music at the same university. At least, this is what he jokingly told the girl. In fact, already a world-famous singer and song-writer, she could have chosen from any college in the country.

Adam had wanted María to join them that evening but she was needed by her cousin Jorge and his Mayan wife, Anna, for baby-sitting duty—something she could never resist. Also, on the way to the restaurant, Adam was to be fitted for his tuxedo for the high school summer prom and she wanted to save seeing him dressed to the nines for the big day.

Adam could barely make out what Chloe was saying over the phone as he stood at the school gate waiting for his parents' car with his cell phone pressed to his ear. If his parents hadn't been late, it would have ended so differently.

"Run, Adam. Just run! Do it! Now! They'll reckon you just wanted to run home."

Adam knew his little sister well enough to realise she wasn't messing him around. He ran without knowing why. Away from the school, along back streets, where he wouldn't meet their car. He ran and he ran until his chest ached and he could run no longer. Then he stopped. For a while he stood, hanging onto a lamp-post, drawing in deep breaths, soaked in sweat. He had no idea why Chloe had phoned, why he'd been made to run from the school, but inside he felt the same awful emptiness that he'd experienced in the Chiapas when María died. María's safety, as always, was his priority, and he phoned her, fearing something might have happened to the girl on her way home from school.

"Hi Adam! What's up? You sound like you've just done a marathon."

"Thank God you're okay, María!"

"What are you on about? The heat must've gotten to your brain, *chico*!"

When he arrived home, Chloe was already there, sitting on the doorstep. She, too, had run from school. Adam saw her face, wet with sweat and tears. Then he knew. He folded her into his arms and his sister's body shook with sobs.

"I tried to warn them," she cried. "I kept on trying with my cell phone, but Momma must have switched hers off. I was too late. It's all my fault, Adam. I should've saved them but couldn't."

They were still on the doorstep when the police car drove up. Adam didn't have to be told, and having the policewoman take him and Chloe indoors and sit them down before telling them what they already knew was one of the most surreal moments in the boy's life.

"It would've been immediate," the officer said. "The doctor at the scene said they wouldn't have felt a thing. That heavy truck, it just went out of control. A burst tyre. And that was it. Who else should we tell, Adam? And someone will have to stay with you kids."

"María," Adam replied weakly "Her family."

All he could think about was his parents being dead, smashed beyond recognition by that truck.

"María? Is she your aunt?" the policewoman asked as she sat comforting Chloe.

"My wife," Adam answered, not thinking.

"What did you just say?" The policewoman looked oddly at Adam.

"Girlfriend to you lot. A few blocks away."

"No relatives then?"

"New York. Two aunts."

"I think we should call them. I'll do it if you..."

"No," insisted Adam. "Just María."

For Adam, María was living proof that death *can* be defied, but he knew that his parents would never come back. Somehow, just then, he only wanted to be with María. For Chloe's sake, too. María and Chloe were very close.

His parents' death was a reminder of the nightmare that Adam had prayed would never recur. María, in tears, stayed with him when he identified the bodies the following day. Aunt Jac and his father's other sister, Germaine, arrived from New York that evening, and for several days Adam and his aunts agonised over what should become of him and Chloe. Aunt Germaine agreed to stay with them until school closed for the summer, but with Adam moving on to Albuquerque in the fall, arrangements had to be made for Chloe. There was only one solution. Chloe had always occupied a very special place in the heart of her ebullient Aunt Jac, the lawyer, writer and leading light in support of the Native Americans' rights. Chloe would move to New York to live with Aunt Jac. The woman would become the child's legal guardian, for there was no one else in the world better suited to look after Adam's extraordinary kid sister than Aunt Jac.

Chloe would soon be fourteen, and arrangements were made for her to join Lee, a twelfth grader, at the same public school in New York in August. The age gap between Chloe and Lee had never been of any consequence for they were devoted to each other. Lee had decided to study photography at college. As for himself, Adam insisted that he should keep on the family home in Houston. It was now *their* home—his and María's. Of course, Chloe was the only other person who knew that they were, in fact, married in Aztec Mexico, their marriage consummated over a hundred years earlier in ancient Colorado.

María was uncertain about still going to the high school summer prom but Chloe insisted.

"I can feel Momma and Papa. They want you to go together. They don't want anything to change for you two. Ever! They know who María really is now, see!"

Who María really is?

When Adam asked his sister what she meant, she shrugged her shoulders and looked away.

"That's all I'm getting from them," she replied. And Adam knew that his sister was, as always, being totally honest.

They went to the prom. María, in a long pink dress, matching shoes, and a pink accessory in her hair, was so stunning that most males present could barely take their eyes off her. But Adam felt no jealousy. That was all packaged away and consigned to his past. Only pride remained, and somewhere within he could feel his momma and daddy sharing that pride. They had both adored the girl who, without them knowing, was already their daughter-in-law. Chloe had been right to insist about the prom.

Adam's sister had been hoping to travel to New Mexico with Aunt Jac and Lee that summer, for the second year running, in her continuing quest to seek out the Puebloan descendants of Eagle Foot, the father of her 'soulmate', Earth Child. Their parents' death put paid to that. The girl realised that it would be wrong to go ahead with the idea. Besides, she was seriously upset, and she feared this might affect her sixth sense, essential for her zany plan. The trip was deferred until the following summer when *she* would be fifteen, Lee eighteen, and both a tad more worldly-wise.

Pepe hung onto Aunt Chloe's arm and Carla allowed herself to be swung, chortling, high up onto Uncle Lee's broad shoulders, whilst Adam took their bags from the trunk of the Oldsmobile. María and Chloe were already happily absorbed in women's talk as they ambled from car to house, with the twins toddling along beside María, occasionally tripping over their little feet as they struggled to keep up. Pepe repeatedly interrupted his mother to add his own opinion about things:

"I think the twins could have my bed, Mama, and it'll be okay if I share the spare room with Aunt Chloe and Uncle Lee. I know Aunt Chloe won't mind!"

"Oh, you do, do you?" laughed Chloe. "And don't you think we should check with your uncle first?"

"No. That won't be necessary. See, he always agrees with you anyway, Aunt Chloe!"

Uncle Lee chuckled.

"'Bout sums it up, Pepe!" he agreed.

"Yippee!" exclaimed Carla. "The twins will be with me—ee, the twins will be with me—ee!" she sang from her lofty seat on Uncle Lee's shoulders.

"And how's your singing going, María?" Chloe asked her sister-in-law. "Any new albums coming up?"

"Yeah, well trying to persuade Adam there to let me retire. Become a woman of leisure. But he won't have it!"

"Oh, my cruel brother, what are you doing to your lovely María? You two have enough money to last through to the twenty-second century."

"She wouldn't be happy to stop singing, Chloe. You know that. We all do. Besides, she couldn't stop. I reckon so long as she's still singing, she might as well let everyone in the world hear her. Wouldn't want to deprive folks of that, would you?"

Everyone in the world? Could it be? No... don't be so stupid, Adam!

Adam forced a grin as he opened the front door for his sister.

"Nope, Adam, I wouldn't," replied Chloe. "Wow, it's always so neat and tidy here, María. You should see our place."

"I like your place, Aunt Chloe. It's nice and messy!" Pepe said.

"You can say that again," Lee chuckled, and Carla giggled as he bounced her up and down.

Pepe knew not to ask his Aunt Chloe until the following day, for she looked so tired after driving all the way from New York over the previous few days. He would have to ask her then, though: ask about those bracelets his father had once given him and Carla. Recently he'd felt a strange power in them. Papa had said never to ask him about this again—and particularly not within Mama's earshot. Papa hadn't been angry. Just kind of upset.

It was all to do with the Golden Jaguar of the Sun and Pepe wanted to know everything. It also involved his Aunt Chloe, this much he knew. Aunt Chloe couldn't hide anything from him, so she would tell him everything, only he had to choose the right time to ask her. Then it could become their shared secret.

All the next day, Aunt Chloe and Uncle Lee were away interviewing people about the hurricane that had devastated Galveston the previous fall. The city was a wreck, a ghost place of sadness and destruction, and Chloe and Lee, convinced that the super-hurricane had been caused by global warming, were hoping to embarrass the extremist Republican government into changing its reluctant stance over the issue. María looked after the twins, with enthusiastic help from their cousin Carla, whilst Pepe spent the day playing in the yard, working out in his mind all the questions he needed to put to his aunt...

Who was the Golden Jaguar, and what happened to him?

Why must he, Pepe, never talk about it to Mama?

Why didn't Papa want to tell him these things himself?

Most of all, why had his father lied to him?

Pepe knew that those golden bracelets with their strange designs weren't just toys as Papa had said.

***

Pepe knocked on Aunt Chloe's and Uncle Lee's bedroom door as soon as he was up the next morning. It would have been so much easier if he and Aunt Chloe were in the same room. They might have had shared dreams, and in a shared 'real dream' she could have led him to the Golden Jaguar. He would never forget the time when they fell asleep together in a hammock in the yard after lunch the previous year and shared a dream about New York. Pepe had never been to the Big Apple, and, in that dream, he flew over the city holding onto Aunt Chloe's hand. Soaring over those sky-scrapers was the most magical moment of his dream life. Afterwards, Aunt Chloe made him promise not to tell anyone else about their shared dream.

The door opened just a crack. It was Aunt Chloe.

"Honey, you shouldn't be up at this hour! Everyone's still fast asleep."

"You're not!"

The woman smiled.

"Guess you're right, there. And I guess you knew that before you knocked on my door, huh?"

Pepe nodded. "I—" Pepe began.

"I know," whispered Aunt Chloe. "Your papa told me."

"What?" Pepe, excited, raised his voice.

"Shhh!" Aunt Chloe put a finger to her lips. "Wait here, Pepe." She disappeared into the bedroom and moments later returned in her dressing gown and slippers. "We can go outside. On the chair swing. Just you and me, huh?"

"Cool!"

Pepe clung to his aunt's arm as they went downstairs and out through the back door to the yard. It was still dark

12

and the security light flashed on, bathing everything in a harsh white glow.

"I think I'd better turn that thing off, don't you?" Aunt Chloe said. "Otherwise they'll think we're a couple of robbers!"

"And put us in jail?" suggested Pepe.

"Don't think they'd do that, honey. But we'll see the stars better with the light off."

Aunt Chloe went back in and switched off the security light. The yard was thrown into blackness. Pepe should have felt scared but with Aunt Chloe that would have been impossible. He never felt safer than when they were together. She took him to the chair swing where he snuggled up against her warm body.

"It's about those bracelets, isn't it, honey?" she asked.

"Papa said they were only toys. I know they're not, and I could see Mama didn't want to even look at them. She's sad about something. And I know it's all to do with the Golden Jaguar, but—"

"Have you ever seen him?" interrupted Aunt Chloe.

"Who?"

"The Golden Jaguar."

Pepe shook his head. "Nope!"

"How come you know about the beast, then?"

"Just do. It's about Papa, isn't it? He couldn't throw the bracelets away, so he passed them on to Carla and me. But why is Mama so scared of them? Why is she always so sad? And why did Papa say to keep them hidden in our secret boxes?"

"Uncle Lee and I were talking about this last night after you and Carla had gone to bed. Guess you must've been awake and thinking about the Golden Jaguar at the same time, huh?" Pepe nodded. "I might've known. Oh, what are you and I gonna do about this telepathy thing?"

"Talk about it?" Pepe rested his head on his aunt's shoulder.

"Yeah, that's what Uncle Lee said. 'One day the boy's gotta know,' he said, 'so maybe that day's come. Maybe he's the only one can find out what's upsetting his Mama. When he knows the whole story.'"

"Uncle Lee told me how Papa rescued him from bad men in New York who were gonna stick drugs into him. Was that to do with the Golden Jaguar too, Aunt Chloe?"

"Yes and no, honey."

"What's that mean?"

"See those stars up there, Pepe?"

"Sure. There's millions of them. No, a thousand million billion trillion. Papa told me."

"And do they look like tiny white dots to you?"

Pepe held up a forefinger and thumb and peered through the gap at the night sky.

"Teeny weeny," he replied.

"And what would you say if I told you that up close those same stars would make our world look like a just a tiny dot!"

"Like this?" Pepe stretched his arms as wide as he could, "And this?" He held up a small hand and brought thumb and forefinger together until they almost touched. Aunt Chloe nodded and both chuckled. "I'd say 'wow!'"

"Makes us all seem kind of unimportant, huh?" Aunt Chloe stared at the stars. "We think we know everything. Got it all worked out. How it's all gotten put together. What's right, what's wrong. But we know nothing about the Great Spirit!"

Without seeing her face, Pepe wasn't sure whether Aunt Chloe was thinking aloud or just thinking.

"The Golden Jaguar... was he good or bad, Aunt Chloe? And why is Mama so scared of anyone talking about him? I can feel her being scared and I don't like it. I love Mama."

Aunt Chloe put her arm around Pepe and held him close.

"We all love your Mama. And as for your Papa, well—"

"Well what?"

"See, Pepe, The Golden Jaguar of the Sun... it's their story. Your Mama's and Papa's. But—" Chloe paused. Pepe gazed at his aunt and saw fear in her eyes.

"You're in it too. I know you are."

"Can't hide anything from my little Pepe, huh? Yeah, I was in it. But only because of your Mama."

"Is it that scary?"

"Scary and wonderful."

"What's that mean?"

Aunt Chloe looked up again at the dark sky.

"It means there's more to the universe than just a thousand million billion trillion stars, honey. Things the Great Spirit keeps hidden. Most of the time."

"Mama doesn't like it when I talk about the Great Spirit."

Aunt Chloe looked uncomfortable. She hesitated, then finally spoke:

"Your mother's a Catholic. But we're not so very different in what we believe. Honey, I can see that I'm gonna have to tell you my bit of the story. Remember, it's just my bit, the bit I saw, like each of those stars up there is only a tiny little bit of the Universe that Pepe Winters can see."

"Does that mean there's a Mama's bit and a Papa's bit to the story as well?"

"Many bits. And ultimately yours, Pepe, and that's the bit that really matters for Mama."

"Will you tell me your story right now?"

"I'll start. But it's a long one, even just my bit, so it looks like the two of us are gonna be up early each morning for a quite a while yet."

Pepe grinned. "Yeah!" he exclaimed, punching a clenched fist into the air.

"But when the sun comes up above those trees there, we stop and wait till the next day. Okay?"

"Okay!"

"And you won't tell Mama or Papa?"

"Nope!"

"You will understand more when we've finished, Pepe. A lot more."

"You won't go back to New York before the story's finished, will you?"

"Can't!"

"Why not?"

"'Cause a certain Pepe Winters wouldn't let me!" Aunt Chloe gave her nephew a playful, gentle punch in the ribs. "Are you sitting comfortably, then?"

"This is the best seat ever! When we're together."

"Hungry? Something to drink?"

"Nope!"

"And you'll let me know if it gets too scary?"

"I'm never scared with you, Aunt Chloe!"

"Then I'll begin..."

Chapter 2: Search for Eagle Foot's Descendants

The three were joined by an old fellow immaculately dressed in a fine three-piece suit and sporting a neat moustache as white as the Rockies in winter. His clothes and bearing spoke of wealth in the life he'd once left behind whilst his physiognomy told a different story. Nose, forehead, cheekbones and chin could only have been passed down through the genes of countless generations of Native Mesoamericans. He was the grandfather of María López, the Mexican girl who had to be brought back from the dead. Although, unlike Papa Pedro, he had never truly embraced the religion so dear to his granddaughter, he now knew how important her life was, together with that of the Beast created with the fire of the Sun God.

It was the scientist who had called for him.

***

"All year Aunt Jac, Lee and I planned the trip. It helped take away the pain of my Momma's and Daddy's death. We would sit together for hours of an evening on the floor of Aunt Jac's New York apartment, with a large map of New Mexico spread out in front of us, surrounded by books about the Puebloans and the Hopi people. I would sometimes search the photographs of those books for faces that reminded me of my friends from the past: Earth Child, Swimming Beaver and Eagle Foot. Perhaps it was that special closeness between Earth Child and myself, maybe the suddenness with which we had to leave the cliffs when the prophecy had been fulfilled, or perhaps it was the horror of hearing what happened to my friend so soon after we'd left. I'll never really understand why I had such a compulsion to seek out the living descendants of Eagle Foot and Moon Water, but I knew I could never feel at peace with myself until I'd found at least one of them.

Adam and María were at college together in Albuquerque, and your daddy was a great help. He was forever sending me information about local Native American groups and activities. He even went along to meet some of those guys, tried to find out if there were any written documents that might have helped me, but more than one or two generations back and the trail always went cold. 'Word of mouth', they would all say. 'That's the history of our people. Can't be torn up, thrown away. Ever since the prophecy, it's been that way. An' folks that know, well they ain't gonna tell, anyways. White man, he may take the land that don't belong to no one, take our crops and our animals, but there's one thing he ain't gonna have: our soul. The soul of our people is in those stories handed down. The true ones. Ain't nobody gonna take those from us; write 'em down then tear 'em up or burn 'em. Do that, an' they burn away our soul. They'd leave behind nothin' but lifeless grey ash.'

"Course, there are the other stories,' they would sometimes add. 'The ones we can tell for White Man to write down. The ones that don't matter for they ain't the ones that come from the Great Spirit or from our Earth Mother.'

Earth Mother? When Adam told me this, I was even more determined. And that thing about Earth Child being Earth Mother's human form, this I never believed. I felt sure it was one of those untrue stories to deflect White Man from the truth.

That year, Lee started his training in photography in New York. We knew his photographic skills would be vital in our search and it so happened that Lee turned out to be the brightest student they'd had for years, and his tutor, an expert on portrait photography, was only too happy to give Lee extra tuition. There were two things I needed from Lee. First, the easier of these, was the use of a camera to highlight different facial features. 'Physiognomy', they call it. The right lighting and shadows, the best positioning, these things would make all the difference in deciding who might be carrying the genes of Earth Child's parents, but what really mattered were the secrets held in the soul. Lee seemed sure that the camera could be used to look into the soul, like opening a door and peeking inside. *'It's in the eyes,'* Lee said. The eyes and the expression, and that's where his tutor helped him. To perfect his portraiture by opening that door to the soul.

I got so excited when I saw some of the photos he took of the black folk in Haarlem. The college said his work was outstanding. Wanted him to have a one man show, Lee being just a freshman student and all, but Lee turned them down. Said he wasn't ready. Truth was, he didn't want anything to get in the way of my project. Nothing was allowed to divert his energies from our common purpose.

Love, they call it. That few years' difference in our ages was immaterial. Like your Mama and Papa, we were held together by love. We didn't have to talk about the things of love. We just knew.

It had been a bit like that between Earth Child and me. Not a boy-girl thing, of course, like it was with Lee, but love all the same. Perhaps that was because we shared so much in our 'real' dreams. I was the only person Earth Child had ever shared her own real dreams with, she once told me. Funny thing was that when Lee and I got real close, my own real dreams stopped. For a long while I had no real dreams at all. In many ways, I was just like any other young teenage girl overwhelmed by first love, though, somehow, I knew he would always be my only love. I knew this the very first time I saw Lee. But, despite that thing between Lee and me, I simply had to find Eagle Foot's descendants. I had to know that my Native friend's suffering, and her early death, had not been in vain.

On a map spread out on the floor we began to put red crosses marking out Indian communities, individuals from Aunt Jac's contacts, from Adam's research, and Lee and I would join up those crosses to plan our routes. Aunt Jac modified these to take into account roads and tracks and commonsense things like that, since our own trail often took us across spaces filled by nothing but empty desert. See, I was just a kid then, and Lee—well, he just said 'yes' to whatever I said. Only wanted to please me. No, sir, roads and such didn't feature much in our routes.

Aunt Jac used to joke about Lee and me. In a kind sort of way, of course. You know yourself Aunt Jac would never wish to hurt anyone. She reminded me once how I used to carry on about women's rights before I met Lee. I'd even complained because Bruno didn't have a sister. Boy, did that change after we first saw each other. He just made me feel so—well, important I guess. Before Lee, I thought Adam and María were the only kids who really mattered. I felt like I just happened to be there, and that if the whole world came to an end then nobody would miss little me. With Lee, I felt different. I knew I mattered to him, and he mattered to me. Terribly. Only twelve, and in love already! Aunt Jac thought we were real cute. And she kept our Daddy right about us before he and Momma gotten themselves killed, for he did worry about me. Didn't know it then but looking back I know now he truly worried with me being so young and serious about Lee.

'Lee's a good boy, Johnny,' I once overheard her say when I was in New York. 'It's okay. Like Adam says, he's young for his age, and Chloe, she's always been a little woman anyways. There really is something genuine between them. As for Lee, he'll always respect your Chloe.'

Respect, Pepe. That's how it started. Yeah, Aunt Jac was right. She was always right. Whatever we had going between your Uncle Lee and me, it all began with genuine respect.

But I was kind of sad that Adam wouldn't be there with us in New Mexico. Even tried to persuade him to stay on in Albuquerque over the summer vacation and join us, but I knew he couldn't. María had to get back to her family. Jorge and Anna were expecting their own child, Anna's second, and nothing could've prevented María being there for the occasion. Besides, they had 'their' house. Even I called my old home Adam's and María's house back then. It was where they'd had their very first kiss. That house was special for them, and of course they were already married. At the time, I was the only other person who knew this. Not even Aunt Jac or Lee knew.

Anyways, soon I overcame my sadness about Adam not being there in New Mexico. It happened on the plane. As we took off from La Guardia, and I was sitting by the window with Lee beside me and Aunt Jac next to him, I felt *so* happy. Aunt Jac had put my hair into braids. I'd gotten her to do that especially for Lee because he told me he liked me in braids. Said that blondes like me were somehow made for braids. Then he added, 'but only for us photographers, of course!' He was always so funny. I never stopped giggling when we were together, and he joked with me on that plane all the way to New Mexico. 'Never mind them Native Americans, Chloe,' he said. 'I think I'll just take pictures of my beautiful girlfriend when we get to New Mexico.'

I was just fifteen. I'd never thought of myself as beautiful. María was the beautiful one, everyone knew that, and yet here was this kind, funny boy calling *me* beautiful. *And* his girlfriend. He'd not called me that before. Must've been the age-gap thing, but suddenly, at fifteen, I looked a whole lot older. Could've easily passed for sixteen. Yes, just then I was happier than I'd ever been. Momma and Daddy were in heaven, I was sure of this, but with me and Lee and Aunt Jac setting off together to seek out Eagle Foot's descendants and Lee calling me his girlfriend *and* beautiful, that was the next best thing to heaven.

We arrived in Albuquerque quite late, what with our flight being delayed and all. It felt strange, us being there and Adam back in Texas, for New Mexico was his place. His and María's. It was like going to someone's home and them not being there. See, I'd not been back to Houston since our parents' death.

'I can't, Adam,' I said one day over the phone from New York to your daddy. 'I can't do it. Like I know our old home is your place now. Yours and María's. But I still feel Momma and Daddy should be there. For me it would be wrong without them. Like it'd be a dead house.'

Adam understood. He came up to New York instead the first Christmas after the accident. I was overjoyed to see my brother again, and he seemed so much older. María stayed behind to be with her family and Adam spent much of the time on the phone to her for he, María and Aunt Jac were busy back then setting up NACSO. The Native American Communities Support Organisation. Adam wouldn't make any decision without first checking it out with his wife.

As we took a taxi to our hotel in Albuquerque, I kept thinking about María. I hadn't seen her for a year and with her now being a secretly married woman of eighteen, it seemed like she belonged to a different generation. But I still felt close to her, and suddenly, in that taxi, I felt sad. I wanted to be with María and hug her and tell her how beautiful she was, like Lee had said to me on the plane. Instead I clung to Lee and hugged him instead, and Lee kissed me and Aunt Jac said, 'Oh don't mind me, you two!' And we all laughed.

At the hotel, Aunt Jac and I shared a room and Lee was on his own a few doors along the corridor. I felt kind of sorry for him on his own. Particularly at night after Aunt Jac turned off the light.

'Can't I just spend one night with him, Aunt Jac? He's very much a gentleman, you know. He'd never do anything bad to me.'

Thank goodness for Aunt Jac! She knew when to put her foot down, and over the matter of Lee and your precocious Aunt Chloe, she kept her foot very firmly down. I may have looked like sixteen, but I was still a child and there were many things I didn't understand. Such as how much Lee would have suffered having me in his room at night and having to protect me from himself. I had no idea what effect my young woman's body was having on him. I guess Aunt Jac was looking after Lee as much as she was looking after me.

The first person we visited in New Mexico was the Native American who lived on his own at the edge of town; the guy I'd seen together with your Mama and Papa after returning from the Mesa Verde. The man who told me about Earth Child dying only five days after we'd left the past behind. We had a hired car, and Aunt Jac dropped me and Lee off at the old fellow's place whilst she went to see a client nearby.

He looked at our map, all spread out on the floor, then disappeared for a few minutes, during which time Lee and I stared at each other and shrugged our shoulders. Then he returned with a red felt-tip. *Great*, I thought! *He's gonna make some useful markings on our map. Perhaps he has information from the kachina spirits*. You can imagine my surprise when he reached down and put a huge red cross over the whole map – like we were wasting his time, or perhaps trying to pry into things that didn't concern us.

I felt I had no right to be doing this, and I was upset. Like really upset, for I'd been planning it all with Lee for a whole year and now the old Puebloan was closing the door on us with that great big red cross.

At first, I thought he was angry, and I felt afraid. But he wasn't. He was trying to tell me something, though not in words. Maybe he was testing me. Whatever—I'll never know for sure. Something had dulled my sixth sense. Perhaps it was my love for Lee. Maybe, because of this, my mind was momentarily closed off to those forces that had always come so naturally to me. I cried. I sat on the floor in front of the outspread map and I wept. Lee came and folded me in his arms and held me close until Aunt Jac returned some forty minutes later. The old Puebloan, still wearing a hat, sat staring at us huddled together on the floor. His eyes, peering out from under bushy white eyebrows, must have been desperately trying to tell me the things I needed to know, but I wasn't seeing them. I only wanted Lee to keep holding onto me, protecting me from my own stupidity in bringing us all that way on such a pointless search—and to forgive me.

When Aunt Jac arrived, Lee and I were standing outside the ramshackle wooden house with my boyfriend still holding me close. The old guy had freaked us out when he began chanting and moving his head about, so we just picked up the map and left him there on his own. Typical Aunt Jac, she was just so kind as she tried to cheer me up:

'Honey, don't worry about it. Poor man must've flipped. Happens to lots of us when Old Father Time gets his way and there ain't nothing we can do about it. Why, perhaps he's in there now thinking he's Abe Lincoln about to set us all free from the tyranny of Darth Vader and his cronies.'

I giggled—a little—but deep down I knew the old Puebloan was right. My idea was crazy. What I didn't know, because I'd closed my inner door on him, was how dangerous it would be. See, I thought that was it when Coyote Spirit fell to his death and the cliff people were saved. But there was so much I didn't know. Couldn't have known, of course. I was heading for a trap, and that old fellow had done his very best to warn me. To save me from myself."

Chapter 3: The Great Trickster

"I always knew," said the wiry old man in the smart suit. "From the moment I first saw her."

"Knew what?" asked the ex-priest. He felt irritated by these newcomers. They had to be put in their place. He smiled to himself when the man appeared to be lost for words. The scientist looked up from her microscope.

"Knew where his granddaughter came from," she explained. "It's why I asked him to join us."

"Oh yes... it's what they've all been saying. But I fail to see why this should concern us."

"Then you're blind!" The one-time Mexican antiques dealer stood up and approached the priest. He knelt and took hold of the other's hand that bore a ring. "Why do you wear this ring?" he asked.

"To remind me," came the answer. "But I still don't see—"

"Then I can't help you!"

***

'Lee, come quick!' I called out through your uncle's door back in the hotel early the following morning. I knocked again. After what seemed an age, the door opened. A sleepy black face appeared, blinking in the bright corridor light. I kissed him awake.

'Lee, it's okay. I saw her. Last night. Had a dream. A real dream. It was Earth Child. I know it.' That, at least, I was sure of. Earth child and I had met up again, but she seemed so frightened of 'them', whoever 'they' were. 'Lee, may I come in, please?' I asked.

I had my hands on my hips. I laughed at his sleep-swollen eyes when he just blinked at me. He smiled, and I kissed him again.

'Sure, Chloe! But what about Aunt Jac? Won't she worry about—?' he began.

'Asleep!' I interrupted. 'Anyways, she trusts you.'

I gave him a playful punch in the ribs as he stepped aside to let me past. Once in his room, I held him close and kissed him on the lips ("Ooh!" exclaimed Pepe) —long and hard till his face warned me we might go too far if I didn't stop. After all, I was only wearing a nightdress. I stepped back from the boy I adored.

'Lee, I'm just so excited! Listen here!'

I took Lee by the hand and led him to the bed. We sat together, Lee in his pyjamas, with his arm around my waist, and anyone walking into the room just then would have thought the very worst, but it wasn't like that at all. Lee sat and listened like a perfect gentleman. He was a great listener—still is—and I babbled on, bubbling with excitement about my real dream, the first for over two years.

'I was in a place like a supermarket, only it wasn't really a supermarket,' I told him. 'More like a place where you look for people, and the shelves they were full of books and files and there were photos of Native Americans everywhere, some in traditional costumes and some in ordinary everyday clothes. They were like the photos you take of people, Lee. Really good! I was trying to see into the souls of the people who owned those faces. And all the time I had three pictures in my hand, pictures I'd drawn of Earth Child, Eagle Foot and Swimming Beaver, and I kept comparing these drawings with those faces, looking at the features and searching for souls in the eyes. Then – 'and this is the honest truth, Lee,' I said, 'I felt a gentle tap on the shoulder, turned around, and there she was. Earth Child!'

'Can you be sure it was her?' your uncle asked. 'I mean, you ain't seen her for over two years. Maybe—'

'I'll never forget her eyes, Lee,' I told him. 'Never! It was her. 'Hi, Living Water,' she said. 'Long time no see!' First, I just stared. There were tears in her eyes. I just couldn't believe my luck. Then we hugged. 'Where are we?' I asked.

'We're in the place where folk look for things,' she replied. 'But it's no good. You'll find nothing here.'"

Pepe looked up at his aunt.

"A place where folk look for things? You mean like Google, only real?" he asked.

Chloe grinned and gently patted the boy's cheek.

"'Bout sums it up, my wise little nephew. Now—where was I? Oh yes. Earth Child. 'Where should I look, then?' I asked her. 'I need to find them. I just have to know what happened to your daddy's descendants. I loved y'all so much!' Oh, you should've seen Lee's eyes just then. You know how big they are. They almost popped out of his head!

'Follow me,' my native American friend said, 'but whatever you do, don't wake any of the sleeping spirits.' With a wave of her hand she indicated those rows upon rows of books and photographs.

The supermarket—I'll call it that 'cause a supermarket's what it reminded me off—it was huge. In that dream, I followed Earth Child between stacked shelves that stretched into the distance as far as the eye could see. Suddenly she stopped and reached up for a large brown book on one of the higher shelves. I had to help her, for I was now taller and older than my friend. She was still only twelve, same age as when I'd last seen her. Together we lowered the book carefully to the ground. She crouched down and opened it. I wondered then what she was doing. The book seemed to be a sort of atlas. A primitive one, decorated with drawings of animals and plants. Then—and this was so totally weird—then the map on the page gradually got larger. I looked down at my feet and I saw I was standing on the book, and still it got bigger and bigger, and then it was like the sky started to grow up from the page of the atlas and up and over our heads, and the painted plants turned into real plants and the animals began to move around and look at us before running off. We were no longer in a supermarket. Earth Child and I were now in a deep forest and what had been a thin line on the map had turned into a trail that disappeared into densely-packed ancient ferns and trees.

'Earth Child, where are we?' I asked again.

'The land of Earth Mother,' she replied. 'Our planet as it used to be and the place she still looks after for the Great Spirit. The one your sister-in-law calls God. Come.'

'Earth Child, are you—you know—really Earth Mother? Were you her all the time when we used to play together?' But Earth Child just smiled that bewitching smile of hers.

'Come with me,' she whispered without answering my question.

I followed her along the path. As in that supermarket, it went on and on, across streams, circling round huge boulders, up and over hills, but still there was that strange forest, those colourful flowers and the sounds of the beasts of the forest. With Earth Child I wasn't the least bit scared. On my own I'd have been terrified.

Lee held me real close when I told him that, and he kissed me on the cheek.

'For me, that's the worst thing in the world, Chloe, you being frightened,' he said. 'I'll never let anything bad happen to you!'

He was so cute, was Lee. Still is, of course.

'Well,' I continued, 'just when I thought we were getting nowhere, like I'd felt with that old guy at the edge of town yesterday with his big red cross on that other map, we came to a village of adobe brick buildings. Earth Child ran on ahead towards a wide space in the centre of the village. She turned and beckoned to me to follow her. There was no one else there, and I walked slowly. It was kind of creepy. Seemed deserted. Earth Child stopped beside a kiva like the one you photographed in the Cliff Palace in the Mesa Verde,' I said to Lee, 'and the hole in its centre had to be a link with Earth Mother.' I knew this from the Mesa Verde.

'Where is everyone?' I asked my little Native friend.

'Not been born yet,' Earth Child answered. 'These are the homes of the people of the future. Who moves into them depends on you, Living Water. And on Leaping Jaguar and White Deer again.'"

"On my Mama and Papa?" asked Pepe.

"Sure thing. 'But that's all in the past, Earth Child,' I protested. 'Remember? Leaping Jaguar killed Coyote Spirit. Your people were saved. And Leaping Jaguar and White Deer, they were already married, anyways. Coyote Spirit could never take her away from my brother!'"

Pepe looked up at his aunt.

"Who is Coyote Spirit?" the boy asked. 'Is', not 'was', as if he already knew.

"We'll come to that later, honey. But your Mama and Papa can never stop being who they really are: Leaping Jaguar and White Deer," Aunt Chloe said. "Lee knows this, and Aunt Jac too, but wasn't no one else in the world who knew it back then. Not even my own Momma and Daddy who are now in heaven."

"Were they always married, my Mama and Papa? Like even before they met at junior high school?"

"A very difficult question, Pepe. But what I couldn't understand, when I stood in that empty village with Earth Child, was how I and your Mama and Papa could have anything to do with the people who would come to live in those buildings. Just made no sense to me. Your poor long-suffering Uncle Lee, it seemed like he'd been presented with so many unanswerable questions. I could see this in his eyes as we sat there together, his arm around me. But he only listened. Said nothing.

'Earth Child,' I said to my real dream friend, 'I only need to know. About those children of Earth Mother. I need to know they were all right after moving away from the cliffs. After the prophecy. Life in those cliff places must have been so beautiful before Coyote Spirit returned from the south full of evil. Even during the great drought. But now I need to know your people found that beauty again someplace else. Only they can tell me. Those that were true to Earth Mother—the descendants of Eagle Foot.'

'I loved my sister, Swimming Beaver,' she replied.

'Sure!' I agreed. 'And from what I heard, her son was one of the wisest chiefs ever. His animal spirit was strong. But what happened after that, Earth Child? Where *are* all your people now?'

'Depends on you, Living Water,' she said.

I began to feel kind of scared. She seemed distant, like death had changed her. Come to think of it, I guess it would have done. Earth Child must have sensed this too.

'Here,' she said, 'look down there into the kiva.'

I turned and peered at the hole in the ground. Writing emerged from it, like someone was drawing on the ground with an invisible stick:

When those that will be, can come together, when time breaks free and blends with the spirits of Earth Mother and White Deer's God, the God of Love, then you shall find me again, alone and still seeking you.

'I don't understand, Earth Child. What's it all mean?' I asked, for I sure felt confused.

'At the weekend, Living Water,' was all she said. 'Remember that. The weekend.'

'What about the weekend?'

'Never lose faith, Living Water.'

'Faith in what? Can't you tell me more?'

Earth Child gave me one of her smiles and I felt a whole load better. I knew then it really was her and not my imagination playing tricks. And she shrugged her shoulders.

'No, I can't,' she replied. 'I shouldn't be here, anyways, but I just had to help the best friend I've ever had. One day you'll understand, Living Water. I promise you.'

Earth Child was growing faint—kind of transparent. I felt the same thing happen when Adam and María were in that kiva in the ancient Mesa Verde pueblo. We knew back then that we no longer belonged in that place and we had to get out quickly. I feared this would be the last time I'd ever see my old friend.

'Take care,' she said, spreading wide her ghost-like arms. I held her close for a few moments and, although she was no longer solid, I felt strangely happy.

'You too,' I whispered. Then suddenly I was alone with my arms hugging the cool air. The buildings had disappeared, the forest was a dim blur, but the kiva was still there, and I knew what to do. I stepped inside the stone ring. closed my eyes and—"

Chloe paused. Pepe grinned.

"And you woke up!" he added.

"Yeah, and at first it felt real weird 'cos it was like I was falling asleep, not waking up. Like being with Earth Child again was the reality. Your poor Uncle Lee looked pretty upset when I told him this.

'What about me?' he asked. 'Aren't I real to you?' I just laughed when he looked at me with those big doleful brown eyes of his. I kissed these and he tried to laugh along with me, but I still felt bad about the hurt in those eyes.

'When I first saw you two years back, honey, I knew I was the luckiest girl in the world,' I reassured him. 'But it's Thursday already. Don't you see, Lee? It's gonna happen this weekend. We'll meet him, her—whoever it is. Eagle Foot's descendant. I'm sure of it. Oh my, I'm just so excited. And you, my big, clever man, who just happens to be the best photographer in the whole of New York, you are gonna take such wonderful photos for me. And Adam's gonna be so pleased when he sees them!'"

"My daddy again?" asked Pepe.

"Your Daddy and Mommy never leave this story. It's been about them all along. But Lee was curious about my little Native American friend whom he'd never met.

'Chloe, have you any idea what your little friend meant with that riddle of hers,' Lee asked, ''cause I sure ain't got a clue?'

'Oh, it'll work out all right,' was all I could say. 'She won't let me down. It was as if—' I paused a while to think '—as if this thing is as important to Earth Child as it is to me. But there is something I don't understand, Lee,' I continued. 'Where Adam and María actually fit in. I mean, for them the whole thing is over. They're just waiting to finish college so that they can marry all over again. Make it official like, for María's parents' sakes.'

'Can't see Adam leaving María behind in Texas,' your uncle said, 'just to meet up with this Native guy, even if you do find him. Or her. Ain't nothing on earth could tear him away from his girl. Not even Earth Mother!' And Lee chuckled. For the first time, ever, I felt a tiny bit cross with Lee.

'Lee. This is serious!' I scolded. 'Earth Mother really is there. Or here. I know it's difficult for María to believe these things, her own religion being that strong, but Adam, he says it's not actually contrary to her beliefs. Just a different way of looking at the same thing.'

That day and the next, Aunt Jac drove Lee and me around the desert near Albuquerque from one Native community to another, as we began to work our way through the list of names given by her contacts, but the reception we got was always frosty to say the least. How naïve I was back then, an eager fifteen-year-old, believing the whole native population of New Mexico would be fighting amongst themselves to be the first to get photographed, and that they all wanted to hear about the ancient Anasazi prophecy in which I'd played a part.

Oh boy! Not one of them knew what I was talking about. The few that Lee photographed agreed, reluctantly, but only after Lee gave them money. Not just a few cents, but three or four bucks each. Poor Lee! I knew he didn't have much money, him being a penniless student and all, prevented by his first and only girlfriend from earning decent cash during his long vacation, but he insisted on paying. Wouldn't hear of it when I suggested that Aunt Jac pay.

As for Aunt Jac? Well, she had the patience of Job. Never once complained or made me feel stupid, but perhaps she knew all along there was more to this thing than a young teenage girl's fancy. In fact, it was she who kept me going as we drove around between those homesteads and Native communities by telling me more about the people that I grew to love so much that summer up there on the Mesa Verde of the past.

After leaving the mesas, the Anasazi people followed what we now call the Rio Grande. They split up and went their separate ways, across the prairies to the east and the deserts and the mountains to the south-west. They met up with their brethren from the Mogollon tribes, and built more villages, but never again did they recreate the great limestone buildings of their ancestors of the mesas. There were wars with the Navajo and with the Comanche, and when the Spanish arrived, they even made pacts with the newcomers from across the seas, learned to ride horses, graze cattle, work leather, but their friendship was betrayed. As with the Navajo and the Comanche, the new lands of their Earth Mother were claimed and taken from them by the Europeans. Worse still, the invaders tried to take their religion from them, peel away their culture and destroy the soul of those peace-loving people. Somehow, they survived.

'But that's just it, Aunt Jac!' I remember saying. 'Eagle Foot's descendants must have been the ones who saved the Puebloans. They'd become indestructible.'

'Honey, I only wish that were true!' your great aunt replied.

On the Friday night, after dinner, Lee and I were looking through digital images of Native American faces on the back of Lee's camera when Aunt Jac came up to us:

'How about you guys taking a break, huh? There's a disco dance at that big hotel two blocks down. I'll drop you off and play the Fairy Godmother. Pick you up before the last stroke of midnight. Seems that's when it finishes.'

'But I'm no good at—' I began but stopped when I saw Lee's face. I could see from his expression that the one thing he wanted to do more than anything in the whole world was to take me to a dance. Your uncle never could hide anything from me.

'Sure,' I corrected myself, grinning at Lee, and he grinned shyly back at me.

We had a great evening. He was a fantastic dancer and he soon got my rhythm going. Never thought I'd ever be able to dance like that, and when he told me I was the most beautiful girl on the dance floor that really did it. I felt like I was up there on the top of the world, floating on a cloud of happiness. I'd forgotten about Earth Child and my quest, about Aunt Jac, about Adam and about my parents in heaven. There was just me and Lee with that kind face of his, and our being together. Aunt Jac had known all along that was exactly what I needed. But about twenty minutes before midnight, something happened that cut into that happiness like a sword slicing through living flesh.

''Scuse me mister, but I think the young lady really wants to dance with me.' It was a Red Indian guy, older and larger than Lee. Lee, usually non-confrontational, but never cowardly, was taken off guard.

'Sorry, dude, but she's my girl!' he said.

The Indian remained silent but came right up to Lee and stood with his face just inches from your poor uncle.

'Hey, Lee. It's okay. Cool it. No big deal. Aunt Jac'll be along any minute. I'll dance with this guy, and you can watch me mess it up, huh? It's okay!' The last thing I wanted was for Lee to get into a fight with someone bigger than him. One blow from one of the Indian's great fists would have sent him flying, though I knew where I was involved Lee would have braved anything. He'd even have taken on a crazed mountain lion if he had to.

I followed the guy onto the dance floor and could feel Lee's eyes trailing us. We began to dance, the Indian and me, slowly and rhythmically, and though I tried hard to keep my distance, I felt myself drawn to the guy. There was something strange about him, something horribly powerful, and, worst thing of all, he was very handsome. I fought hard to keep an image of Lee in my mind, refusing to let go of gentlest person I'd ever known. It was then that I realised things were changing.

First, it was the music. The beat, like. I hadn't noticed any drum beats earlier on. Just the usual electronic sound of disco music, but then somewhere from the depths of that music weird drum beats emerged. They swelled up, got louder and soon dominated everything, filling my mind and forcing me to lift and stamp my feet in the same way as my dancing partner. Then, to my horror, I saw the man himself looked different. Instead of the jeans and tee-shirt he'd been wearing, he had on a colourful tribal costume, a headdress of feathers and anklets of beads and bears' teeth. He was carrying a stick with feathers and an eagle's claw at one end, and he shook this backwards and forwards in time to the music. Not only that, but all the other dancers were also dressed in Native costumes, and we seemed to be dancing as one whilst the music swept us round in a great pulsing circle. And in the centre of the circle was a snake, motionless as if held in a trance by our dance. I wanted to scream out to Lee, for I'm terrified of snakes, but I couldn't. I couldn't even turn around to look at Lee, though I knew he was there, watching me and boiling with anger. I couldn't turn because I was one of them, in some other place, dimension... whatever. I was even dressed like them in a long Native dress decorated with beads.

Suddenly, just when I thought my head would burst with all that drumming, the music stopped. I was standing there, in my short skirt and top again, midriff bared, surrounded by other kids, and there was no sign of the large Native guy. I was holding something. I looked down. It was a kinda carved wooden doll, dressed in cloth and bead garments. I knew already what it was. Lee came up to me and put his arm around my shoulders.

'You okay, honey?' he asked.

'I dunno,' I lied, knowing I was far from okay. I must have been frowning, for Lee stroked my brow then kissed it. He always did that whenever I frowned. Still does."

"I've never seen you actually frown, Aunt Chloe," remarked Pepe.

Chloe laughed.

"Wouldn't want to worry my favourite nephew with a frown, would I now."

"Favourite? You've only got one nephew!"

"Still a favourite of mine. Now, where was I?"

"You'd just come out of a trance or something."

"Wasn't no trance, Pepe. Lee stood gawping at that doll in my hand. 'Give it to me.' he said. 'I'll chuck it in the—'

'No, Lee!' I yelled when he tried to take it from me. I'd never yelled at him before and I felt awful. He jerked his hand back as if he'd been stung. I started to cry.

'Oh, Lee, I'm so sorry! I didn't mean to yell like that. It's just that—look, he wasn't trying to take me from you. I promise,' I tried to reassure your uncle.

'Looked pretty much like that to me, Chloe,' he scoffed.

'No, Lee. It wasn't like that,' I insisted. 'He—well, you know how Earth Child told me I'd know about meeting with Eagle Foot's descendant by this weekend.'

Lee looked away from me. I turned him around and fixed him with my eyes. Your Uncle looked uneasy. Not scared, but uneasy.

'I dunno, Lee,' I admitted. 'Maybe it was him. Maybe someone else. But—' I showed him the little wooden doll. 'This, Lee.'

'What *is* that, Chloe?' he asked.

How could I explain the mystery of a kachina doll at a disco in the middle of the night?

'It's—well, it's a sort of—oh Lee, I can't put it in words. It's a feeling. A connection. I know this is it. Like a key to a different world. It's—"

I expected Lee to be angry, but. as you'll know, anger's not his thing. He was concerned, that's all.

'Chloe, please take care. Things we don't understand are best left alone. Some things are just too dangerous to think about. I'd never forgive myself if anything happened to you.'

'It won't, my darling.' I'd never called your uncle that before, but it was true. He was my darling. Always had been, and he needed to know for I'd never before seen him so upset.

'Chloe, where did that guy go? I saw you dancing away, like you were lost somewhere in the music. You were still dancing when he gave you that doll. Then next time I looked up you were there on your own and the music had stopped.'

'What was I wearing, Lee?' I wanted to know what he saw.

'Why, what you're dressed in now. What a weird question, Chloe!'

'And the music, Lee? Did it sound different to you? Like drum beats and stuff?'

'Not like drums I've ever heard. Same kind of music that played when we were enjoying ourselves, honey.'

I could tell that Lee was slipping into a bit of a sulk, so I put arms around his waist and kissed him fondly.

'Best evening I've ever had, Lee, dancing with you.' I said to cheer him up. 'And remember this. There'll only ever be one guy for Chloe Winters, and that's you. We're like that, in my family, you know. Momma and Daddy, Adam and María and now me and you. We're all single partner people.'

'I'm worried about you, Chloe,' he said, and I saw it in his eyes too.

'No harm will come to me. Earth Child will never let that happen.' I think I was trying to reassure myself as much as Lee.

'But Chloe, in your dream she only said it depends on you and your brother and María. That's hardly protection!'

'Oh look, there's Aunt Jac!' I announced avoiding the issue, for I knew Lee was right. Perhaps Earth Child had only appeared in a real dream to warn me.

That night I slept with the doll on the pillow beside me. Aunt Jac confirmed it was a kachina doll and the sort that the Native red people used to give to young girls to make them fertile. I knew then that the doll was for María, not me, but had no idea that it would lead to a terrifying fate that would engulf both your Mama and Papa."

Chapter 4: A Gold Locket

"So, you wish to return there... again?" asked One Death.

"Yes and no," replied Coyote Spirit.

"Explain. We had a deal last time. Remember? 'You deliver the girl and, as with the Spider Goddess, we leave you alone. But... no girl! And that black-cloaked priest of yours proved less than useless. Why shouldn't we just turn you into a statue? Zotz could use you for a pissing post, so our efforts won't have been completely wasted."

"You wouldn't do that, though. Whilst she lives you still need me. I so nearly had the boy trapped by his own jealousy in an alternate universe of his making that all three of us could have become merged and entered the girl."

"But that didn't happen. The Black Jaguar was killed and the Golden Jaguar within the boy-turning-man grows from strength to strength. How come things would be any different the next time?"

The one-time Anasazi prince drew himself up to his full height, not far short of that of the Death Lord. One Death turned to face Seven Death.

"What d'you think, brother?" he asked.

"I think he hasn't used his real weapon to full advantage yet."

"That being?"

"Trickery!" Coyote Spirit answered for Seven Death.

***

Pepe snuggled up close to his beloved aunt. She'd gone silent, and he knew this was because something big was about to happen in her story.

"So, what happened next?" he asked.

"Well, the next morning I awoke to find Aunt Jac sitting on my bed, looking down at me, just waiting for me to wake up and open my eyes. I blinked a few times then sat up. She hugged me, put something in my hand and closed my fingers around it. I uncurled my fingers and stared at a heart-shaped gold locket on a gold chain. Something inside me kind of lit up when I touched it.

'Wow—it's awesome! Oh, thank you, Aunt Jac!' I said.

'Your granny gave it to me and I told myself when I first saw you that you must have it when you're fifteen, Chloe,' she explained. I kissed her. 'Now open it!' she said.

My sleepy fingers fiddled with the locket at first but finally managed to prize the two halves apart. I looked at the tiny faded photograph of a woman inside. She was young and quite beautiful, with long blonde hair just like mine. I knew she was my grandmother.

'Granny?' I whispered, lightly touching the face in the photo. I felt tears welling. Just then, I felt both happy and sad. Seeing my granny again made me think of Daddy and Momma.

'You dreamt about him last night, didn't you? I heard you calling out,' she said. 'So, I guessed today was the right day for me to give it to you.'

I nodded. It had been another of those real dreams. My Daddy was there in our old house, now Adam's and María's, but Adam wasn't there. Just me and Daddy. Something had happened to my brother. I could feel it.

'Don't you go, too,' Daddy said. Suddenly the floor opened, and Daddy fell through. I saw him there, slowly slipping into the emptiness below, and I tried to grab his hand as he started to float away like an astronaut drifting off into space, but he was just out of reach. I called out to him, but he kept repeating those words, 'don't you go, too... don't you go, too.' Then he vanished.

But I didn't tell Aunt Jac my dream. I didn't tell anyone, not even Lee. See, I knew Daddy was trying to warn me like Earth Child had tried to, but I couldn't stop myself. I'd gone too far. That search had become a part of me. I just felt so bad getting your uncle caught up in it.

For a long while, I stared at the photo of my granny as a young woman. She looked so alive, but I knew she must have died quite soon after the photo had been taken. I'd only ever known Granny from pictures of her.

'Why does everyone in our family have to die young?' I asked Aunt Jac.

'Not everyone, Chloe,' she replied. She sat on my bed and put her arm round me. 'Beautiful, wasn't she? And so like you, honey. To look at and in spirit. She had that other thing too. You know what I mean?'

I looked up at her.

'Sixth sense?'

'Yeah! And funny dreams about things that came true.'

'Real dreams? They are true, Aunt Jac.'

I thought again of what my Daddy said. Go where? Me 'too'? What did he mean?

Aunt Jac picked up the kachina doll from my pillow.

'If you believe in something, they say that may be enough to make it come true. Like these kachinas of ancestors and animal spirits,' she said. I guess I wasn't old enough to understand what she meant. And I was still held by the picture of my young granny. It was like I could feel the strength of her spirit by holding her locket. For me, she was there, somewhere. Was she my kachina spirit? I closed the golden heart over the faded face and slipped the pendant around my neck.

'I must see Lee now,' I announced. 'He's awake! I can feel it.'

Aunt Jac smiled. 'That boy really loves you, Chloe. I can't believe there'll ever be anyone else better suited for you to share your life with, honey, but you're still very young, you know. Just don't get too serious too soon.'

'What do you mean by serious?' I asked, feeling peeved.

'I am your guardian, Chloe. Still have that responsibility for my late brother.'

'Aunt Jac—'

'And I can't have you hurt. I—'

'Aunt Jac, we're not lovers. And it was Lee who said we must wait to have sex, anyways. Says I'm *much* too young!'

'He's a good boy!' she said."

Pepe frowned.

"What are lovers?" he asked.

"Oh Pepe, it's so hard for me to remember you're only a kid. Let's just say two people who love each other so much they share absolutely everything."

"Daddy's always making love to Mummy. In bed. I know it. Are they lovers, then? Like what we got taught in science at school?"

"They sure are. And that's how they made you, of course! Now, where was I? Oh, yes—Lee was awake. As soon as he'd opened his door, he lifted me up in his arms and kissed me, repeatedly swinging me round like I was as light as a kachina doll myself. He put me down gently and touched the pendant around my neck. There was a funny look on his face.

'It's okay, Lee!' I laughed, kissing him again. 'This is from Aunt Jac. Not another Red Indian guy. It's my grandmother. See?' I opened the pendant and showed him the photo.

'Hey, great photo! Wow, she really did look like you. Only not as beautiful! Now wait here. And close your eyes.'

I did. I closed my eyes. But only for Lee, for I knew in a flash what my boyfriend was about to give me. With my eyes still closed I let him place it on the ring finger of my left hand. My heart raced.

'Yes, I will,' I promised after opening my eyes and gazing at the ring. I was grinning from ear to ear. 'But I'm only—'

'Juliet was fourteen,' Lee interrupted.

'I know, Romeo,' I said. Your knowledgeable Daddy told me once, Pepe. Like warning me not to get ideas from Shakespeare 'cos Juliet died."

"Shakespeare?"

"A famous English guy who wrote poems and plays and really understood people."

"Oh!"

"You know, Pepe, I had already seen Lee's ring in my mind. I knew he'd been saving up for it without him having to tell me. But to see it there, on my finger, Lee's pledge to remain faithful to me for the rest of our time together on Earth, it was the happiest moment of my life to date."

"Is that it?" asked Pepe stroking the ring on his aunt's finger. Chloe nodded.

"Awesome, huh? Turquoise set in silver. Native American. 'Where did you get it?' I asked your uncle.

'A-ha!' he exclaimed. 'Some things I ain't telling. Had it made especially, see. And these!'

He took me into his room and picked up two small boxes from the bedside cabinet and gave them to me. One contained a lovely matching turquoise bracelet and the other a set of earrings. I couldn't hold back the tears as he put them on me."

"Can I see them as well?" asked Pepe.

"Later, honey. 'Oh Lee, they're so lovely!' I told your uncle. 'Feel like I'm some kind of princess.'

'Just so long as you'll not mind marrying a poor humble black photographer someday.'

'Oh, stop that silly black nonsense!' I scolded. 'You're no more black than I'm a snow girl! Now, where's the mirror?'

Lee took me by the hand and led me to a long mirror on the wall beyond a built-in wardrobe. I looked in the mirror and screamed. Poor Lee, he was so upset. I turned and buried my face against his chest.

'He was there in the mirror. Behind you!' I sobbed. 'That Red Indian guy from last night.' Lee spun round and looked behind him. I dared to peer over his shoulder again. There was nothing. But I could still feel a presence, a kind of coldness.

'Chloe, I'll understand if you want to call it a day. Go back to New York. Maybe Adam and María could come up and visit you there. Perhaps—'

I shook my head. I had to see this through. Call it destiny if you like. I knew I couldn't avoid it, but I was dead scared. This wasn't what I'd been seeking. I'd come all this way, wanting reassurance about those people I'd been so close to that summer, and now I felt only darkness and fear.

'Can't give up, Lee. Not now. But at least I'll have her with me.' I closed my hand over the gold locket. 'She's like my kachina, Lee. Plus, there's you as well. I've got you. You'll never leave me, will you?'

Lee hugged me.

'Never!' He ran his fingers through my un-brushed hair and kissed away the tears from eyes.

At breakfast, Aunt Jac admired my new bracelet and earrings, but said nothing about the ring on my left hand. But I knew from the way she smiled at Lee that she approved—by default, perhaps. She'd have said so in no uncertain terms if she hadn't done.

'And there's something else, honey,' she said, as if reminded. 'Know how you've been trying to get me to marry my friend Jason, and I said I couldn't, not till his divorce came through. Well—' Aunt Jac smiled. I was so happy for her that the fear I'd felt earlier melted away.

'That's wonderful!' I cried. 'When did he—?'

'Found a text on my cell phone late last night. His divorce has just come through. And another thing—' She was still grinning. 'He's flying to Albuquerque from Los Angeles this morning. I'll go pick him up from the airport. Wants to join us on the flight back to New York.'

Uncle Jason—I'd always called him that—he was just the right kind of guy for Aunt Jac. Quiet, shy and rather dull on the outside, inside his mind was the most amazing thing ever. You know, he kind of reminded me of a fruit preserve factory we visited with our Momma and Daddy in

Vermont, Adam and me, when we were little. I'll never forget that place. Dull grey concrete building on the outside, and I couldn't for the life of me think what we were doing going there, but once we were inside—wow! Awesome! All that fruit – those strawberries and rasps and blueberries—in neat separate containers, getting tipped out onto curled canals where they bobbed around as they got washed clean, the bad ones having been picked out by a row of white-coated, white-hatted workers, then along over a series of conveyor belts, trembling and bursting with juice, they made their way to a large brass vat where they swirled in a hot sticky syrup and finally gave up their flavour. Boy, the scent of those fruits! It just hung there in the air and held me entranced, as I breathed in deep lungfuls of heaven. The jam, still liquid, got sucked up into transparent tubes, up and away and then down towards another belt. This one bore rows of jars, like the ranks of a great army of preserve soldiers, each jar suddenly made solid, given life, when filled with squirts of tasty fruit jelly with mathematical precision. Further along the same belt, the fruit preserve soldier jars got their flat metal helmets and then their regimental labels: 'Vermont Homemade Strawberry Preserve'... or whatever."

"Homemade?" enquired Pepe.

"Well spotted, my wise young nephew. Anyways, with all those jars facing the same way, they were picked up by mechanical crab pincers and without any fuss, because soldiers ain't allowed to fuss, they got put into brown cardboard boxes before being driven off to fight their fruit jelly war on the supermarket shelves. *What if something goes wrong?* I wondered, staring at that eternal march in the Vermont Fruit Preserve Factory. *What if a jar gets over-filled, or another stays empty? What if the different fruits get muddled up and the wrong labels get put on? What if a whole battalion of jar soldiers should fall from that conveyor belt and shatter?* But nothing went wrong, and never would do. I knew that.

See, like that jam factory, Uncle Jason never got it wrong. Aunt Jac—or Jacqueline, as he called her (only person I knew who called my aunt by her proper name)—she told me that. A lawyer who acted almost exclusively for the prosecution in cases of homicide, he saw to it that justice was done.

I say 'almost exclusively'. Once, when the prosecution had in their sights a black guy the police had arrested for a cold-blooded murder of a woman and her child in a car park, Uncle Jason refused to act for them. Said the guy had been framed. Not only that. Said the defence attorney was useless and accused the police of being bent. Uncle Jason became that guy's defence lawyer. Proved without a shadow of doubt the man couldn't possibly have been guilty. The man went free and an investigation was set up into the police methods. See, Uncle Jason, he knew the truth. Not by sixth sense, like me or my granny, but through a process of methodical deduction and an understanding of people."

"What's deduction mean?" asked Pepe.

"Oh, your Aunt Chloe's at it again. Thinking she's talking to an adult. Deduction's like piecing a jigsaw puzzle together and making the picture come whole. It was always a mystery to others how my shy, kind Uncle Jason, ended up working as the lawyer who nailed some of the most evil killers in our society. 'The Electric Chair', some of his colleagues jokingly nick-named him. If only they knew how gentle he really was, I thought. Aunt Jac explained it to me, once. His elder brother, a doctor, had been slain in a senseless killing by fleeing bank robbers. Left behind a young widow and a baby boy. The guys who did it were caught but never charged for his murder. Accidental death, they said. Accidental? They'd aimed their three-ton vehicle at the doctor, who must've seen their unmasked faces, and smashed the life out of him. Uncle Jason only ever wanted to see justice done. If he was certain.

I would have loved to have seen the inner workings of Uncle Jason's mind, like those of the Vermont factory. I thought it was so cool the way he came out with answers to questions not just minutes or even hours later. Sometimes he'd suddenly blurt out an answer the following day, as though he'd spent all that time analysing the issue, turning it over in his mind, making sure he'd considered every nook and cranny of the argument.

I remember, before Aunt Jac and me and Lee went west, I overheard Aunt Jac say to him, 'Have I gone completely crazy, or what, giving in to Chloe like this?' I was in my room at the time, but the door was open. Uncle Jason remained silent. I could see his face in my mind. Blank and expressionless as though no one had said anything.

'No, you haven't,' he blurted at breakfast the following morning.

'Haven't what, honey?' Aunt Jac asked, looking kind of puzzled.

'Gone crazy.'

'Well, thank you. But what makes you suddenly say that?'

'You asked me yesterday if you'd gone crazy giving in to Chloe over this trip to New Mexico.'

Aunt Jac and I grinned at each other.

'Rhetorical question, dear. I just—'"

"Rhetorical?" queried Pepe.

"No answer needed. Like making a statement. But Uncle Jason said, 'No! A very good question. See, I've been thinking about it. About Chloe and her dreams and this mission of hers. It's something that the child must do. No two ways about it. Whatever happens!'

I loved Uncle Jason even more for that. It took the pressure off my guardian, Aunt Jac. Plus, later Uncle Jason would be our rock—especially for Lee and Aunt Jac.

'See here!' announced Aunt Jac in that hotel in Albuquerque the day before Uncle Lee and I were due to fly back home. She took a leaflet out from her handbag. 'A special treat for you and Lee.'

She handed it to me. And she could never have known. Just an advertisement for a fun show for tourists given by a Native American group. Demonstration of basketry, jewellery making and the Puebloan snake dance. It was the sort of show I would now always try to steer clear of. Shows like that turn the Native Americans into kind of circus freaks, but, as Aunt Jac said, they only show the bits they allow the outside world to see. Have to make money somehow when all they've been given by the US government are patches of desert. But I reckoned Lee would be able to take photos and it seemed a better option than twiddling our thumbs all morning. Lee took hold of my hand under the table and squeezed it. That meant 'Yes!'

'Sure, Aunt Jac! It's on the way to the airport, anyways. We'll find stuff to do there, won't we Chloe?' Lee seemed keen, so I agreed.

'Lucky I found it then,' added Aunt Jac. 'It was the only one there on the reception desk this morning.'

I looked at that leaflet again when we were in Lee's room. 'Native American Spectacular!' Earth Child's kachina spirit, if that's who had visited me in that real dream, certainly would not be there. I would've felt her presence in the leaflet. But a snake dance? I recalled that strange dance at the disco the previous night. Had I imagined the snake? There again, the snake and the rain dance, these were the things usually dished out to tourists. *Snake, rain, corn, rain, snake!* And it means nothing to those tourists. Just a colourful display. 'It's so boring!' I'd once overheard some little squirt complain when referring to Native American culture. *Boring?* A civilisation stretching back thousands of years into the mists of early time. A people who were closer to the spirit of the earth and the forces of nature than white man could ever be. A people who didn't need to seek out some hidden meaning in life through organised religion, for they knew. They were a part of it, whatever 'it' is. White Man and his jerky dancing and brain-thumping music, he's the boring one I used to think back then. 'Course, now I know better—about your Mama's God—something I didn't understand then because I still felt so angry with Him for your grandparents' deaths.

'Lee, I'm beginning to doubt what I'm doing,' I said. 'If only I knew what it was that Earth Child was trying to tell me. But I can't see us getting anywhere and I feel so bad about wasting your time. You could have been earning good money now in your summer vacation.'

I was standing at the window of his hotel bedroom looking out at the car park. Aunt Jac was making phone calls, planning her morning, before dropping Lee and myself off at the 'Native American Spectacular'. Lee came up behind me and held me real close. I always liked it when he did that.

'Me work in a burger bar and leave my girl all alone? Prefer to be poor, honey.'

'But—' I began. I stopped. I saw something grey move across the car park. It disappeared behind a car. 'What was that, Lee? Did you see it?' I asked.

'Some sort of a dog, I guess.' I turned and saw Lee was frowning as he squinted at the car park. I looked back at where the grey shape had vanished.

'There it is again!' I said excitedly when it emerged from its hiding place and slunk, camouflaged against the grey tarmac, past a row of cars towards a low wall.

'That's a coyote,' Lee said, still frowning.

'It's so beautiful,' I exclaimed.

In one easy movement, the coyote sprang onto the wall then, a moment later, was gone.

Chapter 5: The Coyote

"I worry for my granddaughter even more now that I know the enormity of her responsibility," said the old Mexican in the smart suit.

The scientist peered down into her microscope again.

"And so you should!" she stressed. "So should we all. What I see down there is not good at all."

The priest made a gesture of irritation with his hand which in another dimension might have been taken as a sign of the Cross.

"Why do you all talk such nonsense? Our Saviour will see that no harm comes to any of us whatever happens down there!" he scoffed.

The old antiques dealer shrugged his shoulders.

"Then there's a lot in the Bible that is also nonsense as far as you're concerned." For the first time in aeons, anger was evident in that place. The priest, muttering incoherently, got up and left the other three.

"He'll come around to our way of thinking soon. When they find the girl."

"The Death Lords find María?" The old grandfather's alarm could have cut through the hardest of steel back on Earth.

"No! The other girl."

***

"'A coyote? Don't think so. Not in a car park. They're pretty shy creatures, you know,' my Aunt told me.

'Lee should know,' I argued. 'He's done a wild-life photography course.' I felt almost annoyed with Aunt Jac for questioning Lee's assertion.

'Well—maybe a tame one?' she suggested.

'Didn't look tame to me.'

As I climbed into the car, Aunt Jac pointed to the kachina doll that I was clutching.

50

'Are you really taking that with you?' she asked. I glanced uneasily at Lee. He hated the doll. I touched his hand. Don't know why I did that. Perhaps an attempt to reassure him that the guy who gave it to me was not important.

'It's just possible it's a kind of message from Earth Child. I don't really know,' I added. 'Don't get any vibrations from it, see. It's just that—well, if I take it to that Native American show this afternoon, I might find someone who knows more about these things.'

The show was in a park off the road to the airport, so at least we didn't have to go far. The kachina doll did extract a response from an old lady in a gift shop. When I showed it to her, she looked at me in a strange way, then at the doll, and shook her head. But I knew already that the doll wasn't for me.

'I think I'll call her María,' I said to Lee.

'Why?' asked Lee, looking awfully puzzled. I'd been unusually quiet at the show. Lee too. He'd hardly said a word all morning. That was Lee's way of telling me something. He never got angry. Still doesn't. Just goes quiet. I knew it was the doll winding him up; and that Red Indian guy who gave it to me, the doll being a kind of fertility thing. You know, as we went up the drive into the park, I'd have given anything to throw the doll out of the window, forget the whole damned thing and just hold Lee close to me. But I couldn't. Something was preventing me from doing that. I felt its power for the first time, and it wasn't coming from the doll. It was connecting with the doll.

'Remember!' I said, snuggling up against Lee. 'The doll's for María. I'm just looking after her until—' I shut up. I didn't know what I was saying, and Lee knew that.

'See you both back here at five, guys,' Aunt Jac said. 'If I'm delayed just hang around. And no running off, Chloe. Like you did two years ago in Colorado.'

'It's okay, Aunt Jac. I'll keep an eye on her!' your uncle promised. Lee and I got out of the car.

'You mind you do that, Lee. More precious to me than anything else in the whole world, my little niece is,' Aunt Jac said.

Lee closed the car door and Aunt Jac drove off. We got tickets for the show from a lady sitting behind a rickety old table at the entrance to the park. Apart from her face, the woman could have come from just about anywhere in the United States of America: shapeless shorts, ill-fitting blouse and well-worn sneakers. There was a marquee, crowded with whites and Hispanics, even a group of Japanese tourists, but not a Native American in sight. Then—and this was the thing that nearly freaked me out—I spotted a large, gaudy tepee beyond the marquee. I felt cheated. The Puebloans lived in houses, like the Hopi, not tepees, like the Apache or Comanche.

'Lee, this is a rip-off,' I complained. 'Just a tourist trap!"

'It's okay! We'll chill out. Find somewhere cosy. Have a little chat. Ain't done much of that today, have we?' He gave me a kiss on the cheek, and I felt better already.

It was whilst we were in the marquee, and I was looking at some Indian bags and jewellery, that I felt a tug on my arm holding the doll. I knew it wasn't Lee. I looked round and saw nothing at first. Then I looked down. A little boy, no more than five, must have pulled at my arm. He was pointing to the tepee without saying a word; just fixing me with big brown eyes that didn't seem to belong to his face. It was like he was mute, or something. I couldn't believe that he didn't speak or understand English. Not in twenty-first century New Mexico.

'It's the doll, Lee. And the tepee. He knows something. And—' I looked down at that little face. It stood out amongst all those tourists. Distinctly Native American, and yet there was something about it. It was like nothing I'd ever seen before.

'Lee, take his picture. Now! Before he runs off.'

The little boy smiled when Lee took his camera out of its case.

'Say cheese!' asked Lee, holding up the camera. The boy said nothing. Only grinned. It was as if he already knew why his picture was being taken.

'Let me see the picture, Lee. His face looks so fam—' The little boy suddenly turned and ran from the marquee.

'Quick! We must follow him. He's gonna show us something. I know it!'

By the time we got outside, the boy had vanished. There was just an empty space in front of the tepee, and the flap of the tepee was closed over its entrance.

'That was so weird, Lee. I'm sure I saw something in his face. Something about his expression. I dunno. Not Eagle Foot's, but I'm certain I once knew him. And now he's gone. Can I have a look at that picture?' Lee showed me a bland image of a little boy. 'That look he gave—it's not there. We must find him. Perhaps—' I was staring at the tepee. Something about it made me think of a volcano about to erupt. 'He's gotta be in there. And if he's there, he's gotta come out. I can wait.'

Lee looked around. There was no one else on the stretch of ground in front of the tepee where we stood; odd considering the whole place was teeming.

'Chloe, there's something creepy about this spot. It's just too quiet. Why isn't there anyone else here?'

I shrugged my shoulders. I'd spent over a year planning this. We'd come all that way, so I wasn't going to blow it just because of a bit of creepiness, though thinking back there was something – particularly with that tepee.

'Ladies and gentlemen, boys and girls, a big hand please for the ancient Puebloan snake dancers!' a speaker announced. It sounded muffled and far away, like a voice from another world. Still that space in front of the tepee remained empty, as if no one else had heard the announcement. I was about to comment on this when the flap opened and a human lava flow of Native Americans in colourful costumes erupted from out of the tepee."

"Lava?" questioned Pepe.

"Liquid fire from inside the earth. Comes out of the top of Volcanos."

"Cool! But not from tepees!"

"And not to the heart-beat rhythm of a hundred drums. Boy, the noise was deafening! Twenty or thirty dancers looped into a moving circle, like had happened the previous night at the disco. And as before, something writhed on the ground in the centre of the circle."

"A snake?" guessed Pepe.

"Sure was. A rattler. But you know, although I'm terrified of snakes, I felt an overpowering urge to join the dancers. My feet were already tapping out the rhythm. I just had to finish the dance I'd started the previous night. Become one with that snake curling and twisting in the centre of the circle. I tried to step forwards, but a strong hand gripped by arm, and held me back."

"Uncle Lee?"

"I attempted to wriggle free. Boy, the weird look on Lee's face! Never seen such a look before. Seemed to me he was trying to ruin everything. Destroy the magic I felt."

"Wasn't he warning you, Aunt Chloe?"

"I see that now, Pepe. Poor Lee! I yelled at him, 'Let go of me! I want to—' I shrieked, then realised I didn't know what I wanted. See, I was kind of possessed, as they say."

"Possessed? Like I possess my football?"

"Just like that—and I was about to be kicked someplace else!"

'Chloe,' insisted Lee, 'I promised Aunt Jac I'd not let you go running off. Please stay with me. Don't go there to dance with those Native guys. Don't do it!'

To this day, I'll never know what Lee must have gone through during those next few moments.

'Lee, let go!' I screamed. 'You're hurting me!'"

"Was he really?" Pepe couldn't imagine Lee hurting anyone or anything.

"Of course not! Lee would never hurt me. Only I thought he might relax a little if I said that. And it worked. He was still holding my arm, but less tightly. I managed to stay quiet for a few moments, but that kachina doll—María, I called her—she was dancing away in my hand. I couldn't keep her still as the beat of the music continued to numb all my senses.

I had never taken bad drugs. Not like some of the more stupid kids at school had done. But I imagined the effect of the strange music must have been like that of a drug. Plus, watching those dancing figures with their masked faces and the writhing of the snake seemed to whirl my brain like it had gotten put into a blender."

"Papa puts fruit in our blender to make smoothies."

"Good one, Pepe. My brain was being turned into a smoothie. Anyways, something then caught my attention. A movement in the entrance of the tepee. It was the Native American boy. Looking straight at me, he was, with that same expression, only I just couldn't work out whether it was Eagle Foot's or not. But I felt sure he was the one I'd waited for all this time. He just had to be. And I wanted him to tell me everything. Show me what happened to my friends from the mesas and guide me to their descendants.

I yanked my arm free from Lee, the worst thing I've ever done in my life, and ran to the tepee. And María, the kachina doll, she ran with me. I could hear her laughing as she ran in my hand, and all I wanted to do—no, all *we* wanted to do—was to escape from Lee. Not for a moment did I think about the effect this was having on my boyfriend. I heard him call out, but it was like from another world:

'Chloe! Come back. Don't go in there!'

Funny, I thought, *but that's just what Daddy said in my real dream. 'Don't you go there too!' Ha-ha! I'm free from Lee, and from Daddy. At last I'm free,* I rejoiced!

And I slipped through the opening of the tepee.”

Chapter 6: The Hurricane

***

Adam was up early to check on the defences against Hurricane Lara which was due to strike land later that morning. They were a good few miles from the coast, so she'd probably get down-graded to a tropical storm, even if they were still in her path, as predicted, but he was taking no chances. They also had the responsibility of Chloe's twins, Jimmy and Kurt. Chloe had left them for her brother and María to look after whilst she and Lee went to interview folk in Baton Rouge about the cruel consequences of Hurricane Katrina some years back. They particularly wanted to meet and film the Vietnamese prawn fishermen, for the irony of the plight of these people was something that they felt would touch many hearts in their documentary on global warning. With their uninsured boats thrown out of the water and smashed by Katrina, for a while they had difficulty competing with the lower prawn prices offered by the importers of prawns from Vietnam – the country from which that they had fled a generation back because they happened to be on the wrong side of a human divide. Lara then added her own irony to the story by changing course and heading for Texas instead of Louisiana, forcing Chloe and Lee to stay another night in Alabama until she'd done her thing and fizzled out.

"Missing Aunt Chloe, huh?" Adam said to Pepe whom he found in the kitchen sitting at the table and drawing with his felt tips. Like his aunt, he was a gifted artist. Pepe said nothing, for, again like Chloe, his concentration was absolute when he drew.

Adam looked at the picture in front of his son: Native Americans dancing, a brightly-coloured tepee—a snake.

"The tepee shouldn't have been there," the boy finally said. "It was wrong. Aunt Chloe told me." Pepe turned around to look at his father. "Papa, what *does* a coyote look like?"

"A coyote? Well, it's a kind of dog."

"Like a fox?"

"More like a wolf, I guess."

"Papa, why was Mama a White Deer? And who called her that?"

"A long time ago, son. Now listen—" Adam pulled up a chair beside Pepe. "Don't let Mama hear you use that name. Understand?"

"Why not, Papa?"

"Because—" Adam suddenly stopped. He caught sight of a painting Pepe must have done earlier, lying partly hidden by the one with the Native Americans and the tepee. He pushed the later picture to one side and stared at the earlier one: a fierce-looking large cat, golden yellow in colour. Its eyes were black with vertical crimson slits, its mouth open, displaying white dagger teeth.

"Did Aunt Chloe tell you about this?" he asked, frowning.

"Oh no! We haven't got to the bit about the Golden Jaguar yet."

"But how—?"

"Oh, I just know about it. That's all. And I know who the Golden Jaguar is too!"

"He's dead, Pepe. Dead! Only a myth. But please, never show this picture to Mama. Or talk to her about the Golden Jaguar. Hear me? Do you promise?"

Pepe, wide-eyed, looked quizzically at his father. He nodded slowly.

"When will Aunt Chloe and Uncle Lee be back?" he asked. "I'm feeling bored."

Adam chuckled.

"Thought you could tell me that, Pepe. With the telepathy thing that you and your aunt share."

"Oh, I can't always tell. But I know she's fine. And she's still in Alabama."

"Well, you and Carla will have enough to do looking after Jimmy and Kurt when we're battened down against Lara."

"Carla's still doing her project with them."

"Sounds good. And how about some breakfast, son? Cereal, bagel?"

"Not yet, Papa. Not till after I've drawn the coyote."

The Ranch House was an impregnable fortress after Adam had finished. Sturdy planks nailed across all the windows, the doors to the outside boarded up and Adam had even been up on the roof, which freaked out María, to check for loose tiles. In the yard, the shouts and shrieks of children had been replaced by Hurricane Lara's cacophonous entry to Houston.

"Go fetch your sister and the twins for lunch, Pepe!" María later called out. "And don't forget to wash your hands." No reply, so she went on a search. Pepe was on his own in the playroom. He looked sheepishly up at his mother when she appeared in the doorway. She was frowning.

"Pepe, where are Carla and the twins?" Pepe was trying to work out how best to answer the question. There was so much he was not supposed to tell his mother. "Pepe, where *are* they?" There was a tremble in her voice. He had to tell the truth.

"She's taken them for their project."

"Their what?"

It was unusual for María to raise her voice, but Pepe understood why she did. She was anxious. But she had no need to be. Because of the golden jaguar bracelets Papa had given them. Carla had put one on each of the twins, and they were really excited at the prospect of being rescued from Lara by the Golden Jaguar of the Sun. The Golden Jaguar might be dead, as Papa had told him, but the bracelets would bring him back to life and he would rescue the twins.

"Where are Carla and the twins, Pepe?" María took hold of Pepe's arm. "Honey, I'm not angry with you. I'm just worried. That's all. Where are they? What is this project?"

"They're gonna be rescued. They're really excited about it. It was Carla's idea."

"No matter whose idea it was. Rescued from what? Where are they?"

"Rescued from Lara. They're by the creek. Carla snuck out with the twins before Papa boarded up the yard door."

With the usual heavy rain storms, the creek would flood two or three times a month every summer. With Lara, it would turn into a raging torrent, whipped up by winds of over a hundred and thirty miles an hour. The hurricane was due any minute and María knew only too well what damage might be left in her wake. According to the media she had already hit land at force 12. No one could survive out there when the real Lara arrived.

"Adam... quick!" she shouted from the playroom. Adam appeared on the landing. "Carla. The twins. Down by the creek," María suddenly seemed almost calm. The horror of their situation had perhaps overridden the panic.

"Oh, my God!" Adam exclaimed, glancing at Pepe. The boy felt bad. He couldn't stop tears from welling. He wanted to hug his Mama and reassure her that Carla and the boys would be okay because of the Golden Jaguar, but he couldn't. He'd promised his Dad not to mention the beast to Mama, and he knew he must never break promises. He watched, with tears trickling, as his Papa ripped the planks away from the yard door and rushed outside. He went and stood at the doorway, in the driving rain, and looked back at his mother seated at the table, her head bent forwards, her shoulders shaking. She was now crying. He figured that if grown-ups cried, they must be *really* upset. If only he could tell her not to worry. The Golden Jaguar would rescue Carla and his little cousins, but he had to keep his promise of silence on the matter.

Lara hit like a predator leaping upon her prey. The house, a terrified rabbit, trembled as Lara the lioness gave vent to her fury with crashes and noises over and above the whistling howl of the wind and the lashing of the rain against the side of the house. Also, there was another sound, tiny and insignificant against the noise of the hurricane: the soft sobs of Pepe's mother. Adam had still not returned with Carla and the twins. Pepe alone knew they would be all right for reasons he could not tell his mother. If only he could, then she'd be happy. Instead he sat on the floor of the playroom with his hands over his ears, every now and then wiping away the tears so he could see better.

Although he knew Aunt Chloe and Uncle Lee were fighting hard to stop it from happening in his life-time, Pepe did wonder whether it was the end of the world when the whole house shook like the wonky tumble dryer that had to be replaced the previous fall. Then came an unearthly bang, as if the gods had discharged a cannon. The roaring sound outside became muffled, after which Pepe heard the most wonderful sound in the world: his Mama shrieking with joy. This was followed by Carla's high-pitched squeals of delight, the laughter and the jabber of the twins and his father's deep, comforting voice; the Golden Jaguar of the Sun comforting White Deer, his Mama. Pepe got up and went to stand in the doorway.

Papa and the children looked as if they'd had buckets of water sloshed over them. Carla, still clutching the golden bracelets, giggled when her Mama hugged and kissed her and the twins. Adam, dripping Lara's tears onto the floor, came over to hug Pepe.

"They're okay like you said they'd be, Pepe. Thank God!" Then he went to fix the boarding over the yard door.

"It was the Golden Jaguar who rescued them, wasn't it, Papa?"

Adam froze, then answered without looking back:

"The Golden Jaguar's dead, Pepe. Remember that! Dead! And he'll never come back."

But Pepe could barely wait to hear more about the Golden Jaguar after Aunt Chloe returned from Alabama. He felt furious with Lara for having kept her and Uncle Lee away for so long.

Chapter 7: The Tepee

The Lords of Xibalba feared the other girl. Unlike the coyote who feared nothing and no one, they knew this girl had the power to destroy them for all eternity, for she had grown stronger than her mother because of what happened after Coyote Spirit's plan to take over on Earth had failed.

***

Pepe could hardly wait for Aunt Chloe and Uncle Lee to get back. As always, he ran up the road to meet their car before its engine was audible from the Ranch House. As soon as they were unpacked, he took his aunt by the hand and led her to the same quiet spot out in the yard where her story would continue to unfold:

"Guess you've been waiting too long to find out why I suddenly became so disobedient, huh? Why I thought I knew better than your long-suffering uncle."

"He loves you very much, Aunt Chloe. Why did you just run off like that?"

"Sometimes, Pepe, there are no easy answers. I did, and that's something I'll have to live with for the rest of my life. But you know, once I was inside that tepee, I felt different."

"How come?"

"Regret, maybe? First, it was like I was totally alone. I wanted Lee so badly. I felt stupid for breaking free and running off. I turned to go back but I couldn't see the entrance of the tepee I'd only just run through. It was like that triangular space for the tent flap had closed over. I couldn't even see the side of the tepee. I was in a kind of swirling mist. I reached an arm out into the mist towards Lee's voice 'cos I could still hear the poor boy calling out for me, but my hand touched nothing. And, oh man, was it cold! Ninety-seven Fahrenheit outside, and there I was in my short skirt and top, belly button exposed, shivering in that mist. It was dark too. Then, as I grew accustomed to the darkness, I made out the face of the little boy I'd followed; the face with those familiar eyes. I realised he was staring not at me, but at the kachina doll in my hand; at María, as I called her.

He turned and vanished into the mist. There was only one thing I could do. Follow him. Besides, I was only in a small tepee—or so I thought. I could hear him ahead of me, his heavy footfall on the rough ground, his shallow breathing. Strangely, both sounds seemed to belong to a man, not a small boy. And I couldn't seem to catch up with the disappearing shape in the mist ahead. The strangest thing was that I was walking and walking and yet never reached the other side of the tepee. I knew I wasn't walking in circles. For one thing, I didn't feel giddy. I felt sick with fear, but not giddiness. And another thing: I could no longer hear Lee's cries. Just my own footsteps, those of the Indian ahead and our breathing, mine and his. Suddenly the boy's footsteps stopped, but I still heard his breaths. I approached slowly. A ghost-like figure of a grown man appeared out of the mist. A Native American in a short tunic wearing a headdress—the very same man who'd made me dance with him the previous night. I looked around, but the small boy was nowhere to be seen.

The guy held out his hand. I knew what he wanted. Not me, but the kachina doll that he'd put in my hand after the dance. Shaking like a jelly, I offered it to him, but he only touched it, grunted, then turned and began to climb. I saw he was climbing a flight of steps towards a high arch. I followed him up the steps. At the top, I could see that the only way on was over a narrow suspension bridge hanging there in the swirling mist. The man was already striding across the bridge, causing it to bounce and swing. Gripping the railings on either side, I followed him.

The mist grew thicker. As if created by a fine silvery dust, it shimmered in the dim light. I might even have thought it beautiful if I wasn't so scared. You're probably asking yourself, Pepe, why I didn't just turn around, find my own way back, escape from the nightmare and be with Lee again. Then apologise and abandon the whole crazy notion of tracing Eagle Foot's descendants. But I couldn't, you see. There was nothing at all behind me. As for that kachina doll I called María, how I hated her! Not the real María, of course. Our María, your Mama. We all love her. But the kachina doll had this strange power over me. I believe it was the doll that had torn me from Lee and forced me to run away from him. I so wanted to throw the doll from the bridge into the emptiness below, but I couldn't. She clung to me like a limpet to a rock. And even if I had managed to prise her free, what then? Who would I be in this strange place, I wondered? Or, more correctly, would I even be? It seemed my very existence there depended on that kachina doll. Without 'María', I believed I would simply vanish.

I struggled to keep up with the Native man, what with those long strides of his, and I was sometimes forced to run, which made it even more difficult to keep my balance and stop myself from falling through the gap between the wooden slats of the bridge and the steel hand-rail, and that doll in my hand she kinda seemed to be mocking me whenever I glanced at her painted face. Just when I thought the bridge was going to go on forever, I noticed the mist ahead was brightening. A tall arch appeared, looming over the shape of the striding man. The entrance to another reality? Beyond, I saw colours. Red, yellow, blue. Thank God, I thought! The park near Albuquerque? And Lee? But no way!"

"Aunt Chloe, why didn't Uncle Lee just come after you in the tepee?"

"Ah! We'll come to that later. Believe me, he did try. Poor boy must have been desperate. Meanwhile, there I was on that bridge wondering how on earth I was ever gonna say sorry to him. *I'll never be able to live this down,* I told myself.

Funny how hope plays tricks on the mind, Pepe. Guess it must be like that with mirages for guys lost in the desert. As the mist thinned, and I began to make out more human shapes ahead, I prayed that the figure standing there, now still and waiting for me, would mysteriously turn into Lee. *Blink*, I prayed, *and that red ground will turn green, those dark shapes beyond will just be tourists, not—oh my God...*

Pepe, I had never been so frightened in all my life as when I emerged from that mist. My Daddy's words came back to me: *Don't you go there too!*

'There' meant 'here'... where I now stood. I knew it. Where your Daddy had brought your Mommy back from the dead. My father had tried so hard to warn me, yet, through my own pig-headedness, I had landed up in this *Place of Fear*, for that's what the ancient Maya called it and that's exactly what it is. Beautiful too, which made it even more terrifying. For a few awful moments, I assumed I'd just died, but something informed me I was still alive—the kachina doll perhaps—and that I was needed by someone or something.

I was standing close to that Native American on the top of a broad hill the colour of blood. The hill sloped down towards an endless plain of bright yellow and blue. In the distance was a massive wall of craggy, snowless mountains. But the weirdest thing was the sky. A curious dull grey, but also luminous, and the mist had turned into a fine drizzle. Soon I was soaking and yet I no longer felt cold. And although it wasn't dark, I couldn't quite work out where the light came from, for the colourful land itself seemed to glow. A sky without a sun that wasn't dark and a landscape that gave off light. Made no sense to me.

At the bottom of the red hill were statues, the figures I'd prayed were tourists in the park in Albuquerque. Each emitted a fear the like of which is impossible to describe. Fear is normally a passing thing. Done and over with after whatever caused it has finished its business. With those statues, it was like the fear that made them that way would go on forever. I tried hard not to look at them, but my eyes refused to be deflected from the nightmare vision. So, there I was, a fifteen-year-old girl from Texas, staring at these things, trembling with terror not cold, despite being soaked to the skin, but worst of all I had no idea what the heck I was doing there or what I should do next. And I held tightly onto María-the-kachina doll, for something told me she was also a key to my survival.

The Red Indian guy turned briefly to look at me—or, rather, at 'María'—then continued down the hill. There was no path. As I followed him, I didn't look too carefully at the ground, but I felt it. It was soft and springy, but I could tell it wasn't red grass. It wasn't made from plants at all. It was the smell that gave it away. It seemed I was walking on a huge hill of congealed blood.

Ahead, I saw low stone buildings beyond the frozen figures of fear, scattered over that colourful blue and yellow plain. I thought we were heading for these, but on reaching the bottom of the blood red hill the Indian did a ninety degree turn and followed the divide between the red of the hill and the blue and yellow of the plain.

We walked for what must have been an hour or so, but my watch had stopped so I had no reference with which to measure time. Perhaps it had only been minutes. Perhaps—and this is what really spooked me—perhaps weeks or months. *Oh, my God*, I thought, *poor, poor Lee. And Aunt Jac!* Would she be back by now? Would she blame Lee for my disappearance?

'It's not Lee's fault!' I screamed out. 'Please don't blame him. He tried to stop me!'

Wherever I was, I wanted the whole Universe to hear me. But I was screaming at no one, at nothing, for that Native man just kept on walking. I followed the back of his head. His long black hair was braided, like my own blonde hair, and on this sat a headdress of feathers. I saw how the muscles on his arms and calves stood out. It felt like they were teasing me. Teenage girls at school in New York would have given anything to have quality time with this guy, yet I only prayed he would suddenly vanish or turn back into that little boy. I couldn't help but think that he was somehow linked to the fear that gripped those frozen statues and that hung like a heavy cloud over the plain; a fear that stretched to the distant mountains on the horizon and beyond.

Finally, he halted again and waited for me to catch up. As I approached him, I felt 'María', the doll, jerk in my hand. She, too, must have felt his power. From the corner of my eye—and I could not look at him directly—I saw him raise his hand and point to something ahead. I squinted then saw it, camouflaged against the red earth: a large blood red building. At first, it seemed more of an outline, like it had been drawn there with a pencil, but slowly it became solid. And it was vast. It had no roof. A kind of stadium. There was shouting and cheering, too, coming from the other side of its high wall.

As we approached, an opening appeared: a crudely drawn door on the red stone wall. Then, as if by some trickery of light, it became three-dimensional. A doorway through which I saw an enormous dark red arena with a central ball court above which were tiered rows of seated Native people. Even from the doorway, I could see their faces were Mexican, different from the guy I was following, and their clothes were weird. Nothing like those of the ancient Puebloans or present-day Navajo of New Mexico.

When I entered the courtyard, every face turned to look at me. I felt horribly vulnerable in my short skirt and clinging wet top as I stood staring back at them, clutching that hateful kachina doll. Suddenly, they began to whoop and jeer, punching air with their fists and shouting in a crescendo of noise. I covered my ears, but it penetrated through my hands and hammered at my brain.

"Stop!" I shrieked.

I felt a tickle of tears trickle down one cheek, but the taunting hoots and teasing whistles only intensified. My obvious distress seemed to excite them even more.

Then my Red Indian guide (my? Yeah, we did seem kind of linked through that kachina doll), he set off again, passing between two rows of yelling 'spectators'. I could tell that's what they were. Uneasy about being left alone with these people, I followed him, trying hard not to touch, or be touched by, any of those I passed. They were evil, and physical contact with someone evil is the worst thing imaginable. I saw where the guy was heading for: a steep stairway up to a floor above the spectators.

Thank God he's not taking me out onto that stinking open ball court (it smelt of blood) *in front of all these jerks,* I thought, though if I'd known more, perhaps I'd have considered this a better fate than what he had in store for me.

The steps led to a balcony encircling the arena. It was empty, and either the crowds had gone silent, or the noise of their jeering was blocked from reaching this upper floor. I wiped away my tears, and trembled before the Native guy, waiting to see what he would do next. If only there'd been a flicker of humanity in those dark eyes set in such handsomely-carved features, but there wasn't. Not one iota of warmth. He was evil personified. My tears were wasted.

Looking at the kachina doll, 'María', he again held out his hand. I wasn't sure whether to feel relieved to be rid of that doll, or fearful. She'd taken me to this godforsaken place, of this I was sure, but I also felt she was helping me to stay alive, as if protecting me against terrors worse than I could imagine, though only to be preserved for some other even crueller purpose. Maybe this was to be the end and I'd never again see Lee or Adam.

But it made no sense to me. The Red Indian would hardly have given me the doll to take me to that place just to get it back from me, when we got there, then kill me. *Or would he?* I wondered. Confused and terrified, I gave him back the kachina doll. He smiled. The first time I saw him smile, but it was an evil smile. The smile of a beast about to play with its prey.

'There!' he said, pointing at the space beyond the edge of the balcony above the court. It was the first word he uttered. I had no idea what the language was, although I understood the meaning perfectly. *There!* And it was an order. Not an observation.

'I can't,' I said, in the same language, edging nervously back towards the balcony edge. There was no wall. I hated heights, like your Mama and Papa. I turned and peered down at the red arena and the crowd, now silent. I prayed they wouldn't see me and start up that awful yelling and whistling all over again.

'Go!' he commanded when I looked over my shoulder into eyes as soft and tender as flint.

'I can't!' I screamed. 'Don't be so stupid! I can't go there where you—' Cut-off mid-sentence by fear, I simply froze when he came slowly towards me. I felt sure he was gonna kill me or throw me down into that court below to be torn apart by those monsters. I had to back away from him. It's all you can do when evil comes at you head on. Then I looked down and gasped. I was standing in space, or so it seemed. Perhaps on glass. I couldn't really tell. Whatever, I was looking straight down at the crowd below. My heart missed several beats, and I dropped onto all fours, searching for something to grab hold of. There was nothing. I looked back at the man. He walked out after me into the space where I crouched, and that's when I recognized Coyote Spirit from the ancient mesas of Colorado.

But Adam killed you, my mind told me.

Quite right, came the answer in my head. *But not here in Xibalba.* As he approached, towering above me, I scrambled backwards, away from him until I was over the centre of the ball court. Then he stopped, standing in the air in front of me, his large feet inches from my hands. He scowled as he held up the doll. A scowl that sent shivers down my hunched spine.

'You'll bring her to me, huh?' he grunted.

'Who?' I replied. I knew very well to whom he was referring. Your mother, Pepe. But I had no idea how I was to do that, or even whether I should if I could. His mouth twisted into a sneer.

'Bring her!' he repeated without answering my question.

He turned and walked back to the balcony. I tried to crawl forwards but couldn't. It was like my knees were stuck to something. Suddenly I fell a few feet closer to that arena. It wasn't glass, after all. I was imprisoned, suspended in a thick, sticky, transparent space that reeked of death. I peered down below at the crowds, then looked up again. The man who had tried to impose his evil on the Anasazi, and whom I'd last seen in an ancient Puebloan village of a Mesa Verde canyon, was gone.

Meanwhile, down in the arena, things were happening. There were two groups of Xibalbans, for that's who these people were: one at each end of the court separated from the crowds by a wall of red blocks. It resembled a long rectangular pit. I realised that there were two teams about to start some sort of ball game, for in the centre of the long court, a huge muscular man stood holding a ball, about the size of a football, in both hands. The 'ball' had a face with blankly staring dead eyes. I didn't look too closely. I'd seen enough."

"A head?" queried Pepe.

"Indeed. A severed head. The big guy shouted a command. The game had begun. He threw the ball high in the air. It shot up just feet from where I was suspended, and the ghoulish face spun round as it flew past, hovering for a moment before dropping down towards the prancing combatants below. Several sprang at the ball, twisting their bodies to avoid colliding with teammates, and one hit the ball with his elbow, knocking it back towards his own team. From that moment on it was an all-out battle. Clearly, the ball had to be kept in the air at all costs, and anyone with the ball, if only for an instant, was a target for the full fury of the opposing team. Arms and legs shot out, the released ball flying off to a hail of shouts and screams from the spectators as more arms and legs and feet flailed in the air to keep it with their owners' team.

I noticed that any part of a contestant's body, bar head or hands, might make contact with the ball. Elbows, knees, even the trunk or the back, but never the head or hands. Perhaps it was the sheer weight of the ball and the risk of causing injury, but more likely, I felt, it was superstition. Maybe head-to-head with the decapitated was considered to bring bad luck; or touching what enclosed another soul might contaminate the toucher. Whatever, there was one thing that was obvious from the fury of the game: it was a matter of 'life' or 'death'... and in the land of the dead! Nothing else could have inspired the violence I saw being played out below me in a thrusting tangle of punching fists and jerking limbs. Down there, I saw a 'single' multilimbed creature enjoying a ghoulish game with that grotesque ball, shifting first in one direction, then the other. Each team appeared to be guarding opposing ends of the ball court. I could only assume the purpose of the game was to fling the ball-come-head through a carved stone hoop high up on one side of the court. In which case, perhaps there was no score at the end of the game. Only death, Xibalba-style, for the losers.

It seemed to me, hanging up there in the air, that evil was so well balanced with evil in this the game that it would go on forever and the ball would never touch the ground, but the end was sudden. A lithe body, perhaps even more charged with fear of another death than the others, sprang high, leapt backwards, rose again and, with lightning speed, shot the ball off his hip towards the stone hoop before any counter-measure could be put into action. The decapitated head sailed through the hole of the hoop.

The game was over and an explosion of cheers and shouts from the spectators shook the air I lay on. The players froze.

What happened next is almost too horrible to relate. Suffice it to say, Pepe, that the man I knew to be Coyote Spirit, the handsome big guy who had brought me there, and with whom I had danced—he suddenly appeared in the ball court and grabbed one of the players. Judging from the man's headdress he was an important player. Maybe the losing captain. His headdress was removed by the Red Indian from Colorado who then drew a knife from his belt and hacked off the other man's black locks. I couldn't bear to watch what I knew was coming next. My eyes remained tightly closed when excited cheers from the crowd confirmed my worst fears.

My eyes popped open again in response to a different sound: a high-pitched whining sound, almost a scream, accompanied by what's best described as the flapping of a large sail. Initially the beast that swept down past me, a giant bat, obscured the goings-on down in the ball court. All I saw was a vast black shape with outspread wings. The huge bat landed beside the headless body of the defeated team's captain, furled its wings then set to work extracting the man's Life-Force from this body. Meanwhile, Coyote Spirit triumphantly held up the severed head, and the crowd roared its appreciation.

Suddenly I remembered. My cell phone was still in my purse belt. My arms were free. I reached out (I was suspended horizontally, face down) and fumbled with the purse zipper. I managed to open it and felt for my phone. Thank God, it was there. I pulled it out. For an awful moment, I thought all was lost when it slipped from my fingers, but by waving my hand about I reached it. Like me, the phone was floating, trapped in the air. I grabbed it, brought it into my line of vision and switched it on. Amazingly, I got a connection. And why shouldn't I have, I asked myself? I was still in a tepee in that park outside

Albuquerque. Bound to get a connection! I keyed in Lee's number. No reply. Perhaps his own cell phone was turned off. I tried your father – Adam – the only person I knew who could rescue me. Once again, no answer. María, perhaps? The same. It made no sense. Adam and María always left their cell phones on. Without having my sixth sense, it was their only means of communicating with each other when not together. They've always been inseparable, your Mama and Papa. So, I texted Adam:

Adam save me. Stuck in air in t p Albuq. Death soon. — C.

I didn't know what else to say. Wasn't used to texting. Normally it was all there, somewhere inside my head, as if texting or phoning were superfluous, but in Xibalba I had no reception in that headstrong head of mine. Some kind of interference was stopping me from getting through and I knew where it came from: Coyote Spirit. I'd felt this once before in the mesas when I was trying to seek out Eagle Foot after he'd given himself up to Coyote Spirit to release those women who'd been captured and threatened with human sacrifice.

I sent the message okay, praying for a reply asap. It came almost immediately. I thought I had passed the worst moment in my life, watching that ball game and the awful bat monster, but Adam's texted reply pushed me even further into the depths of despair:

Welcum 2 Xibalba litl sis.

That's all he said in his message. My hero brother! The one person I thought I could always rely upon—the person who'd saved the lives of María and of my boyfriend, Lee. It seemed like my only life-line back to the real world, out of this nightmare, had been severed. At that moment, I just prayed I might die there and then. I felt evil had won and that I could take no more of it.

Then I noticed something below me as I tried to blot out the grisly proceedings in the ball court; something dangling from me, something gold. I focused on the object:

my granny's heart-shaped locket with the picture of her on the inside. My ancestor spirit, my very own kachina. I put the cell phone back in my purse and reached for the locket. I closed my fingers around it and held it in my clenched fist. It felt warm. Not temperature warm, but spirit warm, as if love radiated from it, and this love from my granny seeped into me and found my soul, and I felt strong again. Adam or no Adam, I would fight them. I would not let them kill me and turn me into a ball for another of their cruel games. My granny, whom I had never known, would protect me. I believed in her like nothing else mattered at that moment. Not Adam. Not even Lee..."

Chapter 8: The Kachina Doll

"That's in the past," said One Death.

"But we know already how the future can change the past," observed Seven Death. "Change the future and it'll all come right. We'll rule that dimension they call Earth for as long as she remains with us here... an eternal statue of beauty."

"He wants more from her. And for the present he's our only link to her."

"That too might change."

"The other girl?"

"If we can find her."

***

"What did it feel like when Aunt Chloe ran into the tepee and kinda disappeared, Uncle Lee?"

Lee, startled by Pepe's directness, looked up at the boy. He had been explaining the documentary movie playing on his i-pad whilst Chloe and Adam were out in the yard clearing up after Hurricane Lara, and María was playing with Carla and the twins. He stared into his nephew's inquisitive brown eyes. Although those eyes were of a very different colour to his wife's, he saw so much of Chloe in them. "She's been telling you that story then, Pepe?"

"Yeah, only it's not really a story, is it? Not a story sort of a story. More like what you and Aunt Chloe are doing in with your movie. A kinda documentary."

"Your aunt ain't been scaring you, has she? See, your Mama, she's none too happy about all that stuff."

"I know. And I never talk to Mama about it. About the Golden Jaguar. I'm not allowed to. Papa says it's too painful for her. But I can sort of see it when Aunt Chloe—"

"See it?" interrupted Lee. "See the story?" Pepe's serious little face studied his uncle.

"Not with my eyes seeing. More like I know it's there, but I need the words to help me. And Aunt Chloe says I have to get it right because one day I'm gonna have to know who I am and who Mama and Papa really are and perhaps that day's gonna come soon."

"So," began Uncle Lee, closing the i-pad and opening his mind for Pepe, "that tepee business, right? Well, first it was like my life had come to an end. We were that close, your aunt and me, and for her to suddenly break away and go running after that Red Indian kid, carrying the doll some hunk of Native American muscle had given her, I was like—well, kind of devastated, I guess. Know what that means? Devastated?"

Pepe nodded.

"Like my life had folded over and there was no purpose to it any more. See, I ran after Chloe, but as soon as I reached the flap of the tepee through which your aunt had disappeared, the tepee became kind of solid. More like a rock than a tent. I circled round and around the thing, repeatedly. I tried to look underneath it, but it was well and truly stuck into the ground. I banged on it and darn near broke my fist doing that. It seemed like it had no inside. Just a painted solid rock which had swallowed my darling Chloe.

You know, Pepe, there are times when things seem so terrible you can't even weep. That's how I felt then. I sank to the ground outside the rock-come-tepee and I refused to budge when one of the events organisers came up to me.

'I ain't leaving here till my girlfriend comes out of that thing,' I insisted.

'Don't know what you're talking about,' the guy said. 'The tepee's empty. Apart from the dancers' belongings. And they're all in the marquee over there enjoying well-earned refreshments.'

I turned and saw that the opening in the tepee that had been there, then hadn't, was back. No longer solid rock. I looked through the opening and, as the man had said, it was just an ordinary tepee, empty apart from a few bags and small piles of clothes belonging to the dancers.

'Is there another way out of this tepee?' I asked.

'Another way out? You crazy or somethin'? Ain't nothin' but a fake anyway, this here tepee. Now get along with you!'

'Sir—my girlfriend just went into it. Ran off, see? When I tried to follow her in, it just turned into solid rock. The flap had vanished.'

'Look, son, I don't care if you're into drugs or something, but I ain't got no time to waste listening to your bullshit. Clear off!'

That drugs thing kinda upset me. See, it was from drug pushers that Adam rescued me in New York. I'd never done drugs. The whole idea of an artificial life through drugs was abhorrent to both Chloe and to me. I only just managed to stay calm.

'I'm telling you, I am not moving. Not till my Chloe comes out."

'Well, she ain't gonna come out of nothin', is she? Don't give us no trouble, black boy.'

That did it! I really did lose my cool. Ashamed to say, I raised my fist. Then my cell phone rang. That guy was darn lucky. Since being with Chloe, I worked out in the gym a lot to become strong for her. She always did seem kind of vulnerable to me. In need of protection. One thump and I'd have knocked him senseless, but instead I answered my cell phone. It was my Ma.

Jeeze, Pepe, I got one helluva shock. Turned out my Dad was sick. Like seriously sick in hospital. Would I come back to New York immediately, she asked? For a few seconds, I felt like I was being pulled in half. My face must've shown the turmoil I felt, for Mr Ever-So-Lucky Native American dude just walked away, leaving me alone. In truth, I had no choice. I felt bad about my Dad, but there was nothing I could do for him and I'd never leave that place until Chloe came back from wherever she was—

and I knew this to be somewhere inside the tepee. I explained this as best I could to my Ma over the phone, but it wasn't easy with the state I was in just then. Then I went to the side of the tepee, hidden from the Red Indian who missed getting my fist in his face, but within sight of the tepee entrance. I waited for Aunt Jac and Uncle Jason to arrive, and that's exactly how they found me three hours later, slumped against that tepee staring at the entrance hoping and praying that my Chloe would just reappear like nothing had happened.

'She's done it again, hasn't she?' Aunt Jac asked. "Run off like she did two years back. Oh Lee, I am sorry. Please don't blame yourself. It's Chloe. She's so strong-willed, and sometimes she can't—'

'It wasn't her fault,' I interrupted. 'It was the doll's. She insisted on calling it 'María', for some reason. It pulled her away from me, I know it. It brought her to this tent. Plus there was a Native American kid the doll was following. I'm sure he had something to do with the big guy she'd danced with last night and who gave her the doll.'

'That kachina doll? She never said a Native American gave it to her,' Aunt Jac sounded concerned. 'I thought they were just giving them away, or something.' She sat down on the grass beside me.' 'Last time, Chloe, Adam and María came back within minutes. Funny thing is, they reckoned they'd been away for weeks,' she said. 'But this feels different. Look, Lee, if you want to get back to New York to see your Dad, I'll stay here. Jason will take you to the airport. Help you get a flight.'

I shook my head.

'I ain't leaving her, and that's final!' Aunt Jac got my message. She sent Uncle Jason over to talk with the event organisers. They listened to him, being a lawyer, and I was thankful for that, but I still felt pretty cut up about that other guy treating me like scum. Truth is, I guess he looked a little too much like the man who asked Chloe to dance."

Uncle Lee smiled at Pepe.

"I was jealous, see. First time in my life I'd felt such a thing over a woman. Jealousy, huh! And it darn near killed me knowing she'd gone in there with that Red Indian boy, and God knows who else, and disappeared. But praise the Lord for Aunt Jac and Uncle Jason! We sat together, and your Uncle Jason, he told me we would sit there for as long as it took for Chloe to come back. He and I talked man to man, for that was my other first. Realising I was a man, no longer a kid, and would have to face this thing like a man.

Just as Aunt Jac was about to go and get us a couple of hot dogs, her phone rang, and when she answered it her face dropped like it had fallen twelve hundred feet from the top of the Empire State.

'That was María,' she said after coming off the phone. 'Adam's vanished. Poor girl was so distraught she could hardly speak. He'd never do that without saying anything. He loves her too much. Lee, this can only mean one thing. It's all to do with María, not Chloe. Be brave, Lee. You'll get her back. I promise'"

'What?' I asked. 'I don't get it. How come this has anything to do with María back in Houston?'

For a few moments, Aunt Jac didn't answer. She stood there like she was racking her brains to work out how to tell me. Like she was embarrassed that I'd think she'd gone crazy.

'The Golden Jaguar of the Sun. He's been called,' she said. 'And it's María who's in danger. Not Chloe.'"

Pepe's jaw dropped.

"So, he's not dead, like Dad said he was?"

Lee shrugged his shoulders.

"I'm not the best person to ask, Pepe. If your Dad said he's dead, then he had a reason for saying it. But you must understand, death ain't so easy to explain away in one word."

Chapter 9: Beast and God

"Can't we just wait till she dies again? She'll not be that lucky next time. The Hero Twins have grown weak."

"You're forgetting something."

"The coyote?"

"Yes... there's him too. Grown strong whilst Hunahpu and Xbalanque have grown weak. No, her, the other girl."

"The coyote says she's here. He can sense her."

"What?" roared One Death with such force that the swing bridge to Xibalba quivered in the mist like a released bowstring.

***

"I'd better go and help your Papa and Aunt Chloe outside," Uncle Lee said to Pepe. "Lara brought down some pretty big branches. Told your Papa I'd cut 'em up with a chain saw."

Lee stood up, but Pepe remained seated at the kitchen table. The boy's mother was playing with Carla and the twins in the playroom, and from the emerging noise it was clear that they were having a whale of a time.

"I've seen it," Pepe announced. "The Golden Jaguar. Like inside of Aunt Chloe. But why can't I talk to Mama about the beast? The Golden Jaguar's good. He'll always protect her."

"There are things that happen to each of us that are best forgotten, Pepe. Like they should remain buried somewhere deep inside of you and never again get dug up. You see, talking about something bad can be like digging up those memories. Brings back the pain. And maybe next time you try to bury it, you can't. Just listen to your Mama now. She sounds so happy singing away in the kitchen. Keep her like that."

But Pepe knew how truly unhappy his Mama was, and it pained him to know this whilst wishing that he could help her.

Uncle Lee headed for the door to the yard.

"Can I help you with the chain saw, Uncle Lee?"

Uncle Lee chuckled. "Man's work, Pepe," he replied. "Can't have you losing any arms or legs, can we?"

"I could hold things. Fetch things. I'm good at that."

The man smiled at his nephew and held out his hand. Like an excited puppy, Pepe jumped from his seat and ran to his uncle. He took hold of Lee's hand. It felt big and strong.

The Golden Jaguar is big and strong too...

This much the boy knew. But there were other things he wanted to know about the beast, and it seemed too long to have to wait until he and Aunt Chloe would have their special time together at dawn the next day, sitting on the chair swing in the yard. The bits that he thought he knew were all jumbled up in his mind like the scattered pieces of a vast unassembled jigsaw puzzle.

Lee took the chain saw from the garage and placed it in the wheelbarrow.

"May I have a ride please, Uncle Lee?" Grinning, Uncle Lee placed an over-sized cycle helmet on the boy's head and lifted him into the wheelbarrow beside the chain saw that smelt of wood and grease. They laughed together as the barrow bumped along the path and over the grass to where the boy's Papa and Aunt Chloe were raking and picking up twigs and smaller branches... and talking. Mostly, they were talking:

"Well, hi there, Mr Space Man!" Aunt Chloe exclaimed.

"I'm Uncle Lee's right hand man today," Pepe proudly announced.

"Oh, you are, are you?" his dad said.

Pepe scrambled out of the wheelbarrow and soon busied himself by lifting the smaller logs, cut up by Uncle Lee, into the barrow. His Papa and Aunt Chloe quickly forgot that he was there and talked on:

"You've got to talk to her, Adam. There's something terrible troubling her. I can feel it. You only have to listen to those latest songs of hers. They're just so deep. All I know is it's to do with—" Aunt Chloe glanced in Pepe's direction, suddenly remembering his presence, and the boy put his head down, pretending that he wasn't listening.

"I can't rake it up for her again, Chloe. And bring back the pain," replied Pepe's dad.

"But we must know what this is about, Adam. Have you no idea? When you called me, I thought it was gonna be so easy. But that wife of yours, she's giving nothing away. Too deep for me to read her mind."

"Chloe, I'm at my wit's end and I'm shit scared. Scared that asking her again could be like lighting a firework. With no turning back."

"There's only one thing, Adam. He's got to know everything. That's why I'm putting it all together for him."

"She tried to make me think it was me. Worrying about her. You know. That business in the Chiapas all over again. Her way of trying to reassure me—or put me off the scent, perhaps. Yeah, it was a relief for me to learn back then that she knew all about what happened to her in the jungle without any harm coming to her. But it's not only that. I know there's more to it." Pepe's dad paused. "Of course, there is her religion."

"Making her unhappy?"

"No. Helping her."

"María's true religion is love. Pure and simple. That's the real María for you. Of all people, you should know this. Somehow I can't help thinking that her love is behind everything."

Chloe stopped what she was doing and leaned forwards on the rake. Pepe, all ears, struggled with a pile of broken-off branches.

"I sometimes wonder whether you and María think Lee and I have gone crazy over this Earth Mother business.

Gaia, as some call her. Guess she's buried deep inside me now and I can't get rid of her. Like María's God is inside of her. You know, talking to young Pepe has brought it all back to me as well, like you said it might. And the pain of losing Earth Child forever—and never knowing who she really was. I used to call her my soulmate, but I'm not sure what I meant by that. After all, no one could ever be closer to me than Lee. But with Earth Child, it was different."

"So very different, Chloe? I mean, what you and María feel about things? Her God, your Earth Mother and the 'Great Spirit' you used to go on about? Remember? It's all about love, isn't it? What you felt for your friend, what you feel for Lee, what you're trying to do for the planet? *Her* planet? Is there really a difference?"

"But it's like María has so much more with her belief. Like whatever happens to the world, it'll be okay because He's there, all the time. But—" Chloe paused.

"Same with the Great Spirit, surely? Same thing, different name?"

"You know," continued Chloe, "Lee says it's because I still feel bad about having left Earth Child so abruptly. And then Earth Child dying because of us. Because of the prophecy. He says it's like I'm trying to prove something. To Earth Child. Or perhaps myself. But he says—"

"My little sister, you don't need to prove anything. No one could do more than you!"

"Yeah... well, Lee says what the heck if I am trying to prove something. Just so long as it's the right something!"

Pepe heard his father laugh.

"Sis, don't you go worrying about that. It'll always be the right something where you're concerned."

"And telling little Pepe about the Golden Jaguar? Is that the right something? Am I scaring him for nothing?"

"No. You were right. Who better to put María's mind at rest than Pepe? I can't. Perhaps it's all to do with me, anyway. No, Chloe, I'm just so grateful to you and Lee for coming down and finding an excuse with that documentary. It's so very much the right something to help María."

"But the documentary is for real, Adam. We have to make it."

The following morning, young Pepe was up before dawn. In the darkness, he sat cross-legged on the landing outside Aunt Chloe and Uncle Lee's bedroom and waited. Aunt Chloe must have sensed he was there, for quite soon the door opened. She almost fell over the boy.

"Oh my, you gave me such a fright!" she exclaimed in mock alarm. "And you look just like a little Buddha sitting here in the lotus position." Pepe giggled as he stood up and took his aunt's hand to lead her downstairs and out into the yard where they sat together again on the chair swing.

"Was it really scary the first time you saw the Golden Jaguar for real?"

"No, honey. See, already I kinda knew who he really was. And seeing the Golden Jaguar wasn't half as scary as believing your father had sent me that awful text message when I was stuck up in the air looking down at those Xibalbans."

"How big was he?"

"How big do you imagine he is?"

Pepe strained his arms as wide as he could—which wasn't very wide—and he grinned.

"Oh, much, much bigger!" laughed Aunt Chloe. "Ginormous! But you know, it isn't only size that counts."

"The teeth? Do they count more?"

"Sure, but—"

"I know," announced Pepe, folding his arms. "It's the claws. They're huge, aren't they."

"More than size and claws and teeth, Pepe. More than all of that. See, once upon a time the Golden Jaguar was the most terrifying of all the beasts in the *Forest Without Time.*"

"How come you can have a place without time, Aunt Chloe?"

"As the Golden Jaguar once said to your Papa, there are many worlds, each with its own possibilities, but some things are greater than all these separate worlds put together. They kind of link in with everything. That's what you and your Mama believe, right? When you go to chapel with her?"

"Don't you?"

"Sure, honey. Not inside a church, that is, but I believe in a different way, I guess."

"So, what's this to do with the Golden Jaguar and its claws and teeth? Is there something about it that's even bigger than claws and teeth. Like God? Or that Great Spirit you talk about?"

"The Great Spirit? Oh, He and God, they don't need claws and teeth. But just then, I was glad to see the claws and teeth of the Golden Jaguar, for I knew he was on my side, even if I believed my own brother had abandoned me."

"Would Papa ever do that?"

Aunt Chloe shook her head then smiled.

"Let me tell you about those claws and teeth. That's what you want to hear about, huh? That's why you got up so early today!"

Pepe nodded and snuggled up against his aunt, for he was more than just a little bit scared, but her body felt warm and comforting.

Chapter 10: Death of the Beast

"Then we must find her and destroy her, brother! We'll summons every force in Xibalba. Our all-seeing gods and demons must search for her and not stop until we have the child in our hands."

"And then?" grinned Seven Death, looking at his spade-sized hands.

"Yes... then!"

Their laughter shook the distant mountains. Even One Monkey, recovered from his beating from Art Weissenbach, and the Great Spider Goddess, never quite the same after being part-sucked into the vacuum created by the Old Woman of the Hills—even they felt the rumbles of the Death Lords' mirth.

***

That morning, Pepe sought warmth and comfort not only from his aunt's body but also her soul. He could hardly wait for her to get to the bit about the Golden Jaguar of the Sun.

"When's he gonna appear, Aunt Chloe?"

"All in good time, Pepe. Now, where was I? Oh, of course! My big brother. Your Daddy. It just made no sense that Adam had betrayed me like that, and as I hung there above the red ball court stinking of blood, trying to ignore what was going on down below, I racked my brains for what I'd done wrong to get sent to the *Place of Fear*. Not one thing came to mind.

I've always worshipped your papa. Too much, perhaps, I wondered. Not given him enough space when we were younger, maybe got on his nerves by being around when he wanted to be alone. Thing is, he'd never once given me that impression. He was the big brother every young girl would dream of. And since we'd been parted, after your grandparents got killed, he was on the phone to New York every night, checking that I was behaving myself

"

at Aunt Jac's, asking if I needed anything, and he and María, they paid for everything. My clothes, school stuff, travel expenses. Aunt Jac was well-off and told him that paying for me was nothing, but your papa insisted. It was his brotherly duty, he told Aunt Jac.

'So, what about this?' I whispered, weeping, to myself after seeing that text message. 'Is this your duty too, big brother?'

I shivered as the giant black bat, having finished its gory business, spread its leathery wings and lifted itself up from the ground. Harsh shrill bat shrieks threatened to burst my ear drums. The creature hovered right in front of me. I saw what looked like blood, *Life-Force* in Xibalba, drip from its sharp teeth whilst its sightless eyes turned towards me. Like a leaf in a strong wind, my body shuddered in response to its sonar waves. I thought, *this is it, Chloe girl. Lee, will you ever forgive me?*

The bat vanished in a flash, startled by another noise: a snarl, a growl—the sound of anger over the misfortunes of millions of others, perhaps? I honestly don't know how to describe it. Plus, I'd never before seen the Golden Jaguar with my own eyes."

"Hooray!" cried Pepe, raising his head from its resting place on Chloe's lap. "I knew it!"

"And I kind of knew about the beast from the real dream I had when Adam and María were lost in the Chiapas jungle. In the mesas, I saw what it did, but Adam never wanted us to see the jaguar face-to-face. Like he was protecting us from something. But that growl! If you'd heard it, you'd understand why even a monster as terrifying as Zotz would have taken fright.

At first, I saw nothing to explain the sound on looking down at the ball court. Coyote Spirit, holding a knife in one hand and the doll I called 'María' in the other, looked up at me and it seemed like the evil in his eyes was mocking me up there in my little skirt as I helplessly kicked my legs in whatever it was that he had me trapped. And there was cruel pride in those eyes for what he'd just done with that knife. Like he was warning me that I'd soon share the same fate as the captain of the losing team. He'd already tossed the head of the doubly dead player into the centre of the ball court, but the man's body had gone. Then I noticed something wriggling about on the ground. Vivid blue against the red blood.

My God, I thought. *That's all that's left of the decapitated captain, shrunken down to a squirming headless blue thing, its Life-Force sucked out by Zotz. Doubly dead, yet not dead!'*

I thought about tales of vampires from Eastern Europe, about Dracula and the un-dead, but this was far worse than a rubbish horror movie. The shrunken blue thing got picked up and it froze as if still able to feel fear. Then I heard that growl again, louder and clearer, before he came into view. For a few moments, I held my breath in awe.

It's not just the sheer size of the Golden Jaguar that causes your heart to miss beats and beads of sweat to break out on your forehead. It's the perfection of the creature, Nature's ultimate killing machine. Its form, packed with steel-hard muscles, is programmed to respond to every sense. The precision of each purposeful movement and its stealth — things once crafted by the servant of the Great Sun God himself—seemed miraculous to a schoolgirl like me."

"Mama doesn't believe in that stuff."

"She doesn't need to. But the rest of us are kind of different. Except for..." Aunt Chloe cupped her hand over her mouth, realising whom she was speaking to.

"Except for what?"

"Never you mind! Now, where were we?"

"The Golden Jaguar."

"Yeah—well those muscles were magnificent and those teeth too and the claws, but, oh boy, when I saw his eyes! I'd once painted them like burning coals after that real dream I had about my brother and his girlfriend, but on seeing them for real the first time, I reckoned I hadn't done them justice. In fact, to paint them properly would be impossible. Fire, yes, but it was a fire that was depthless. Like those eyes were not only from another dimension but remained connected to different worlds. Different universes, perhaps. I'll just never forget the moment I first saw the eyes of the Golden Jaguar of the Sun. For a while I even forgot the hopelessness of my predicament, but I was thankful those eyes weren't fixed upon me.

It was Coyote Spirit who now stood transfixed by the stare of the Golden Jaguar. He dropped the doll and the knife, and, for a few moments, I saw fear in his eyes, saw his great muscular body shake a little as the jaguar slunk slowly towards him, sinking down onto his haunches. That's when I knew the Golden Jaguar was on my side. That's when my despair melted away and turned into anger. Anger over the decapitated team captain who had only tried his best, anger for Lee being hurt by my disappearance; anger for the cruel and sudden death of my parents. That huge Native guy down there was, for me, the embodiment of all the bad things that had happened in my young life.

'Kill him,' I muttered, gripping my granny's locket as tightly as I could. I knew then that it was the ancestral kachina of my grandmother who had delivered the Golden Jaguar to me there in Xibalba, and that he would respond to my commands through her.

Just when it seemed the beast was about to spring; the Red Indian underwent a weird change. First, he shrank, and I thought, *great, easier for the Golden Jaguar to kill him with one blow from his giant paw.* But with that shrinking, his body began to look different. He dropped onto all fours, and his clothes fell from him like loose rags. I saw that he now had a long tail and fur. His face elongated into a canine snout with pointy ears, and his sneer seemed a thousand times worse. It was the same coyote I'd seen in the car park. The one that I'd told Lee was 'so beautiful'. The Red Indian was the coyote; the coyote was the small boy, and the sneer was the sneer of Coyote Spirit I saw in the Great Kiva when he snatched María away from my drugged brother.

It was all coming together like a nightmare-turned-real: Coyote Spirit, still 'alive' in Xibalba, with María, the object of his insatiable desire, having brought about his downfall in the prophecy, in his sights again through me now caught like bait in a trap. If only I hadn't been so pig-headed in my search for Eagle Foot's descendants. The whole exercise had been monkey-dumb crazy. If only others had been less kind and told me the truth. But Adam? Where did he fit in, and why should he want to destroy me too, I wondered? And how on earth did Coyote Spirit plan to reach María?

The coyote was no match for the Golden Jaguar. It seemed ludicrous that such a diminutive creature should even try to pit itself against the power of the giant cat. I half expected to see it turn and run, with the Golden Jaguar bounding after it, but that didn't happen. The dog-like animal bared its yellow teeth, and, crouching low, began to slowly circle around the Golden Jaguar. I couldn't believe it. Then, with blind foolhardiness, it ran at the cat, snapping at the air before the jaguar cuffed it aside, sending the creature sliding over the bloodied ground of the ball court. Immediately, the coyote picked itself up, ran back towards the Golden Jaguar, and resumed its game of circling around the beast. It took another run at its foe who once again struck it aside with a blow from his paw. I noticed that the Golden Jaguar's claws were retracted. The coyote's bravery now caused me concern, but I could only hope that the Golden Jaguar was playing with the creature as a cat would with a mouse. *He'll kill it when he decides to*, I prayed. Perhaps he believed I might be entertained by his play, but in truth I was still terrified.

The 'game' seemed to go on forever, the crouching jaguar cuffing aside the grinning coyote each time the dog ran at him, with his fiery eyes burning bright in the dim *Xibalban* light. Then I noticed a change in the Golden Jaguar. Almost imperceptible. His ears turned back, he sank right down onto his haunches, his great muscles tensed, like the string of a bow, his tail flicked—just perceptibly. When he sprang, you'd have missed it if you'd blinked, it was that quick. He hit the coyote with full force and in an instant the dog was down on the ground, held helpless by the weight of a huge paw, with the jaguar's claws now digging deep into its flesh. The coyote yelped like a puppy.

Just when I expected the Golden Jaguar to sink his ivory teeth into the scrawny neck of the coyote, my attention, and, that of the beast himself, was diverted by a disturbance at one end of the ball court. The red ground mushroomed up like a mini-volcano without fire; the same thing happened at the other end. Each red mound separated from the ground and gradually transformed into a recognisable shape: that of an ancient Mayan man, huge and naked apart from a loin cloth, and totally red. One had a single feather in his hair, the other seven feathers. They were easily as large as the Golden Jaguar, if not larger. At that moment, I just wanted the giant cat to hurry up and finish the job.

'Kill the coyote and do it quick!' I whispered. I didn't know what these blood-red apparitions were. After all, no one at school in the U.S.A. teaches you about One Death and Seven Death, the evil Lords of that Mayan Place of Fear, Xibalba. That they, too, were evil was obvious, but I had no idea how evil. Least of all, I was unaware that the seemingly invincible Golden Jaguar of the Sun was no match against these two monsters in their own domain.

The beast must have known this. Perhaps all along he'd known that to try to rescue me in that godforsaken place was to attempt the impossible. What soon became horribly clear was that the tide had turned, and the Lords of Xibalba were about to play cat and mouse with the Golden Jaguar. Abandoning his own whimpering prey, he charged at one of the giant red rubber Indians only to be bounced backwards by the blow of an enormous club. He sprang at the other Indian, but his teeth seemed unable to gain purchase on the flesh of the rubber thing, if, indeed it had any.

Now a baited beast, the jaguar ran this way and that, snarling and snapping his jaws, whilst One Death and Seven Death, rolled, bobbed and danced about unharmed, occasionally clubbing the weakening jaguar. I shed tears for my would-be saviour. I knew he was good. Terrifying, but good, and nothing else in that place had any goodness about it. If I could have freed myself, I would have jumped down and fought those cowardly rubber things bare-handed, but all I could do was to weep and wait for the cruel show to end.

I watched as the wallops from those huge clubs started to take their toll. The jaguar began to sway, as if disorientated, but he refused to give in, and the coyote, now recovered, again began to encircle the wounded cat, still keeping a safe distance from those giant paws. I knew the jaguar couldn't take much more. When he finally managed to lock his jaws around One Death's leg, clinging on with bull-dog determination, and even bringing the rubber lord to his knees, I could see the end coming. Seven Death tore into the Golden Jaguar with his club, smashing his skull with one mighty blow. The cat jerked sideways. Released, One Death limped away and the coyote, its sneer intensified, slunk slowly up to the twitching cat. Still nervous of the beast's paws, it hesitated just beyond the jaguar's reach. Those eyes of fire, half-closed, were now little more than smouldering embers. Only when their glow had faded to nothing did the coyote leap over those paws and sink its needle teeth into the golden neck of the jaguar. For a brief second, the beast's eyes opened wide, the fire returned, and a deep-throated growl of despair emerged. It was an awful sound, for it was like the pain and the anguish of all those people he'd witnessed being sacrificed to evil, throughout his many thousand years' existence, shrieking out in a final plea for release from suffering. It was the cry of the damned, and, oh, how I now felt for those damned souls, for I was soon to become one of them.

The Golden Jaguar's eyes flickered then went black. His head sank to the ground. The coyote's jaws released their grip on the jaguar's throat. The dog stepped back, immediately transforming into Coyote Spirit, now naked. But it was the next bit that made me scream out. Not only did the coyote change back into a man, but the Golden Jaguar himself slowly shrank and assumed human proportions. Oh, my God, how I screamed, for the human lying limp, with blood trickling from his neck, was none other than your dad, Pepe. My beloved brother, Adam.

'No, no, it can't be! That's not you, Adam. Say it's not you!' I screamed over and over.

But it was. *He* was the Golden Jaguar."

"Papa?"

Pepe's eyes had grown so large that Chloe feared they might pop out. She nodded then put a comforting arm round the boy's shoulders and held him close.

"The pain of seeing him lying there was compounded by guilt for having believed he'd betrayed me, and for calling him to rescue me in the first place. The wounded One Death limped over to the body of my brother with a large flint knife in his hand. I knew what he was about to do, I shrieked out for him to stop. Whether he heard, I have no idea, but I don't think it was my screaming that prevented his hand from severing Adam's head from his body. It was Coyote Spirit.

'Wait, One Death. We must finish this properly. I have yet more pain for Leaping Jaguar and his silly little sister, Living Water, before we make use of them both for the ball game. Remember how you once promised me that one pleasure if I worked for you all those hundreds of years back: that of taking White Deer for myself. You, too, were both denied her when she came here as Princess Arima. Remember? Allow me to put the boy's soul, what's left of it, up there with his little sister. I can make use of him for one final time. His body, at least. Then we shall both have White Deer, huh? He can watch me take her as my queen, Eagle Spirit, something he denied me in the past, and then she and I together shall watch a double ball game using the heads of the great Golden Jaguar and his feeble little sister.'

After hearing these words, One Death merely limped to one end of the ball court whilst Seven Death ran to the opposite end. Each seemed to collapse and sink into a lump of quivering red jelly as if it had just been plopped out from one of those aluminium moulds your grandma used to use to make party jellies. Rapidly, each jelly lump spread out and merged with the blood-earth of the ball court. Triumphant, Coyote Spirit waved the kachina doll, María, in front of the body of Adam.

Why do that? I thought. *You've killed him already! What more harm can you do now?*

Then I saw what he meant with his words to One Death. The fingers on Adam's outstretched hand moved. They were clawing feebly at the ground. He was still alive... just. Whether I should have been pleased is another matter, knowing Coyote Spirit had only spared his life to make him suffer even more by seeing María taken in front of him, but that faint flicker of life in my brother gave me hope.

Coyote Spirit lifted Adam off the ground and up over his broad shoulders, then carried him like a sack across the ball court to the steps. Soon I heard the man's heavy breathing close behind me. As I turned my head, held as I was in that transparent aspic prison above the ball court, he raised Adam high in the air with both hands then pitched him like a discarded puppet into the space beside me. Adam landed suspended, like me, face down, as if on an invisible mattress, and only a few feet away.

'Enjoy the show together," sneered Coyote Spirit. "It'll be a good one. Remember how she chose me when I gave her the choice?'

I remembered only too well. When Adam had been drugged by the poor, simple Swimming Beaver, and María had been tricked into believing she would be saving the life of Eagle Foot, and therefore others.

Coyote Spirit returned to the court below, and I called out to Adam:

'Adam, please stay with me. Stay alive. We beat him once, and on his own the Golden Jaguar would have beaten him again—easily. Just stay with me. Please, Adam!'

Tears had blurred my vision, but I saw Adam's eyes open just a crack. I knew he'd heard me.

'Want to see some real magic now, girl?' Coyote Spirit shouted up from the arena.

I knew his ghoulish show had only just begun. I looked down and he began to change again. He was shrinking, his features became less angular, less coarse, his skin and his hair lightened. It wasn't the Indian boy this time, that was for sure. As this transformation was taking place, a twisting trail of vapour seemed to connect Coyote Spirit to Adam, and when I looked at my brother, I saw that he, too, was changing; becoming transparent. To my horror, Adam was being turned into a soft, glass shell, but when I looked down at the ball court, there was my brother standing where Coyote Spirit had been, complete with jeans and tee-shirt. A perfect clone. I was too gobsmacked to say anything. My mouth hung open, but no sound came from it.

'Think it suits me, girl? My new body? Not as handsome, ay?' asked Adam who was Coyote Spirit, in perfect English and grinning. Adam's voice. Adam's smile.

'I don't think much of these muscles, and a bit small down there where it counts, but it'll still do the job, huh? I'll lure her back here with this puny body and then I'll give her a taste of a real man. Right here. For your entertainment. He can watch too. Then she can watch a double ball game when I've satisfied her.'

Adam the Coyote Spirit pointed at the soft-glass-see-through-Adam by my side.

'Great entertainment, huh?' he added. 'And when she's mine she'll become my Queen for eternity. At long last I'll be an all-powerful leader and she'll want for nothing. As for you two, my Xibalban friends here have their teams ready. So, enjoy whilst you can!'

Suddenly Adam-who-wasn't-Adam was gone. It was the weirdest thing, seeing Adam vanish down there, knowing it wasn't him, whilst being stuck suspended in space beside an empty soft-glass shell of a brother. I had no intention of looking at any more Xibalban ball games, so I closed my eyes and thought back to when Adam and the Golden Jaguar defeated Coyote Spirit in the mesas. Well, perhaps 'thought' isn't the right word. When you have this sixth sense, as you well know, Pepe, it's more like floating in some other dimension, like reaching out with your mind. I reached out to my brother and immediately got reception. The real Adam was still there, in that transparent body. I knew it. He was too weak to reach back to me, but I could feel his inner strength there, and it was fighting. Guess you could call it his spirit. I don't really know. The bit that doesn't need a body to exist. I felt him fighting. Whom or how, I had no idea, but he was there, and it was like I was with him, telling him not to let go, telling him he would win. And when I opened my eyes and looked at him with all my concentration, I saw he wasn't just a glass shell. He was changing all the time. Like the colours of a bubble change as it floats in the air, so the substance of Adam (not the right word, I know, but no word can properly describe what I was looking at) altered over time. All I can say is that sometimes he seemed to be there, a soul trapped, and at other times he wasn't. Like I was only looking at a shell. My chief fear, however, was that he was slowly dying.

'Stay alive, Adam. Please stay with me,' I whispered, over and over and over."

Chapter 11: María's Secret

On the Aegean island of Patmos, a lone figure sat in a lean-to shack under the overhang of a cliff. He was well cared for by the islanders who were fascinated by the man who told them about the Son of God and how the Roman overlords had banished him to their island paradise for believing in one man's claim to be able to save Mankind through His Father. From where they stood, it seemed they only needed saving from the Romans, but this man, who simply called himself 'John', did have extraordinary eyes that spoke as well as saw, and these eyes seemed, at times, like mirrors into the future.

"He may be dead," said the eyes of the man called John, "but He'll rise again, as He did once before, and return when the world is ready."

Some of the things his eyes spoke of, he wrote down in that little shack of his; other things were either too terrifying for words, or, being from another dimension, beyond the scope of mere words.

***

Pepe brushed away tears with the back of his hand.

"I didn't want the Golden Jaguar to die, Aunt Chloe. Not so soon. Why did he have to die?" he asked.

"Honey, things don't always work out how we want them to. Not in real life. Only in make-believe stories can you have control over things like that. And the 'why' bit? Who's to know? The Native Americans would put it down to the Great Spirit trying to tell us something. But look! Uncle Lee's up. And you know what? He's gonna need a bit of help with his movie editing today. The bit about the hurricane. Think you can do that? Help your Uncle Lee tell our extremist right-wing administration about the bad things they're doing to our planet?"

With eyebrows raised, Aunt Chloe pointed to her half-awake husband who stood in the doorway. Somehow, he reminded his wife of a zombie who had unwittingly walked out of a horror-movie on a cinema screen and was trying to work out where he was. As she had often informed her nephew, he was not a 'morning person.'

"Does that make Uncle Lee like a great spirit too, then? Because he's helping the planet?"

"We're each of us a small part of the Great Spirit, just like your dreams are a part of you, Pepe. Thing is, do we always listen to Him?"

"D'you mean God? Mama says there's only one God. But I do like listening to Uncle Lee. He knows *so* much."

Aunt Chloe was still staring at her husband in a funny way. "Knows some things I don't know, that's for sure," she said quietly.

Later, after Pepe had spent much of the morning at the computer with Uncle Lee, and Chloe had talked for hours, over the phone, with various top people about the documentary (were they, too, connected with the Great Spirit, the boy wondered?), Pepe and Uncle Lee took a quality time break on the boy's favourite spot: the chair swing. His Papa was working indoors, preparing a series of lectures about the interrelationships between different communities in pre-Columbian North America, whilst his mother had taken Carla and the twins shopping at the mall.

"When Aunt Chloe said that you know things she doesn't know, Uncle, does this mean you know what's happening to Mama? That's what it's all about, isn't it? Mama being so sad. I know it's the real reason why you're both here. Not actually that documentary business, is it?"

Uncle Lee nodded.

"Can't hide anything from you, little man, can we?"

"Nope!"

"Yes, Pepe, there are things that Aunt Chloe doesn't know. Not even now. Things that happened a long time ago, before you were born, but they're stuck in my mind like they've gotten attached there with super-glue."

"Can you really stick memories with super-glue?" Pepe asked.

"Only 'super' super-glue."

"Is that like Great Spirit superglue?"

"Pepe, I know Chloe believes in that stuff, but your Mama and you, you have other beliefs. I don't think she'd want to hear you talking about the Great Spirit like this, being a devout Catholic."

"What happened, Uncle Lee? When you were outside that tepee with Aunt Jac and Uncle Jason, and Mama called to say my Papa had disappeared? What happened after that? What did Mama do?"

Uncle Lee looked uneasy.

"Aunt Jac, she tried so hard to keep calm. Uncle Jason was real kind, you know. What with me and Aunt Jac near hysterical over the loss of first Chloe and then Adam, he kept us sane. Kept on saying that they'd both come back, sure they would. Said we might worry—and should do, for it's only human to worry—but said not to make ourselves ill with the worrying thing 'cos they were coming back and they'd not be wanting us to make ourselves sick.

Just talking to Uncle Jason made me feel better. He was that kind of guy. Reassuring. Strong inside. I knew then that Chloe would return, but I also knew it wouldn't be an easy ride for any of us. When María called again, half-an-hour later, to say Adam had turned up, we felt sure we'd not need to worry about him anymore."

"Hooray! So, Papa got free!" Pepe asked, jumping from the swing and punching the air with a clenched fist.

"If only," Uncle Lee said. "Look, what are you like at keeping a secret—a very special secret?"

"The best, Uncle Lee!" Pepe grinned at his uncle and sat down again. He loved being in on secrets.

"See, when your Mama told me what happened after her first phone call, I kind of promised her I'd never tell

Chloe or your Papa. She said she had to tell someone, she felt that confused, and back then it didn't seem to matter too much, but this sadness of hers of late, it must be because of what happened then. Aunt Chloe, she has this hunch that only you can help take that sadness away from Mama. But to do that you have to know Mama's story as well. One day she'll thank us for sharing her secret together."

"Does Mama's story join up with Aunt Chloe's story, then?"

"Aunt Chloe would say the Great Spirit makes all stories join up, Pepe."

"Is Mama's story as scary as Aunt Chloe's?" Uncle Lee put his arm around Pepe's small shoulders.

"You're a brave boy, Pepe."

Sitting next to Uncle Lee, Pepe felt like the bravest person in the world when he rested his head on the man's broad shoulder and listened to his mother's story as told by Uncle Lee:

"For that awful half-an-hour or so, María was frantic with worry. Hearing that Chloe had vanished had hardly registered in her mind. Your aunt was always taking off following some sudden whim, but she was never truly 'lost'. She could look after herself with that sixth sense of hers. Adam, on the other hand, never wandered off. He never did anything without letting María know. He had only just called her, and asked her to come around to his house for 'singing practice'—which usually meant making love..."

"Making babies?" interrupted Pepe. Uncle Lee scratched his head. It was all too easy to forget that Pepe was only a child.

"Let's just say that every second they had together as man and wife was truly precious to them. Anyways, when your momma rang the doorbell there was no reply. She ran back home to fetch her own key and returned to your Daddy's place. She walked from room to room, shaking with fear that something awful had happened to Adam and that she'd find him slumped to the ground somewhere—an electric shock, perhaps. She checked all the cupboards in every room, the loft, the garage. Nothing! He'd simply vanished without leaving a message. There was no sign of a struggle. She checked his bedside cabinet, and the two golden jaguar bracelets were there, where he always left them.

It was at this point when María phoned Aunt Jac. She wondered whether Adam might have called his aunt for some reason. Of course, she was upset to hear about Chloe running off, and about my daddy being in hospital, but she couldn't think why either of these things should have any bearing on Adam's sudden disappearance. She sat on the settee, with the phone in one hand, wondering who else to call. Her own family home was swarming with children, her mother was up to her armpits with washing, her Papa at work. No point in troubling them. She'd tried Sam Royal's wife, but they'd heard nothing from Adam. Jorge and Anna were the only other people she could think of, and she was just about to call Jorge when Adam came through the door leading into the kitchen which she'd already checked out. For a few moments, she looked at him as if he were a ghost.

'Where were you, Adam?' she cried out looking up from the settee where she'd feared she might drown in her own tears and waving the phone at him. She felt her Latin temper coming to the boil as relief turned to anger. 'What on earth were you doing in there? I've been looking all over for you! Even called Aunt Jac in Albuquerque. I feel a right dummy!'

'Honey, what's up with you? Been out there in the kitchen all the time. Preparing a little surprise for my girl. Today's the day, huh?' he said.

'Adam, don't joke with me! It's not like you. You're reminding me of that jerk Spike, only...' Adam came up to her, behind the settee, and encircled her with his arms.

'Only a lot more handsome, right? But *chica*, you ain't seen me at my best. Ain't seen my muscles, felt my strength as you should.'

'Adam, please stop acting so weird! So, what is it, this surprise? Better be good, Adam Winters, because I've had one hell of a bad time here worrying for nothing. I thought—I don't know, I just had this strange kind of feeling that something awful–" Adam frowned. He gripped her shoulders, only a little too tightly.

'OW!' your momma cried out.

'Sorry, honey. Here, come with me. I'll show you.'

Adam took María's hand and led her into the kitchen. María looked around and saw nothing different. Nothing on the sideboard, no flowers, no romantic meal prepared. Just a kitchen.

'What?' she asked. 'Where's this surprise?'

'Here,' replied Adam. 'Me!'

Before María had a chance to explode with full-blown Mexican fury, Adam took her in his arms and kissed her long and hard on the lips, caressing her body with his hands, and María's anger melted like frost in warm sunshine. She smiled up at him when their lips finally parted. She reached up with her hands and stroked his cheeks.

'And?' she queried.

Adam lifted her up in his arms and kissed her lips again.

'The whole me,' Adam said. "Every little bit! Feels kind of little down there, but it'll do the job, girl!"

Girl? He never calls me 'girl', your mama thought.

'I already know the whole you, my dear husband,' María said, still stroking Adam's face with her fingers. "What are you talking about?" Adam smiled and shook his head.

'There's more, my darling. So much more.' He lowered her to the ground. 'We must get married properly. And soon.'

'Adam, we already are—'

'That wasn't for real, María.'

'What do you mean? Papa Pedro—Father Pedro—he was there. And he was a priest. It's been our thing for so long, Adam. Ours and Chloe's secret. It's how we defeated that evil Coyote Spirit in the mesas. Remember? God, that was a close one!' An odd look flickered across Adam's face. María couldn't fathom it. 'What is it, Adam?' she asked and squeezed his hand.

'Need to get somewhere, María. That's all. Do something with my life. Become—'

'Become a professor?" offered María.

'Do not tease!" Adam rebuffed, gripping your mama tightly again. He saw he was hurting her and relaxed his grip. 'Don't you dare make fun of me!'

"Adam, what is up with you?' she said. 'You're a born academic. You'll make a brilliant professor. It's what you've always talked about.'

'María, I've decided I'm gonna become a great leader. I can feel it. The world needs me.'

'But Adam, you've always—' María halted mid-sentence on seeing the look in your daddy's eyes. She backed away. She had never before seen such hardness in them. It reminded her of Colorado when she felt she'd been abandoned by the Golden Jaguar and had planned to kill herself rather than yield to Coyote Spirit. *Are all men the same at the end of the day?* she wondered. Nope! This wasn't the boy she'd fallen in love with and with whom she'd shared so much."

"I knew it wasn't Daddy," added Pepe.

"It gets worse, Pepe. Can you handle the truth? As told to me by your Mama?"

Pepe's eyes gave Lee the answer. The man continued...

"'As for you, girl (*girl again*? she thought) I can tell you badly need what only I can offer in that department.' Adam nodded towards the bedroom door. 'You'll feel it too, María. This new strength in me. Left the weakling Adam behind!'"

"My real Daddy?" offered Pepe.

"Uh-huh! 'Adam, have you gone crazy or something?' your mama asked. 'What on earth...?' A shadow slid across Adam's face. 'You mean we should get married again before graduating? In a church. Live as man and wife at 'Univ' in Albuquerque?'

'For a start.'

'A start?'

'Sure, Eagle Spirit! But there are better places for a queen like you!'

'Eagle Spirit? Please don't make fun of me, Adam. You know how upset I got in Colorado. I could never, never be like that evil monster wanted me to be,' your momma said.

Adam pressed himself up close to María. Frightened and confused, she sought some indication from his face that this was the Adam she loved. She felt something firming up against her."

"I know what that was, Uncle Lee."

"Yeah... well there's not much you don't know. Your mama was so scared by then. 'No, not now. Please,' she begged. 'We could—' She told me she was searching her mind for an excuse for them not to make love. She couldn't face it with Adam being like that. He seemed hard and uncaring, not strong, but she didn't dare tell him. It was so odd for her to be with Adam and yet not dare tell him everything on her mind. Why she should feel frightened of her husband, she had no idea, but she was frightened as hell.

'The wedding, then,' Maria offered as an escape route. 'If we're gonna marry soon, I'll want a proper wedding dress this time. Not that strange pink one like last time.'

Adam just stared at María for a few moments like there was an enormous struggle going on in his mind.

'Wedding?' he queried, and his eyes turned wet with tears. 'What wedding are you talking about?'

'Ours, honey. You just—oh Adam, you're acting so creepy. Only a moment ago, you—'

'How long have I been in here? In the kitchen?'"

"That was my real dad then!"

"Sure thing, Pepe. And your mama was over the moon to have him back. 'Seems like you were hiding away a long while doing I don't know what!' she scolded. And when she looked again into his eyes, they too were different. Kind, and loving, as always."

"I love my papa so much!"

"Yeah, it was the Adam she knew and trusted, and she kissed and tasted the tears in his eyes.

'Come on! We'll go to the mall at Katy Mills. There's a bridal shop there. And I'll do the driving!' she offered.

Adam looked around at his own kitchen as if he'd just walked onto the stage set of a play in which he had no part and for which there were no lines.

'Just now, María—it was like I was somewhere else,' he said, 'only I can't remember a thing about it. Not one thing. And what's all this about a bridal shop?'

Your mama held him close.

'We were talking about getting married again. Soon. In a church. You were so definite about it, and I thought, yeah, maybe we should. Not keep it a secret any longer.'

'But Papa Pedro... he was a priest. And he came back to you for your confession. Remember? He was there in ancient Mexico. He married us.'

María frowned at your daddy.

'That's what I just told you, Adam. Then I reckoned you were right about us re-marrying soon.' Adam's eyes clouded over, turned dark, flickered then became bright once more. María frowned again. 'We shouldn't have to pretend like this to my parents. It's not like they don't know we're made for each other. Anyways, we'll go to Katy Mills. I'm all fired up about a bridal dress now. Beginning to see it in my head. A real wedding.'

'The other was totally real for me.'

'Not what you said just a moment ago, honey. Come on. You've been working too hard. Get in the car.'

'Pink again?'

'What?'

'Your dress? Will it be pink again?'

María laughed. 'You're not listening to me! I said *not* pink! And certainly not with all those strange birds on it? Yuk!'

'It was so beautiful. You were beautiful!'

'Come on, Mr Day Dreamer,' urged María, pulling Adam towards the front door.

On the way to Katy Mills, María chatted non-stop, pushing to the back of her mind Adam's unsettling behaviour. She talked about all the guests they would invite, where the reception should be held, what the cake would be like, and the bridesmaids...

'Now they could wear pink,' your mama suggested. 'Like at Jorge and Anna's wedding. And Chloe—would she look okay in pink? What d'you think, Adam? She'll be my principal bridesmaid.'"

"Aunt Chloe in pink?"

"Your aunty looks lovely whatever she wears. Mind you, it annoys her when I say that. Tells me I'm not being helpful."

"I like to be helpful!" stressed Pepe. "Particularly for Mama."

"Which is why I'm telling you this. Now Adam didn't answer your mama. She glanced sideways at him, and the car swerved a little when she saw the look on his face.

'Adam, what is it?'

'Chloe—she... I don't know, María—it's like—'

'Did Aunt Jac call you about Chloe or something?' your mama asked. No answer. 'Adam, I just asked you a question. Did Aunt Jac phone you about Chloe running off again? Like she used to?'

'She's in trouble. I know it. Oh, my God, I've no idea why or where, but she's in terrible trouble. We must turn back. Quick. I've got to—' Adam stopped mid-sentence.

'I can't turn around just now. Not here on Interstate 10. Adam, what is going on?'

'Turn around? Never! We're gonna buy that wedding dress for you, Eagle Spirit!'"

"Who's Eagle Spirit?" Pepe asked.

"Someone your mother must never be, Pepe. 'Please, Adam, stop playing horrible games with me' your mama begged.

'Won't say that when I really play with you, girl. You'll be saying "don't stop, please, please never stop!"' When he said this, your daddy was grinning like a dog who'd just been offered a bone. The bewilderment had vanished.

'And this thing about Chloe?' asked your mama.

'You can forget all about my stupid little sister (Pepe gasped) after the ball game!'

Ball game?

María just did not know what to say. The return of this dark Adam she'd never known before truly terrified her. It was as if two people, poles apart, sat in the same passenger seat beside her. She drove on in silence, parked the car, and they entered the mall. María wished to keep a distance between herself and 'stranger' Adam, but he wouldn't allow it. He kept her close, fondled her and in front of everyone. It was as if he wanted to make a public exhibition of his possession of her, for that's what he made her feel like. A possession. And choosing her wedding dress was no pleasure, for she began to see herself being only that: her husband's prize possession. Nothing more.

'I think we should go home now,' she said after looking through a few books of wedding dresses and trying on a couple. Adam's impatience unnerved her.

'We're just wasting effing time, Eagle Spirit,' he'd complained as she stood in front of a mirror trying to decide between two dresses.

María glowered at him. She felt her blood turn to fire. She wanted to slap him, slap away this Adam she didn't recognise, but somehow managed to keep her cool. It was a López thing never to make a show in public. Her family was refined, almost 'aristocratic', and not from the back streets of Mexico City. But what happened in the mall on the way back to the car was too much. She blew a fuse. Back to his fondling thing, Adam suddenly raised her skirt, exposing her underwear in public."

"How awful! That most definitely wasn't daddy!"

"No, it wasn't. 'Should be red, not white!' this Adam remarked as María fought to pull her skirt hem back down. Whether anyone had seen anything or not was immaterial. She swung around and walloped him across the face.

'Don't you ever treat me like a slut again, Adam Winters! You know, I've had it up to here with you! I'm honestly having second thoughts about this wedding. Perhaps it's a divorce we should be looking at, right? Maybe—'"

"We Catholics can't divorce," Pepe informed his uncle.

"Like you said earlier, it wasn't your daddy did that thing! This other Adam, rubbing his reddening cheek, silenced your mama with his stare. He gripped the arm that had slapped him and squeezed it so hard María let out a cry.

'No woman tells me what to do or what not to do! Drive me home. Now! I'll tame this wild streak in you, huh? Show you what a real man does to a woman who disobeys him!'

María hardly knew what to do. Turn and run from the boy she'd always loved so much? Phone Jorge again? There was certainly no dark side to Jorge, unlike the boy she thought she knew better than anyone else in the world. Could Jorge advise her? Or should she just go back with this Adam and pray the one she loved might return to her, never again to change back into this stranger? In the end, she chose the easy option. Dutifully, and without any further word, she followed Adam to the car and drove him home. As they turned into the drive, she heard Adam doing something he would never normally do in front of her: cry. He glanced sideways at her with the eyes of her own dear Adam. She stopped the vehicle, opened the driver's door, got out and ran around to the passenger door and helped him out, for he seemed done in. With one arm around his waist, and sobbing herself, she took him into the house and placed him on the settee. She began to kiss him, all over his face, stroking and caressing him. He touched her cheek."

"Do all grown-ups in love kiss as much as my mommy and daddy?"

"I can only answer for your aunt and me and—well, for us I guess it's a 'yes'. And just then your daddy was pretty cut up. 'What's happening to me?' he asked. 'I love you so much, and yet there's something fighting inside me. Something—'

María flung her arms around Adam and kissed him on the mouth. She undid his jeans, removed his tee-shirt, and then slipped off her own clothes. ("Oh!" remarked Pepe.) Adam stared at the bruise on her wrist where he'd gripped her hard in the mall.

'My God, María, don't let me ever harm you. Kill me first if I try to do anything bad. Promise me, princess!'"

"I've heard him call Mama that, but she doesn't like it too much."

"Because it's true, perhaps. Anyways, María silenced your daddy with a finger to his lips. On the settee, they came together as if this was the first time that they'd made love as adults, and even when they lay together afterwards, exhausted, each continued to fondle and caress the other.

'Princess—it's Chloe,' Adam said after a while. 'I have to get back to Chloe. Something's pulling at me. I must know what's happening. Have to. How—why—?'

'Chloe? But she's in New Mexico. Adam, you're acting so odd. And back there in the mall? Don't you even remember what you did?'

Adam appeared vacant for a moment then grabbed Maria's arms with both hands.

'Ouch!' she screamed, wriggling free and rolling backwards off the settee. She reached for her clothes in a hurried attempt to cover her nakedness.

'I haven't even begun, girl. (*'Girl'* yet again? This so puzzled your mama.) So, let's do it properly this time!'

María backed away, shaking her head. The coldness in her husband's eyes had returned. An awful thought occurred to her. She'd been tricked by the unknown Adam and given herself to him. Screaming, she ran to the front door holding up her skirt and blouse. The very moment she reached the door, it opened, and a familiar figure brushed straight past her into the house. A large man with flaming red hair and beard—Art Weissenbach."

"Mama's guardian angel, right?"

Lee nodded.

"Your mama made a futile attempt to hide her Venus figure with her skirt and blouse.

'Boring, boring!' Adam shouted from the settee. 'They've told me all about you, and how you're becoming a bit of a nuisance back here.' After slipping on his jeans, he stood up to confront Art. 'You ain't got no right to deny me my conjugal rights, Hunahpu!'"

"One of the Hero Twins. They're also Mama's angels, aren't they?"

"Sure thing. 'What are you doing here, Art?' gasped your mama.

'Stand back, María,' warned Art. 'Jeannie will be along any minute now. She's parking the Austin-Healey. Your own car was blocking the drive. Did this monster touch you? In that way?'

But María could only weep. Adam said nothing, but began to circle around Art, baring his teeth in a dog snarl.

'You can't stop me, Hunahpu. I'm stronger, now. I've the strength of the Golden Jaguar as well. Give her to me. Let me have my Queen and I'll leave you alone.'

Art said nothing. He stood motionless, watching the younger man's every move.

'Oh, my God, Adam, what's happened to you? Please don't be like this,' María begged. 'Look at me!'

But Adam, positioning himself as would be expected of the Texas junior karate champion, ignored her. The girl was merely his prize and not a person with whom he wished to converse. Like a snake striking its prey, Adam leapt at Art, kicking at what should have been the other man's head, only Art was too quick. In a flash, he'd turned, arched backwards, and caught Adam's foot with a flick of his wrist, sending Adam sprawling to the ground.

'María, did he touch you?' Art asked again as Adam calmly picked himself up and resumed his predatory circling. Both men fixed each other with animal eyes. It was as much a battle of stares as one of muscle or speed.

'I—I don't know!' wept María. 'We're lovers. Have been for over two years. We're married. It's been a secret, but—'

'Eagle Spirit is mine,' interrupted Adam. 'The Golden Jaguar is dead, and now she's mine. Just go, Hunahpu!'

Jeannie entered and María ran into her arms.

'Jeannie, stop them! Please stop them! Adam's gone crazy, that's all. He's not himself. Tell Art. Stop the fight. Just stop them,' she sobbed.

Adam sprang and stabbed at Art again, bringing his leg up to overbalance the older man, but once again Art was too quick. With lightning speed and minimum effort, he cuffed Adam on the neck, twisted his arm and sent him spinning across the room, causing him to crash into the TV before hitting the ground.

'Stop it, please stop it! Leave him alone!' shrieked María, tugging at Jeannie as the other woman tried to restrain her. 'I can't bear it. You've all gone mad. Leave Adam alone. I'll talk to him.'

'María, that ain't Adam,' Jeannie said. 'Believe me. It's not. Whoever it is wants to destroy us all plus take away your soul. And you are so very important to us. Let Art do what he has to do!'

'It's Adam!' screamed your mama. 'Just now. When he made love to me. It was Adam. I know it.'

Art glanced momentarily at Jeannie. Adam saw his chance. He shot forwards, like an arrow, toppling the other man who in an instant was on his back, Adam's hand at Art's throat, squeezing. If it hadn't been for Art's super-human strength his wind-pipe would have been broken. Instead, Art swung his head and body sideways, flipping Adam over, and slammed his forearm into Adam's face. When Adam staggered to his feet another swift blow from Art's fist sent him reeling backwards. To María's horror, Jeannie grabbed Adam from behind, allowing Art to slug him three more times in the face, following which the boy sank down onto rubbery knees, swaying, his swollen eyelids half-closed. He appeared to be trying to focus on María as he weakly struggled against the Jeannie's firm grip.

'María, what's happening. Where am I?' he asked in a barely audible voice.

'I love you!' María cried out.

For a few moments, the look in Adam's eyes softened; he tried to say something, but nothing came out. Art remained still, as if deciding how to finish off his opponent. Or was he waiting for something to happen...

A sneer reappeared on Adam's bloodied face. The softness was gone from his eyes.

'So you should, my queen. So you should... forever!' he gulped like a monstrous frog just before Art hit him for the last time.

His neck snapped backwards. Jeannie let go and Adam's head hit the floor with a bang. María screamed and ran towards the still body of her husband, but when she was only half-way across the room the body had gone. The blood smearing the floor too. It was as if Adam had never been there. She turned to Art, speechless, with her arms stretched out silently beseeching the man to bring Adam back to her. But Art, too, was changing. Jeannie as well. They were already transparent, like figures from another world—ghosts."

Lee felt unable to tell Pepe Art's final words to his mother:

'The child must be destroyed!'

Instead, he explained that María had told him how she'd simply stared in disbelief as the figures vanished whilst Art's words '...*must be destroyed,*' still echoed inside her head.

Lee left the boy sitting alone on the chair swing. He did not want Pepe to see a grown man's tears.

Chapter 12: All-Powerful Leader?

"You mean to say there's another one?" began the priest. "No, this cannot be!"

Fed up with his own company, he had returned.

"Another what?" queried the one-time Mexican antiques dealer from Houston.

"Mother."

"It's the other father you should be concerned about. And the other child. The one for whom every day is a birthday after the sun has risen again."

***

For the rest of the morning, Pepe hardly saw anything of Aunt Chloe and Uncle Lee. They were working towards a deadline for their documentary, and the sponsor was unhappy with a sizeable chunk of the movie. Much to Pepe's disappointment, his dad's sister and her gentle husband spent hours huddled around a laptop in their room, editing. They barely seemed to notice him when he brought them juice and cookies mid-morning.

After hearing his mother's story from Uncle Lee, Pepe so wanted to comfort her and tell her that Papa was fine and not to worry, but he couldn't. He had to keep his promise. Uncle Lee had said she mustn't know that Pepe knew her secret, although the boy couldn't understand why. Anyhow, just then, she, too, was busy in her and Papa's bedroom practising her singing. She was preparing for her next album. He always loved the sound of her voice when it filled the house with that haunting blend of happiness and sadness, but that day it seemed to be only sadness and, after hearing her story, this sadness made him feel kind of empty inside. He wished he could take it away for her. *So* wished he could make Mama happy again.

Pepe couldn't work out how his knowledge of the Golden Jaguar story was going to help her. Not now that he knew the beast was dead. He felt certain there was

116

something else in the 'Mama story' that Uncle Lee hadn't told him. '*Must be destroyed*', his uncle had said. Somehow, he assumed he was referring to the little Red Indian boy in Chloe's story. The one who had lured his aunt away from his uncle and who turned out to be the coyote who killed the Golden Jaguar. Probably, the same creature had pretended to be his daddy. Pepe would kill it himself with his bare hands given the chance. He would destroy the monster and make Mama happy again, if that's what the problem was. For Pepe, his mother's happiness was the most precious thing in the world. That's partly why he liked Aunt Chloe and Uncle Lee coming to stay, because his mother seemed more like her old self again when playing with Carla and the twins.

Papa was also working that morning, so it fell upon Pepe to look after, and amuse, Carla and the boys. With all that talk between the grown-ups about bad leaders not believing in global warming or caring about wanting to save Planet Earth, he decided to play 'World Politics' with them. He didn't truly know what the word 'politics' meant, but he liked the sound of it and, in his game, he would be the all-powerful leader of the United States of the World. Of course, he would be a good leader, not like the present president whom Uncle Lee disliked so much. He would stop global warming from happening and save the planet, but only he, Pepe Winters, could make the laws and tell people what to do. And these laws would be the right ones so that all his people (Carla and the twins) could be happy. Carla would be minister for children and for singing, because, like Mama, she was a good singer, and Kurt, minister for travel since he was so keen on toy cars. Pepe couldn't immediately think of a useful role for little Jimmy, the other twin, so decided the best title for him would be 'spare' minister. His skills (Pepe wasn't sure what they were, but he reckoned the child had to have 'skills') would be brought into play during times of world crisis.

All morning the children played happily at 'World Politics'. Pepe had them tidying up the living room, sorting out the trash (essential for the survival of the world), organising Carla's dolls and stuffed animals (the world population) into neat rows, checking on food resources in the fridge and the vegetable plots in the yard whilst monitoring the world's 'electric things' (a torch, the vacuum cleaner and Pepe's remote-controlled Porsche). They had world council meetings, presided over by Pepe and fuelled by soda and cookies, and when the twins doubled up as the 'bad guys' the game became more like hide-and-seek. The grown-ups, of course, represented the different ethnic groups: Mama, the Mexicans and other Native peoples, Papa and Aunt Chloe, the whites and Uncle Lee, the blacks. Pepe told the twins not to upset these 'different ethnic groups' by bursting into their rooms. This could cause 'ethnic wars', he warned.

By lunch time, the kids were ravenous.

"We saw to it that world food supplies will be saved," Pepe said to his mama when they were all seated at the table. She was serving pasta, starting with the little children.

"Sure, honey," she agreed.

He was so pleased to see her smiling. There had been too much sadness in her singing that morning.

"It's great being an all-powerful leader, Mama. There's so much you can—" Pepe stopped. His Mama looked like she'd just been stung by the worst stinging creature he could imagine. She was trembling.

"Don't say that, Pepe! Don't ever say that!" she cried. She dropped the serving spoon and fork and ran weeping from the room. The boy's papa pushed his chair back and ran after her.

"María!" he called out.

Pepe, too, began to cry. He must have hurt his mama, but just didn't know how, and this was the very last thing he would wish for. Carla and the twins sat, wide-eyed and silent. Chloe came up to Pepe and put her arm around him.

"It's okay, Pepe. Mama will be all right. We'll sort this thing out for her together. Be brave."

She glanced at Lee. The man raised his eyebrows and shrugged his shoulders.

Later, Pepe, standing outside their bedroom door, overheard Aunt Chloe and Lee arguing. They never argued, and he felt bad all over again, for he was sure it was because of him.

"I only said what she told me. Like we agreed. It's not as if he's given away a secret. And she doesn't know we've been speaking to him."

"Maybe that's why she's so upset."

"Anyways, it was your idea, honey. I had my doubts, as you know." Uncle Lee sounded sulky, and this was so unlike him.

"Lee, we have to do this. I feel it inside me. That's why. All I'm saying is, well—we must be careful about the words we use."

"You mean like not tell him certain bits. Censor it! Well, I never told him exactly what—"

"No, no! He must know everything. It's just that – oh, I dunno. Guess it's getting us all down. And I still feel guilty for starting up the whole thing back in the Mesa Verde. Then afterwards searching for my friend's descendants."

They went quiet. Pepe put his ear to the door in case they were now whispering. He could only hear Aunt Chloe crying, so he ran to his room, lay on his bed and pulled the covers up over his head. If only he could cut out the world, the Golden Jaguar, dead or alive, and hide from all that misery. But the following morning he was up even earlier. Aunt Chloe, too. It was as if they both knew the story had to be finished. For Mama's sake.

Chapter 13: Austin-Healeys... Great Cars!

The Death Lords of Xibalba were in no hurry. Whatever the Coyote had or hadn't done was of little consequence to them for he was merely their plaything anyway. The other girl would be found.

***

"Well, Pepe, when Adam, your dad, called out to me it was the most wonderful moment of my life. I had my eyes closed at the time. The noise of the ball game below was blood-curdling and I couldn't bear to watch it. I knew that it was all about death and the desperation that comes from our universal desire to avoid death, the destroyer of all things. We all of us have a kind of common instinct for self-preservation, I guess. But for me, the ball game signified unimaginable horror. I believed that soon, though I didn't know when, Adam and I would become a part of it. At least, our heads. As balls. Then I heard your dad's voice...

'Chloe?'

My eyes flicked open and I stared at my brother. He was looking straight at me. He was whole, no longer transparent, though there was still blood about his neck where the coyote had bitten him.

'Adam? Is it really you?'

'Oh Chloe, I'm so sorry. I just thought—thought I was stronger.'

'Adam, have you always been the Golden Jaguar?' Your daddy shook his head. 'There's so much I just don't understand, Adam. But that was Coyote Spirit, wasn't it?'

'Sure was!'

'And it was you who killed him back then, in the mesas? When he tried to take María from you?'

'Uh-huh!'

'And this place—it's where you took María before bringing her back to life by overcoming that giant spider?'

120

'Xibalba. The 'Place of Fear' of the ancient Maya. Their sort of underworld. But she must never know that, Chloe. Know that she once died.'

'Sounds like she'll know all right when he brings her here. That's what he intends to do, Adam. When you were kind of asleep—stunned or something—he said he'd bring her here. Make her his queen. In front of you.'

I peered down at the game below. Violent yet strangely coordinated and even beautiful. Saw the 'ball' dance from hip to elbow to knee to thigh, always in the air.

'I remember so little, Chloe,' your daddy said. 'Just that I was trying to kill the coyote, trying to rescue you, then—'

'Then those big red rubber bullies came up out of the ground. It was so unfair, Adam. You were beating Coyote Spirit. I didn't know it was you but, boy, I felt real proud of the Golden Jaguar. But those red bullies appeared and, well, the Golden Jaguar didn't stand a chance. He fought to the very end, you know. And all the time it was you!"

'Yes and no. We were like together, Chloe. Two in one. Kinda merged. Happened back in the mesas the last time I fought the coyote. Seemed more convenient that way. Being together. Guess I must have gotten weaker when the jaguar was dying. Can't remember a thing. Not even like in a dream. It's just... blank."

'It was so weird, Adam. Somehow, I knew you weren't dead when you went all sort of transparent. Coyote Spirit said he'd spared you anyways—so that he could watch you suffer when he and María did 'it' down there in front of you. Then he lifted you like a rag doll and carried you up here before chucking you to where you are now—onto whatever it is we're stuck in. Feels like being suspended in invisible jelly, don't you think?'

'Can say that again,' said Adam, squirming and trying, unsuccessfully, to raise his arms.

'Anyhow, although you looked half-invisible, 1 knew you weren't a ghost either. Same as I know this is no dream. You were horribly still, though. Like you were immobilized by something. Then you kind of came back again, became more solid, more alive-looking—stronger—only to turn all see-through and weak again. I thought my big brother was a chameleon with all that changing going on!"

Pepe giggled.

"'Chloe, I've no recollection of any of this,' continued his aunt. 'How did I even get here?' your papa queried."

'You're asking me? How should I know?'

'You called me... I think. It happened so quickly, I'm not sure. Just remember your voice – calling for me—or was it for the Golden Jaguar? As I said, María and I were like together. Talking about—you know...'

'Like what happened in that cave in the Mesa Verde canyon, right?'

'Kind of!'

I was staring at the golden locket dangling from my neck.

'It's our granny's. Has her picture inside. Aunt Jac gave it to me.' I reached out for it to show Adam. 'She—oh, my God!' Suddenly Adam fell about ten feet as my fingers closed around the locket. I screamed and dropped it.

'Wow! What did you just do, Chloe?'

'Only took hold of the locket. Like just before the Golden Jaguar appeared. I thought Granny's kachina spirit was all I had then. And it was like something electric. It happened again just before you dropped down.'

'When you held that thing it was as if I'd gotten a massive surge of energy. Like when I was the Golden Jaguar, only stronger. Chloe, it was—" Adam grinned. 'Like I had ten thousand sun-loads of power in my veins. When did you let go of it?'

'Just now. When you dropped like an astronaut falling to earth.'

'No. Before. When the Golden Jaguar was here.'

'Dunno. When those red rubber bullies appeared. Guess I freaked out as they rose up out of the ground.'

'Do it again, Chloe. Hold the locket. Hold it tight and don't let go this time. And think about your granny or whatever else you were thinking back then.'

'*You*, big brother. I was thinking about you.'

'Do it, Chloe! Now!'

'Adam—I'm so sorry about all of this. I should never have—you know—when we were in the Mesa Verde with Aunt Jac. If it wasn't for my—my—'

'Sixth sense? Sis, that prophecy had to happen. Otherwise the past could have changed the present. Momma might never have met Dad. Anyways, you had no control over it. We're only finishing what you started. That's all. We'll do this thing together and she's gonna help us.'

'She?'

'Our grandma. Dad always said you're just like her.'

'That's what Aunt Jac told me too.'

'Okay, now take a hold of her locket. And think about us. And about Momma and Dad and the granny we never knew.'

I did just that. Took hold of the golden locket, pressed it into my palm and folded my fingers over it. I closed my eyes and I thought of the times we had together, Adam and me, and of how I looked up to my brother, how much his kindness has always meant to me, and I thought of the love we felt as a family, of Dad and Momma, and I tried to imagine my granny, tried to bring her to life in my mind from that tiny photo. Then I opened my eyes. Adam was no longer there. I looked down at the ball court where a wave of excitement seemed to have spread through the spectators. They were cheering and yelling as if they'd never seen such play in a ball game, and then I saw that it was Adam down there in the ball court and the focus of all the excitement.

I'd often watched him at his karate tournaments. María never went. She said she couldn't bear to see him get beat up, though in truth he never did. He invariably won and without hurting his opponent. 'All about speed and timing', your daddy told me. And 'exposing the opponent's weakness'. Then I remembered him telling me that he imagined María was there, and that he was protecting her, so, as I watched him caught up in that ball game, flying this way and that, always too quick for the opposing team (somehow, he seemed to have joined one of the teams), I thought of María. The lovely María. And I heard her singing in my head and tried to mentally transmit her beautiful voice to Adam.

I guess neither of us knew where this was heading, and for those few minutes I even forgot that Adam and the others down there were using a human head for a ball. I just willed Adam and his team to win, and, to be honest, with Adam playing there was no contest. Soon, he had full possession of the ball, keeping it in the air. He wove around and in between his opponents like they were standing rocks, spinning, twisting, turning and leaping, bouncing the ball off different parts of his body, and on reaching the side of the court he batted it high in the air and straight through the stone ring. The game was over, and his teammates, strangers only moments before, lifted him high in the air to a tumultuous applause from the audience.

I, too, was delighted, but not for long. *What now*? I thought. I expected Coyote Spirit to suddenly reappear any moment, together with María, and then finish off his ghastly promise. Adam and I were still doomed.

But Coyote Spirit didn't come back. Adam's team circled the court three times, holding their new hero up for all to see. My brother looked kind of out of place in his jeans, tee-shirt and Texan kicks, whilst all those other guys were dressed in ancient Mayan costumes with painted faces and naked brown limbs. Then a large man with an elaborate headdress leapt from the wall into the court. He held a long flint knife. He grabbed the cowering captain of the opposing team and dragged him across to Adam. He handed your daddy the knife, and forced the team captain to his knees, holding the man's head down.

'Adam,' I shrieked out, 'you can't do this!'

I was afraid my brother had become one of them. But Adam shook his head, and, holding the knife in both hands, he snapped it in half, like it was no more than a candy stick, before throwing the pieces to the ground. The cries from the crowd were a mix of amazement and horror. Then the man with the headdress let go of the captain and, red with rage, strode towards my brother. He reached out as if to seize him, and my heart did a somersault, but, in a flash, he was flung to the ground by Adam. When he attempted to stand up members of both teams ran forwards and pinned him down.

'There'll be no more ball games in Xibalba! No more killing of the dead!' Adam shouted to the players and the audience. The losing team captain stood up straight, unable to fully comprehend the sudden turn in his fate. But the bloodthirsty spectators were far from happy. They got up and punched the air with their fists, shouting abuse at Adam. Some, armed with knives, climbed over the wall and jumped down into the ball court. But the players, with the two teams now merged as one, were stronger and fitter. Although outnumbered by the spectators, the players, who, in Xibalba, had only ever known that game of death, fought bravely, dodging the slashing knives, the thrusts and stabs, and flinging spectators to the ground in all directions.

'Resist them!" Adam yelled.

All very well, I thought, *but this isn't getting us anywhere. And I'm still stuck up here!*

Then I saw them, again, those huge red rubber dudes, the Lords of Xibalba, One Death and Seven Death, arise from the blood-soaked ground into which they'd vanished after the Coyote had killed the Golden Jaguar.

'Adam, watch out for One Death and Seven Death!' I screamed.

'Wait!' he called back. He spoke hurriedly to the ball game players, about a dozen of whom immediately formed a human pyramid with their teammates protecting them. Adam ran at the pyramid, and, pulled upwards by the strong arms of the players, scaled it in no time. He reached up, inches from my free arm, just as One Death began to take human form. I managed to wriggle forwards in that invisible goo until my fingers touched Adam's. With a thrust of his arm, my brother gripped my hand and pulled me towards him. It felt as if I was being tugged through wet cement that was just about to set. Adam curved his arm about my waist, let go of the player's arm supporting him and leapt some twenty feet or so to the ground. The other players dismounted from the pyramid and ran at One Death. Forming a barricade, they grabbed his club and slowed him down as I hurried on, beside Adam, towards the entrance.

Spectators eager for blood blocked our exit. Worse still, Seven Death had also risen and was approaching with slow, determined strides, swinging his weapon with both hands.

'We've had it,' I cried.

'Just grip that locket, sis. I'm gonna—' He closed his eyes for an instant, but enough for me to panic when a spectator lunged at him with a knife. The spectator ended up with his face pressed into the red earth, Adam's foot on his neck as he wrenched the knife from the man. Just then, a familiar but totally inappropriate sound, from beyond the entrance, caught my attention: the chug of a vintage car engine. I turned and saw a red Austin-Healey hurtle into the ball court. It circled, scattering spectators, cheered on by the players, before skidding to a halt beside us.

'Jump in, kids!' shouted the plump, blonde-haired woman in the front passenger seat, swinging open one of the rear doors.

'How—?" I began.

'In!' ordered Adam, pushing me into the car and jumping up behind me. The car lurched forward, just soon enough to avoid a vicious swipe from Seven Death's club, shot out of the arena and continued to bump along over the red blood earth. I turned to see spectators pouring out from the ball court before spreading themselves over the hillside, up towards the top of the hill above which loomed the high arch of the swing bridge. Our escape route was cut off. Then One Death, followed by Seven Death, emerged, dwarfing all humans.

'Chloe, remember Art and Jeannie? From San Antonio? When María got spotted by a talent scout from New York?'

'Hi, Chloe!' said Jeannie, turning and smiling at me. 'Oh my, you're no longer the child we knew back then.'

'Where are we going?' I asked. 'And how do we get outa this place? What about—?"

'Too many questions, Chloe!' chuckled Art. 'One at a time, please.'

'Well... how the heck did you two get here? In this old crate of all things? Yeah, I remember the car all right. It's the one that took Adam and María downtown during that vintage car rally in San Antonio. But how on earth—?'

'Let's just say you and Adam called me. As for this little beauty, she's too magnificent to call a mere car. And certainly not a crate! Why, she an' me, we're just about inseparable. Next question?'

'Where are we go—?'

'That depends on where you wanna go, my child.'

'Just want to be with Lee again. And say sorry for being so stupid.'

'And what about One Death and Seven Death? That was the next question, huh?'

'Sure!'

'Only one way out. And it's blocked. The bridge we're driving away from as fast as she, my ole beauty, can take us.' Art patted the side of the Austin-Healey with pride.

'Then why—?'

'Not even I could fight off that lot. Not with the Lords of Xibalba on my tail. No, you'll have to take the alternative route.'

'The alternative route?'

'Uh-huh!'

I glanced back at the red hill and the red arena building. Already they seemed a long way off, but the hill was crawling with Xibalban spectators. One Death and Seven Death had either vanished or were camouflaged against the red earth. We were now driving over the blue and yellow plain. A strange sound was coming from the ground as we sped over it. A kind of screaming. I looked at Adam.

'Don't listen, sis. Just cover your ears,' he said.

I hated that sound and did as he said. It was later that he told me it came from the never-ending screams of souls trapped in the stinking soil like everlasting flowers, their *Life-Force* sucked out by the bat god, Zotz.

Soon, I saw buildings ahead. I thought it had to be some sort of a village and prayed that the inhabitants would be friendlier than the ball game spectators. As we approached, I realised it was no ordinary village. The motionless people I'd seen from afar turned out to be stone statues, only horribly life-like, and their expressions sent a chill down my spine. I thought I knew fear, but those faces showed me something way beyond any fear I could have imagined. Zotz again, as I later discovered. Art pulled up alongside one of the buildings.

'Out, you guys!' he ordered.

'Here?' I queried. I hated the place, as I hated everything in Xibalba.

'Look back at the red hill, Chloe.'

'Oh, my God!' I exclaimed.

Like a trail of ants, Xibalbans now streamed after us across the blue and yellow plain, their numbers multiplying all the time. Art and Jeannie, already out of the car, prodded the statues.

'Some of 'em kinda fall apart. Turn into dust. Need four that don't and that we can lift into the car. And you guys, slip off your tee-shirts. We're gonna need 'em.'

I felt embarrassed standing there in my bra, but happier when Jeannie stripped as well, and I soon saw what this was about. Adam and I helped Jeannie and Art pull our tops over four of the statues that were solid enough, and together we carried these to the Austin-Healey then lifted them into the seats. The car pointed towards a far-off chain of gigantic mountains. Art started up the engine, slipped it into gear and eased the foot of the statue in the driver's seat onto the accelerator pedal. He leapt backwards when the vehicle shot forwards.

'Great cars, Austin-Healeys!' he said as we stood watching the vehicle speed towards the mountains. 'Should give us a bit of time.'

I squinted at the red hill. The ant-trail of Xibalbans following the car had been deflected towards the mountains.

A thought occurred to me: María.

In our haste to escape certain death, we'd forgotten all about María. Coyote Spirit had planned to take her back to the ball court for a public performance of what he claimed to be better at than any other man."

"But he wasn't, was he?" questioned Pepe.

"Pepe, the Coyote was evil. Pure evil! But I was frightened for your Mama's sake. And I just couldn't seem to feel her with my sixth sense."

"*Our* sixth sense!" corrected Pepe. "Yeah, sometimes mine gets blocked out. Like when I want to know what's in Mama's mind and she's not letting me in."

"Back then, I feared she'd be there on her own, at the mercy of those Xibalbans. I begged Art to go back for her, but Adam interrupted me:

'She's not here. Not in Xibalba.' Your daddy hesitated. 'But she thinks I'm dead. Which is why we're gonna have to hurry."

Chapter 14: Coyote Cure?

"You've failed us again, miserable dog!" roared One Death. Coyote Spirit, neither man nor dog, licked his wounds and said nothing. He'd lain with her, in another's body. But the power his lords spoke of would soon be his... as they would also be.

***

"Mama, will you play with us this morning?"

"Not 'World Politics', I hope, Pepe?" María asked.

"Oh, it was getting boring and the twins didn't want to be the bad guys any more. Anyways, I'm fed up being an all-powerful world leader."

María flinched.

"What would you *like* to play, honey?"

Carla piped up:

"Can we play hospitals, Mama?"

"Sure, guys. Sounds great. And my voice needs a break from singing."

"You could sing in our hospital. It would so make the other patients happy!"

"Other patients?"

"Carla's dolls and soft animals. Oh, you've gotta be a patient, Mama. We want to make you better, see," explained Pepe.

"Better?" The woman's features tensed.

"Sure, Mama. Come!" The boy took his mama by the hand and led her into the playroom. "You have to lie down there on the floor."

María laughed.

"Don't you have proper beds for your patients in this hospital of yours?"

"No, we sold all our beds. So we could have enough money for the making-Mama-better medicine," Pepe said, before fetching a blanket with which to cover his mother as she stretched herself out on the carpet.

131

And for the next hour or so the children fussed around María whilst she lay on the floor pretending to be sick. They gave her medicine in the form of orange juice and pills which she was informed had been specially made up to look and taste just like candy. They jabbed her arm, as gently as possible, with a mock syringe and Pepe, the doctor, frequently put his ear to her chest, as his father had once taught him, to listen to the beating of her heart.

"Sounds good, Mama-patient," he announced, "but I'm afraid we're gonna have to operate to take away your worries."

"Worries? Worries about what, Mr Doctor?"

"That's what we have to find out. Nurse!" Carla skipped obediently up to her brother. "Fetch the scissors, nurse. Got to do a big operation."

"Big?" María pretended to shiver with apprehension.

"As big as this, Mama!" said Carla, stretching her little arms as wide as possible.

"Will I be safe in this hospital of yours?" María asked.

"Nowhere safer, Mama."

"And the twins. What part do they play?" The twins sat in a corner of the playroom, seemingly oblivious of the important surgery about to take pace.

"They're—" Pepe appeared thoughtful for a few moments. "They're the people who take you home."

"In an ambulance?"

"Sure!"

Pepe and Carla busied themselves stroking their Mama's hair and pretending to cut around the top of her head with make-believe scissors.

"We've found the worries, Mama!" Pepe exclaimed.

"We've found the worries," echoed Carla, grinning.

"Hey! Good job. That was cool, kids. Can I go home now?"

"Yeah. Only you'll have to come back as an animal for more tests." María sat up in alarm.

"As a what?" she asked

"This is an animal hospital now, see."

"Oh dear. I've only just gotten over my operation. Not a sick animal, I hope?"

Carla, still grinning, nodded.

"What kind of animal must I be?"

"A deer," said Pepe without hesitation. María looked away from her son. "A white deer."

"And I'll be a kangaroo nurse because I'm good at jumping, and the twins, they can be birds to fly you home when you're better," Carla added.

"And you, Pepe? What kind of animal doctor will you be?" María asked her son, still looking the other way.

"A coyote?" Carla suggested. "They're smart. Uncle Lee told me. Only—" Carla scowled. "They trick people, though. Uncle Lee said that too."

With tears welling, María hurriedly stood up and ran from the playroom.

***

Chloe sensed something had gone wrong with the children's play. Back on the chair swing in the yard, she told Pepe that neither he nor his mother was ready yet:

"There's more to the story, see."

"But you said only I can draw this worry out of her. It's all about Coyote Spirit, isn't it?"

"Only partly. As for that devil and his cronies, it seemed to me your mother's guardian angels had the measure of them.

'Art, you're a genius!' Jeannie said staring at the Xibalbans heading for the decoy car. 'Coyotes aren't the only ones who can trick folks.'

'Been tryin' to tell you that for years, honey,' replied Art. 'Thought you'd never come around to believing in me!'

'Who else can I believe in?' joked Jeannie. But in that place, Adam and I weren't into joking.

'If María, in Houston, thinks I'm dead—' Adam began. Art's grin left him as Adam fixed him with a gaze that unnerved even me. Of course, I'd already witnessed Coyote

133

Spirit turning into Adam, or whatever it was that happened back there in that ball court, and had put two and two together, but I couldn't figure out why my brother was suddenly talking about María back in Houston.

'Then I must—' began Art, but Jeannie cut in:

'She'll worry, Adam. What woman wouldn't with you disappearing like that. That's why we need to get you back quickly."

'But—if she thinks I'm dead, and then I'm not, so to speak—" Adam continued, then went blank, as if he, too, had been transformed into a frozen statue.

'We can't waste time discussing hypothetical issues!' interrupted Jeannie, unaware of your dad's sudden change, but I saw it and knew somehow it had to be linked with Coyote Spirit and what happened in the ball court. Was he somewhere else, or closing off his mind to us whilst he tried to remember something? One thing is for sure, though: later, my brother had no recollection of any of this.

'That building over there, kids. Quick!'

Adam snapped back into the here and now. He was with me again, and for a few moments wore a 'where the heck am I?' sort of expression. Art had just pointed to the largest of the buildings.

'Been there before, Art. Remember?' said Adam. 'With María. Both of us came within inches of being terminally transformed by Mr Batman!'

'In there?' I asked weakly. I shuddered, for an awful sensation filled the building. Even its stone walls seemed to mock us.

'Zotz? He's harmless so long as you stay close to me, guys,' added Art.

I believed most things that Art told us, but Zotz harmless? No way! I knew only what I felt, and I clung to Jeannie as we entered the place, and, without a top, feeling totally defenceless.

It was dim, dank and difficult to make anything out at first. A strange painting decorated a dark grey stone table on a plinth, but that's not what really caught my attention. Cut into a large flagstone on the floor was the roughly hewn image of a bat from which flowed a desolate despair that would have chilled even Satan."

"I don't believe in Satan," said Pepe.

"Not sure I did till our present president took up office. Anyways, Art tried to cheer me up making light of everything. 'Guess Dracula ain't at home,' he remarked. 'Just as well. He can get tiresome! Now help me lift this flagstone, Adam."

I saw that there was a thick metal ring attached to each carved-out bat wing. Art pulled at one of these whilst Adam grasped the other and together the two men slowly raised the flagstone and lifted it to one side of a gaping black hole. 'Behold the alternative route out of Xibalba! When Zotz is in residence, ain't many folk who come this way by choice. Likely he's busy gorging himself back at the ball court jus' now. Must be a fair number of bodies there.'

I peered into the hole.

'In there?' I queried in a barely-audible voice.

'You'll be fine,' reassured Jeannie. 'Honest!'

Art climbed down. There was a ladder, and I watched as his red hair disappeared. Jeannie followed. Adam turned and gave me a brotherly hug. I wished it would never stop. He felt so strong."

"He is!" agreed Pepe.

"Sure. Strong yet gentle. 'Wanna go next?' he asked.

I shook my head.

'Don't wanna lose sight of you, Adam.' Tears had cooled my cheeks. 'Not whilst we're still in this horrid place. I—' He kissed me on the forehead then squeezed my hand.

'And don't you be worrying about Lee. He's strong too. He'll be okay. Maybe a bit mad at you for running off like that, but he'll be all right.'

'What about you? Are you mad at me?"

Adam touched my cheek and smiled. He, Aunt Jac and Aunt Germaine in New York were my whole family now. They were all I had, apart from Lee, and, of course, María my secret sister-in-law. In my brother's smile was a warmth that melted my fear. It was like the sun emerging from behind a cloud on a cold winter's morning, an expression of that wonderful bond between siblings. It was love. Not a boy-girl thing, like with me and Lee, but it was love, all the same. Family love. Those moments when I thought he was dead were the worst in my entire life, and the instant I realised he was still alive, the very best."

Pepe snuggled up against Aunt Chloe. He wanted to tell her she was like his sun but felt curiously shy.

"You know what your daddy said to me?"

Pepe shook his head.

"'Little sis, I could never, *ever* be mad at you. Just mad at those who try to do you harm. Be brave now! Okay?'

I nodded. Adam always made me feel better. Ever since I took my first faltering steps in this world of ours and discovered how it could, at times, be a painful place, Adam had been there to comfort me.

'Not too fast, Adam,' I begged as he lowered himself into the shaft.

Suddenly, I was thrown to the ground by a piercing shriek. I'd heard the same terrifying sound up above the ball court when the giant bat, Zotz, appeared for the *Life-Force* of the decapitated team captain. The room blacked out. A vast dark shape was blocking the doorway.

'Hurry!' shouted Adam's voice from the darkness below. A hand reached up out of the gloom, searching for mine. I stretched down, gripped this hand and stepped into the shaft. There was a rustling and scraping behind me. I descended the ladder as quickly as my feet would allow, fearful not only of the bat, whose hot, sticky breath curled around the back of my neck like a scarf of burning gas, but of losing my hold, tumbling into the abyss and taking Adam with me. I half-expected the huge creature to shrink and flutter into the shaft to sink its teeth into me. But it didn't. Gradually, the shrill sonar squeaks faded as we went down, down and down. The shaft sloped then levelled off until we were walking in a tunnel. This widened out till your daddy and I could walk on hand in hand. A dim light ahead silhouetted the figures of Art and Jeannie.

'Who really are Art and Jeannie?' I whispered to Adam.

'Depends,' he whispered back. 'Sometimes they're just Art and Jeannie running a haulage business in Iowa, other times they're the Maya hero twins, Hunahpu and Xbalanque, and the ancient gods of the sun and the moon. But I think they're really 'thingies' for María.'

'Guardian angels?'

'Something like that.'

'Now that the Golden Jaguar's dead? I hope—' Adam squeezed my hand.

'Hope can also be the Devil,' he whispered. I chuckled, though I didn't know why. Release of tension, perhaps. But—*the Devil? Why?*

'Think I'll just stick with Art and Jeannie!' I said quietly.

Art and Jeannie stopped at what seemed to be the end of the tunnel.

'This it?' I asked Art. 'The Bridge?'

'If only!' Art said. 'This here, Chloe, is the true Xibalba. Where the Xibalbans 'live'. If you can call it living. Up there are the evil gods of Xibalba and our old friends One Death and Seven Death. That's where most Xibalbans end up if they try to escape, with their Life-Force sucked out of 'em. An eternity of pain. See, for the Xibalbans, that bridge leads to paradise 'cause they're already dead as we know it, but for you two it leads back to life and to your loved ones. Think of Xibalba as a half-way house. Sooner or later the Xibalbans all try for paradise, but there ain't many who make it.'

'What are Xibalbans like?' I asked. 'Other than those zombies up there.'

'You see them every day back home, Chloe.'

'Like us?'

'They are you. You, Adam, Lee, your aunts, anyone and everyone, only they're 'dead' as you'd call it. Here, of course, death is something a whole lot different.'

'But what about heaven? Going straight to heaven?' I asked. I was thinking about my poor momma and daddy ending up in this awful place. Adam squeezed my hand again. He must have had the same thought.

'Good question, Chloe,' responded Art. 'A while back, I might have answered differently. But you know, after feeling that special love between Adam and his girlfriend María, my beliefs kind of changed. And the Golden Jaguar changed with me.'

'He's dead,' I said.

'Is he?' Art and my brother exchanged glances. 'What I mean to say about the Xibalbans is that to you they'll seem like ordinary people. Good and bad. Up there, above ground, the ones hungry for *Life-Force* and the bitter-sweet taste of victory over defeat, they're only a part of the ball game. And it's a game that seemingly never ends. Not even after your Universe has gone silent. But I guess you saw what happened when Adam joined in. The players' hatred of each other vanished. The two teams became as one 'cause of your brother. He had that effect on them. Same as he had on me and the Golden Jaguar on account of a love inside of him that comes from María.'"

Pepe punched a fist into the air.

"Yeah! Mama!"

"It's in you too, Pepe. I know it. But this is what we have to show her."

"Can't her guardian angels just tell her?"

"It's about showing, not telling. Getting back to those guardian angels, Art explained to me all about the spectators. 'They're different, see,' he said. 'Take away their hatred and ain't nothin' but a hollow space behind two eyes. We all know people like that, and the Death Lords use 'em as spectators for the game. Here in Xibalba, it's like there are two kinds of souls: the spectators, caught up in an unending cycle of evil, then the players and those who hide down here until they're forced to become players too. Those seeking paradise. The spectators are forever combing these dark tunnels for more players, training 'em, and every player someday gets to be captain of his team. And then – well, like folks back in your place in the time of the ancient Maya and Aztecs got told, the losing captains get fast-tracked to heaven by decapitation. But don't believe what people say.'"

"Show don't tell again?" Pepe checked with his aunt.

"It's what Lee's always saying about our documentary movies. Gotta show the world what's really happening. Show folk the starving kids in Alabama, then perhaps the truth about what some call 'God's country' will out!"

"God doesn't need a country, does He?"

"Nope! Anyways, there we were at the end of that dark tunnel with me praying we'd soon be out of Xibalba. 'This place is so horrid!' I said to Art.

'Place of Fear, Chloe! Worse than horrid.'

'Why are you telling us all this stuff? Can't we just get the hell out of here?'

'Not that simple. See, Jeannie and I are gonna have to leave you two now. When One Death and Seven Death realise you're not up there, they'll know you're down here. The spectators are one thing, but here we'd struggle against some of the creatures hidden in these tunnels. As for the Lords of Xibalba, they'd drag you both back to the ball court – and, well, you know the rest. No, Jeannie and I must go back to challenge them to a ball game. Distract them a little. Pretty even match up there on the ball court,

139

'cause what we lack in size and muscle we make up for with brains and agility. Down here, we'd likely get sandwiched between them with one at either end of a tunnel. They'd move in towards each other, then... bingo! for the Death Lords. A red currant jelly sandwich. No, better we stay away from you guys.'

I looked nervously at Adam.

'Which way to the bridge?' he asked.

'All tunnels lead to the bridge,' replied Art.

'Yeah, but that means you can either go towards it or away from it. We could be going round and around down here forever and never get any closer.'

'You'll find out from the walls.'

'How?'

'By listening to 'em.'

'Listening?' I asked. I was beginning to think Art and Jeannie had gone crazy and that Xibalba was just a giant evil madhouse.

'Put your ear to the wall. The thing you most want to hear, or the thing in life you find most beautiful, it'll call to you from across that bridge. Its echo will travel along the walls of the tunnel to wherever you are in Xibalba. The walls will always tell you where the bridge is, Chloe. So just think... walls!'

I put my ear to the wall. From afar came the most beautiful sound anyone could imagine. And being so distant, yet so clear, added to its sweetness and sadness. Tears streamed my face. I looked at Adam.

'It's her,' I told him. 'Listen!' Adam put his ear to the wall, and I knew from his eyes he'd heard the same thing. The voice of María. Singing. Adam took my hand again.

'We'll make it, Chloe. For her sake,' he promised.

'Well, guys, Jeannie and I must get going,' Art said. 'Retrieve our beautiful car. She won't have gotten far. Was almost out of gas, anyways.'

'Will we see you again?' I asked.

'Back there, everywhere! And all the time, Chloe. In the mirror, too.'

I don't know what I expected for an answer to my question, but Art's answers always seemed to lead to more questions. I glanced at Adam, as if he might provide one, but his face looked as blank as mine felt. I was about to ask Art what he meant, but to my horror both he and Jeannie had simply vanished.

'Adam?' I whispered, gripping my brother's hand more tightly.

'To hear her singing was his answer, sis,' he said. 'Quick. We mustn't stay here a moment longer than necessary.'

Without Art and Jeannie, I felt as helpless as a chicken in a fox's den. Cold, too, in just my bra without a top. We walked on into a wide, empty space which turned out to be a meeting point of five tunnels. After pressing our ears up against each wall, we took the tunnel in which we could hear María's voice. I was getting used to the dim light and could now make out a faint glow ahead coming from beyond a bend. It got gradually brighter until the tunnel straightened out, and I saw that it led to a large open area. I heard voices. Murmurings at first, but soon clearly audible as distinct voices. Men's and women's voices, and the words they used were recognisable. It wasn't English, but I understood it.

'Mayan?' Adam queried.

'How come I understand it?'

'I really don't know, but—' He looked at our granny's locket around my neck. 'Perhaps that thing you're wearing? Like with the golden jaguar bracelets.' I fingered the locket and Adam shrugged his shoulders.

'Granny's locket? Because she looked like me?'

'More than just looked like you, from what Dad once said.'"

"And I'm like you too, Papa says. Not to look at, but inside," Pepe informed his aunt.

"We have to convince your mother of that, Pepe. In the tunnel, hearing those voices, and knowing Xibalbans weren't all like those horror movie dummies, the spectators, I asked your Papa whether they might be friendly.

'We'll soon find out,' he replied.

We proceeded slowly into what seemed to be a kind of market place. It smelt of unclean bodies and damp. I was holding Adam's hand so tightly that I was afraid I might hurt him. He must have felt me tremble for he put his arm across my shoulders.

'It'll be okay so long as we stay together,' he assured me.

Nothing could have prised me away from my brother. There was certainly no need for him to worry about me running off.

We halted, unsure whom to approach.

How odd, I thought, *to have a market underground in the land of the dead.*

It was crowded, with dozens of stalls, though many of the goods were spread out over the ground on colourful rugs and the people were either standing in groups, talking, or moving around, mingling, looking at the displays on offer.

At first no one took any notice of Adam and me as we walked on. I was concerned to see not just one but at least six other tunnel entrances opening into the hall. There might have been more, but it was too dim from where we stood to make out anything in detail. I wanted to test each tunnel entrance, unobserved, by pressing my ear to the wall and listening for the voice of María, but our luck in remaining undetected ran out. A hatchet-faced man caught my eye and came towards us. Then another and another, and soon we were surrounded by a bunch of Native guys, all men. The one with the hatchet-face pointed to me, stepped forwards to stroke my arm a few times, then tugged at my blonde braids. I wished I hadn't donated my tee-shirt to that statue we put in Art's car. I felt like I was half-naked as the ugly brute ogled and fondled me. I'd never let anyone other than Lee touch me like that before.

'Adam?' I said weakly, rooted to the spot. I felt Adam's fingers tense like the coils of a spring. We would be hopelessly outnumbered if it came to a fight. Even though my brother was the Texas junior karate champion, we wouldn't stand a chance in that place. As for me, I'm the biggest scaredy-cat in the world.'"

"Papa says you're the bravest woman he knows."

"Your papa's too kind, sometimes. Uncle Lee is forever joking about the way I cling to him for the least reason. See a small spider in our room and he has to lift me up in the air."

"So, what happened next?"

"'I give you feathers. I give you cloth for her,' the man said to Adam, running his hand up and down my shaking arm. It was obvious that he thought Adam had brought me to the market place to sell. Your daddy hesitated. He always did that in karate, too. Like he was testing his opponent, waiting to decide when and how to strike. Meanwhile, I was terrified. Suddenly, I got grabbed from behind. I turned, trying to break free. Adam raised his hand, but I shouted out: 'No, Adam, don't!"

The man gripping my arm was old. He had straggled white hair. There was a glint in his eyes, but they were kind. Not like those of Hatchet Face. *His* were as hard as stone.

'This old guy is okay,' I said to Adam in English.

'He brought her here for me,' the old man said. 'We've already done a deal.'"

"You felt him, didn't you, Aunt Chloe? Like I do sometimes."

"Sure thing, Pepe. And when I looked at his eyes, I knew he was trying to help us too. I nodded at Adam. He'd already read my mind.

'Like the man says,' Adam said in Mayan to Hatchet Face, 'she belongs to him now.'

Hatchet Face's eyes narrowed to knife slits.

'An old fellow like Lizard-by-the-Water? She'll get no pleasure from him! Hasn't used his staff of joy for hundreds of years. Doubt whether he knows what to do with it.'"

"What did he mean?"

Aunt Chloe had again forgotten she was talking to a child. Often, she thought of Pepe as a wise old man.

"Sorry, Pepe. I think he realised the old guy was trying to save me from a fate as bad as anything in the ball court. And I shuddered at the thought of having any kind of 'pleasure' with any of those others encircling us."

"Uncle Lee gives you pleasure, doesn't he?"

Chloe laughed.

"Of course he does! Anyways, someone else in that market seemed to be on our side. 'Cool it, Power-of-the-Eagle,' another man said. Hatchet Face dropped his hand. He stood staring at me for a few moments, then pointed to the old man.

'I'll have her when she tires of you, Lizard-by-the-Water. For one feather. You give her to anyone else and I'll see to it that the spectators seek you out. Fancy a ball game, huh? Heard they're looking for a new captain!'

His laugh was as hard as his eyes. And the smell of him even worse. I was so relieved when he and the others wandered off, though the horrid man kept peering back at me with those knife-sharp eyes of his. The old man, the one they'd called Lizard-by-the-Water, stayed with us. He still held onto my arm, but gently and clearly without malicious intent.

'Follow me,' he said quietly.

We followed him out of the market place, along one of the tunnels. There were doors in this tunnel, possibly belonging to 'dwelling places'. He opened one and ushered us into a small room lit by two flickering lamps stuck on the wall. There were several floor mats, and Lizard-by-the-Water beckoned for us to sit on two of these before squatting down himself.

'The bridge?' he asked. I shouldn't have been surprised, for we were obviously not the usual Xibalbans.

'Yeah,' Adam replied, 'and by the quickest route possible.'

'There's no way of knowing that in Xibalba,' the old man answered. 'What seems fine just now may be totally not fine a few breaths later. But you're not dead. I can tell. Why are you here?'

Adam looked at me and suddenly I felt guilty. However much Art might have tried to persuade me that I'd only taken us along a path marked out by fate, I had, after all, been a free agent. Just as two years before, nothing had forced me into stepping back into the ancient mesas when I ran on ahead of your parents to meet up with Earth Child whom I'd only met in my real dreams. This time, try as I might to blame the doll I'd called 'María', it was my choice again to run off after that Indian boy.

'I was searching,' I said. 'I'd lost a close friend a while back. A long while back. I wanted there to be more than that. More than never seeing her again. Not knowing what really happened to her was so awful. And my brother, well—he—he kind of—well—' Your daddy completed my sentence:

'My sister called for me!'

'Brother and sister. I thought so. Close, then. Look… erm?"

'My name's Chloe. And my brother's called Adam.'

'Strange names.'

'The Cliff people called us Living Water and Leaping Jaguar back then.'

The old man smiled.

'So, you flow like a stream that seeks out the Water of Life whilst Adam has the courage of the most fearless of forest beasts.'

'There's someone else, too,' I said. Lizard-by-the-Water looked into my eyes. Somehow, he knew.

'The one calling you back? The one they call 'special'?'

I nodded. 'Adam's wife. María. Most beautiful girl in Adam's school. Perhaps in the whole of Houston. Or Texas. Even the world.'

'More beautiful even than you?' I felt embarrassed. I thought Lee was the only one who found me vaguely pretty.

'Much more!' I blurted. 'And her voice when singing is every bit as beautiful as she is.'

'Someone like that calling you to the bridge might improve your chances of getting back.'

Might? The man's choice of words chilled my insides. He turned to Adam:

'First we must find something for your beautiful sister to cover herself with. Those men out there see too much of the girl.' He disappeared through another, lower doorway at the back and returned holding a patterned shawl. After wrapping it around my shoulders like a poncho, he used two colourful clips to fasten it at the neck and across the chest. Already, I felt less vulnerable.

'My wife, from where you came, made things like this. And sandals and baskets. Flower-by-a-Rock and me were so close. She'll be in paradise now, of course, I know it. And she'll be waiting. Across that same bridge. I've been trying to get to the bridge for as long as I can remember, but this place defeats me every time.' I saw sadness in his eyes. 'Just so much evil.' I placed my hand on his arm.

'You could come with us,' I suggested. He looked from me to Adam.

'Me? Come with you to the bridge?'

My brother agreed:

'Why not? I've done it before. Went back across that bridge with María.'

'You've been here and back to the living world already? Is this possible?'

Adam nodded.

'We could do with another friend here. For the kind of help you just gave us,' he said.

'See, these guys, Art and Jeannie, they were kind of helping us,' I added. 'They called this is the alternative route to the bridge, but they've gone back to the ball court.'

'The ball court? They're spectators?'

'No, no. They're gonna challenge the Lords of Xibalba to a ball game.'

'Impossible! Unless—"

'She's telling the truth,' insisted Adam. 'They're also known as Hunahpu and Xbalanque.'

'The Hero Twins? You met the Hero Twins? Who are you people?' The old man's eyes now betrayed unease. Adam laughed.

'We're just two kids from Houston, Texas. Look, come with us. Please! I think we all need each other.'

To Lizard-by-the-Water, we must have seemed like mysterious messengers from the world of the living, a world he'd all but forgotten about apart from a distant memory of the love for his wife, Flower-by-a-Rock. Our connection with The Hero Twins, also Art and Jeannie, must have made us seem like a pair of angels."

Chapter 15: The Devil Within

The 'other girl' aside, they had interminable arguments about what the man called 'John' really meant, but one thing seemed certain: He, of whom John spoke, would return.

***

"Why is the president of the United States so all-powerful?" Pepe asked his Uncle Lee.

"Good question," Lee replied. "Can't really answer it. It's just the way things are."

Not only did Uncle Lee worry about the new bearer of that title, but the whole world feared the man. That is apart from the few who sought to gain from his empty promises. Some described him as the 'Anti-Christ' and others as the 'Beast of the Book of Revelation'. Who- or whatever he was, one thing was clear: neither the man, nor much of the country he now 'led', had even the remotest interest in the catastrophic changes that were catapulting the world, that he and his wife so obviously enjoyed with their $billions, towards cosmic oblivion.

"Why won't he listen to you and Aunt Chloe? You told me your documentary was like a wake-up call for the world. To pave the way, Aunty said. Pave the way for what, Uncle Lee?"

There were things that Lee and Chloe discussed in private that each had promised the other to disclose to no one else, including family. Especially family! The man said nothing, but he took hold of the boy's hands. For Pepe, this was enough:

"We must find someone to stand up to him and slow down global warming, right?"

Uncle Lee nodded.

"I agree," the man said. "As for the most important job in the world, I guess some of those in power start off with good intentions. Maybe. Say that they're doing the best thing for people. Or kid folk that they are. Trouble is, it doesn't always end up like that. Good intentions turn sour, good guys can hide their bad bits no longer, or power corrupts and something else takes over."

"Like the Devil?"

Lee knew that the boy had read media reports on the views of others, the intelligent minority who had tried to show the world who or what the new president would turn out to be.

"We can all change, Pepe. Sometimes for the better, mostly for the worse."

"Mama and Papa won't change, will they? I'd hate it if they ever changed!

"Not in that way, they won't."

"Will I change one day?"

'You'll grow up!' remarked Uncle Lee, but he knew what the child was really asking. The same question that had troubled his mother ever since that time when Chloe simply vanished into a tepee all those years back. This was the real reason behind their trip to Houston. The documentary was but a convenient smoke screen.

"What about that bad guy? The one called Coyote Spirit who pretended to be my father. Was he ever good?"

"Well, you know that's one question I did ask your Aunt Chloe. 'Maybe he was,' she said. Like the president of the United States of America, he probably wanted the best for his people. Once. Guess it was power changed him. Magnified the evil."

"You mean like Lucifer? Could the same happen to me, one day?"

"Nope!" It was all Lee could say in reply. He could hardly have said, *we don't know and that's why we're having this conversation.*

"Why not?"

"Because you're Pepe Winters and your Mama and Papa are who they are. Particularly Mama. Something very special about her, your Aunt Chloe has always said."

"I know."

Pepe so yearned to ask his Mama why she was sad all the time because it seemed to be getting worse, and he knew this was to do with him: whether he would be bad one day, like the new president, and not listen to Uncle Lee and Aunt Chloe. But he realised he had to know the full story from his uncle and aunt before he could take away that sadness. Until then he would be the perfect son – do everything he could for Mama and Papa, take care of Carla and play with the twins. He so loved to see his Mama smile when he did these things.

It was his Mama's music that showed him the depth of her sadness: the songs from her new album she was preparing called '*I Know Only Love*'. Pepe couldn't truly understand the title, and neither could his father when the boy asked him what it meant:

"Your Mama's very deep," Papa had replied.

Why do deep and weep rhyme? Pepe wondered.

"What's deep mean?" Pepe asked. "Person, not water deep?"

"It means she feels things even more strongly than the rest of us."

"What sort of things?"

"Things that link us all together. Loving, hoping, worrying, praying."

"She prays a lot. I've heard her. Not only at church. Can't you just ask her why she prays so much and why she's so sad, Papa?"

"Wish I could. No, Aunt Chloe's right. It's gotta be you, son. When she's finished telling you about the Golden Jaguar, you're the only one can make Mama happy again."

"But it's such a long story, Papa, and Mama's getting sadder every day."

"She's afraid for you, Pepe. She knows you're learning about the story, and at first she was pretty much against it, you hearing all that stuff."

"Too scary?"

"That—and perhaps other reasons too. She wouldn't say. But your Aunt Chloe insisted, and you know your aunt. There's no one in the world who can refuse her when she has her mind set on something."

But all Pepe could think about was the new president, the Devil and the Devil within people.

Guess I do believe in Satan, he told himself.

***

"Shall we continue our story?"

"How will it make Mama better, Aunt Chloe?"

"I wish I could answer that. Trouble is, there are bits that none of us knows. That's where you must come in."

"But I can't make things up!"

"No one's asking you to. Now—wanna hear what happened to your aunt and your dad in the tunnels of Xibalba?'

"Okay!" Pepe wasn't sure that he wanted anything other than for his Mama to be happy, but he listened anyway:

"Lizard-by-the-Water was hesitant. And in that awful place I could hardly blame him. Nothing, apart from death, seemed certain in Xibalba. Death, evil, suffering—and trickery.

'Oh, please come with us,' I begged after looking long and hard into his sad old eyes.

'My wife wasn't as beautiful as you, Chloe, but her soul was pure. And she was so warm. A great mother. She made the best corn-cakes in our village.'

'Please!' I insisted.

He looked thoughtful.

'Well, if I end up as captain in a ball game, as a result, then at least—' He gave me a wink. 'At least I'll have the thought in my head before I lose it that I've tried to help a beautiful woman. What more can a man ever hope for, huh?'"

"I think you're beautiful too, Aunt Chloe. And I know Uncle Lee does. He told me."

151

'Well, then I was only fifteen, remember. Still a child even if I looked like a woman. Anyways, together the three of us left his dwelling place and returned to the darkness of the tunnel. I put my ear to the wall. Already María's voice was louder, clearer, and I was determined we'd reach the bridge, but there was something else. A child crying."

"Child?"

"Uh-huh! And that's partly why I'm telling you all this."

"Who?"

"I... I can't be sure. And I had no time to find out. I couldn't waste precious moments and destroy the only chance that kind old man might have to reach his wife — and paradise.

Lizard-by-the-Water took the lead and we followed close behind. Apart from the sound of our footsteps, the tunnel was silent as a tomb. The noise from the market place had dwindled to nothing. There were interminable twists and turns. Just when I began to think this tunnel would never end, it branched into two. One of these seemed to be a shade brighter, and after putting my ear to the wall of each, I was relieved to hear María's voice ahead of me in that particular one. In the other, only silence."

"What about the crying child?"

"Nothing. But I felt sure María's voice would lead us to the bridge. The tunnel got brighter, but it was a different kind of brightness. As we got closer, I saw light streaking in pencil shafts from narrow slits in the ceiling, and the patches of grey high above us were little bits of Xibalban sky. When I looked up, spots of Xibalban rain cooled my face. These fell through air vents just large enough to illuminate the tunnel with a ghostly grey light. The tunnel was wider at this point, and several other side tunnels opened into it.

'This way,' said Lizard-by-the-Water, pointing to one of these. I checked that María's voice was still ahead of us and we followed him for a few yards, stopping when someone called out from behind. We all turned at once. It was a woman.

'You can't go that way,' she shouted. She was dressed, like the men of Xibalba, in a short breechcloth and was bare-breasted, but her paucity of clothing was more than made up for by elaborate jewellery. Beaded necklaces looped around her neck like the rings of Saturn, and she had on gold bracelets and anklets. From her ear lobes hung large gold discs, and filigrees of gold thread were braided into her long black hair.

'This is the way, sister,' Lizard-by-the-Water called out to the woman. 'I've been further than this before. This time I'll reach the bridge and there is no other way.'

'Certain death, that way,' she said. 'And who are you?' She pointed to me. I hated her immediately.

'Me?' I was never any good at that 'who, me?' thing. Always disliked being singled out.

'It's you, isn't it? Came here searching, turning over the past, trying to reshape our futures.'

I felt guilty enough as it was, and tears welled in my eyes.

'I only want to get home. Be with Lee again.'

'Couldn't accept Earth Child dying, huh? Couldn't accept that part of the prophecy?'

'How do you know these things,' I asked. 'They're nothing to do with—'

'Everything's to do with me!'

Adam stepped forward:

'My sister was Earth Child's friend. That's all. She's tried to change nothing. She doesn't belong here. Neither of us do. We just need to get back.'

'Oh, the Golden Jaguar of the Sun has grown horribly weak. Once he was strong. Feared by all. And I used to command him. As high priestess of the Sun God, it was my right to call him to our magnificent temple. My duty. But he became contaminated by the weakness of a puny little boy from a parallel world. The world of the future. And that slut of a girlfriend of his. To think he not only prevented the gifting of her blood to appease the Rain God, but by deceit he stole the Golden Jaguar from us. Ugh!'

I felt angry. No one was gonna rubbish my hero big brother like that, or his girlfriend. Particularly not María!

'You're talking about the junior karate champion of Texas, you cow!' I said.

'Cow, huh? Then he can enjoy a little game with the Lords of Xibalba!' She turned her dark eyes on Adam. *Oh, why didn't I keep my big mouth shut?* I thought.

'Run!' cried your papa, but we were too late. The way ahead was blocked by a large cage, the door of which was open. The tunnel between us and the cage was filled with armed spectators pointing spears. More appeared behind the high priestess. I felt myself prodded on the butt by the sharp end of a spear.

'Don't even think about it,' I whispered to Adam when I saw him freeze as he used to do in karate contests. He studied the competition and agreed:

'Good advice!' he whispered back.

The high priestess had either overheard or read my mind. Possibly the latter, for I was aware of the same sort of evil energy force interfering with my sixth sense as I'd experienced with Coyote Spirit.

'Pity you won't be able to use that clever martial arts stuff for the ball game,' she teased. 'And by the way, your sister will be the ball. Ha-ha! Oh, and your old friend here will be captain of the other team. Your rival. Problem for you is that back on earth he was an expert at the game. Unbeaten. Did he forget to tell you?'

All three of us were herded into the cage, the door snapped shut, fastened with strong cord, and the cage was lifted with long poles. I felt like an animal being taken for slaughter. Four hefty spectators, one at each corner, raised us onto their shoulders, and we were bounced along, away from María's voice and from the bridge.

'It's okay, sis,' whispered Adam, wiping my tears with his fingers. 'I'll come up with something. These Xibalbans seem pretty thick. Her included.'

But I knew he was worried. I could tell from his eyes. Adam has never been able to fool me, although I realised then that he was trying his best to allay my fears. I felt his comforting arm reach across my shoulders as tears continued to trickle down my cheeks. We were taken back past the skylight air-shafts, and, from there, along a different tunnel. I felt a tap on the shoulder and turned around. It was Lizard-by-the-Water.

'The Snake Goddess,' he whispered, keeping his eyes on our cage bearers.' That gold necklace you wear—'

'What? My grandma's golden locket?'

'You keep rubbing it. As if it has special powers.'

'I thought it did have. Once. But the Golden Jaguar's dead and Art and Jeannie, they're—' I broke down. Never had I wept so much. It felt as if all the fear and anger the world had ever known were flowing out from me as tears. 'Guess they're dead, too, by now,' I added. 'Killed by those red rubber brutes!'

'The Lords of Xibalba?'

I nodded.

'Look, child, lizard and snake work hand in hand, if you get my meaning – not that the snake has any hands. She won't ever harm me or mine, I can vouch for that, but a bunch of juicy spectators might go down very nicely inside her long body. You wouldn't mind if I have a go with that thing of yours, would you? It's gold, so has to have strength.'

Strength?

Before then, I wouldn't have let anyone other than Adam touch our grandmother's locket, but now, knowing I was about to die and have my head used in a ball game, it made little odds. I slipped it off and handed it to the old man.

'You must hold it as well,' he whispered, placing it carefully in my palm. 'We'll only be able to reach her through the spirit of your grandmother. Let me put the flat of my hand over yours, so...'

We sat facing each other, bobbing up and down in that cage, with the golden locket sandwiched between our hands. I closed my eyes, and saw, in my mind, a huge whip-curl of terror slithering along a darkened tunnel. I heard a distant noise, like a faraway train, but speeding towards us. It got rapidly louder, until the cage crashed to the ground when the four bearers dropped us and ran off, screaming like banshees:

'The Snake Goddess!'

The approach of the Snake Goddess was heralded by a crescendo of shrieks, and a smell like that of concentrated sewage, before her ridiculously-hideous head burst into view. Her forked black tongue flicked out like an uncoiled slimy, plastic rope, feeling the cold air, whilst green reptile eyes searched the gloom for a meal of *Life-Force*.

'This doesn't seem such a great idea,' I said to Adam just before the head of the snake smashed into our cage, carrying us forward in front of her enormous nose and sabre-sized teeth for a hundred yards or so. Suddenly we were hurled sideways through an opening in the tunnel, as if we were merely in her way. Soon afterwards she must have reached her prey, the cowering Xibalban cage bearers; the tunnel echoed with their piercing screams. Then the train-roar of her crusty body slithering over the rocks faded into silence.

The three of us were all tangled-up with each other, dangling upside-down in the cage wedged in a narrow opening. Several bars of the cage had been split by impact with the Snake Goddess's head. After righting ourselves we began to pull the broken bars free, for Adam and I shared a thought: whatever Lizard-by-the-Water's allegiance was with his reptilian alter-ego, we had to get the hell out of there before the snake returned to enjoy a dessert of

American teens. After the screams were silenced, I'd become aware of another sound: that of rushing water.

'She knows who I am,' our companion grinned. 'That's why she dropped us off here. Back on earth, I was born beside a fast-flowing river where my parents used to go to fish. A lizard ran over the rock beside my mother as Earth Mother released me into the world. That's how I came by the spirit of the lizard. Don't worry! She'll not harm us.'

'Is that running water?' I asked. 'Like an underground river?' I knew the ceaseless Xibalban rain had to end up somewhere.

'Of course there's water down here,' he replied. 'How else could we survive – if you can call death survival? Up there, where the gods rule, there's no need for it. Only the blood of our souls. *Life-Force*. That's all they want up there.'

Adam helped me out through a gap in the cage. A little further along the tunnel we were standing on a kind of shelf to one side of which was a steep drop, and the sound of rushing water arose from the darkness below. I put my ear to the wall, hoping to hear María's singing, but all I could hear was the noise of the river.

'What do we do now?' Adam asked Lizard-by-the-Water.

'Just as all rivers find the sea back on Earth, here, in Xibalba, they all lead to the Great Emptiness at the Cliff of Oblivion.'

'Great Emptiness? Cliff of Oblivion?' I queried. I prayed his reply wouldn't confirm my fears, but it did.

'The void spanned by the bridge.'

My brother had told me about that bridge over Hell even before I followed Coyote Spirit. I already knew how terrifying it was.'"

"From when Mama died?"

Chloe looked in awe at young Pepe's face. How could she not, in the presence of someone whose wisdom spanned millennia, whatever his age in years?

"Yeah... but she didn't, did she? Die, that is. Her God knew that her time hadn't come. Because of you, Pepe. Your mama saw you in the *Forest Without Time* even before she got taken to Xibalba. Anyways, when that old man confirmed there was running water, I had visions of us being swept along by an underground river only to be spewed out into that bottomless void at the mouth of the tunnel. And ending up in—"

Chloe paused.

"In Hell? No way, Aunt Chloe! Not you!"

"You're right. No way! Not then, anyways. There was a path by the river. Lizard-by-the-Water told us it's where they got their water to drink from."

"Still seems strange that dead people need water." Pepe looked puzzled.

"Even if I knew what 'death' is, I'd probably agree with you, Pepe. But I guess in Xibalba water is to *Life-Force* what our water on Earth is to our blood. Anyways, the old fellow told me there were lots of watering holes in all the tunnels. 'Any good at climbing?' he asked.

Well, I'm not good with heights. Never done any of that rope stuff. Not much opportunity in Houston which is as flat as a pancake, or in New York where they're unlikely to take kindly to folk scaling the sky-scrapers. Your dad's scared of heights, too."

"I know. But I'm not! I'm trying to teach Carla to climb."

"Don't give your mama kittens!"

"Can people really have kittens?"

"Just an expression, Pepe."

"Like what I gave Mama when the kids were out in that hurricane? Carla said afterwards that Papa's eyes were on fire."

Chloe drew in a deep breath.

"Hmm! Poor María! Now back to Xibalba. See, the old guy told your dad and me that if we took a certain path, we would eventually reach the cliff. And beyond that, zilch.

We were gonna have to climb to the top with nothing but a void beneath us and hope we didn't come out too far from the bridge because there'd be no cover at all up there. No place to hide.

'What about the red hill?' Adam asked. 'Could daub ourselves with the red mud up there? Camouflage?'

Lizard-by-the-Water shook his head.

'That's where the Death Lords come from. Where all the evil of Xibalba is concentrated. No, once up on top, a sprint to the bridge, huh? You okay with this, Adam? But what about that thing you have with heights?'

Your daddy tried to smile. My only consolation was that I knew he was the bravest guy alive."

"Alive in the land of the dead?"

"Uh-huh!"

"You said, 'was', Aunt Chloe. Shouldn't that be 'is'."

"Most definitely! And he somehow made me feel brave too. 'If the cliff's got no bottom, then it's got no height,' he said. 'Not one you can measure, anyways. So, no height, no fear, little sis! We'll do it, you and me!' And we high fived. I think Lizard-by-the-Water wondered why we were slapping our hands together.

'As for me, I'll be fine!' he said. Lizards are good on cliff faces!'

Groping in the dark, he led us down a narrow path to the river. The roar of the water deafened us as we followed that path along a stony bank. All the time I prayed we wouldn't encounter more spectators, and we didn't. We came across the occasional solitary soul: an old woman, who said nothing at all, a young man who talked a lot, and wanted to know all about Adam and me before wishing us well for our journey to the bridge. Then we saw a young woman ahead, and soon caught up with her. She stopped to tell us her story. She'd died in childbirth and was desperate to be reunited with her baby in paradise. She was crying so much that she'd probably added a significant amount of water to the river."

"Can you have rivers of tears?" asked Pepe.

"Well, I guess if everyone in the world cried at once then it might be possible."

"Could a river like that carry Mama's sadness away?"

"We'll need more than a river of tears when the time comes, Pepe. Which is why I'm telling you all of this."

"What about the crying child, Aunt Chloe? I have to know more about her."

Her? For a moment, Chloe's vacant expression informed her nephew that something had occurred to his aunt. Before he could ask, she continued the story:

"I don't know any more. 'So, you too have chosen to try your luck with the cliff?' Lizard-by-the-Water asked this woman.

'It's the only way for me,' she said. "The bat, the spider, the snake, I can face them, but our own kind who have become spectators, they're the evilest of all. They rarely make it down here, by the river, for they only come to steal players for the ultimate sport of death: the ball game, and the chance of catching splattered drops of *Life-Force* that we used to call blood.'

So, Rain-on-the-Corn, an intriguing name, joined our little group as we slowly made our way along the path towards the mouth of the underground river. It's impossible to say how long it took us, for there, in Xibalba, time isn't as we know it here, Pepe. Although Rain-on-the-Corn must have been dead for many centuries of Earth time, it seemed, for her, that she had only just been separated from her child.

The first indication of our approach to the mouth of the river was a feint luminescence ahead. Gradually, this became brighter, then, on rounding a bend, I saw an oval of light in the distance. As we got closer, this grew until I could make out an opening, twenty to thirty feet wide, like the gaping mouth of a cave.

It's one thing having no head for heights, but when we emerged from that tunnel, and watched the river cascade soundlessly into the oblivion below, with the cliff face dropping into horizon-less infinity, I felt something way beyond rational fear. Even terror would be far too weak a word to describe that feeling when you realise you are only inches away from nothing. Nothing at all. To fall off would have meant falling for eternity. Hell. We looked up towards the top of the sheer cliff, tinged with red. I guessed it was a climb of about fifty metres, and I could tell we weren't the first to use this route, for the footholds appeared well worn.

There was one thing that gave me the encouragement I needed to keep going and not turn back: the bridge. I could see it in the distance through a haze of mist. At least the start of it, for the other side was lost in the mist. For me the bridge also meant a chance to return to Lee and the life I knew; for Adam, showing his love for your mama, and for the other two, reaching paradise.

We looked at one another, evidently with the same thought going through our minds. Who should go first?

'Me,' suggested Lizard-by-the-Water. 'I'll lead, and if I fall then you'll know that I've have taken the wrong route.'

Adam was determined to keep his eyes on me all the time, so it was decided that I should follow Lizard-by-the-Water, with Adam behind me and Rain-on-the-Corn in the rear. As I edged my way up the cliff behind our new friend, concentrating all my energy on each slippery hand grip and foothold, I prayed that Zotz wouldn't suddenly soar down from above and pick us off one by one. By God, did I pray! To Granny, the Great Spirit. And your God. Anything I thought of the bridge. Of Lee. And I just kept on going. Up and up and up, until at last, clutching the red spongy ground, I scrambled over the lip of the cliff, and lay there, gasping."

Chapter 16: A Voice from Another World

The man on Patmos who called himself John knew nothing of the Old Woman of the Hills. If he had known her, he might have had an answer for those who keep asking "...But when?"

Nor had any of those gathered together, in a dimension outside time, seen the Old Woman of the Hills. But the deceased Mexican antiques dealer knew about her from his young friend back in Houston. He had heard how, without her, the boy would never have uncovered the second Golden Jaguar bracelet and thereby rescued the girl from becoming eternally enslaved to Tezcatlipoca. And later, he'd been sent to the Forest Without Time to provide the boy with a glass tube with which to catch venom from the Great Spider Goddess in Xibalba, and from which the old lady would make anti-venom to prevent the girl's death. For these reasons alone, the old Mexican fellow knew that she was important for that world down there but had no idea why.

***

The next day, Chloe had an interview downtown with the Governor of Texas. It was for the documentary. She'd wanted Lee to come too but, on this occasion, he felt it would be better if he were to stay out of town. He had a 'thing' about politicians. They drove him insane and there was an excellent chance that he might lose his characteristic cool with a guy who, like the president, had never shown the slightest interest in the dire effects of global warming upon his own state, let alone the rest of the world. Chloe, on the other hand, had always managed to charm the most unlikely of people with her naïve, though direct, questioning. And her blue eyes and bewitching smile. Plus, she was pretty. So, Lee stayed at home, looking over photos, on his laptop, of the havoc caused by

Hurricane Lara. Pepe was at a loose end as it was raining, and Carla and the twins were playing 'schools'. Not a game that enthused him. He crept into his uncle's room to see the photographs.

"Do you have any photos of that tepee, Uncle Lee?" he asked.

"The one your aunt disappeared into?"

Lee looked quizzically over his shoulder at Pepe.

"Did she really disappear, or was it that you just couldn't see her?"

"Comes to the same thing, Pepe. And no, I took no photos. Didn't seem right. Maybe I'm superstitious, but I dreaded preserving anything that reminded me of her being gone. And remember, back then I honestly believed I would never see her again."

"It still makes you cry, doesn't it, Uncle Lee!" observed the little boy, for tears started to well in the man's eyes.

"Sure does. But back then, I was kinda beyond tears. Kind of half-dead, and you know, if it hadn't been for Uncle Jason, I do believe I might have died. Three days I sat there, outside that tepee. Wouldn't move. Hardly spoke, and for three days Uncle Jason stayed with me, fed me, gave me water. Aunt Jac, she never told no one else about Chloe's disappearance. Said the worst thing would be to have the place teaming with family, with police and reporters. Spent her time contacting Native American chiefs and medicine men—shamans, they're called—'cos she knew this thing was way out of the ordinary. 'Not White Man's stuff,' she said. And it was because of Aunt Jac that they let me stay there, her doing so much for the Native Americans with her legal work and all. They treated me good, too. The guy I nearly thumped apologised every time he saw me, and he kept bringing me burgers and hot dogs and coke and stuff."

"Yummy!"

"How can you say that, Pepe, with your Mama being the best cook in the world?"

Uncle Lee gave Pepe a playful punch in the side.

"Well, we never get to eat junk food. So, it has to be yummy!"

Uncle Lee laughed.

"Did you know then that Papa was in there with Aunt Chloe?" the boy asked.

"Only knew what I told you. That he'd vanished and reappeared back in Houston."

"But he wasn't really killed, was he?"

Lee shrugged his shoulders.

"Like I said, it wasn't no White Man's nor Black Man's business going on there inside that tepee. Maybe one day your aunt will tell you more about Native beliefs, about their religion. They have a whole different view on life and death. Same as they see themselves and nature around them in a different way."

"But that's what this is all about, isn't it, Uncle Lee? What happened in that tepee, and whether Papa really was alive or dead?"

"Jeeze, Pepe! You know, sometimes you make me feel like the little kid. Chloe warned me I'd not be able to keep anything from you. I only know what your aunt and your mama told me. Your papa, he won't speak about it, and your mama—see, this is all about Mama, anyways. About you making her better when you know it all."

"I tried wishing with the golden jaguar bracelet to make her feel better. I put Carla's on as well. I sat there and I thought, *please, please make Mama happy again, and make her music happy and not just those sad songs that make me want to cry.* Then I went into the kitchen and she was sitting at the table and her head was in her hands and—and she was crying. I hugged her and told her she was the best mom in the world and that I loved her, but she cried even more."

"We all love her, Pepe. We'll do it, this thing. You'll do it. All righty? When Aunt Chloe's told you everything?"

Lee held up his right hand and Pepe high fived with the man.

***

Later, on returning home, Chloe wiped away the tears from Pepe's eyes using a hankie embroidered with a Native design. She took him by the hand to the chair swing then continued with her story:

"First, I heard Adam panting. Then his head appeared at the edge of the cliff. I leaned forward and offered him my hand as he pulled himself up onto the stinking red ground. Oh boy, that smell! Then, together, we helped Rain-on-the-Corn over the top, and for a while we all four sat there, grinning stupidly. I mean, to grin when you're only inches from a sheer drop into the emptiness of Hell, ay? Perhaps it was just the thought of being that much closer to the bridge."

"I don't always know why I grin!" offered Pepe.

"No? Well, be that as it may, the arch of the bridge looked as if it was only a short sprint away from where we were sitting, though it was uphill, and distances in Xibalba are, like time, deceptive.

'Rain-on-the-Corn? How did you come by that name?' I questioned the young woman. 'You people have such strange names.'

'When my mother was with child with me we had a terrible drought. There was hardly any corn that year, and I was told I was lucky to have been born at all. Through my name, I was linked with the Rain Goddess in the hopes that I'd bring good fortune to our tribe.'

'Did it work?'

'Never had a drought as bad again. That I do remember being told. Mind you, my memory of life back there has become hazy.'

'Hardly need to pray to the Rain Goddess in this place,' I said looking up at the wet, grey drizzly sky. 'Tell me, down in those tunnels—those rivers—where does the

165

water come from? Seems kind of odd to me. The river up here is dark red.'

'*Life-Force*... blood of the spirit. Down there, some believe all that water comes from the tears of those lost souls seeping through the ground. It's said that they never stop weeping,' replied Lizard-by-the-Water. 'And the ground in Xibalba is like sodden moss that passes on that sorrow to us Xibalban folks who never know what's in store for them. Plus, this rain must go somewhere. But you saw the endless drop down from the cliff face. Just nothing as far as the eye can see and beyond—probably forever. There are other people who say the land turns to water, the water turns to air and the air then gives way to nothing. Like the emptiness under the bridge. To tell you the truth, no one knows.'

I must have looked uneasy since Adam and I had both drunk from the underground river, and the thought of slaking our thirst with the tears of tortured souls sickened me.

'It's only water, Chloe, wherever it comes from,' Adam reassured, placing his hand over mine.

'And what about your names?' asked Lizard-by-the-Water. 'Do they mean anything?'

'I... well—' I suddenly felt I'd missed out on something by not knowing who I truly was. Adam helped me out:

'Chloe's a Greek name. Means green shoot. So, she could never belong here 'cos there is no green in Xibalba. And Adam, well, he was like the first man on Earth. In the Bible. Created by God. María's God.'

'The Great Spirit?' queried Lizard-by-the-Water.

Adam glanced at me, as if uncertain.

'Sure,' I agreed. 'The Great Spirit.'

Even then, I was more into Native religion than my brother was, but I knew deep down there could only be one universal truth."

"Why?" asked Pepe.

"Has to be. We don't live in different universes, do we?"

"Suppose not."

"Anyways, I explained how your daddy's Bible namesake, the first man, once lived in a place called the Garden of Eden. A sort of paradise on Earth, I said. And that things went kind of pear-shaped when the serpent persuaded Eve, his woman, to eat an apple. Because of this Adam and Eve were kicked out of paradise.

'So?' Lizard-by-the-Water looked puzzled. 'No big deal! Earth Mother would have put the fruit there for a purpose. Surely the Eve you speak of could only have made Him happy by doing that. Making use of the food He gave to the first man and the first woman. And the serpent, my totem animal spirit, was just helping her, don't you think?'

Adam laughed.

'We see things kind of differently, I guess,' he said.

'And your totem animal, Adam. How does he help you?'

Adam had to admit that the Biblical Adam, who had nothing to do with the Americas, was totally irrelevant to his own existence on Earth.

'But my brother has the Golden Jaguar instead!' I blurted out, feeling uniquely proud of your papa. 'Maybe—' I wasn't sure whether I should have said 'has', 'had' or even 'was' or 'is', but Adam frowned at me, so I shut up.

By then, we'd recovered our breath after the climb and we discussed how to get to the bridge; whether to make a dash for it, or go slowly, either as a group, or spread out— even run—one at a time. In the end, we decided to stick together. I had my granny's golden locket with its mysterious power, and Adam had... himself. Either of these, or both, I hoped, would help our new friends on to paradise.

We would run together at the pace of the slowest, we decided. We stood up and embraced (funny, I thought, how an embrace has such a timeless and universal meaning), and, as though competing in an Olympic two hundred metre sprint, we ran. Lizard-by-the-Water, being old when he died, was the slowest, and the rest of us adjusted our pace so that he could keep up. The slope was steeper than we'd anticipated, but thankfully we seemed to be the only moving things in sight. Myself, I was spurred on by the thought of being reunited with my huggable Lee. *We'll soon be at the bridge,* I thought, hoping he might hear me inside his head. I felt almost relieved as the arch of the bridge got closer, but I quickly learned it wasn't gonna be that easy.

Ahead of us, half-way to the bridge, the red ground changed. I wasn't looking at ground at all, but at a huge red stone wall. The wall of the ball court arena. A dark space appeared in the wall. The entrance to that awful place. In Xibalba, nothing is more terrible than the ball court. Now it was the only thing that stood between us and the bridge. We stopped. Adam took hold of my hand.

'Be strong, sis!' he whispered.

Two figures emerged from the entrance, instantly recognisable, and I breathed a sigh of relief. They waved at us.

'Art and Jeannie,' I screamed in my excitement. 'Look, Adam. It's Art and Jeannie! We've made it!'

I ran on ahead. I knew Adam had told me not to go running off again, but I couldn't stop myself.

'Chloe—wait!' Adam shouted after me.

I turned and called back to the others:

'Hurry up! They'll get us to the bridge. Quick!'

'Chloe, just a minute. I need time to consider. Like in karate!' Adam responded.

I took no notice and shot off again. Adam ran after me shouting, 'Chloe, Chloe!' whilst our new friends stood watching. Of course, neither knew about Art and Jeannie, but they did know about the Hero Twins of Xibalba. For them, these guys would have seemed different.

'Oh my, you're looking just great!' said Jeannie as I ran into her arms and hugged her. She stroked my hair over and over. In fact, looking back, I guess she was perhaps a little too interested in my head, but it was so lovely to feel her comforting body against mine and to hear her infectious laugh. 'Have they been looking after you okay?' she asked, peering over my shoulder at my brother and our two new friends.

'Sure have!' I said.

'Art said you'd make it here!'

I broke free from Jeannie and went over to Art.

'It's so good to see ya, kid,' he said, enveloping me with his huge arms. He, too, ruffled my hair. 'Colour of ripened corn, huh?' he said. 'Shame to see it go!' Looking back, that should have given me a clue. Guess I'd always relied too much on my sixth sense, and I was getting nothing bad back from the man.

'Adam,' I said, turning to my brother. 'Come and—' I stopped. I knew that look in Adam's eyes. From the karate contests in Texas. More than that. There was a fire in those eyes as I'd seen with the Golden Jaguar. 'What is it, Adam?'

My brother just stood and stared. Art still had his arm around my shoulders.

'Will you escort us? To the bridge? With our friends?' I asked Art.

'What's the hurry, guys?' our friend from Iowa, in that other world, said. 'Come and watch the next game.'

'What?' I asked. Still, the penny hadn't dropped, but I couldn't believe what I'd just heard. Why should he want me to see another grizzly ball game? *Art? Jeannie?* I looked from one to the other, and felt, at the same time, the man's grip on my shoulder tighten. It was painful and I tried, in vain, to pull myself free.

'Only joking!' Art exclaimed relaxing his grip a fraction. 'Jeannie, call for the car. Me and Adam, we got some real serious stuff to figure out.'

Art went over to Adam and shook him by the hand, and the fire in Adam's eyes shone like it was being stoked with gasoline.

'Yoo-hoo! Austin-Healey! Where are you?' cooed Jeannie through a grin the size of the Grand Canyon.

'Jeannie, I think we can make it on foot,' I protested. 'I mean, it's not far. I just wanna get back to Lee. Back home. And Adam, he really needs to be with María. And those two Xibalban guys with us over there. They've suffered enough. They deserve to go on to paradise, don't you think?'

A familiar car burst out from arena entrance: the red Austin-Healey, only now—and this was the odd thing—now there was no driver. Remote control? Or imagined? Who knows? It came to a halt just a few yards from where we stood.

'She's in there,' Art whispered to Adam, loud enough for me to hear. Adam only stared. He said nothing. 'She's in there,' repeated Art. 'María. They've got her. You'd better come with us now or her head will be in the next ball game.'

Still Adam remained silent and motionless as in a karate tournament. After all, we had both heard María singing from afar in the tunnels, so she could not have been in the ball court at the same time.

'Coyote Spirit says she's well and truly his now, you see. We can't stop the Death Lords on our own. Not this time,' continued Art.

I felt strangely empty, as if all hope had just been taken from me, and, if they spoke the truth, María was in that godawful place at the mercy of both the coyote and the red rubber monsters. I addressed your dad:

'How come, Adam? It can't be. What's he talking about? Is it really Coyote Spirit with her? Or really María?'

'Chloe, you have to persuade your dumb brother. If he leaves her here, there's no telling what those Lords of Xibalba will do to her. For eternity, remember. That's a heck of a long time. In fact, time doesn't even play a part in the equation.'

'Adam, say something!' I begged my brother. 'Please! We'll have to risk it. You can't leave María in that place. What's happened to you?'

'Good, Chloe,' insisted Jeannie. 'At least you can see sense. Get in the car. Adam's in a state of shock. He'll join us in a moment when it sinks in. He'll not want María to go in such a horrible way. You know, they say you can still see from your eyes when your head's being knocked around in the ball game. And such a pretty head she has, don't you agree."

'We'll have to shave her hair off first, of course,' said Art, turning to look at me, still grinning.

I knew in an instant why Adam had remained totally still. Whether it was what Art had just said, or the glint in the man's eyes, I can't be sure now, but I knew, and my mind became receptive to Adam's thoughts. These two were not Art and Jeannie from Iowa. As Art stepped forward to take hold of my arm again, Adam struck out. Art toppled and Jeannie, who had grabbed me, began to push me into the Austin-Healey. Adam slammed her against the side of the car, with her arm twisted back, and she fell on top of Art. Your dad pulled me free from the tangle of limbs and together we ran on towards the bridge.

From the corner of one eye, I saw that Lizard-By-Water and Rain-On-Corn had also started to run in the same direction. I heard the revving of a car engine behind me, and in moments the Austin-Healey, with Art and Jeannie in it, swung around in front of us, blocking our path. In a futile effort to escape from them, Adam and I headed back down the hill, but only for the car to overtake us again. We stopped and stood back to back, and I prayed like I'd never before prayed. I didn't know to whom I was praying — the Golden Jaguar, Lee, the Hero Twins even, for this Art and Jeannie sure weren't the ones we also knew as Hunahpu and Xbalanque. The Art and Jeannie lookalikes got out of the car and came towards us... slowly, teasingly.

'Ain't no need for all this fussin' around, Adam!' Art said. 'Just come with us, all nice and quiet and we'll see who gets your girl in there, okay? We're real generous, Seven Death and me. She's already ours, but we'll give you this last chance to get her back if she still wants you. Win the ball game, and you take the girl with you. Ball's right there beside you, a-waitin'! What a pretty little ball your sister will make, huh? We'll have real fun watchin'—'

He was interrupted by a shrill sound high in the sky. I'd heard it before: the sonar of Zotz, the bat god. Lizard-by-the- Water and Rain-on-the-Corn, now approaching the bridge, had been spotted, and Zotz was swooping down towards them. I closed my eyes. I couldn't bear to watch their end, now so close to that of my own. An awful scream from the direction of the bridge, not a human scream, flipped my eyelids open...

A massive condor, the size of a small airplane, had the bat in its claws and was stabbing at the thing with its great curved beak. Red stuff streamed out of the bat onto the bridge below. Art and Jeannie stared open-mouthed at the macabre scene up in the sky, and, in a flash, Adam was there, between the giant lookalikes, sending both flying in opposite directions. At the same time, accompanied by shouting and yelling, spectators began to stream out from the entrance of the ball court. For Adam and me, it was gonna be either them, the spectators, or One Death and Seven Death masquerading as Art and Jeannie. Adam chose the spectators. Grabbing my hand, he pulled me up the hill. Most of the spectators appeared to be armed with knives and clubs. I just hoped the end would be quick and that I wouldn't feel a thing. Just as Adam let go of my hand and felled the first three spectators as if they were merely shop-fitters' dummies, the condor released its prey and swept down from the sky, attacking spectators with such ferocity that the few survivors, overcome with panic, fled in all directions.

Then I realised that those spectators had not been running after us; they had been fleeing from something every bit as terrifying as the giant condor. Out of the ball court strode the golden figure of a giant ancient Mayan dressed in a golden breechcloth, his flaming red hair tied back, and he was wielding an enormous club of gold. With each swing of his club he took in three or four spectators, launching their smashed bodies high into the cool, wet air; the real Art, magnified way beyond the believable.

'Run!' he boomed out, as he cut a swathe through the screaming crowd of spectators. 'Run, Adam and Chloe!'

'Hunahpu, they're mine!' the 'other' Art, also swelling, roared. Running, I turned to see the fake Art and Jeannie change in front of my eyes. Their smiles gone, faces becoming red, features hardening, they grew in height and girth till their clothes dropped off, and soon the Art and Jeannie we loved so much had become those evil red rubber guys, One Death and Seven Death, just as I'd seen them earlier in the ball game.

Adam grabbed my hand and we ran again towards the bridge. Lizard-by-the-Water and Rain-on-the-Corn were already there, waiting, and still in a state of shock after their close encounter with Zotz. All the time, I expected a large red hand to grab me from behind, but after we reached our friends, I looked back and saw why this hadn't happened. The Lords of Xibalba had been driven back by a relentless attack from the vast condor, Xbalanque, and the golden giant, Hunahpu. They were being bounced around like rubber toys. Each had a red club of his own, but these seemed powerless against the twirling golden club of Hunahpu and, slowly and inexorably, One Death and Seven Death were being driven towards the edge of the cliff and towards the oblivion of Hell.

'Oh, my Golden Gods!' exclaimed Lizard-by-the-Water, 'I have never before seen the Hero Twins looking so

– so powerful. Normally they're like puppies before the Lords of Xibalba. Something must have happened here to change them. Made them grow stronger. Could it be—?' The man looked from Adam to me and then Adam again. 'Could it come from you two? From the world of the living? Something you brought with you? More powerful even than the golden locket you wear, Chloe?'

Adam shrugged his shoulders, his thoughts elsewhere.

'María!' he said quietly, without realising he'd given them an answer by announcing your Mama's name. 'I have to go back for her. Back to the ball court. You go on ahead over the bridge, sis. At least you'll be okay, even if I never come back.'

'No, Adam. Don't!' I said. My face was wet with rain and tears. 'Don't leave me. Don't go back inside that place. Please, no!'

'She's right,' said Lizard-by-the-Water.

'If María is there, I have to. I am so sorry, Chloe.'

'Then I'll come with you,' I insisted. 'You can't stop me. I'm not afraid—' I heard something and held up my hand. 'Wait – d'you hear that sound?' Through the mist, from across the bridge, I heard singing. It came from so far away, from another world, that it was barely audible, but I recognised the voice; the same voice I'd heard in the tunnels. The voice of María. 'I can hear her, Adam. It's María. She's not in the ball court. Those monsters were only trying to trick you.'

Adam frowned as he strained to hear what I so clearly heard. I knew that look of his as he struggled with the dilemma of whether to believe me or the Lords of Xibalba. I removed my grandmother's locket and slipped this over his head. I took his hand and closed his fingers around the locket.

'Listen!' I instructed.

Adam closed his eyes and listened, and slowly his lips curved a smile.

'I saw her!' he said quietly, opening his eyes. 'You're right, Chloe. As always! And she needs me quick. She's lying there on our bed in Houston, singing to herself and — and she's crying at the same time. I've got to get to her. Gotta hold her in my arms. Tell her it's all over here in Xibalba.'

If only! I thought but didn't say.

'What are we waiting for, brother?' I asked.

He gave me back my locket. I took one last look at Xibalba and at the battle being waged, now close to the cliff. Although the Death Lords had been driven to the brink of the precipice, we didn't wait to see them being tipped into that infinite nothingness of Hell. Accompanied by our two friends, we ran onto the bridge, Lizard-by-the-Water in the lead, under the tall arch and into the mist beyond. With four of us running and sliding over its wet planks, the bridge swung and jerked like crazy. I grabbed the metal railing which was all that separated me from that eternal drop into Hell. The two Xibalbans were a merged blur in the mist ahead. The blur withered to nothing. I turned my head to reassure myself that Adam was following, for the silence over and above the sound of my footsteps had a bleakness that made me fear there was only me and the flapping of my feet on the bridge, and that I was otherwise alone in a pointless universe. Thank God, he was there, not far behind.

Two fading blurs were the last I saw of Lizard-by-the-Water and Rain-on-the-Corn.

Chapter 17: A Lesson on Love

The more the old Mexican thought about the Old Woman of the Hills and the man on the Island of Patmos who called himself John, and the more he saw of what was happening down there, the more it began to make sense.

***

"Uncle Lee, how come those Hero Twins gotten stronger just because of Aunt Chloe and my papa?"

"The whole thing is a mystery to me too, Pepe, but I'll tell you what I think. I think it's about love. Those evil Lords of Xibalba knew about your papa's love for your mama and they made use of this by trying to trick him into playing a ball game with them. They thought he'd do anything to save María again. But they hadn't reckoned on your papa loving other folks like his sister as well. No way was he gonna let your Aunt Chloe be used like that, even if it was the only way to save his wife. That's real love, son, and it's strong. Some say it's the strongest goddamn force in the universe. Whatever, I believe that force flowed from your papa to the Hero Twins when they realised he'd protect Chloe at all costs. Maybe it also weakened the Lords of Xibalba. Who knows? Like water flowing over a fire, perhaps. Your aunt's Native name was Living Water."

"I know. But Uncle Lee, who was the Old Woman of the Hills?"

"Who *is* the Old Woman of the Hills, Pepe? Who indeed? Now there you have me!"

"I think I'll give Carla and the twins a lesson in love today. We're gonna play a game after breakfast in our make-believe schoolhouse. Carla said she wants to learn about love. And she can be the Old Woman in the Hills, and the twins'll be the Hero Twins!"

Lee laughed.

"Awesome, Pepe! Your aunt will love that. Our little boys heroes, like your papa, huh? A true American hero for saving me from drug pushers all those years back."

"Mama's sadness is something to do with Papa and me, isn't it?"

"Ain't for me to go saying, son. But Chloe, she sure believes you'll fix it."

"I do love Mama, Uncle Lee."

"Who doesn't, Pepe? And know what? Your Mama loves you. And little Carla too, of course. Loves you both like crazy."

Pepe finished his breakfast with Uncle Lee and ran off to help Carla set up her school house in the living room using boxes and chairs and a coffee table. Lee waited for Chloe to finish her shower, then the two of them went for a jog before the ferocity of the Texas sun could change their minds.

"You know, that kid is pretty remarkable," Lee said as he and Chloe panted together along the path beside the muddy bayou.

"Yeah, they know it too, honey," Chloe said. "It was the school that started this whole thing up, I think. About him needing to see an educational psychologist. Too bright for the system. An IQ off the top of the scale. María got really upset. Like she didn't want her son to be labelled a genius. Didn't want him to be different from others. It totally freaked her out. That's why Adam called me. Couldn't figure out why María began crying about it. Thought she should be pleased they had such a brilliant kid. But I understood. Being a mother myself, I guess."

"Understood what? He's brainy like his Dad. That's all there is to it. Both goddamn clever!"

Chloe stopped jogging and stretched down to grip her shins whilst catching her breath. Lee also stopped, turned around and ran back to her.

"He is so like Adam, don't you think?" he asked. Chloe looked up. "Funny thing is, María keeps saying that all the time. Like she needs reassurance. Haven't you noticed?"

Chloe said nothing, and they ran on.

Back at the Ranch House, as the children played at 'schools', and Pepe taught his attentive little students all about love after boring them with a synopsis of the plot of Romeo and Juliet, pointing out that their love brought warring families together, his mother withdrew to the parental bedroom to perfect the songs for her new album.

All morning, Adam sat in front of his computer preparing a series of lectures on the integration of tribal culture into modern industrialised American society. María's voice sounded so distant, and hauntingly beautiful, that his eyes filled with tears. He knew why María was unhappy. He'd known all along, and he wished they could talk about it in the same way they could now talk about her once dying and being brought back to life, but he knew they couldn't. Not until he had answers for the questions that she would ask him. And as he searched his brain for those answers, and listened to her ethereal singing, he wept like a child.

***

"Ready, Pepe?"

Pepe nodded, and Chloe picked up from where she'd left off. On the bridge to Xibalba...

"I stopped and turned again after passing under the arch at the far end of the bridge, at the top of the steps that led down and away from the mist. Adam soon caught up. We stood together and peered back into the grey space beyond which lay that awful Place of Fear. The silence, apart from our own breathing, was absolute.

'Where are Lizard-by-the-Water and Rain-on-the-Corn?' I asked. 'What's happened to them?' I felt tears well, for I'd grown fond of our Xibalban friends. 'They vanished before I got to the arch. Do you think—?' I began.

My brother finished my sentence:

178

'That they've ended up someplace else?'

I nodded. He grinned.

'Paradise?' I suggested. Somehow, I knew. 'But I wish I could've said goodbye properly. I mean, it was a bit of a rush, wasn't it?'

Adam laughed. Then he took me in his arms and hugged me.

'Thank God you're okay, sis. And our friends? I don't think you'll need to be worrying about them anymore, all righty? For them the bridge ended where they should have gone to in the first place after dying.'

'And Rain-on-the-Corn will be with her baby?'

Adam chuckled again.

'That baby might have grown up some by now after a thousand or so years. But who knows?'

'Adam, I am so sorry I brought you there. Got you involved. All that stupid business about finding the descendants of Eagle Foot and to be with Earth Child's people again. It seems so unimportant now. And I've put you through hell. Lee and María too.'

'Sis, don't you go feeling bad now. You were trying your best. Plus it may yet turn out to be the most important thing anyone's ever done. In the whole history of Mankind.'

Anyone other than your daddy saying this, and I'd have pouted and said they were making fun of me, but not Adam. He always had a way of making me feel better for as long as I can remember. Even as a little girl, whenever I'd gotten into trouble with our Mommy or Daddy as a result of following my 'feelings', or running off like I often used to, even then my big brother would hug me and make me feel better.

'What now?' I asked.

'You've gotten the answer there, sis. Round your neck.'

I looked down at our granny's locket and closed my hand over it. No longer did I hear María. I saw Lee sitting alone outside the painted tepee. Poor boy! I really did cry then, like I hadn't cried for a long time, and Adam held me close.

'It's okay, it's okay,' he repeated, stroking my hair.

'He's real close, now,' I said. 'I can feel him. It's like my sixth sense has suddenly come back. That's the tepee, just there. See it? But I don't hear María any longer.'

'Let me try.' Adam took hold of the locket. I saw him fight back the tears. He pointed a finger in the direction opposite to where I had pointed.

'She's there, lying on her bed just crying. I can see her. The singing's stopped. We must both hurry, sis.' He kissed me on the forehead.

'Say sorry to María. From me,' I begged as we parted, standing in front of a tepee which Adam couldn't see.

Adam grinned.

'I'll say nothing of the sort,' he told me. 'Quick, get back to Lee. Before they send the police out to look for you!'

Swirls of mist were beginning to envelope us. Adam was turning into a ghost shape. After taking a few steps towards where I knew I would find Lee, I shouted back into the mist:

'I'll phone you when I get back!' But Adam was already gone. There was only mist.

I started to run. Slowly at first, for it's a strange feeling running into thick mist, not knowing if you'll bump into something any moment, but I soon speeded up. I could barely wait to be with Lee again, and I ran as fast as my legs would go. The cold air cooled my face, wet with tears, but gradually the air grew warmer and the mist lighter. The grey gravel path turned into grass and the grass into canvas flooring as I ran on in the tepee. I had to stop abruptly to prevent myself from crashing into a table strewn with pamphlets. I looked at one of these. It advertised the Native American Community Show, promising spectacular dancing, awesome drumming, plenty of fun for kids and 'great corn dogs!'.

'Lee!' I shouted at the loose flap hanging over the entrance of the tepee. The flap was pulled aside, and a startled black face appeared. How I loved that face."

"And still do?"

"And still do, Pepe. 'Lee, oh thank God it's you, Lee!' I sobbed, running into his arms. How wonderful it was to feel those strong hands again as my boyfriend lifted me off the ground and swung me round and around like a human merry-go-round. Our lips met, and we remained like that, locked in a kiss, me still up in the air, for what seemed an eternity of bliss.

'Hey, let that girl down, Lee! She's gonna need to take another breath sometime!' someone called out.

Lee lowered me gently to the ground. He still hadn't said a word. Just kept on smiling at me like he'd never seen me before and really liked—no, loved—what he saw.

Uncle Jason came up and hugged me as well.

'Where did you get that cloak?' he asked, frowning.

'I looked down and saw that Lizard-by-the-Water's woven cloak was open and my bra was showing.

'Oops,' I said, pulling the cloak discretely across my chest. 'A friend gave it to me.'

Lee looked worried, and I giggled through my tears. More from embarrassment, I guess.

'Don't worry! He was at least a thousand years old!' I said before kissing Lee again. 'You know, I just don't want to stop kissing you, now. Never!'

'Better find your Aunt Jac first, young lady! We need some kind of an explanation. When we're all together, and in your own time, though.'

'Can I please call Adam before we do that, Uncle Jason. I have to know he's okay.'

Uncle Jason looked from me to Lee and back.

'He... erm, María called. Three days back. Same day I flew in from New York and you ran off into this tepee. She called to say he'd disappeared. In quite a state, she was, your Aunt Jac said. Then she got a message to say he'd turned up. María hasn't called back since then, and your aunt got no answer when she tried phoning her. Like the girl had left the phone off the hook, or something, and her cell phone was switched off, too. No message from Adam, either.'

I bit my lower lip. Poor María. I really did feel awful.

'When did she say Adam showed up again?' I asked.

'Three days ago.'

Oh, my God! I thought. *That was Coyote Spirit! Suppose? No!* I couldn't bear to think about the worst thing ever!

'What have I done?' I whispered to Lee, taking hold of his hand.

'It's okay,' he said, squeezing mine. 'Look, give Adam a call. God alone knows what happened when you disappeared into this tent thing, but just call Adam now, honeybunch.'

I called my brother's cell phone. María answered. For a few moments, I stood stunned. I just felt utterly stupid and didn't know what to say.

'Hello?' María repeated. 'Is it Adam Winters you're wanting?'

'María, it's me. Chloe. Are you okay?' I so wanted to say sorry to her, but it was as if I'd seized up and couldn't.

'Sure, Chloe. I'll go get Adam.'

'Is he okay? Adam, I mean. Like himself?'

She laughed.

'You can say that again. Working too hard, as always. But, yeah, he's fine. Just a moment, Chloe.'

Am I mad? Did any of that actually happen? I was wondering.

I remained rooted to the spot, with tears streaming down my cheeks, almost afraid to speak to my own brother, wondering what he might say.

'Hey, Chloe, how's it going?' I paused, gripping the cell phone tightly. 'Chloe?'

'Sure, Adam, I'm fine. And you? I mean are you okay? After... you know?'

'Oh that! María says not to worry about that phone call she made to Aunt Jac. I'd gone to the library without telling her. Pretended I was in the kitchen all the time. See, she thinks I'm working too hard. It *is* our summer vacation, after all.'

No mention of what we'd been through together in Xibalba. It made no sense to me. Most of all, Adam telling a lie about going to the library. Your dad just never tells lies. After I rang off, I had an odd feeling that perhaps the whole thing had all been in my imagination. Had I just been hiding away in some corner of that tepee for three days and three nights, with all that stuff happening in my mind and Lee not being able to see me? *Impossible!* I kept telling myself. The tepee was empty apart from a few chairs, a table and a couple of cardboard boxes on the ground. Both too small for me to fit into. Then I had another, even more terrifying, thought: who was the man at the other end of the phone with the voice of your father?

What happened later, at Adam's end of the line in Houston, Uncle Lee should tell you, because he was the only one María confided in. As for me, I felt I was in some kinda dream as the three of us walked out of that park, away from the tepee, to seek out Aunt Jac. I kept pinching myself to make sure I wasn't still back in Xibalba, suspended above the ball court, waiting to have my head used in a ball game of death.

Aunt Jac was terrific. It's not that Lee and Uncle Jason weren't. They were, but poor Lee, he was just so relieved to have me back, wherever I'd been, and he wouldn't let go of my hand. All he did was gaze at me as though I might disappear if he were to look away for an instant. And Uncle Jason, he just seemed done in. For three days and nights he'd used every ounce of his energy to keep Lee going, talk to him and support him, and now — he looked like he could do with a hundred years' sleep. So, it was Aunt Jac I spoke to when we sat together in Starbucks over coffee and doughnuts. And I knew Aunt Jac would believe every word of my story, for the two of us had grown so very close since living together in New York, what with our shared interest in Native American affairs and culture.

'Oh my!' she exclaimed, patting my hand when I'd finished. 'I am so proud of you, Chloe.'

'Proud?' I queried, looking at Lee whose face still showed the hell he must have been through after I ran off. 'Don't you think I did a terrible thing? Poor Lee was hurt real bad, and you and Uncle Jason too, and then—' I went quiet. My call to Adam had left me with a strange feeling inside. I felt like I was in some kinda jigsaw puzzle with a key piece missing. The whole thing had been about Adam and María, and yet over the phone, Adam made it seem as if nothing had happened — that we'd never even been together in Xibalba.

'Adam... María? Perhaps for them it's not over,' Aunt Jac said. 'I know you're telling me the truth, but there must be so much we still don't know or understand. This time, Chloe, you had no choice. Don't you see that? Coyote Spirit knew exactly what you were seeking. That's the downside of having sixth sense. Others with even stronger powers than you can probably read your mind like a book. Guess he did that and used you. You were just the bait, my poor little Chloe. For him to get to María. But it seems like the bait almost destroyed the predator for a change. No, I'm real proud of my favourite niece!'

She always called me that when she wished to cheer me up. A recurring joke, for I'm her only niece."

"So that's where you get the 'favourite nephew' thing from!" grinned Pepe.

"Sure is, young man. But back to Aunt Jac. 'I agree something ain't quite right,' she continued. 'Adam never lies. Maybe he's just so relieved to be with his girl again. And she with him. So, they're kinda blocking out what happened. You see, I've never heard María so upset as when she phoned. Then me not being able to get in touch with her or Adam the last couple of days. But Adam was with you. Are you absolutely positive María wasn't also there in Xibalba?'

I nodded.

'Her voice—her singing—definitely came from across the bridge. And Adam—' A sudden look of horror must have shadowed my face. Aunt Jac squeezed my hand.

'What is it, Chloe? What's the matter?'

An awful thought occurred to me. Was the Adam I'd been with in Xibalba Coyote Spirit? After all, I had witnessed my brother's body stolen by the evil monster, leaving behind only a weakened ghost. Seeing that ghost turn back into Adam had been the happiest moment of my life, but had I been tricked into believing this to be my brother? Had Coyote Spirit brought María back with him, hidden her in the ball court, then returned with her to Houston to live again as Adam Winters? I knew that Coyote Spirit would have done anything to get María. I felt so confused.

'No, honey. I honestly believe that you'd know,' Aunt Jac tried to reassure me after I'd explained my fear. 'You could never have done all those things with Adam back there, been through so much together, and not have known. You, of all people. Besides, from what you say, a guy like Coyote Spirit would want to have María as himself. Too proud to masquerade as a puny mortal like—'

'Adam is not puny!' I objected.

'Sorry, honey. Bad choice of word. But from what you've always said, Coyote Spirit sounds like one big hunk of Native muscle and man.'

Lee looked uneasily at me. I patted his hand, to reassure him that this monster could never be my man.

'Guess he did look like a Hollywood star, but I wouldn't want him anywhere near me, and that's a fact!'

Then Aunt Jac, with talk of Hollywood, changed the subject. Her romance with Uncle Jason had always been a bit of a Hollywood story and finally seemed to be coming to a happy conclusion. She told me they were to be married in six weeks, in Houston. Not a church wedding, for neither belonged to any particular denomination, but they wanted to hold the reception, a small family affair, at Jorge's restaurant, and they were very much hoping María would give a live performance for them. Adam too, if he felt up to it.

'Why not New York?' I asked, having grown very fond of the Big Apple. Also, I couldn't bear the thought of being in Houston again without Lee. Aunt Jac read my mind:

'And you will be our photographer, won't you?' Aunt Jac asked Lee.

'Dangerous request,' Lee replied.

'How come?' Aunt Jac looked upset. She must have guessed I wouldn't go to the wedding if Lee wasn't there.

''Cos you might find I'll only be taking pictures of my girl. Particularly if you have her all dressed up as a bridesmaid!'

I gave Lee a playful punch in the side, so happy that he seemed to be back his old self.

'Looks like we're gonna have to follow Chloe around to get into those pictures, Jason.'

'You gonna call Adam again? Let them know too?' I asked.

Aunt Jac looked at me for a few moments, like she was working out in her mind how best to deal with this. She knew my determination better than anyone.

'Okay, honey. I'll have a go. I'll call your brother. See if I can get any sense from him.'

She did—but she didn't; did call him, did ask him where the heck he'd been, and why his sister was so upset, but no, she didn't get any sense from him. Your daddy was like a clam shell, all closed up, and no power on earth was gonna prise him open.

We returned to New York. All four of us. I'd lost interest in my search for the descendants of Earth Child's tribe, though not my love for the Native peoples of America or what they stood for. It's just that after what I'd been through, I only wanted to be with Lee all the time, with my aunt, and my new uncle, and I wanted to stay in the present, to forget the horrors of Xibalba, those red rubber Death Lords and even the Golden Jaguar. I wished to be a normal fifteen-year-old but very much in love. Like Juliet! Being bridesmaid at the wedding would, I reckoned, help me to forget my nightmare in Xibalba for the romance of a wedding is enough to draw any teenage girl back to the land of the living. And I insisted that Aunt Jac let Lee in on the design and choice of material for my bridesmaid's dress.

'He's a photographer!' I pleaded. 'He's got an eye for that sort of thing!'

Aunt Jac grinned.

'When my favourite niece puts it like that, how on earth could I say "no"? Sure, honey, he can choose, but do remind him that the other bridesmaid is darker skinned, has black hair and never has it done into braids like you do.'

'She did have when we were in the mesas together,' I replied, thinking back to when María was 'White Deer' in ancient Colorado.

Of course, I saw the wedding as something different, though could never admit this. So did Lee. For us, it would be our big day, our coming together, with me as a young woman and no longer a child. As for Adam, I hoped we'd find someplace quiet where we could talk together, if only to reassure myself that the Xibalba nightmare hadn't been a symptom of my own impending madness. And that he was truly the brother I knew and loved.

And so, as the day drew near, with pre-wedding excitement occupying all my thoughts, and with frequent telephone calls to Jorge and Anna about the reception arrangements in their restaurant, my bags packed and me counting the hours till our flight down to Houston, I managed to forget all about your mama and papa until the phone rang the day before we were to depart. As it rang, I knew it had to be Adam before Aunt Jac answered it. There was nothing wrong with my sixth sense. And I knew it was to do with something that in time would affect us all.

'Well I never!' Aunt Jac exclaimed on coming off the phone.

'They've gotten married already!' I said.

'How did you know, honey?'

I knew just before Aunt Jac answered the phone.

'How could they do this?' I asked. 'I just don't understand!'

I was both angry and saddened, and felt tears spill from my eyes, for I feared this would change everything.

'Don't feel upset," soothed Aunt Jac. "There'll still be *our* wedding. Jason's and mine. Though with only one bridesmaid. You. But that's fine with me. And our reception won't be any different, only they would like to ask a few of their own friends along as well. See, their wedding was a very simple affair. The priest married them yesterday. María's parents were there, but no one else, Adam said.'

Aunt Jac held my hands and kissed the tears in my eyes.

'He also said he hoped that one day his little sis would forgive him and understand. Said the one person he always wanted to be at his wedding was you. Chloe, he was trying to tell us something. I know it.'

If I hadn't been so uptight, I might have known it too; known the real reason for their lightning wedding, but my sixth sense got drowned by those tears. It never worked when I was all pent-up. I would always lose reception or whatever it's called.

'What about María's bridesmaid's dress?' I asked. 'What's she gonna do with it now?'

'Ah, she's worked that out already. She'll wear it one day at yours and Lee's wedding. As a matron of honour instead of a bridesmaid, if you'll allow her to, Adam says.'

'Good job Lee insisted on pale blue!' I said, wiping my tears. 'The pink María suggested would never have gone with my hair!'

'For my wedding, Chloe Winters will be the loveliest bridesmaid ever! And Lee's photos will prove it. I know they will.'

'Oh well,' I said, 'I guess I'll get used to calling them Mr and Mrs Winters one day.'

Aunt Jac smiled at me.

'They've been that already, haven't they? Ever since you three re-appeared in that kiva together in the Mesa Verde, right? I could tell María had turned from girl to woman in those three minutes.'

'I know,' I replied. 'And I so wish I'd been at their first wedding in ancient Mexico. They said it was like a dream, but I knew it was more than just a dream.'

At the reception after Aunt Jac and Uncle Jason got married, Adam took me aside to explain. María was pregnant. With you, Pepe."

Chapter 18: Sins of the Father

With Tezcatlipoca a spent force, evil had to find new outlets. Underneath the trusting, unwatchful eyes of his masters, One Death and Seven Death, the man with the spirit of the coyote grew in strength and evil and, like them, knew that having a child by the girl who had been called 'special' could change her world in ways that would make resistance to his power pointless.

***

"No, I can't do it!" screamed María.

Adam was jolted from a deep sleep to find his wife sitting bolt upright in bed, staring wildly ahead at a blank wall and gripping the bedclothes.

"Honey—sweetheart—what is it?" Adam asked, turning over and reaching for his wife's hand. "Please tell me."

María only glanced at him. He couldn't bear to see the pain and the fear in those eyes he loved so much. He sat up and tried to cuddle her, but she broke free and left the bed.

"I can't, I can't," she repeated, looking away. "Can't do it!"

"Darling, *please* tell me! Can't do what?"

But María wouldn't answer. She ran, sobbing, from the bedroom. He looked at his watch. Two-thirty in the morning. Wearily, he eased his legs out of bed, and followed his wife. He heard her sobbing in Pepe's room where he saw her kneeling on the floor beside their son's bed cuddling the boy in her arms. Pepe stirred in response, but his eyes remained closed.

"María," whispered Adam, "please tell me what's wrong. We can't go on like this. Look—" He knelt beside her and gently rested a hand on her shoulder. "If there's something bugging you, you've just gotta get it off your chest, honey."

190

But María only shook her head and kept muttering, "I can't... I can't..." as she continued to hug Pepe.

Pepe opened his eyes.

"I wanna go to the bathroom, Mama," he said.

"Okay," she said, stroking his hair. "I'll come with you, sweetie."

Adam didn't think to ask why a boy of Pepe's age should need to be accompanied to the bathroom. Pepe climbed out of bed, rubbing his sleep-heavy eyes, whilst María stood up and took hold of his hand.

"Listen, when you get back, you and me, we're gonna have a talk, María," Adam insisted. "We'll just go back to bed, put on the light and have a good long talk. Then we'll kind of—yeah!"

Seeing his wife's shapely curves from behind he had a sudden urge to take her in his arms, pull her nightdress up over her head and make passionate love, but commonsense was telling him this was the very last thing he should do. For several weeks, she'd been far too distracted to respond to his love-making as she had ever since they first made love in that cave in the ancient Mesa Verde. So, instead, this night he reckoned they would lie together and talk and talk until daybreak if necessary. He wasn't going to let sleep overcome him until he knew what it was on her mind. What it was that she 'couldn't do'.

Adam sat on Pepe's bed waiting for them to return from the bathroom, turning over in his mind the thought that had tormented him for so many years; the thought he had tried repeatedly and unsuccessfully to bury...

That Pepe was not his child?

He feared that the thing she couldn't do was to tell him this, and her reluctance fuelled his doubts and threatened to resurrect his old enemy. Jealousy! During those three days in Albuquerque, nine months before Pepe was born, for which his mind remained stubbornly blank, had she sought solace in the company of his old rival, Fernando? Was Fernando Pepe's true father?

"Papa?"

It was Pepe at the door. Alone.

"Where's Mama?" asked Adam.

The boy shrugged his shoulders.

"Can I go back to bed now, Papa?" he said.

"Sure!" Adam stood up and watched the boy climb back into bed. "But where is Mama?" he asked again.

"Think she must've gone downstairs," Pepe replied with a yawn.

On leaving the room, Adam bumped into Chloe as she stood pulling a dressing gown around her shoulders.

"What's up, Adam? What's all this carry on about?" she asked.

Lee stood gaping vacantly from the doorway of their bedroom, wearing only a pair of boxer shorts.

"María's worse," Adam muttered. "Bad dream, or something. I dunno. She won't tell me. Came into Pepe's room and gave Pepe a hug. She was crying. Then she took him to the bathroom. But—"

"But what?"

"It was her screaming out that woke me up. 'No, I can't do it!' she was saying."

"Oh, my God!" exclaimed Chloe, pushing Adam aside. She ran downstairs. "Lee!" she shouted.

Lee, galvanised into action, hurried after Chloe. Adam, engulfed by panic, followed his brother-in-law. The door to the yard was open. Chloe, with Lee, ran out into the yard shouting:

"María, stop! Don't do this!"

For a minute or so, Adam stood in the kitchen, unable to move. Despite all that he'd been through, he felt utterly helpless. Then something inside him took over. His legs sprang into action. He ran out to the yard, to the bushes beyond the chair swing where, in another dimension, he had seen himself and María sitting together and playing with their unborn children. At first, he couldn't see María.

But Chloe would find her. He trusted his sister more than anyone.

She knew where Moon Water's body lay. But Moon Water was dead.

Dead?

Adam stopped at the bushes that partitioned off the lawn beyond. His mind tried not to see María, stretched out on the grass, and Chloe beside her with dark red stains on her nightdress that could only have been blood. Lee stood with a knife in his hand. Adam's head went swimmy and he sank to his knees and thumped the ground with his fists.

"María!" Adam shrieked. He felt a heavy arm across his shoulders and looked up. It was Lee.

"She's okay, Adam," his brother-in-law soothed. "Chloe took this from her just before she could do anything stupid. You should've seen the way she threw herself at María. Man, it was awesome! But the blood is Chloe's. The knife caught her arm."

"Adam?" It was María. Chloe was now cradling her in her arms. "I'm so sorry, Adam. I just wanted to—I couldn't—"

Adam went and knelt beside his sister and stroked his wife's hair. She still wore it long, like a teenager.

"It's okay, honey. Let's just go inside. Have a cup of cocoa. Mexican style with chilli, huh? Just give it time to come out, darling. I shouldn't have pressurised you."

"Hold me, Adam. Like before. Like when—you know—after you rescued me from that coyote creature."

Adam lifted María into his arms and carried her back into the house. In the living room, he gently lowered her onto the settee, whilst Chloe, holding a bloodied hand over the gash in her arm, sat beside her.

"I'll go get a bandage, Chloe," said Lee. He put the knife on top of a bookcase, out of reach from María, and left to find a bandage for his wife.

"I'm sorry, Chloe. I feel so awful," María sobbed. But Chloe only smiled.

"Don't worry. We've been down this road before, Maria." she said, referring to the episode outside that cave in the mesas when María thought Adam no longer loved her. "Guess that's what a sister-in-law's for," Chloe added. "To help her brother out." She looked accusingly at Adam.

"I—I was only trying to—" Adam stuttered.

"María, we haven't been totally honest with you," Chloe interrupted. "Our documentary was just an excuse. Kind of. Though we do have to make it. Real reason we came here was to sort this whole thing out. Adam asked me, and I said I thought I knew what the problem was, only I wasn't certain, and sure as hell I didn't know how to get to the truth."

"That dream! It keeps on coming back. Night after night after night," María said faintly.

"A real dream?"

"Dunno what that is."

"Like more real than life."

María nodded.

"Suppose so. In a way, it is. Look, can I talk to Lee about it? Alone?"

María looked anxiously at Adam. The look seemed to confirm the awful thought that had plagued him for so long, and yet he still loved her. He had always loved her, ever since middle school. However painful the revelation that was about to unfold might be, and even if Fernando did turn out to be Pepe's true father, he would still love her.

"Honey, however you want to play this, I'm easy. If—" he started to say.

"Adam, this isn't a game. It's just that... I really don't know how to put this—"

"I'm sorry. Didn't mean it like that."

"Adam, I love you. There'll only ever be you. You know that, don't you?"

Adam inwardly swore at the tears forming in his eyes.

She wants to tell Lee that I'm not Pepe's father because she thinks he'll know better how to break the news, man-to-man. The knife of words pierced where it hurt. He was too upset to talk. He just nodded. Chloe took hold of his arm.

"Let's leave them, brother. We have our own talking to do," she said. "Lee!" She looked pointedly at her husband.

"What... me?" Lee appeared as vapid as anyone might after being forced out of bed in the middle of the night and flung into the climax of a television soap drama.

"Lee, you are about to sit next to the most beautiful woman in America and you're only wearing boxer shorts!"

"Jesus, María, I am sorry! Just a minute!"

"It's okay, Lee," María responded. "To be honest, I hadn't even noticed."

And so, Lee sat beside María, ready to listen. He was a good listener, which was why she chose him. Plus, he wasn't close in the same way as Chloe, her parents, Jorge or Aunt Jac. And Lee was never judgemental. María was sure she would be cruelly judged and terrified that Adam might leave her. Talking to Lee seemed the only way forward now that the option of killing herself had been taken away.

Then there was that thing she could never do. Not in a million years.

"Upstairs, big brother!" Chloe said before pushing Adam up the stairs to his and María's bedroom.

"You do believe her, don't you?" she asked as they sat together on the bed.

Adam nodded.

"But Pepe? What if—?"

"Adam, just take your mind back to that summer. When you suddenly turned up in Xibalba. When you saved me. When you—" Chloe paused. "When you were the Golden Jaguar."

Adam totally ignored Chloe's question:

"It's Fernando, isn't it? He's the father."

"Oh, do shut up! Don't ever say such a horrible thing about María again. You know she'd never cheat on you. Look, every time I tried to talk to you about what happened back then, it was like there was a brick wall there. You seemed to be denying it ever happened. You really freaked me out for a while. Then I just said to myself 'forget it, Chloe. Pretend it didn't happen'. But it did. I know it did, and so does Lee. So, think back, Adam, 'cause that's the only way we're ever gonna help María. That's what this thing with Pepe's all about. I don't know what the dream is that's been tormenting the poor woman, but I know one thing. It's tied up with what happened to you when you were hanging up there all kinda suspended like a jelly fish in the air above that ball court."

"Ball court?" Adam stared at the floor in front of him and slowly shook his head. "That's just it, Chloe. I remember nothing. All that talk about going back to Xibalba —and please don't think I didn't believe you—but for me Xibalba was just about bringing María back to life. Getting snake venom from the Snake Goddess and preventing that awful thing from happening. Preventing her death after it had happened. It's like there's a total blackout for those three days you speak of. And yet that business about María phoning Aunt Jac because I'd vanished. Then me coming back and saying something to her about being in the kitchen all the time." Adam glanced sideways at Chloe. "I know she wouldn't lie to me. But don't you see? You saying I was with you in Xibalba during those three days and María's been saying I was with her in Houston. Makes no sense. Then she tells me a couple of months later she's pregnant. And I always took precautions back then. I almost asked her once. About Fernando. Whether he and she had—you know—but I couldn't. And she was so happy about our baby. If I can still call Pepe 'ours'. But that's the thing. She's always made such a thing about him being like me."

Adam's eyes were wet.

"And you don't know why?"

"Chloe, how could I even suggest that to her? When she was so over the moon about Pepe?"

"Adam, you've gotta think back. You've got to prove to her that Pepe's yours. Look, there is something I didn't tell you because we never got around to talking about it."

"What?"

"The Golden Jaguar. When he'd gotten killed by that coyote, after being battered senseless by those red rubber brutes, he turned into you and the coyote became Coyote Spirit. You were still just alive. He wanted you that way for a purpose. It was like Coyote Spirit sucked something out of you and—well, he kinda looked like you. He *was* you, in fact, but you were also still hanging up there, a transparent jellyfish stuck in the air just beside me. I couldn't reach you because we were kind of trapped like fossilised insects in amber. But I felt your soul was still there somewhere inside that jellyfish thing, and I knew you were fighting because you kept changing—like sometimes you seemed to be getting your body back, then you'd lose it again. But the thing is, I feared Coyote Spirit was gonna use your body to get to María, bring her back to Xibalba and make her his queen. It's what he said he'd do. He was gonna force us to watch this before that ball game thing. Using our own heads, yours and mine, for balls. He vanished, then instead of him returning with María, you came back to life in that jellyfish, Adam. Like you were your old self again. And it was definitely you. Not only that. It was like you'd gotten stronger. As if the Golden Jaguar had become you, and its spirit was still there, rather than the other way around, as before."

"What are you trying to tell me, sis?" Adam frowned. "That now I'm really Coyote Spirit living as Adam Winters?"

"No! I know you're not. It's just that when Coyote Spirit became you—I mean looked like you—well, neither of us knows what happened after that."

"You mean he came back to Houston and did 'that' with María? God, I'll bloody kill him!"

Chloe chuckled.

"You've done that already. Look, Adam, the whole thing was so weird, then the Lords of Xibalba turning into Art and Jeannie—who were really the Hero Twins—"

"Like before?"

"Yeah, well it was like I didn't know who was who in that place, and my so-called sixth sense was useless. Only thing that had any sort of power was our granny's locket."

"Dad always said you were like a clone of Granny."

"Look, Adam, somehow we've gotta find out who was who and where and when. María will talk to Lee, I know it. She must. And, poor woman, she wants answers, because she's gotta know who it was who made love to her and brought little Pepe into this world. She never willingly cheated on you, Adam. She thought it was you. Because that's who was in bed with her when the boy was conceived. But now she thinks it was someone else."

"Coyote Spirit?"

"Hardly likely to have been Fernando, huh? He wasn't gonna suddenly turn into Adam Winters for a date with his favourite girl, was he?"

"Then that's it, I guess! Pepe is Coyote Spirit's child."

"No, that is not it! I just know Pepe's one of our family. Sixth sense can't fail me on this one."

"But if that monster used my body, perhaps he also used my genes."

"Nope! You're his father. *I* know and *Pepe* knows. Somehow, we must prove it. Nothing else will bring María back to you. Adam, you've no idea how she's suffered over this thing. And after all these years, I still wonder whether you really realise how much she loves you. I mean for you to suggest that she could possibly have had fling with Fernando is unthinkable!"

"I'm sorry. I'm pretty much—I dunno what it is—like I—"

"I know, Brother Nerd! Never really regained self-confidence after being teased at middle school, despite later becoming Regional Junior Karate Champion. Look, those devils in Xibalba want her back. Don't you see? They say she still belongs to them, and they want her like Coyote Spirit wanted her. To keep. If she'd killed herself out there in the yard, that's where she could be right now. In Xibalba. With them. Adam, this is getting so serious."

"You told me over the phone back then that Art and Jeannie had killed them. Pushed them over a cliff or something."

"Thought you weren't listening! That's what we both hoped for, Adam, but we never saw it happen."

"For years, I was too terrified to even talk about Xibalba. I really believed this might have killed María."

"Later this morning, before María gets up, you and I and Pepe are gonna sit down there on that chair swing together and work out how to bring your memory back. And we're not gonna get off it till we've done that. Okay?"

Adam put his arm across Chloe's shoulders.

"What the heck would I do without my little sister?" he asked.

"For a start, you and María you wouldn't be in this mess."

"No! Do not go blaming yourself again. Or that religion of yours. Oneness with Nature, or something, isn't it?"

"I keep telling you, Adam," chuckled Chloe, "I don't have a religion. But those Native Americans did have something wonderful before we white guys destroyed it. Less of a religion than a feeling for Nature. For Life and the Universe."

"And ancestral spirits, eh? Like our granny?"

"Shhh! I hear them coming upstairs. I'll get Pepe to wake you up later, but now just show María how much she really means to you. Take her in your arms and make love to her, brother. Okay?"

But as Adam Winters made love to his beautiful wife, he imagined himself to be a handsome muscular Red Indian called Coyote Spirit, and afterwards, when María had fallen asleep, with his mind still blank for those three missing days, he wept.

Chapter 19: Search for the Truth

The scientist spoke as she continued to peer at the world through her microscope:

"I see changes."

"What is she talking about?" asked the nervous ex-priest. "She really does annoy me."

"And you're beginning to annoy me," retorted the dapper Mexican in a suit. "Your people all but destroyed mine."

"Come now, let's not argue," said the one-time antiques dealer from Houston. "His people also brought us the God of Love. Remember that!"

"Changes," repeated the scientist. "It may all be over sooner than you think. Unless..." She looked up from her microscope.

"Unless what?" A row of celestial faces stared at her.

"The other child," replied the woman. "Her genes. Blended with His."

***

"Are you sure that's what she said?" Chloe asked Lee whilst prodding him to prevent him drifting off to sleep again after the alarm clock went off. She could not relax until she had a better idea of what happened in Houston over those three days. There had to be something. A word perhaps? Or a vision that would help Adam to recover his erased memory. Lee opened his eyes and looked at her.

"Yeah! Adam seemed strange, not himself, she told me. Said odd things that kind of upset her. But he would also suddenly return to normal, like. Then, again, he'd go all weird. Said he really freaked her out."

"And that was when he reappeared?"

"Yeah! Soon after she'd made that call to Aunt Jac. The kitchen's where he said he'd been all the time. Then he kept vanishing. Said he'd been to the library each time."

"Even at night?"

"Slept behind a bookcase after they'd closed, he told her."

"Which was when the real Adam Winters was a jellyfish suspended above that ball court in Xibalba?"

"And they made love only once."

"But that's just it. Who made love to her? And what about Art and Jeannie?"

"Poor María! Art suddenly appeared from nowhere, he and Adam had a fight, Adam gotten himself killed and then disappeared again. Before he, too, vanished, Art said 'destroy the child'. María went back to her parents' house and took to her bed and wouldn't stop crying and, apparently, no one could get any sense from her. Then Adam came back again. Just like that. And poor María thought she was seeing a ghost. Or going mad. But she wasn't. It was her own Adam, she could tell, and he said he had no idea what she was talking about when she went on about the fight with Art and about vanishing."

"Only once, then?"

"What?"

"They only made love once during that time, right?"

"Guess so. Look, she was pretty upset last night, you know. It's very hard for the poor woman. What with those dreams and all. Art keeps coming back to her and the dreams seem more real than real, and night after night he's telling her to destroy the child. Of course she could never do that."

"That's it!"

"What's it?"

"That wasn't Art. Here in Houston, when this all happened back then. Or in her dreams. Oh, don't you see? It was one of those Death Lords. One Death or Seven Death. I saw them turn into Art and Jeannie in Xibalba. They wanted María for themselves. Somehow, they'd morphed into Art and Jeannie. And piggy-backed onto Coyote Spirit, whom they later killed as 'Adam', so they could get María for themselves. It's so obvious, now, Lee.

They've been tormenting her, hoping she'll end it all by killing herself and arrive back in Xibalba for all eternity as their plaything! Or worse, use her to take over our world as well as Xibalba."

"But I thought you saw them pushed over the cliff by those giants, whatever their names are."

"Hunahpu and Xbalanque, the Hero Twins? Didn't actually see that happen. Only assumed it. Boy, they'd grown huge, and the red rubber guys looked so weakened, but it seems that in Xibalba anything is possible. And who knows, they could've been killed and brought back to life—well, into some kind of existence, anyway. I see it all now. Perhaps they were afraid that Coyote Spirit's son by María would be even more powerful than them. They'd also know she'd rather kill herself than her child. We simply must not let her out of our sight till this is sorted."

"Sorted? How?"

There was a timid knock on the door and a familiar little voice:

"Aunt Chloe? Are you ready?"

"Look," said Lee, climbing out of bed, "it doesn't seem right for me to be in my boxer shorts with María, in her bedroom, standing guard whilst you and Adam discuss things with Pepe. Besides, I'm sure it was only a cry for help. And she knows she's getting that now. I'll take the twins to her instead. Tell her they want to be with her. Okay?"

"Guess you're right, honey. You wake them up, then."

Chloe opened the door whilst Lee shook their sleepy sons awake.

"Aunt Chloe!" Pepe exclaimed, hugging his aunt. "It's gonna work, isn't it? We're gonna make Mama better? You and me?"

"You, me and Papa. You want to wake him up? After taking the twins into your Mama's bedroom to keep her company?"

"You mean to stand guard?"

Chloe could keep nothing from her nephew. She crouched down and stroked his cheek.

"Not exactly, Pepe. Uncle Lee has work to do, and we can't have them getting up to mischief, can we? Is Carla still asleep?"

"Sure! You know what Carla's like in the morning!"

"There you go, then. It has to be Mama looking after the twins."

"Aunt Chloe?"

"Pepe?"

"You are my real aunty, aren't you? I feel as if you are."

Chloe kissed the boy's forehead.

"So, you know what this is all about, huh? And I feel it too, honey. Like right here!"

She patted her chest where her heart was. Pepe fetched the twins from their bed as Chloe went and tapped softly on the door of Adam's and María's room. A weary Adam emerged.

"She's still asleep," he whispered.

"Won't be for much longer. Enter the terrible twins!" announced Pepe.

Chloe stepped back and the twins toddled past her then ran to the bed like playful kittens. They climbed onto the cover, jumped up and down a few times then kissed María awake.

"She'll be fine with them. And Lee will be downstairs in the kitchen. Come. We've work to do!" she said.

Adam felt a gentle tug on his arm. It was Pepe. He lifted the boy up and Pepe put his arms around his father and pressed his face into the hollow of his neck.

"He knows, and I know, Adam," Chloe said. "So, we're just gonna sit there on that chair swing together till we've found an answer, 'cause you and María, you have to know too. At least now you can see why."

On the way to the chair swing, Adam told Chloe how María opened up after they'd made love during the night.

She told him everything that she'd told Lee, all that she knew, and how Art kept returning to her in those nightmares, telling her to destroy the offspring of Coyote Spirit before it was too late.

"But you're my dad!" insisted Pepe, hugging Adam even more tightly. He remained with his cheek up against his father's as the three sat together on the chair swing. Chloe spoke first:

"That's not the real Art or Hunahpu in her dreams. It's One Death. Or Seven Death. One of them, anyways. Makes no odds. He killed Coyote Spirit. The real Art could never have done that in case it was you, but One Death, he wouldn't give a damn. Besides, killing Coyote Spirit would only bring the Anasazi guy back to Xibalba. Weakened, perhaps."

"Why did the Death Lord leave María if he wanted her so much?" asked Adam. He sat looking blankly ahead, stroking the back of Pepe's head.

"Good question. Wish I could answer it. Maybe they can't exist here in the absence of Coyote Spirit."

"You know, I often used to recall that vision of me and María sitting on this very bench after she'd died—" Adam clapped his hand to his mouth realising what he'd just said in front of Pepe.

"It's okay, Papa. I know as much as Aunt Chloe, anyway." He gripped his father's hand and squeezed it with his small fingers. Adam continued:

"The Golden Jaguar took us to this place where we're sitting now, in the Forest Without Time. From the past. Only we saw our futures together. We saw you and Carla, Pepe, before either of you were born. And Mama wasn't that much older than you are now. And I thought then, so that's what it'll be like. That'll be the end of all this business."

"And it is, Adam," Chloe said, patting her brother's knee. "She's alive, you've had so much happiness together, you have two of the greatest kids. And Pepe and I both know you're his dad, and maybe the Death Lords did get killed and these dreams of María's are no more than that. Bad dreams."

Adam shook his head.

"Adam? Were you listening to me, brother?"

The man turned to look at his sister.

"Sorry! I was just thinking of her at our wedding. The real one. In that city beside the lake in ancient Mexico. Can't believe it's the same place as modern Mexico City. She looked so lovely. If only you'd been there, Chloe." He paused, briefly. "Papa Pedro was there. Before he died and hundreds of years before he was born. And he married us. What the heck is going on, Chloe? It makes so little sense to me."

"Maybe she can tell us." Chloe held up their granny's locket and stared at it. She was about to say something when Pepe tapped her hand and looked up at her.

"Aunt Chloe?" His questioning eyes sparkled in a curious way. Chloe knew something had just entered his little mind.

"Yes, honey?"

"Tell me more about the Old Woman of the Hills. About what she can do."

"Your Papa's the best person to do that. I've never met her."

"Papa?"

Pepe now fixed his inquisitive eyes upon his father.

"You've been reading my mind again, haven't you?" Adam asked, grinning. The boy nodded. "She's the strangest person you could ever meet, Pepe."

"Scary strange?"

"Nope! Nothing scary about the Old Woman of the Hills except when—" Adam frowned.

"She wasn't real then, Papa, was she? That Native girl told you. Came from inside your head."

"Gosh, Pepe. What more can I tell you? Yes, the other Old Woman of the Hills in that weird City on the Plain,

Coyote Spirit's city, she came from me. But the real Old Woman is not crazy like some people believe. She — like when she looks into your eyes, it's as if she—oh, Pepe, I'm not that good with words. Not like your aunt. The Old Woman seems to be—"

"Is it your soul she seems to be looking into?"

Adam stared at his son.

"Wow, Pepe! When you put it like that, I suppose that's about it. She's looking right into your soul. And she speaks with whatever language is there inside you. It's totally weird, but when you're with her it all seems so natural."

"And she calls Mama a princess, doesn't she?"

"Mama is a princess. In another world."

"Are all princesses as beautiful as Mama?"

"No. Mama's special. Mama's—"

"Adam, that's it!" interrupted Chloe. "María's special for them too. Special for all of us, sure, but for them as well. And for the Old Woman of the Hills. Pepe feels it, don't you, Pepe? And I've known since I first met her. Oh, why didn't I see it? All these years, and poor María suffering so!"

"I don't get it, Chloe. You and Pepe have left me way behind. What's this got to do with the Old Woman of the Hills?"

"She's the answer to everything, Adam. God, I am so stupid at times!"

"Oh, you're never really stupid, Aunt Chloe," observed Pepe. Chloe chuckled.

"He said it!" agreed Adam. "My amazing little sister is never really stupid. So! Spill the beans, sis."

"Just a hunch, Adam. But—"

"When are we going to Mexico, Papa?" asked Pepe, eagerly bouncing up and down on the chair swing.

"To where, Pepe? I'm afraid you've lost me again."

"To Mexico, Papa! To see the Old Woman of the Hills!"

"No, Pepe. Just wait a minute! We can't go rushing off to Mexico just because Mama's sad."

"But that's it, Adam. That's why you have to go. To save María again, because, by golly she needs saving now. From that torment inside her. Thinking little Pepe is Coyote Spirit's son must be simply awful for the woman. And you, for sure, cannot reassure her that he isn't!"

"I'm not, I'm not!" shrieked Pepe, hugging his father again. "This is my daddy!"

"You and I know, but Mama doesn't, and until Papa remembers everything that happened, she's gonna suffer more and more with all that worrying."

"I know all about how babies come into the world!" Pepe announced. "I told Carla about it. It's when mommies and daddies really love each other, like Mama and Papa do. And the daddies put their things into—"

"Okay, Pepe! That's enough! In your case, I'm sure that was true. Just gotta prove it."

"I still don't get it, Chloe. Besides, it'll only make María feel worse if she sees the Old Woman of the Hills again. If she's reminded once more."

"He didn't say her. He means just you two. It's all about you and Pepe now."

"And the other girl," added Pepe.

"Other girl? Oh, that's your Aunt Chloe, son!"

Chloe merely frowned.

"Oh, Papa! When can we go? How about right away? My bag's packed already." Adam laughed.

"Oh dear, oh dear! I can't drop everything and run off to Mexico like this."

"Can't you?" questioned Chloe. "You saw what happened last night. Can't you just do this for María?"

"Please, Papa! I want Mama to get better!"

"But—?"

"No buts, Adam. The boy's right. Go straight onto the internet, get the earliest possible flights for you and Pepe — then I'll phone Jorge and he'll tell Tia Bea and Tio

Federico. Do it now, before the kids have María up and about. Before she can say 'no'. And just make up some garbled excuse for the university."

Adam, still sceptical about what he was doing, went back into the house and logged onto the internet. Chloe remained with Pepe on the chair swing. She saw him staring at her granny's locket.

"It's the locket, isn't it, Pepe? Your great granny's kachina spirit. You can feel her too. She's telling you something. Am I right?"

Pepe nodded.

"Did you never see your granny?"

"No. I never did see your great granny. She died young. Like your granny and grandpa."

"But in your real dreams, Aunt Chloe? Did you never see her in one of those?"

"Nope. Never done that. Never dreamt about her."

"I dream about my dead granny and grandpa. Often!" Pepe announced casually. "They're very nice! And they're not in that horrid place with giant bats and things."

"Bats and things, ay? Well, the Hero Twins easily overcame Zotz, the Bat God. That I did see."

Then Chloe listened in disbelief as Pepe described her mommy and daddy perfectly, and she smiled to herself as she realised how right she had been to tell Pepe the story about the Golden Jaguar of the Sun.

Chapter 20: Trickster Tricked

"What do you mean, 'He'll return'. We know that. It's why we're here. Waiting. But with no mixing of genes when He does, I hope."

The scientist looked at the ex-priest.

"Yes. Waiting and doing nothing. And when it's over, what will we do then? Without a purpose, will we even exist?"

***

"Last two seats on the plane, Pepe," Adam said to his son as they sped along the beltway towards George Bush International Airport. "Goddamn lucky, huh?"

"She'll have kept them for us, Papa."

"Who's that?" Adam asked, grinning.

"Her!" the boy replied. He peered down at the golden locket which seemed disproportionately large up against his small chest.

"After we've gone through security, you just keep Aunt Chloe's locket hidden under your shirt, Pepe. And particularly in Mexico City. Might get kidnapped if they think you're a wealthy young man."

"But we are wealthy, aren't we, Papa?"

"Yes. very. Because of Mama. Her famous voice. Her looks. But we don't keep her wealth just for ourselves."

"I know. Aunt Chloe told me. About what you and Mama and Aunt Jac are doing for the Mayans and the Native Americans, and the help you both give her and Uncle Lee."

"What else did she say?"

"About Mama being kidnapped once. Only I'm not supposed to tell anyone. But I can tell you, can't I? Because you know."

Adam frowned.

"I know all right, son. That was one hell of an awful moment when I had to watch your Mama being snatched away from me by those drug thugs."

"So, you weren't the Golden Jaguar then, Papa, or you would've chased that vehicle and caught up with it."

"Pepe, that's another thing you must never talk about. The Golden Jaguar. Just think of it as a fairy tale."

"But it isn't a fairy tale, is it?"

"No more and no less than the fact that Mama's really a princess."

After passing through security, Adam helped Pepe to tuck the golden locket out of sight under his tee-shirt.

"Do Tia Bea and Tio Federico know about the Golden Jaguar or the Old Woman of the Hills?" the boy asked.

"Best not mention these things, Pepe. Then we don't have to lie about why we're going to Mexico. Your aunt told Jorge I had some affairs to sort out there and, well, I do have some real work to do with charities and agencies supporting Mayan communities in Southern Mexico."

"Does Mama give them money as well?"

"Sure does! And she's paying for Anna's friend, Manuel, to become a doctor. He qualifies next year."

"What does 'qualifies' mean?"

"Means he can work in a hospital as a proper doctor."

"Why can't I tell about the Golden Jaguar and the Old Woman of the Hills?" Adam had to trawl his mind for an answer.

"Let's just say it's to do with their beliefs. Going to church and that. They're devout Catholics. Like Mama."

"And me! But if Mama believes in God and these things will help her, then it can't be going against God, can it?"

"Sometimes, Pepe, there are no easy answers."

"Aunt Chloe says that God and the Great Spirit of the Native Americans are the same only with different names."

"Your aunt is very wise, Pepe. Now, how's your Spanish? Better than mine, I'll bet, with Mama talking away to you two kids in Spanish half the time!"

Pepe and Carla were both fluent in Spanish. Adam as well, but their accents were perfect, and they could easily pass as Mexican children. So, in Mexico the man let Pepe chatter away to him in Spanish — English, he said, was banned — as they travelled about the city. Pepe, like his mama, was an expert at 'chattering away', but anyone listening in to the discourse would have been taken aback. The topics alone would have taxed the most learned of professors at Harvard or Yale, but the child's analysis and understanding of those topics were awesome...

The evolution of religion in the West, the impact of Christianity upon the social structure of black American culture, the cosmos and the Great Spirit, and the interplay between gravity and dark energy in the universe. Such things the child talked about as if they were merely to do with a big screen blockbuster for kids. And then he would switch to a blockbuster, like any other kid, or chatter about what he and Carla could get up to doing with old cardboard boxes in the yard back home. He was both child and wise old man moulded into one.

It was extraordinary, but also one reason behind María's fear of what Art's voice kept telling her: fear that a child bearing the seed of a centuries old Indian spirit might well show signs of superior (and supernatural?) intelligence. Adam, too, had been brilliant at school. María remembered well the shy young academic teased mercilessly by her previous boyfriend, Spike O'Driscoll, and the boy with whom she fell in love at middle grade school even before he realised he loved her. But with Pepe it was different. His genius seemed more than a mere biological phenomenon.

Recently, Pepe's principal had commented on his intelligence. She called Adam and María into school one evening and went on about IQ testing and educational psychologists and devising a special programme for him, for he was surely some sort of a prodigy. María, instead of being pleased, became upset. Unreasonably so, Adam thought, and he had to take his wife out of the room when it looked as if her Latin temper might get the better of her. Outside, she burst into tears and ran to the car, and Adam had to sprint after her.

"Honey, what was going on in there? What came over you?" he asked. "She was only trying to do her best for little Pepe."

"I'm sorry," María sobbed. "but I just want him to be normal. Like any other child."

"He is. Only he's super bright. That's all."

But he was unable to console her.

"It's just as I feared," she said.

"What is? You're afraid of him being clever? Come on, María! You should feel proud. Happy!"

"No. Different from others. Like—" She paused and looked directly at Adam. He saw pain in her eyes, and it hurt him to see it there, but he felt unable to reach out and take away the pain. That evening, he phoned his sister, and Chloe told him enough was enough, that they had to help María and that it was all to do with Pepe.

***

"Will it take long to get there?" Pepe asked as he and his father sped, in Tio Federico's car, towards the mountains beyond Mexico City.

"To the Old Woman's cave? Oh, an hour or so."

"It feels funny. Kinda warm," the boy said.

"What does?" asked Adam, bemused. He never quite knew what his little son was going to come out with next.

"This locket of Great Granny's"

Adam glanced sideways at his son. Pepe's small hand was in front of his chest clasped over the locket which he had just pulled out from under his tee-shirt.

"Well, it would do, having been under that tee-shirt of yours."

"No, a different warm, Papa. Like when I hug Mama, and when I play with Carla. That sort of warm."

Conchita Gonzalez, the wife of Papa Pedro's old friend, was with them to show them the way. She'd become quite frail and her memory wasn't what it used to be. Twice they got lost. Adam tried hard to memorise landmarks that might help him find his own way in the future, for perhaps the old lady hadn't much time left on earth. Soon she might pass across the curtain of death and join husband, José, and son, Santiago, but just now he badly needed her to get to the cave, although he had no idea how seeing the Old Woman again was going to help them. Chloe and Pepe seemed to know, though, and that was enough.

"Will you be okay here on your own?" Adam asked Conchita in Spanish when they'd pulled into the familiar lay-by at the foot of the path leading up to the cave.

"Fine," she replied. "Me and my memories will be just fine together. If I close my eyes, I can hear Santiago playing his guitar and singing to me, and that gives me peace. That's all I ask for now. Peace."

As Adam climbed the steep path, followed by Pepe, he heard María singing and, in her voice, he heard a yearning for the same 'peace' of which Conchita had spoken.

"Is coming to see the Old Woman again like coming home for you?" Pepe asked his father.

He is your child!

Immediately the boy had asked his question, these words appeared inside Adam's head. It was like when he talked in his mind with the Golden Jaguar, all those years ago, whilst protecting María.

"I know," he said.

"Know what, Papa?"

"Sorry, Pepe. Thinking about something else. The Old Woman like coming home? Yes and no, I suppose."

"How come 'yes and no', Papa?"

"Well, home is all about Mama and you and Carla. But this place here is where I can find the truth. About your daddy. Here is where—" But the man could not find the right word to describe the feeling that Pepe must have sensed in him as they neared the cave. And it occurred to Adam that he wasn't the slightest bit breathless despite the steep climb. He was reminded of when he ran with his dead girlfriend in his arms, up the very same path, in a desperate bid to return the girl to the land of the living. The Old Woman had done that for him, and given him happiness beyond his wildest dreams, but here he was again in a bid to retrieve not life but reassurance for María. In this case, of course, a paternity test kit would serve no useful purpose.

The strength of the Golden Jaguar had resurfaced. In fact, the more he thought about it, the more he realised this had never truly gone away. The Golden Jaguar wasn't dead, as Chloe had told him, for he was the Golden Jaguar. Coyote Spirit's big mistake had been failure to acknowledge this.

"*¡Hola!*"

Father and son called out together from the cave entrance where they stood holding hands. A faint tapping sound, a stick feeling the ground, a shuffling noise then, like an apparition from another world, the face of the Old Woman of The Hills was in front of them.

"Pepe! You are so like you're father!" This time she spoke in perfect English with a Texan accent. Leaning on her stick, she reached down and gently stroked Pepe's cheek with the back of her hand. "Johnny will be real pleased to hear this. And Ann, too."

My parents? She knows them?

"It's about—" began Adam.

"Princess Arima, of course. Your lovely wife. I know. Pepe's told me already. Told me everything. And he knows you're his true dad, but we'll have to do some fishing, you and me. Help each other. Are you prepared? If so, y'all better come on in!"

"I'm afraid I don't—"

"Don't be afraid. Never be afraid. Fear grows, swells up, takes over. The poor princess, how she now suffers because of her fear. No, Adam, don't let her suffer no more. Give her back her happiness. She deserves it."

"Have I—I mean... her suffering, that's been my fault, hasn't it?" The Old Woman smiled, and he felt her smile touch his soul like Pepe said. He wanted to weep yet couldn't. "I should've known. And Chloe, she tried to tell me something was wrong. It's just that I couldn't bear for anything to come between María and me, and this business with the missing three days, I—"

"Get along inside with you, Adam! A-fishing we shall go, huh? You like fishing, Pepe?"

"Never tried it," the boy replied. "Are you everyone's grandma, then?"

Adam felt Pepe give his hand a squeeze as the Old Woman turned and headed off into the blackness of the cave without answering.

"Grandma?" he whispered. "Why did you call her that?"

"She's the whole world's grandma, Papa, I'm sure of it," the boy whispered back.

The world's grandma?

Adam had no idea what Pepe meant as they followed the Old Woman of The Hills deep into the cave. Just any grandma was one thing, but Pepe had been quite specific. The 'world's' grandma, and for Pepe it seemed perfectly natural that the world should have a grandma. Adam thought about his own long-dead granny who, like his mother, had died young. Maybe the Old Woman's seemingly timeless age made his son say that.

"Is she also the kachina spirit of the world?" whispered Pepe. "Like my great granny is Aunt Chloe's and mine?"

Adam looked at the bent back of the Old Woman ahead and he wondered.

The shaft of light, the bend in the cave, these things he remembered, and soon they were in that magnificent high hall deep inside the mountain, with an eerie glow streaming from a natural skylight way up in the cave ceiling, its walls adorned with ancient paintings. They sat together on a bench beside a rickety table, Pepe sandwiched in between Adam and the Old Woman. Pepe handed her the gold locket. She opened it out to gaze at the image of the young woman with blonde hair.

"Your granny was so like little Chloe. But we mustn't waste time. Wear it always, Adam. Hold it when you need to. And remember this. I'll be here all the time. Together with you and Pepe. Think of this cave as your boat whilst you two are the fishermen. Out there."

"Out where?" asked Adam, taking the golden locket back from the Old Woman.

She smiled again.

"Here," she said softly.

"Fishing for what?"

"Memories. Fishing for memories, Adam."

He pressed the locket into the palm of his hand and immediately felt that warmth of which Pepe had spoken – an intense feeling of love for María and for Chloe and the children. He closed his eyes, and as he did so he seemed to rush forwards in his mind. It reminded him of the *Forest Without Time* when he was swept along with María on the back of the Golden Jaguar, and once again he could feel the silk-soft flick of her hair streaming across his cheek and the warmth of her lips against his. But this time he was also the Golden Jaguar.

Chloe had called him. She was in terrible trouble and he was her big brother. He had to save her. He opened his eyes and saw the green blur of the forest. If he looked real hard, he could make out faint ghost images imprinted upon the green of the forest: his son Pepe and the Old Woman of the Hills. He closed his eyes and the Forest didn't change. It was there, solid, but only in his mind. Or the jaguar's mind. The vast trees and ferns, the vivid splashes of colour, and the bloodcurdling animal sounds, he remembered well, but he had no fear. He knew he was the Lord of the Forest as his huge body smashed through the undergrowth. The trees thinned out. It was brighter ahead, and he slowed down. Beyond, he saw the tall arch of the bridge to Xibalba, and beyond that, swirls of grey mist. In one bound, he leapt over the steps leading up to the bridge, then sprinted, like a cheetah, over the springing planks into the thick mist. The bridge bounced drunkenly from the weight of his great body, and he remembered the voice of the Golden Jaguar, his own voice now, once saying he would surely die in Xibalba for there were creatures and Gods more powerful than he was there, but he was also Adam Winters, and, powered by Love, nothing could prevent him from rescuing Chloe.

In no time, the arch at the far end of the bridge appeared through the mist. Two more bounds, and he'd passed on under the arch into Xibalba, but he didn't stop. He sped down the blood red hill towards the great red stone ball court and the jeering and the shouting, and on through the doorway of the ball court where he came to a halt.

The dim, leaden Xibalban sky shed its ceaseless tears over the dark red of the ground and the sea of swarthy Mexican faces. The place reeked of terror and of death. Suddenly, tens of thousands of spectators, tiered along the four sides of the arena, above the ball court, went quiet, apart from the occasional gasp of fear.

Fear of me?

A powerfully-built Red Indian, whom Adam recognised at once, stood at one side of the court, holding a wooden kachina doll. Adam remembered the man who stole his girl from him whilst he lay grovelling in doped confusion in that kiva at the foot of the ancient mesas; the man he later killed. Coyote Spirit. And he smiled to himself, as far as a big cat can smile, on seeing the man tremble when he transfixed him with eyes of fire.

But the doll troubled Adam. Somehow it seemed to be linked to the spirit of María. The man was still a threat to his beloved wife and to Chloe, of whom he was aware in the space above. Whilst the fire in Adam's eyes burned incandescent, Coyote Spirit dropped the doll, shrank down, changed form, and in an instant the man was replaced by a coyote dog.

He watched the coyote, head down, tongue lolling, staring at him with its cold eyes. Way up in the air, suspended above the court, was the body of a young girl with braided blonde hair, wearing a short blue skirt. His little sister trapped, it seemed, by invisible bonds. She was looking down in terror, and he could hear her voice inside himself pleading for him to save her.

The Golden Jaguar-come-Adam slunk forwards to the centre of the court, sank down onto his haunches and waited. The coyote, with a leer on its sharp face, began to encircle him. A puny creature, to be sure, but Adam knew from his karate never to underestimate anyone or anything. He would wait for the coyote to make a wrong move, exposing its weakness.

Adam always kept the animal within his field of view, turning his head slowly as the coyote circled first this way, then that. When the attack came, it was sudden and ferocious, but no match for the power Adam felt in his huge body. With a swift swipe of his great paw he cuffed the creature aside, sending it sprawling across the bloodied gravel. It picked itself up, licked its wounds, and began circling again. Once more it lunged at him, only to be knocked flying by a further blow from his paw. Over and over, the coyote attacked him, and each time it got weaker as blood flowed freely from its deeply gouged flesh. Adam, unmarked, waited until he was sure of a kill. The coyote, circled once more, saliva drooling from its evil mouth. Adam sprang. He slammed the beast to the ground, his massive claws fanned out and pinned the little creature down. The coyote whimpered, but just before Adam could close his skull-crunching jaws around its head, something happened. The Lords of Xibalba rose up from the red ground.

The giant red rubber figures of One Death and Seven Death soon stood, legs apart, one at either end of the court and each wielding a giant club. Adam would have to kill them first. The easy skirmish with the coyote must have been part of their game. He was their sport now, and the crowd of spectators began to jeer again, taunting him. He leapt at one of the rubber figures, for he too was immensely powerful. Meanwhile, the injured coyote slunk to the side of the ball court, out of harm's way. The Xibalban Death Lord stepped aside and took a swing at Adam with its club, but the cat was too quick. As the coyote had done with him, he repeatedly attacked each giant in turn, but some of the blows from those clubs found their mark and took toll. He felt his strength starting to ebb. He would have to pull one of them down. He crouched low, waited, then sprang. This time the Lord of Xibalba was too slow. Adam sank his teeth into its red rubber tree-trunk leg, twisted his head and with an earth-shaking crash the monster fell to the ground. Immediately, a terrific blow from the other Lord's club sent Adam into a sickening spin across the blood-dirt ground of the ball court. For a while he lay still, stunned. Slowly, painfully, he managed to get back up. The injured Death Lord was hobbling, but the other one, swelled even more, stood with his club at the ready. Adam felt his body sway. He sank down onto his haunches again. If he could weaken both, he stood a chance. He'd forgotten about the pathetic coyote; his fight was now with the Lords of Xibalba. He gathered every precious ounce of strength into his tensed muscles, flicked his tail and shot into the air. A searing pain caught the side of his face. He dropped in agony, limp as a rag doll. This time he was too weak to get up.

Moments later he felt the sickening, warm breath of the coyote on his face, heard its rhythmic panting and, through glazed eyes, glimpsed the sneer on its face and its needle-sharp teeth. He felt the pain those teeth inflicted as they sank into his throat, and he became even more aware of the foul stench of the dog and the smell of death as life drained from him. The frantic screams above seemed so far away. They came from a girl called Chloe.

The cat was dead, but the boy's vision was clear enough for him to see the coyote turn back into Coyote Spirit, the man. The man spoke, and his words ignited Adam's inner fury, but all he could manage by way of movement was a slight twitch of his fingers, the fingers of a boy. It reminded him of when he was drugged by Swimming Beaver in ancient Colorado. He heard the man's laughter and sensed the man's power bore into him, tearing him apart.

Adam was aware of being lifted across the Coyote Spirit's shoulders, being carried, floppy and useless, then getting flung into the air. The air stuck to him like glue. He was floating, weightless, like a frozen bubble. He had no paws, no claws, no golden fur. Just the hands of a boy, transparent as glass, and legs as useless as dangling cucumbers. But he could see. Somehow his eyes still worked, and he saw his sister hanging just feet away from where he lay suspended like a chalked figure at a police crime scene, and, down below, in the ball court he saw himself. Upright, proud and very much alive. He was too dazed to think clearly, but this seemed just about as bad as it could get, to see himself, but not himself, down there, picking up the kachina doll from the bloodied ground. Something told him that the doll would take the man, the 'other' Adam, straight to his darling María. And the monster would touch her, kiss her and, God forbid, he would make love to her. He recalled Coyote Spirit boasting, just before being killed on that cliff in the mesas, how he would take her 'over and over' again. The pain, for

Adam, of watching Coyote Spirit as himself, in his own body, suddenly vanish to collect his prize back in Houston, was indescribable. And in that half-dead state, Adam could do nothing. He could neither lift a finger to fight the man, nor move his lips to cry out.

From that moment on, the here-and-now-Adam, the one sitting in that cave with Pepe and the Old Woman, with his eyes closed, felt he was watching a movie, and yet he *was* the movie. Then something strange happened. He heard a voice inside his head, as in the past when he spoke with the Golden Jaguar, and, more recently, when he *was* the Golden Jaguar. It was Chloe begging him to stay alive. And he felt strength in her voice, as if it was some sort of spiritual fuel stoking the fire still smouldering inside him. As Chloe's voice fanned that fire, he thought of María and of the danger she was in from that coyote bastard. The life in the fire was pulled two ways: to stay and save his sweet sister from a cruel death or chase after Coyote Spirit and prevent him from taking María.

After struggling with this dilemma, Chloe or María, there seemed only one option: to chase after Coyote Spirit by travelling through the fire kindled by his sister's voice. He would hunt down his own body in his mind and repossess it before Coyote Spirit could use it to take María. Chloe had given him back strength from somewhere deep inside the fire. The power of the Golden Jaguar was still there.

So, Adam found himself in three places at once. Sitting at a table in the cave of the Old Woman of The Hills, his son by his side, his eyes closed; suspended motionless in the air, above that ball court of evil and death, beside Chloe; and now travelling inside himself, journeying into that fire.

The fire took over. There was no heat about it, no burning coals underfoot, for he had no feet in that place. No body. Only his mind. The fire changed from a red glow to orange to yellow, its intensity brightening until he felt himself in a space that was incandescent white. It was a space without distance, without sky, ground or corners to it. It felt limitless. And yet things were forming there. Images in his mind. His house. María. And someone who looked like himself. *Was* himself... but wasn't.

He, that other self, was talking to María. Thank God, she was fully dressed! He reached out in his mind for his body, his own body, and something dark and powerful leapt out from the Adam Winters figure, rushing at him, swirling and circling, changing all the time like a swarm of killer bees. But he was strong. The intense light all around him was himself. His true self. He got closer to the physical body of Adam Winters, and as he did, María became more solid. He could hear her voice, make out her words. With a surge of energy, he pushed aside the darkness.

For a split second, everything went blank. Then he found himself back home. María spoke of a wedding. They were standing there in the kitchen in Houston, their home since his parents had died, and María had apparently been talking about getting a proper wedding dress.

"Wedding? What wedding are we talking about?"

María gave him a funny look.

"Ours, honey. You just—oh, Adam, this is so totally weird. Only a moment ago, you—"

"How long have we been here? In the kitchen?"

"Seems like you were somewhere a long while doing I don't know what! You'd vanished then reappeared from nowhere."

He gazed into her eyes. He felt their warmth, their loving, and she kissed his own moistening eyes.

"Come on," she said. "We'll go to the mall at Katy Mills. There's a bridal shop there. I'll tell Mama—and *I'll* do the driving!"

"Just then, María—it was like I was someplace else, but I can't remember a thing about it. Nothing. What's all this about a bridal shop?"

María hugged him.

"We were talking about getting married again. Soon. In a church. You were so definite about it. And I thought, yeah, maybe we should. Not keep it a secret any more."

"But Papa Pedro was a priest. When he came back to you in the confessional."

María looked both puzzled and annoyed.

"That's what I just said to you!" She mellowed. "But you were right. We shouldn't have to pretend like this to Mama and Papa It's not like they don't know we're made for each other. Come on, lover-boy. We'll go to Katy Mills. I'm all fired up about that bridal dress now. Beginning to see it in my head, even. Our real wedding, huh?"

"The other one will always be real for me."

"That's not what you said a moment ago." María was frowning. "Come on. You've been working too hard. Get in the car."

"Pink again?"

"What?"

"Your dress? Will it be pink gain?"

Oh, that sweet laugh of hers! How he loved it when she laughed.

"With all those strange birds on it? Hardly!"

"That dress was so beautiful. You were beautiful."

"Come on, Mr Day Dreamer!"

Grinning, she pulled him along to the door, and out to the car, as if he were a child. Once in the car, she chatted away as usual about all manner of things, and he let her sweet voice flow through his troubled mind like a stream of healing holy water. Suddenly, in a flash he saw Chloe. *Oh, my God,* he thought, *what's happening to my little sister? Where is she?*

María had gone quiet. Adam grabbed her arm. The car swerved.

"Adam, what is it?"

"Chloe—she—I don't know, María—it's like—"

"Did Aunt Jac call you about Chloe then? Aren't they in Albuquerque?"

Adam knew something awful was happening to Chloe. If only he could remember—somewhere up in the air—that smell of death...

"Adam, I just asked you a question. Did Aunt Jac phone about Chloe running off again? Like she's always doing?"

"It's Chloe. I know it is. She's in terrible trouble. Oh, my God! I don't know why or where, but it's something awful." Adam felt himself slip into a whirlpool of panic about Chloe. "We must turn back. Quick. I've got to—"

The black bee swarm engulfed him like a dark shroud. He broke free. He could only think of Chloe, poor little Chloe, hanging only feet away from him. María was gone. But hadn't he just been with María? He looked down at the ground and at the horror of the ball game. He called out to Chloe. The girl opened her blue eyes. When she looked at him, they widened, and he saw hope flicker, in all that terror, like a nearly-spent candle.

"Adam, is it really you?"

"Chloe, I am so sorry. I thought—I thought I was stronger."

"Have you always been the Golden Jaguar?"

Adam shook his head. He felt confused. He'd been called to rescue Chloe, that he knew, but he had no idea how, or why they were suspended above the ball court of Xibalba. He just felt utterly defeated, as if everything was coming to an end.

"There's so much I don't understand," the girl said, "but that was Coyote Spirit, wasn't it?"

Adam remembered fighting the coyote. It had seemed an easy battle. He'd had the evil creature pinned to the ground and was about to bite off its head when those giant red rubber monstrosities appeared, rising out of the ground as they'd done before when he was there with María... the Lords of Xibalba.

"Sure," he said.

She spoke about what had happened. It was still a jumble in his mind. Chloe didn't seem to know where she was.

"Xibalba. Means 'Place of Fear' in Mayan. A sort of Mayan underworld."

They talked about the last time he was there, and he spoke of the importance of María never knowing about Xibalba or about her death.

María? Coyote Spirit?

He felt a sudden surge of power, of movement. A fire, burning like a thousand stars, welled up inside him. Without warning, he dropped about ten feet towards the ground. Chloe screamed. Adam looked up at her. She was holding something in her hand. He remembered. He'd been distracted, thinking of María—María and Coyote Spirit together—but Chloe had been speaking about their granny's golden locket and had just taken hold of it.

"Wow, what did you just do?" Adam called out to his sister.

"I only picked up the locket. Like I did before the Golden Jaguar appeared. I thought Granny's kachina spirit was all I had to help me."

"Chloe, when you took hold of that thing it was like I had this enormous burst of energy. A strange kind of power. And everything came back to me. It was as if I had—" A thought occurred to Adam. He asked Chloe when it was that she'd let go of the locket whilst he was fighting the coyote, and she told him it was when the Lords of Xibalba had risen from the ground. He got her to do it again, to hold the locket in her palm and concentrate her thoughts on him. That power must have come from Chloe and their granny's kachina spirit together, and it worked. He dropped to ground, not only alive and fit, but with a feeling that he could tackle anything, conquer all evil.

Having been catapulted into the ball game, he dropped like a stone and arrived in one of the teams. When they saw him cast aside opponents like discarded dolls, taking possession of the ball, and dodging all attempts by the opposition to retrieve it, he immediately became their champion, their hero. The game didn't last long. Adam bounced the ball off his thigh through the stone ring, then did three laps of the ball court with the winning team, raised up on the shoulders of two teammates, and to loud applause from all spectators. A large guy with a feathered headdress and clutching a knife leapt down into the court. The captain of the losing team was brought before him and pushed to the ground onto his knees. The big fellow handed Adam the knife.

"You can't do this, Adam!" screamed Chloe.

But Adam had no intention of beheading the man. He snapped the knife in two. The man with the headdress, incensed, tried to grab hold of him, but Adam was too quick, and he flung the guy to the ground.

"There'll be no more ball games in Xibalba," Adam yelled. "No more killing of the dead!"

Team players on both sides cheered him, but the spectators, horrified by such an unwelcome display of compassion, began to hiss and boo, and those in the front row jumped down into the court, armed with clubs and knives. Others followed, and, in the ensuing fight, Adam and the players were soon outnumbered, but the players were agile and strong. No spectators could get anywhere near Adam.

"Adam, watch out for One Death and Seven Death!" screamed Chloe.

Sure enough, they rose again from the red ground.

"Wait!" Adam shouted back at Chloe.

He quickly arranged for a group of players to form a moving human pyramid whilst other players shielded them from the fray. He was pulled by a chain of hands to the top of the pyramid, just below Chloe. He reached up as his sister reached down. They made contact. He gripped her firmly around the forearm and pulled her with ease through the invisible force that pinned her to the air.

Several players helped him to the ground with Chloe safe in his arms.

The Lords of Xibalba were now laying into the players, sending them flying in all directions with blows from their tree trunk-sized clubs. Chloe was crying.

"We've had it," she sobbed. "Poor Lee! Poor María!"

Something jolted free inside Adam. A memory? To do with María?

"Just grip that locket, sis. I'm gonna have to—"

Adam closed his eyes. That inner fire burned so strongly he momentarily lost vision, but as his eyes searched the fire, he saw María and himself. Another self. In a car. His eyes filled with tears at the thought that he might be too late. A black cloud shot from out from the body that was also himself, circled and swirled and tried to destroy him, but his brightness soon dispersed the cloud. He was in his body and María was beside him in the driver's seat. He remembered nothing of Chloe, or Xibalba, when he entered his body, but his face was wet with tears, and his cheek felt sore, as if he'd just been slapped. The car had stopped, but he felt too shattered to get out. María looked at him. At first a puzzled look, but it quickly changed. She, too, began to cry. She got out of the car, walked around to the passenger's side, opened his door and hugged him. She helped him out of the car and supported him with her arm about his waist as they went on into the house. They sat on the settee and she kissed him over and over.

"What's happening to us, my darling? I love you so much, but there's something inside me fighting. Something I don't understand."

María flung her arms around him Her kiss silenced his lips. Then, with hands almost frantic in their haste, she unzipped his jeans and removed his tee-shirt. Quickly, she slipped off her own clothes. For a few blissful moments, he sat looking at her, unable to believe how beautiful she was. Every time he saw her naked, she seemed lovelier, but this occasion was special. Then he noticed a bruise on her arm. He touched his slapped face. Did he cause that bruise? Had he hurt her when his mind had gone blank? He couldn't bear the thought of this

"My God, María, don't ever let me harm you. Kill me first if I try to. Promise me, my princess," he said.

She gently placed a finger over his lips, pressed her body up against his, and they came together in love on that settee. As two-in-one, they discovered paradise. Finally, spent by passion, their bodies parted, and they lay still, holding hands and looking up at the ceiling. He turned over and looked at her again, feasted his eyes on the soft curves of her body and her shapely breasts as he stroked her cheeks. Suddenly he thought of that other person he loved so much, but in a very different way: his little sister. He wondered about her. Why? There was something there at the back of his mind. Those blank periods — they had something to do with Chloe.

"Princess—I have to—Chloe—she's—I dunno—something's wrong—I have to know what's happening to her. Why? And how?"

"Adam, do you really not know what's happening? You were so weird earlier. And back there in the mall! Yuk! Don't you even remember doing what you did? And now you're banging on about Chloe again. What is up with you?"

Chloe?

That black cloud re-appeared and suffocated Adam. He gasped and coughed, then felt a pulling on his arm.

Chloe!

That's where he was. In the ball court, with Chloe frantically tugging at his arm as a spectator lunged at him with a knife. In an instant, the man was sent sprawling across the red earth, his knife knocked from his hand by Adam's swift response. At the same time, there was a screech of tyres as a red Austin-Healey sped into the arena, swung round in an arc and skidded to a halt yards from where Adam stood with his sister.

"Jump in!" shouted Jeannie.

Chloe hesitated.

"In!" insisted Adam, pushing her into the familiar vehicle after Jeannie had swung open the car door. He climbed in after her. Only just in time, for, as the car lurched forwards, Seven Death's club only just missed his head. The Austin-Healey raced out of the ball court, scattering bewildered spectators in its path.

"Chloe, remember Art and Jeannie? From San Antonio?"

His sister looked puzzled.

"Hi, Chloe!" Jeannie greeted.

"Where are we going? And how can we get out of this place?" Chloe asked.

"One question at a time, please," laughed Art.

It transpired that Chloe did remember Art and Jeannie, remembered them taking Adam and María for a ride downtown in San Antonio in the back of the Austin-Healey the day after the girl was offered her first recording contract, but she couldn't for the life of her work out what those two were doing in Xibalba. And with a vintage car, of all things. When Art explained that she and Adam had called them, she seemed none the wiser. Adam would have told her all about the Hero Twins of Mayan mythology, but they didn't have time. As if multiplying by the second, spectators poured forth from the ball court in pursuit, and had begun to spread out over the red hill, blocking their path to where they needed to get to: the great swing bridge to and from Xibalba.

The car bounced down the hill, away from the crowd, and on towards those grey stone buildings and frozen statues that Adam remembered so well; where Zotz, the bat God, had almost, but for Art and Jeannie, sucked out the *Life-Force* from himself and María, freezing them, in pain, for eternity.

Art came up with a plan. Adam felt bad because it involved himself and Chloe stripping off their tee-shirts, draping these over two of the statue-figures and lifting them into the Austin-Healey. Poor Chloe was left standing in her bra, but the plan made sense. Art started up the car's engine, slipped it into gear, leapt back and watched as it sped off towards to the mountains. The ant-trail of spectators bent and changed course towards the car and the mountains. They'd been fooled, and Art explained how he and Chloe would have to make their way to the bridge via the alternative route, through the underground tunnels of Xibalba, which they could only enter by raising the flagstone in the building ahead. The flagstone that Adam knew was also the resting place of Zotz.

A rapid fast forward, then Chloe said, out of the blue, they'd have to go back to the ball court for María. He had no idea what she was talking about until he learned of Coyote Spirit's plan to take his girl back to Xibalba and make her his queen. Adam stood speechless as he listened to his sister. That fire reignited inside him. He closed his eyes, disappearing into the fire, and María was there in their living-room back home. She looked terrified and his own body was slumped on the floor, his face bloodied. Art and Jeannie were there, too. That same dark cloud emerged from his broken body trying to drive him off, but it was weaker. He had to get to María, and he felt himself easily slip back into his body. The pain in his face and his neck was agony, and he could move neither arms nor legs. María appeared blurred through his hazed vision.

"María, what's happening? Where am I?" His voice sounded so faint.

"I love you!" María called, and her words echoed in his fast-emptying brain. He saw Art come towards him and knew the man was about to kill him. In a flash, he returned his body to the dark cloud in the knowledge that Coyote Spirit could now never take his María.

"She's not here in Xibalba," Adam said to Chloe on opening his eyes. She looked at him. She could read his mind and her face showed relief. Art and Jeannie stood beside her.

Adam opened his other eyes, the eyes of the man sitting in that cave with his son and the Old Woman. It was as if the movie had been switched off, but he remembered everything. He took hold of Pepe's hand and smiled at the boy.

"*My* son," he whispered.

The boy hugged him.

"I know that, Daddy."

"But Mama needs to know it. My poor princess. She thought—" Adam felt the eyes of the Old Woman of the Hills trying to tell him something. "It's over," he said. "This is just incredible! I'll call María on my mobile and tell her I remember everything. We'll go home tomorrow."

"If only it were that easy," the Old Woman said.

"What do you mean? I'm Pepe's father. I was there, in my own body, when we made love. Oh, my God, it was wonderful! Pepe comes from me, from our love. It's okay. Poor María has no reason to worry any longer."

"But you do," the Old Woman said.

Adam frowned.

"I don't understand. That's what was worrying her. That Pepe is the son of Coyote Spirit. That—"

"Because One Death has told her to kill the boy because of this," she interrupted. "That's why you have to worry now."

"One Death?" From the tone in his voice, Adam seemed to imply the Old Woman was crazy.

"Who was it who killed your other body there back in Houston just then?"

"Why, Art of course. He had to, to stop Coyote Spirit from—" He glanced anxiously at little Pepe. "From taking María."

232

"And who were you with back in Xibalba as soon as you escaped from your dying body?"

"Chloe and—" Adam stopped mid-sentence. "Art and Jeannie," he added slowly, staring at the Old Woman. "You mean—?"

"They want her, Adam. They want her in Xibalba. The two of them. They fooled Coyote Spirit into believing he could have her, but all along they've wanted her back. Ever since they saw her in that car after you'd gotten that spider venom for me. They knew she could never kill her own child. They knew she'd kill herself rather than do that. Then they would have her for all eternity. There's only one thing you can do now."

Chapter 21: Return to Xibalba

And when the Death Lords had gone to scour their land of dead souls for the one that really mattered in their old world, the coyote sat in the ball court and watched as a spectator, invisible and invincible. He had no interest in the other girl. How could he have? She was only a child when she died... Both times.

***

The Old Woman of the Hills stood up and hobbled across to the corner of the cave. She stooped to pick up something from the ground and returned to the table, placing a small knife in front of Adam.

"What's this?" the man asked.

"They should never have crossed over," she said. "Something happened there to allow them to do that. Like something between this world and Xibalba. The Lords of Xibalba shouldn't be able to cross over, but with Coyote Spirit entering your body something must have happened to enable this. María is no longer safe. Chloe neither. See, it was like this..." The Old Woman sat down again. "Once the Death Lords were men on Earth, just like you, Adam. Twin brothers. They were powerful men, great leaders, but they grew greedy and their greed allowed evil to enter their bodies. The Great Spirit had to banish them forever to the underworld, a place of trial between Earth and Paradise. But they took over. They made themselves the Lords of Xibalba. They became masters of fear, and of the Place of Fear, the testing ground for deceased spirits. You know the rest. And the difference you made."

"Why should *we* have made a difference?" Adam asked, unable to see what she was getting at.

"Your love, Adam. Yours and María's. And your love for your sister."

"So?"

"It'll have awakened their memories. Memories of a long-forgotten world. The world of Man. Somewhere, back there, they'll have known love, however evil they have now become. They'll have known its power, but of course now their very existence is to deny love and destroy it. Now they've felt its strength again. They want to capture it, hold onto it... and change it. Maybe their memories acted like a key to allow them back into your world, Coyote Spirit being the lock."

"And María?"

"Perhaps once there was a princess, a long time ago, in the world of Man, a princess so beautiful, so loving that she even stole the hearts of those twins."

"Princess Arima?"

"There's much even I can never know, Adam. But whatever went on in the distant past will make no difference to the future. The Lords of Xibalba are pure evil, they want María for themselves and for all eternity. María has not one shred of evil in her. Her Latin temper boils over sometimes, but only when she sees injustice being done. But those spectators in Xibalba are merely empty souls who have absorbed the evil of the place, become part of it. For María to end up there would be an eternity of torment for her. There's only one thing left for you to do, Adam." Adam stared into the Old Woman's depthless eyes. "Destroy One Death and Seven Death."

"Me?"

"You, Adam Winters!"

Adam looked at the small knife on the table.

"With that thing?" he asked.

"No, Adam. With your brain."

Adam glanced at Pepe.

"I'll help you, Papa," the boy said. "We must never let those nasty death men get to Mama!"

"Men? If only they were just men."

"The knife, Adam. It'll cut through anything but cannot kill the Lords of Xibalba. Not even the Golden

Jaguar of the Sun, nor the Hero Twins could do that. But you, Adam, *you* can. If you take the right path.”

“Path?”

“We’ll do it, Papa. We will!”

“We?”

“I have to come with you.”

“No, Pepe. You can’t.”

“I have to. Aunt Chloe knows why. Because of the other girl.”

“Your aunt is that other girl, Pepe.”

Pepe turned to face the Old Woman of the Hills.

“You understand, don’t you?” he asked. The woman nodded.

“Of course I do! Of all people, I should know of whom you speak. If only I could do it myself, but I can never go to Xibalba because of who I am. There, I would no longer exist.”

“I know,” said Pepe.

“But how will I know whether Art and Jeannie are the Hero Twins or the evil Death Lords if we meet them again?” Adam asked.

“It’s true that both can turn into your friends as you know them in your mind, Adam. Pepe, come here, my child.”

Pepe jumped from his seat and ran to the Old Woman who whispered something in his ear. The boy nodded, grinning.

“And don’t tell your Papa,” the Old Woman cajoled. Pepe shook his head. “He’ll know what to do, Adam,” she added.

“So, how—?”

“You’ve no time to lose. After all these years, suddenly it’s become urgent. They can no longer reach María through those dreams and she hasn’t yet returned to Xibalba. So, they’ll come for her. Somehow. You must return to Xibalba to stop them. By using the locket. Hold Pepe close to you, on your lap, and grip the locket tightly in your fist. Whatever happens, Adam, do not remove this from your neck. And think about María, Chloe, Pepe and little Carla. They'll give you strength. Your granny too. But your brain must do the rest. Meanwhile, I pray for you."

"Pray? To whom?"

The Old Woman looked at Pepe.

"He'll know," she smiled.

Pepe, so excited at the thought of helping his Papa save Mama, climbed up onto Adam's lap and put his arms around the man. Adam slipped the knife into his jeans belt. Both shut their eyes tight and the father closed his fingers around the golden locket that dangled from his neck and squeezed it. He thought of his beloved María, of Chloe and of his son and daughter, and he let himself free-fall into that incandescent white light that shone inside his mind.

***

"Papa?"

A small hand patted Adam's arm. He opened his eyes. He was sitting on a rock with Pepe on his lap.

"Who are those funny statue people?" Pepe asked, pointing to a group of stone figures with grotesque faces.

They were on the blue-yellow plain of shrunken souls near the Temple of Zotz.

"They never made it," Adam said. "They're the souls that never got to paradise. Those too," he added, indicating the myriads of blue and yellow 'flowers' stretching to the horizon.

"Mama's gonna go straight to paradise when she dies, isn't she?"

Adam was staring at the terror frozen onto the face of one of the statues.

"When the time comes, Pepe, yes. But not for a very long while if we can help it."

He tucked the locket back inside his tee-shirt and lifted Pepe down to the ground.

237

"I wish I didn't have to step on these souls," the boy said. "Does it hurt them, us walking all over them?"

"Pepe, that's all they are now. Hurt. Nothing but hurt left in them. So, I guess walking over them will make no difference."

"When can we kill those Death Lords?"

Adam smiled at his son's enthusiasm.

"Gotta find them first, son. But I've a pretty good idea where they'll be."

"The ball court? Aunt Chloe told me how to get there."

"She did, did she?" Adam said, still grinning. "She's some girl, that aunt of yours!"

"Yeah, and I know what she's doing right now. She's playing tag with Mama and Carla and the twins in the yard."

Adam laughed.

"We won't need to send them a post-card, then, Pepe. You can just tell Chloe what's happening here."

"Oh, I wouldn't do that. The Lords might get to Mama that way. Granny thinks they can reach her through me and Aunt Chloe."

"Can you reach Granny too, in that young head of yours?"

"Oh, I've always known Granny," the boy replied.

"So, show me the way, son."

"You have to go into the bat's house."

"Zotz?"

"Yeah! Aunt Chloe said you and Art lifted a flagstone and this took you into the tunnels. If you put your ear to the wall of a tunnel you can hear Mama singing. Her voice will lead us to the bridge, and the ball court's near the bridge."

"There is another way. Just beside that red hill over there. A short walk."

"No, Papa. We must find her. The girl. Aunt Chloe heard her. She was crying."

"Pepe, who are you talking about?"

"I love her. And so does the Old Woman."

Adam had to concede to his son's greater wisdom. For years, he'd wondered why everyone went on about María being 'special'. Now he understood. She was the mother of a very special child.

"Just hold onto me, son."

Adam took Pepe by the hand and led him to the temple of Zotz. They halted in the doorway, for the dark shadow of the bat god lay flat on the stone in front of the altar table with the map. Aware of their presence, the shadow changed shape.

"I just knew he hadn't been destroyed. Only weakened," said Pepe.

"Let us through, Zotz!" Adam demanded. "In the names of the Hero Twins, Hunahpu and Xbalanque, let us pass, and I'll spare you."

Pepe tugged at his father's arm. Adam looked down at him. The child beckoned with a small finger. He whispered something and Adam nodded. He let go of Pepe's hand, and crept round behind the altar. The boy now stood right in front of the flagstone. Adam's heart missed few beats as he watched the shadow of the bat arise from the ground, expanding and turning solid as it did so. His son stood still until his father gave the 'sign', then Pepe put his thumb to his nose, wiggled his fingers and stuck out his tongue at Zotz. Angered red eyes sprang to life in that black bat face and Adam immediately jumped out from behind the altar and plunged the Old Woman's knife deep into the back of the creature. An ear-splitting scream filled the room. Adam, slashed downwards, carving a deep gash. Like thick blood, *Life-Force* poured from the wound, and Adam jumped back, wiping the knife on his jeans. He grabbed Pepe's arm and pulled him to one side, and together they watched the monster shrink down to the size of a football. Still black, its edges became blurred, fuzzy, like a small dark cloud suspended above the flagstone, but the gash remained, and the stinking red fluid continued to flow from it. The screaming stopped. Adam realised the flagstone would soon be covered, and the whole building would fill with *Life-Force* which, by now, was tipping out of the doorway and forming a stream over the blue-yellow carpet of shrunken souls outside.

"Quick!" he said to Pepe, attempting to lift the flagstone. But it wouldn't budge. Not even when he put every ounce of strength that he had into it.

"Papa, you're not doing what the world's granny told you," Pepe said. Adam, panting, looked up at his son. "Think about Mama!"

Adam closed his eyes and cleared his mind. María was there, alone, in his mind, and she was singing from her latest album, singing of love, of past happiness, of sorrow and sadness, and he reached out to her with his own hankering love, and he pulled on the stone. Slowly, it moved. Up, up, up — and then to the side. With a thud, it fell to the floor, splashing *Life-Force* over his jeans. Adam gathered his son in his arms and slipped though the opening, climbing down the steps into the tunnel below. Once down he ran on, carrying Pepe, as a slow waterfall of congealing red goo tipped down the steps behind him. He didn't stop running until he was well clear of the entrance, and until he saw illumination ahead. Pepe, grinning, raised his right hand and Adam high fived with the boy before lowering him to the ground.

"Now put your ear to the wall," Pepe told his father.

Adam did as he was told, and to his amazement he heard María's voice.

"Can you hear Mama?"

"Sure. But how do you know these things?"

"Aunt Chloe told me. And you were here with her last time."

"Yeah! The rest of that movie, I guess!"

"You missed the best bit, Papa!"

"Tell me later. So, I follow Mama's voice. Right? And that takes us to—?"

"To the bridge. Near the ball court. But last time you went a different way. See, there was a great big snake. The Snake Goddess. Only it was the spectators she was after 'cos you were with this lizard guy who protected you. Snakes and lizards are cousins, see. And you were prisoners in a cage till the snake came along."

Adam took his son's hand and they walked on towards the strange light.

"What else happened that different way?" he asked.

"You and Aunt Chloe and the lizard guy and a sad lady—-on-the-Corn, or something—you had to follow an underground river till y'all came out on the side of a cliff."

"*The* cliff?"

"Yeah! The one that drops down for ever and ever and you never reach the bottom if you fall off. 'Hell', Aunt Chloe says."

"Sounds great, Pepe!" His son knew he hated heights.

"You made it okay the last time, Papa."

"Maybe this time I'll just follow the sound of Mama's voice, eh? Might come out closer to the ball court."

"Yeah! That's where the spectators take the people they pick up. The other Xibalbans either hide from the spectators or they try to reach the bridge. Yuk! That knife stinks, Papa! So do your jeans!"

"I think Mama will be busy washing my clothes when we get back, huh?" Adam imagined himself arriving at Tio Federico's, and boarding the plane, still wearing blood-soaked jeans.

"You could wash them in the river."

"Good idea, son! Show me the way."

They passed underneath the lofty sky-lights which gave the tunnel its strange luminescence, then on into the market place, now empty...

Voices!

Adam stopped. He drew his knife. Half a dozen spectators, armed with clubs, appeared ahead, silhouetted in the dim light. They halted and stared at Adam and Pepe.

Two shouted something unintelligible, raised their clubs and ran at them, but froze just feet from where Adam and Pepe stood.

"Let us pass," Adam said calmly.

"Let you pass," repeated the two spectators together, in English, as if in a trance, their faces aglow from the fire in Adam's eyes. They remained motionless as father and son walked on. The other four spectators shrank back against the wall, fearful of Adam.

"Let you pass," they echoed.

Adam and the boy walked on, unmolested, as the spectators stood back, stock-still.

"Hey, Papa, that was so cool!"

"Keep moving, Pepe," Adam whispered.

They came to a fork in the tunnel. Adam put his ear to the wall, smiled at his son, and continued walking.

"She's singing one of Carla's favourites," he said.

"Will Carla become famous too, one day?"

"Whether that's a 'yes' or a 'no', she still has the prettiest little voice in Texas."

"Over there, Papa!"

Pepe pointed to a low opening in the side of the tunnel.

"Must be one of the holes that lead down to the river. You can wash off that horrible red stuff."

Adam realised that the sight and smell of *Life-Force* on his jeans and tee-shirt upset Pepe. He stooped under the overhang of the side tunnel, keeping a hand on his son's shoulder. He heard the rush of water in the distance, getting closer as they edged forwards.

"Yuk!" cried Pepe. He'd stopped and was flailing his arms about as if they were caught in something. Adam reached out in the dark. His hand brushed a thick, sticky steel-like rope. He grabbed Pepe and pulled the boy free.

"It's her!" he cried.

Holding Pepe's arm, he turned and hurried back towards the dim light of the main tunnel.

"Who? It can't be the girl," Pepe called out, but Adam didn't reply. A dark shape filled the entrance, blocking their return to the main tunnel, cutting out all light. It moved quickly towards them, legs wavering like branches in a wind, feeling the way. It stopped and spoke, and its voice was deep and grating. The language, Adam understood, though it wasn't English or Spanish. He saw the creature's face, illuminated, saw the red-tipped fangs, the multi-faceted eyes with their many points of bright yellow light: his own reflected eyes.

"They told me I'd find you again, one day. Down here. You cheated me out of that juicy girl, so rich in *Life-Force*. Not this time, though! You're both mine now, you and her child. And when you're nicely bound and wrapped up, you can watch me suck out the boy's *Life-Force* first. I'll give you that little bit of pleasure before I get to work on your own miserable carcass."

There was a burst of light and the great spider turned her head to the side to avoid its intensity, scraping her foul body backwards, for a few yards, over the rough ground.

"Cheat, huh?" roared Adam. "I gave you a chance. A chance of happiness in paradise, but you chose greed instead. Greed and deceit. I warned you not to strike my single eye."

"Not your single eye! You have two."

"Back then you thought it was. That's what matters. This is the end of the road for you, Spider Goddess!"

The spider shot forwards, unable to pounce within the confines of the tunnel. Adam was too quick for her. In a fraction of a second, he had the knife in his hand, and with two swift slashes had cut through the creature's front legs causing her to slump forwards onto her hideous face. He picked up one of her cut-off legs, still twitching, and poked the spiked end into first one eye of the spider, pushing and twisting, and then another and another, until all her eyes were put out. The spider, blinded, growled:

"You cheat again, sapless human. I'll destroy you and the boy, if it's the last thing I do. You'll never get past my fangs. I'll suck out your *Life-Force*, grow new eyes and become stronger than ever before."

Her hollow scimitar fangs, useless without eyes to guide them, stabbed at empty space. Adam leapt onto her back, avoiding the other six jerking legs, thrust his knife downwards into the spider's neck, pulled it to the left and to the right, again and again, until the head, still growling, "stinking cheat—human scum—", fell, severed, to the ground.

"You—!" the bodiless head exclaimed, then no more words emerged. Beheaded the Xibalban way, the Great Spider Goddess had been forever silenced.

When Adam looked at his son, the boy's face beamed in the light of his eyes.

"Awesome, Papa!" Pepe exclaimed. "Your eyes are all shiny and bright. They're like little suns! Can I do that?"

Adam laughed.

"Let's hope you'll never need to. Come, I must clean myself up."

He jumped down from the back of the dead spider, hacked a hole through the steel cable web, and together they backtracked to the river where they drank, refreshed themselves and Adam washed his jeans and tee-shirt. Pepe suggested his dad get a transfer made for the tee-shirt with *I killed the Great Spider Goddess!* written on it, but his father persuaded him this wasn't a great idea.

"It would upset Mama," he said.

"Yeah, guess so," agreed the child. "She still has bad nightmares about the giant spider jumping onto you when you had that funny hat on."

"She told you that?"

"Nope! I just know it!"

It seemed strange to Adam to see in Pepe what he'd gotten so used to in Chloe. What was so striking with both his sister and his son was the almost casual way each just accepted that extraordinary clairvoyant gift. For them, it meant little more than being able to hear, see or smell things. It truly was another sense.

Now clean, but cold and soaked, Adam led Pepe back, through the slashed spider web and over the dead monster, to the main tunnel. His eyes still shone like torches, and this light helped them hurry on their way. Further on, there were doors on either side of the tunnel, but they were all shut. Adam had the impression the place was abandoned, until Pepe suddenly halted and tugged at his arm.

"What is it?" he asked, looking down at the boy.

"In there!" said Pepe.

The boy turned and pointed at a door a few paces back.

"What's in there, Pepe? There's no one here. The place is deserted."

"The girl. The one I love. In there. I can feel her. She's crying."

Adam walked back to the door and put his ear to it. All he heard was the voice of his wife singing from another world somewhere ahead of them.

"Pepe, it's just your imagination."

"It's not, it's not!" Pepe seemed very upset. "I don't need to imagine things, anyway. Open the door, Papa!"

Adam really did not want to waste time, but to ignore his son would have been foolish. He pushed at the door, but it was bolted fast on the inside. He shouted for whoever was on the other side to open the door, but nothing happened. Finally, he pulled out his knife and plunged it into the thick wood. It was like stabbing into butter. Quickly, he sliced out a large chunk of door, and peered in. His eyes lit up the room, and there, crouching in one corner, hiding her face from him, was a young Native girl, much the same age as Pepe. He recognised her straightaway. Pepe pushed past his father and ran to the girl.

"It's okay," he said to the other child, hugging her trembling body. "I'm here for you. And my dad's a good man. He won't harm you."

"What language is that?" Adam asked his son.

"Don't know, Papa. It's her language, anyways."

"What's her name? Ask her, Pepe."

Pepe didn't need to ask her.

"This time it's Mountain Flower, Papa."

Adam frowned. *Must have been mistaken,* he reckoned.

"And why—?"

"She doesn't know. She's been waiting for hundreds of years. She only knows that she's frightened, Papa. Of the spider and the people with the clubs and—" Pepe stroked the girl's tangled hair when she began to cry in his arms. "She's afraid of the giant red men."

"The Lords of Xibalba!" Adam muttered. "Tell her to come with us. We'll take her to the bridge. From there she can get to paradise. Join her mommy and daddy and never be afraid again. Take her by the hand, Pepe. She'll trust you. I'm sure she will."

Pepe helped Mountain Flower to her feet, and the girl clung to him as a drowning person would cling to a life belt. They stepped out into the tunnel, and Pepe and his new friend ran along beside Adam as they journeyed on, round bends, sometimes climbing up steep gradients, then dipping down again, deeper and deeper into the earth. The child had stopped crying, but whenever Adam turned to look at her, he saw only fear on that small face. There was no sign that she remembered him, so he must have been wrong. but there again he had grown into a man since then. She had large brown eyes, just like Carla's, and if it hadn't been for the terror in those eyes, and the dirt smeared on her cheek and forehead, she'd have been as pretty as a picture. From the look of concentration on Pepe's face, he could only guess that his son was talking to the girl inside his head as if she too had sixth sense.

They came to another fork in the tunnel. Adam tried one wall, then the other. He raised both thumbs at his son.

"This way, guys," he said, and they ran on. From there, the tunnel only climbed. It became brighter, not from Adam's eyes but from a reddish glow ahead. Adam warned Pepe and Mountain Flower to stay back when they neared an arched opening on the hillside. He held his knife at the ready.

Soon, they stood alone on the red hill, equidistant between the ball court and the bridge the top of which was just visible above the brow of the hill. The bottom of the red hill merged with the blue and yellow plain, and there was a cruel beauty about the plain and the grey sky hanging over it. Indeed, there was something both wondrous and fearsome about the whole of Xibalba. Would María yet become queen of this place? A queen shared by two evil kings who could turn themselves into whatever they wished. Perhaps into whatever she wished for, too? Himself, even. Would she 'live' here for eternity with a pair of evil Adams?

He looked back at the children. Mountain Flower suddenly gasped and hid behind Pepe. The boy laughed and told her not to worry.

"Papa was only thinking of Mama," he reassured the girl. "He felt angry when he thought about what they might do to her here and that makes his eyes light up. It's the Golden Jaguar inside him, see! His totem animal."

Yes, Pepe. That she will understand.

"Do not let go of Mountain Flower's hand, Pepe," Adam warned. "We're going in!"

Mountain Flower shook her head when Pepe tried to explain to her what his father was planning to do. Her eyes were like little pockets of alarm. Gradually the boy managed to calm her down. In her own language, he told her how his dad had killed the bat god, Zotz, and the Great Spider Goddess, and that he had a strength, a good strength called 'Love' back on Earth, because of his Mama, and that not even the Lords of Xibalba could overcome him now. Pepe reassured Mountain Flower that his father would destroy One Death and Seven Death and that he would lead her to paradise.

Adam had discovered that he understood every word his young son spoke to the girl when he held his granny's locket. He felt proud of the boy. Pepe was showing this Native child the greatest love of all: love for a stranger.

Or was she? But for her name, this had to be the girl whose spirit Chloe had sought for so long. Younger, perhaps, but her all the same.

"It's okay, Papa," Pepe said. "She can't wait to see her mommy and daddy again."

Adam smiled at the girl and she beamed back at him, but he felt saddened that these two children would never be able to become friends back on Earth.

With Pepe and Mountain Flower beside him, Adam walked on towards the ball court. Pepe, who must have read his father's mind, told him the girl's story:

"She became separated from her parents when they all died in an earthquake. It happened in the middle of the night. The ground opened and most their house, with her parents in it, was swallowed by the ground. A pile of stones had fallen on top of Mountain Flower, and she was trapped at the edge of a big hole and her legs hurt something awful. She cried and screamed all night long, and she tried to think what she'd done wrong to make Earth Mother, her real mother, so angry." Pepe paused and looked up at his father.

Her real mother? This must be the same child! But the story's wrong.

"She shouldn't have done that to her own child, should she?" the boy questioned. Adam shrugged his shoulders. "Then the ground started jumping about again and there were lots of horrible noises, but most of the stones on top of her fell into the hole. She tried to crawl away. She said she couldn't crawl far because her legs wouldn't move properly. They were broken and hurt a lot. She tried to pull herself along with her arms, but never got far. Just lay there the rest of the night, exhausted and too weak to call out. After the Sun God had woken up and climbed high in the sky, she could see that there was nothing left of her village. Just rubble. She called out again, but she says her voice was so weak not even a mouse would have heard her. Besides, there was no one else left alive, she was sure of it. She says it was so quiet, even her breathing sounded loud. The Sun God beat down on her broken body, and she wondered what on earth she'd done to anger him as well. She prayed to him and to Earth Mother, and she prayed for rain to cool her body, and for food to give her strength, but nothing happened, and she got weaker and weaker."

Adam looked at the girl and she smiled again.

I know it's her! Why does she say nothing?

"For two days and two nights, she lay there until life fell away from her body and she found herself here. At first, she searched for her parents, but she knew this wasn't paradise and that she'd have to somehow get there for her to ever see them again."

"Is she Mayan?" Adam asked.

Pepe spoke to the girl.

"Yes," she replied. "But before she was something else. In another life."

Of course! Why didn't I think of re-incarnation?

"She knew Lizard-by-the-Water and Rain-on-the-Corn," Pepe said, "but they disappeared a while back."

"Who are they?"

"You really don't remember, Papa?"

"Nope!"

"Guess you never got to that part of the movie either. You and Aunt Chloe escaped to the bridge with them. Aunt Chloe thinks they went on to paradise."

Pepe turned to Mountain Flower:

"You'll meet up again with your mommy and daddy in paradise, I know it."

As they approached the entrance to the ball court, Adam heard a familiar noise behind him. The chug of a vintage car engine. With an arm around each child, he turned and watched as the red Austin-Healey bounced over the red earth towards them. Even from a distance, he could make out the flaming red hair and beard of Art, and the perpetual smile on Jeannie's face. But who were this Art and Jeannie? From what he'd seen in that 'movie', in Xibalba there was no way of telling. In Texas, too, perhaps?

"I'll find out, Papa," Pepe said, aware of his father's concern.

The car bumped over the rough ground and came to a halt a few yards from Adam and the children. Jeannie waved happily, jumped from the vehicle and came running towards them. Art followed at a more leisurely pace, swinging his club.

"Where's María?"

Why should Jeannie ask about María? Adam's face felt the heat of the fire in his eyes as he gripped the knife. He remained frozen to the spot whilst the woman hugged Pepe and Mountain Flower. She held her arms out wide for Adam. "Adam?" she queried, concern evident in her cheerful face, but he remained rooted to the spot.

Art came up and ruffled Pepe's hair.

"Good job he's gotten María's looks," he joked. "Carla too, by all accounts. And her mother's voice. Remember that song of hers back in San Antonio, Jeannie? The one you loved so much. Adam had to translate the Spanish for us."

The way they spoke, moved, smiled—everything thing about them—informed Adam that these were his true friends from Iowa. And yet—

"How did it go, Jeannie? '*Your hands caress my soul with Love—*' or something? What was it, now?"

Jeannie helped him out.

"'*Your hands caress my soul with Love like the gentle breeze of dawn... Your voice gives me strength like the wind sifting through the trees... Your kisses... erm... your kisses trace words of happiness on my lips as I yield my Love to your body and to your soul...*'"

"Well remembered, Jeannie. Look—" began Art. It seemed as if Art and Jeannie were warier of Adam than the other way around. They held back.

"Your little boy — what was his name?" Pepe asked Art.

"They never had a little boy," Adam muttered through his teeth.

"Yes, we did," said Jeannie, her smile gone.

"Luke," Art added. "Name was Luke. Died after three days. Never gotten that chance to get to know the little fella."

"He'll be in paradise, now, won't he?" Pepe asked.

"Wait a minute—" Adam was puzzled. Something didn't make sense.

"They're the right Art and Jeannie," his son announced. "See, Papa, that bit about the boy, the Old Woman told me in the cave. You didn't know that, so it wasn't in your head. One Death and Seven Death could never have known if it wasn't in your head."

"So, you two are Hunahpu and Xbalanque as well? But how did you know about Art and Jeannie having a son who died if I didn't know? After all, you found Art and Jeannie there in my head when I first came here with María."

Art grinned from ear-to-ear when he winked at the boy.

"Let's just say a certain little person told me. Okay?"

"It was kinda like sending an e-mail in my head, but only to the Hero Twins' mailbox," explained Pepe. "The Old Woman's idea. Her mommy." The boy looked sideways at Mountain Flower.

Earth Child's real mommy? The Old Woman of the Hills? Earth Mother? Adam shook his head in disbelief. His son never ceased to surprise and confuse him.

"Another ride in my old beauty?" suggested Art, opening the car door for Adam and the children. "I'm gonna miss her when you're gone for good from here, Adam. Mind you, I have an identical one back on your place. Earth."

Adam climbed in after Pepe and Mountain Flower. Art and Jeannie got in the front and the big man started up the engine. Even from a distance, Adam could hear the shouting and jeering of spectators in the ball court.

"So, it wasn't you who killed Coyote Spirit?"

"Nope. Indeed not! You were kind of doing that already, Adam. By the strength of your will. Only trouble is, you were being pulled in two directions. By your love for your wife and your love for your sister. But for you, Chloe would have perished here all alone. You know, learnin' from what you did gave us more strength."

"Papa?"

Adam was thinking about María and how scarily close he must have been to losing her to Coyote Spirit. How bizarre it was that One Death had killed the man out of greed to have her for himself. The Old Woman was right. The Lords of Xibalba had been his greatest threat all along. But one thing puzzled him. Having killed Coyote Spirit, why didn't One Death just kill María? Then he recalled reading once, way back, that only folk who died naturally ended up in Xibalba. There again, how come killing Coyote Spirit had landed the dog in Xibalba. Easy, his brain told him: for the Anasazi man's totem animal, being killed by another animal (him) could be 'natural'.

"Papa?"

"Pepe?"

"Papa, can Mountain Flower come back with us? She wants to, and I'd like her to. I don't think she was meant to have died in that earthquake anyways. It's what her real mother wants, I know it. Because of me."

Adam looked at the girl's large, questioning brown eyes, and he wondered what on earth she would make of present-day Houston.

"We'll let the bridge decide, huh?" he replied.

The Austin-Healey burst through the entrance to the ball court, skidding into the arena after Art slammed the brakes. The noise of the crowd stopped. It was like turning off a blaring radio. The ball game players halted. Someone spotted Adam, recognized him and broke the silence by shouting something to the other players. The players of both teams, abandoning their game of death, ran towards the car as Adam stepped out.

"Look after the kids," he said to Art.

The players surrounded Adam, lifted him onto their shoulders, yelling and punching the air, as they carried him over to a large man with a feathered headdress, who wielded a knife. The ball game 'overseer', Adam reckoned. With eyes of fire, Adam only had to look at the Native guy, and the other man, fearful, scrambled over a wall behind him, falling amongst the spectators who backed away from the edge of the arena when Adam approached. The players lowered him to the ground.

"One Death and Seven Death!" Adam called out in Mayan. "We'll finish that ball game now, if you dare! The last ever ball game in Xibalba!"

Silence.

Adam and the players stood in a group to the side of the vast ball court and waited. The crowd, now uncertain, waited as well. The thrill of the ball game was all they knew. Now this visitor with the flaming eyes talked of ending it all. He, the beast with eyes of fire that had been killed by the coyote, had returned, and was now challenging the great Lords of Xibalba. As before, he had joined with the players from opposing sides. The spectators just stood and stared whilst, slowly, the red ground at each end of the court rippled, changed and took shape. Two vast red rubber figures rose up from the earth, one with a single feather sticking up from the back of his head, the other with seven. Each carried a club the size of a redwood.

"It's Death against Love, One Death and Seven Death!" Adam called out, firmly gripping his granny's locket. "And here we all stand together. We play for Love, not Death." With a sweep of his hand he indicated his loyal group of players. "You're on your own, you two! The spectators are too cowardly to move!"

"It'll be less painful for you if you let us take you now, thing!" roared One Death.

Adam recalled their previous taunts, belittling him as 'thing' in front of María. Then, they'd fired his anger by reminding him of Spike, in middle school, teasing him with taunts of 'Snowflake!' He glanced back at the car to check on the children. Art was out, beside the vehicle, holding his own club, and he too had grown enormous.

"Come and get the ball! See what you can do, you little red rubber puppets!"

Adam took the ball, a head with sightless eyes, and ran with it towards Seven Death, followed by a stream of players, whilst others stepped back to block One Death. Seven Death swung his club in the air, smashing it down onto the ground, missing Adam by inches. Adam darted off with two players in a different direction, whilst a group of players encircled one of Seven Death's legs, and struck his foot repeatedly with their own clubs. He staggered backwards, and swung his club again, sending one of the men sprawling onto the red dust. By stepping sideways, he prevented Adam from reaching the stone ring. Again, Adam dodged the club, and ran back to join his teammates, helping the stricken man to his feet. They huddled together as Adam spoke to them in a whisper, then fell apart. It reminded Pepe, who was watching from the car, of American Football on television.

Half of Adam's team charged at One Death, the other half at Seven Death. Meanwhile Adam ran, keeping the ball in the air with different parts of his body, first in one direction, then another, weaving in and out of his teammates. The Lords of Xibalba became confused as they tried to work out not only where Adam was, but in which direction he was travelling, at the same time fighting off incessant attacks from the players darting around their lumbering feet.

Suddenly Adam stopped. Several spectators had climbed into the court and now encircled the Austin-Healey. Art was whirling his club at them, fending them off, but two had crept round the other side of the car and grabbed Mountain Flower. She started to scream, the most harrowing sound Adam had ever heard. He dropped the ball, pulled out his knife and ran at them. He slashed straight through the arm of the one holding Mountain Flower, before flinging the man to the side. The other man fled. Adam looked back. The ball had gone. It was in the hands of a spectator who'd taken off with it in the direction of Seven Death. Just before Adam could reach the man and prevent him from passing the ball to the monster, he saw the Xibalban Death Lord reach down and pull something up from the ground: a net of steel cord. In a split second the net was over Adam, and he was being dragged, helpless, over the rough ground. The man with the ball watched, laughing and jeering. A quick pass of the ball to Seven Death, and it would have all been over, but the man, too jubilant in his own glory, lost that vital fraction of a second.

As in karate! Adam thought.

By circling his knife above his head, he cut a hole in the net, through which he leapt, clinging onto its cables. Like a monkey, he climbed up onto Seven Death's hand and up along his arm to his shoulder. In a panic, the spectator flung the ball in the direction of Seven Death. Adam launched himself into the air, caught the ball, somersaulted with it firmly in his grasp, and, behind Seven Death and well out of reach of the creature's club, he knocked the ball straight through stone ring. It was all over and had been so easy.

Like excited kangaroos, the players jumped with joy. They cheered. Then a most extraordinary thing happened. Most, if not all, of the spectators joined in. It seemed their allegiance had switched on seeing the invincibility of their Lords thus challenged. More jumped down into the ball court and swarmed around One Death and Seven Death, preventing the Death Lords from reaching their champion. Adam ran back to the car.

"Cool one, Papa!" Pepe exclaimed as his father climbed into the Austin-Healey.

"Look after Mountain Flower," Adam said. "The worst is yet to come!"

Art started up the engine.

"Tell me one thing!" Adam shouted back at the struggling Lords of Xibalba. "How did you get back to my world to kill Coyote Spirit? They say you can never leave Xibalba.

The spectators went still. It wasn't over. Their taste for blood and death was still there, ingrained in their trapped souls.

"Let's say we took a piggy-back ride on a defeated, love-sick Adam Winters. We knew you'd go back to her. To try to stop Coyote Spirit from taking her."

"Well," shouted Adam, "how about another ride! Go for it, Art!"

Art slammed his foot down on the accelerator and the car shot towards the exit. Adam turned, just in time to see the Lords of Xibalba changing. Not shrinking but changing shape into one of the fastest of animals in North America: the mountain lion, each the size of the Golden Jaguar.

"Faster, faster," Adam urged as they sped up the red hill towards the beckoning arch of the Bridge of Xibalba, part-enshrouded by mist.

"Ain't no mountain lion ever had a six-litre engine like this little beauty," joked Art.

Adam looked back. The players had formed a tiered semi-circle around the entrance of the ball court, effectively caging in the mountain lions. He knew it wouldn't last for long, and the Austin-Healey began to chug and splutter as it approached the top of the hill. Adam saw the human cage collapse as players tumbled from friends' shoulders. Two gigantic red cats sprang over them and on up the hill in the direction of the car. Art stopped the vehicle.

"Run!" he shouted after Adam had collected the children from the vehicle and taken off towards the crest of the hill, a child dangling from each arm. Art and Jeannie climbed out, no longer as Art and Jeannie but the Hero Twins, resplendent in colourful, feathered headdresses and tunics, and they met the red mountain lions head on as the beasts bounded up the hill towards Adam and the children.

Adam ran down the short slope to the steps leading to the bridge, scaled the steps three at a time and lowered the children underneath the arch.

"You go on ahead," he said to Pepe. "And keep hold of Mountain Flower's hand."

The boy, grinning, followed instructions and ran with the girl into the mist.

"I really do hope you'll come home with us," Adam had overheard his son tell the girl in the car. "I don't think you're meant to go to paradise yet. Because you're special as well."

Adam waited for One Death and Seven Death, merely slowed down by the Hero Twins, to catch up. He wanted them to follow him onto the bridge. He was their willing bait. He shouted out to Art to let them pass, then he ran after Pepe and Mountain Flower over the bridge into the mist. The only sound was the chatter of his son's voice ahead. He slowed down and walked on in the wake of that voice, clutching his knife in one hand and gripping his grandmother's locket in the other. The light from his eyes cast an eerie glow into the haze. Suddenly, he felt a change in the swing of the bridge. Something, or things, had gotten onto the bridge behind him. A great weight was making him bounce like a baby in a baby bouncer. Despite this, he speeded up.

"Hurry on ahead!" he called out to Pepe. "They're closing in behind me!"

He heard the children's running steps grow fainter, and he ran to catch up. The jolting of the bridge increased. He heard breathing behind him. He was acutely aware of the bottomless drop below, sharpened by his fear of heights. He turned, and through the mist he could make out the looming red shape of One Death, now in human form, gaining on him with vast strides. He prayed he hadn't miscalculated the timing. What if they were to take his body and pass on into the world of man together with Pepe and his little friend to claim María forever and destroy her son, the chosen one, plus the daughter of Earth Mother?

At last, through the mist, he could make out the arch at the other end of the bridge.

"Get off the bridge! Quick!" Adam shouted to the children.

"You're too late, thing!" One Death called from only a few yards away.

"Am I?" said Adam. He stopped and gripped the steel railing. Using the Old Woman's knife, he slashed through first one cable, then the other. The bridge swayed crazily. One Death halted and held on. Adam, grabbing the other end of the cable, pulled himself backwards.

"Princess Arima needs us, Adam Winters. We're real men. She'll want us to satisfy her for all time. You wouldn't deny her such eternal pleasure, would you? Not if you really love her!"

One Death's taunts had the reverse effect. Instead of weakening, Adam's eyes blazed like an exploding star. With a phenomenal surge of strength, he turned and ran on under the arch. Once he was off the bridge, his knife turned into raw anger, hacking through the boards and supports of the bridge as if they were made from cardboard. One Death and Seven Death were within feet of the arch, and firm ground, when the bridge gave way, swept downwards by the weight of the Death Lords. He watched them struggle to hold onto the cables as it disappeared into the mist below, and he heard deep, muffled screams as each lost his grip on the bridge and was sent plunging into oblivion. Their seemingly eternal reign of fear in Xibalba had come to an end.

Adam ran from the mist and down the steps to join his son. The girl stood serene, beside the boy, holding his hand, and smiling. Adam smiled back at the child.

"So, the bridge made the choice!" he said. "The right one for sure, judging by the look on your face, Pepe."

Chapter 22: Earth Mother's Orphan...

"She's gone!" someone behind him shouted.

Coyote Spirit looked up. A spectator stood at the entrance to the ball court. Red stuff, called 'blood' in the old place, trickled down his face from a gaping gash on his forehead.

"So have they!" added another spectator.

The coyote, indistinguishable from those around him, felt his lips curl a smile as other Xibalbans re-entered the ball court from the red hill outside.

"Never mind the child. Tell them to come back! What fun will the ball game be without our lords?" asked someone standing below the coyote.

"Bring them back? How? The bridge has gone and so have they." The coyote's grin broadened, and all his sharp teeth showed. "How indeed?" he whispered.

***

Adam ran with the children through the tunnel in the mountain ahead, then out into the *Forest Without Time*. The path wound between huge furry fern trees, past giant fan-shaped leaves and luxuriant bushes studded with colourful flowers. They passed strange creatures, many fearsome, but Adam paid no head to their savage stares for he knew that he was Lord of this forest. They reached a clearing from which five paths disappeared into the undergrowth, and Adam stopped, uncertain which to take.

"The locket, Papa! Use your granny's locket!"

Adam grasped the locket and felt himself being drawn towards one particular path. They followed this path until there was light ahead. On leaving the forest, they were confronted by a steep hillside and a narrow continuation of the path led to a cave. A cave that, by now, seemed almost like home to Adam.

"Keep hold of my hand, Mountain Flower," Pepe said in English. "You'll be okay. The Old Woman's very nice. I'm sure you'll like her. After all, she is your true mother."

Adam followed the children up the slope.

"You spoke English to her," he said to Pepe.

"Yeah! I can't seem to speak that funny language any more. But I can think things as I speak, and she seems to understand me."

"Guess she'll have to stay with Cousin Jorge and Anna when we get home. So that she can learn English." Anna, Jorge's Mayan wife, was now totally fluent in English.

"Oh no!" protested Pepe. "She has to stay with us. Mama and I will look after her and I'll teach her English. I know what she's thinking most of the time. Anyway, Anna's having another baby. She'll be far too busy! And she doesn't speak ancient Mayan, anyway. Or that other language Mountain Flower used to speak before."

As spoken by the ancient Anasazi?

That Anna was pregnant was news to Adam. He knew nothing about yet another little López. But Pepe was right. Mountain Flower would have to stay with them, but not with a name like that. Nor as Earth Child.

"How do you know Anna doesn't understand ancient Mayan?" he asked Pepe.

"Oh, I just do."

They reached the ledge in front of the cave, and the Old Woman of the Hills was there already, standing at the mouth of the cave, leaning forwards on her curved stick.

"Pepe told me you were coming," she said. "And about Mountain Flower, too. What a pretty little thing you've become, my dear child. It's been so long, I'd forgotten how lovely you are." She stroked the child's ruffled black hair. "Need a bit of a tidy-up before you go out there, huh?" she added, gently running the back of her gnarled hand across Mountain Flower's muddied cheeks and forehead. In an instant, the girl's face was clean, her hair sleek and shiny. Nothing astounded Adam any longer.

"It's done," he said, returning the knife to the Old Woman.

"Of course," she said. "Couldn't have been otherwise. Ain't nothing stronger than that love inside you, Adam Winters. From the Princess. And all because of Pepe."

Pepe? So, my son's the 'special one' after all?

"Are you really like Pepe said?" Adam looked down at the golden locket hanging round his neck.

"The world's grandma? Is it true, you're asking?"

The man nodded, and the Old Woman laughed.

"I'm what you wish me to be, Adam."

Adam lifted the locket, as if to remove it and hand it to the woman, but she held up her hand.

"Keep it," she insisted. "One day, Chloe might need it for her work. Pepe too." She turned to face the boy. "So," she said him, "you're just like your Papa, huh? You, too, have a princess. A little princess *and* a friend."

Pepe looked happily at Mountain Flower and softly squeezed her hand. She smiled back at him when she knew, from the words he spoke inside her head, that she'd been called a princess.

"Go back to her, Adam. To *your* princess. Go back, and never again be afraid for her. Her time to return to the place she came from is a very long way off. Longer than yours, but she'll know that you'll wait for her there when your time comes 'cause that's how it is with you two."

"And Chloe? Her work?"

"Another story, Adam. A whole other story. As for—" The Old Woman looked down at Pepe and Mountain Flower who still held hands. "As for that story, it's only just beginning. Because of Princess Arima. Santa María. That's how it has to be, this time. Two children. Mine and hers."

"What about the Hero Twins? Art and Jeannie? What'll happen to them, now?" Adam feared he had stranded his two friends in Xibalba by destroying the bridge.

"Like you, they've done their bit in Xibalba. They can get on with just being Art and Jeannie. For your wife's sake. And they're not the only angels back there in my world, you know."

Angels, thought Adam?

For a few moments, he stood reluctant to leave the Old Woman, the 'world's granny', or whosoever she might be, for something was telling him he would never see her again.

"Go, Adam. She needs you. Don't waste time here in Mexico."

Adam turned and peered over the ledge, down the slope. The Forest had gone. Tio Federico's car was there, in the lay-by at the bottom of the hill, and slumped asleep in the back seat was Conchita. He looked at the Old Woman, held out his arms and gave her a hug, and in that brief contact, he felt her warmth, her strength and her love. She hugged the children, turned and walked back into the cave. At the precise moment when she disappeared, so did the cave entrance. The man stared at a bare rock face. There was nothing to indicate that there had ever been a cave.

"That was my real mommy," Mountain Flower said in perfect English and in a matter-of-fact sort of way.

Earth Mother... Earth Child?

Adam shrugged his shoulders and glanced at his watch. The minute hand had moved on only ten minutes from when he and Pepe had left the car to climb the path up to the cave. Following the same path down to the road, he repeatedly turned around to make sure Mountain Flower was still there and that it hadn't all been a ridiculous dream. Thank God, the Mayan-Anasazi child was still holding onto Pepe's hand. Both children knew the destiny of one was bound to the other.

Adam took care not to slip and fall as they descended the steep slope. What a dreadful irony it would be if he were to fall to his own death after sending One Death and

Seven Death into the oblivion of Hell from the Bridge to Xibalba.

Once inside the car, Pepe took pains to explain to his friend what this was, for her expression told him she needed reassurance. After seeing Art's Austin-Healey, maybe she associated cars with the Mayan Place of Fear. In his head, Pepe explained to the girl that cars belong to the world of Man, and that the red Austin-Healey in Xibalba had come from his father's head anyway.

After strapping himself into the driver's seat, Adam turned to explain Mountain Flower's presence to Conchita, in the front passenger seat, but only as much as was needed.

"She's an orphan. We're gonna take care of her."

Which wasn't entirely accurate if what had been said in the cave was true. Conchita shrugged her shoulders. Her age allowed her to believe anything.

Adam started up the engine and they drove back towards Mexico City. He smiled to himself on overhearing his son teach the girl English. For all Pepe knew, the child may have been conversant in every language on Earth:

"Papa — *Pa-pa*," he said, pointing to their driver. "Or 'Daddy', as some say." Pepe was proud of his Mexican heritage.

"Papa, Daddy," repeated Mountain Flower, also pointing.

"Seat," Pepe said, indicating the seat they sat on.

"Seat," echoed the girl.

"Door."

"Door."

"Road."

"Road."

The children giggled and played together in the back as if they'd been friends for all their short lives, whilst Adam drove on towards the world he knew, towards Tio Federico's and Tia Bea's place in the city, towards María's family and towards María. He could barely wait to get back to María.

Mountain Flower was a delight. María's family in Mexico City adored her. She spoke no Spanish, nor, apart from the few words Pepe had taught her, English. The sentence she spoke in the presence of the Old Woman, he reckoned, came from her 'mother'. The child was sublimely polite and appreciative at being brought back to life, though a certain sadness lingered in her big brown eyes, a sadness at having left her latest 'parents' somewhere back in the mists of time. Adam had no idea when she had last died, only that she knew nothing of the 'bearded white men' from the east, the Spanish. That would have put her previous life at least as far back as the late fifteenth century, or beyond. Before that, another life in thirteenth century Colorado. And afterwards, hundreds of years in Xibalba. He couldn't begin to conceptualise this, although he realised that time in Xibalba and in the *Forest Without Time*, was a different dimension to that experienced here on Earth. One thing about the child was apparent to Adam: not once did she appear to remember their time together in the pueblos of the Mesa Verde.

Adam asked Pepe to tell Mountain Flower to keep her origin a secret. All she should say, if asked, was that her natural parents were dead, and that there were no living relatives. As it happened, Pepe barely let her out of his sight, and he would intervene, in Spanish or in English, if anyone tried to press the girl about her past. They bought her western clothes, trimmed her hair, and soon she looked like any other Native Mexican girl apart from being unusually pretty and having a disarming smile.

Tio Federico's friends in government pulled strings to get the adoption papers formalised quickly and a passport was issued for the child. Someone suggested the name 'Bella', so she became 'Bella López'. She loved her passport photograph and would sit for long periods talking to it in ancient Mayan as though it should talk back to her. She seemed chuffed that a little piece of paper could look exactly like the face she saw reflected in water or in a mirror.

At first, the plane journey to Houston terrified the girl as she sat sandwiched in between Pepe and Adam, hardly daring to move. During take-off, Pepe hugged her and repeatedly whispered to her "you're all right, it's okay" over and over. Gradually she calmed down, and for the remainder of the flight, the boy gave her an English lesson. After landing in Houston, she was able to say, "I'm an American girl", "God bless America," and "I want chocolate chip cookies with my ice cream."

Her passport seemed to puzzle the man in US immigration. He spent ages examining it and looking at the girl. After Pepe whispered something in her ear, she smiled. The man returned her smile, patted her on the head and let her pass on through.

From that moment on, Mountain Flower was known as 'Bella', their adopted Mexican orphan, and with Adam's fame as a champion of the Mayans and other native North American peoples, few questions were asked. Never again did she say who her true mother was. María accepted without question what Adam told her over the phone but advised him not to forewarn Chloe as to who Bella was. After all those years spent searching for Earth Child's descendants, she feared her sister-in-law might freak out. As for who the child really was, Adam reckoned this should remain a secret until her time came. Even then, who would believe that an old woman living in a mountain cave somewhere in Mexico was actually 'Gaia', or Earth Mother and that her only daughter would have a part to play in an, as yet, unfulfilled prophecy?

As it happened, Chloe knew bits of the story already from Pepe, even before the plane had touched down. And she sensed her nephew's newly-found happiness. She felt excited though couldn't fathom why.

Chapter 23: Or Someone Else?

The coyote slipped unnoticed out of the ball court. The question, he suggested through bared teeth, should be:
"Why, not how? Why, if she can still be mine, should I want them back?"
He overheard talk of 'falling into the chasm because of the bridge having been destroyed by the golden beast-turned-boy'.
"That accursed jaguar not dead? So much the better! I will always have access to her world having shared the boy's body."

***

María stood with Lee in the arrivals lounge at Houston airport. She ran into Adam's arms. He held her tight, kissed her till she complained, laughingly, of not being able to breathe, then whispered into her ear:

"It's okay. I know everything! He's my son."

"Mama!"

María turned and hugged the boy.

"He killed them, Mama! Papa killed them both forever! Sent them to Hell!" he shouted excitedly. Two other travellers, overhearing, stopped and stared in alarm.

"He must have been watching a really bad in-flight movie!" María explained. They almost smiled whilst Maria laughed nervously. God, how Adam had missed that laugh!

"Killed off any possible doubts, the boy means," Adam added for the benefit of the two sceptical travellers.

María looked at the small Mayan girl standing beside her husband.

"So, this is Bella!" she said, turning to give the child a hug.

"I am an American girl!" Bella proudly announced.

"Then that makes us both American aliens," María stated, kissing the child on each cheek. "Adam, where did you get this dress for her?"

"Pepe chose it."

"Oh, you men! This is a Mexican party dress! She can't go around in clothes like this! Bella... tomorrow, you and I, we're going to Katy Mills. Gonna get you a whole new wardrobe, girl!"

"God bless America!"

"Oh, God bless you, honey!"

When Adam saw the tears in his wife's eyes as she hugged the little girl yet again, he realised he should never have worried about whether, because of the past, he had made the right decision in bringing home Mountain Flower.

"Pepe's been teaching her English," he said.

"So I see! Come and say hello to Uncle Lee, Bella."

María took the girl's hand and led her to where Lee stood apart from the family group. Bella looked at him, wide-eyed. She'd grown used to white people over the previous few days but, so far, hadn't met a black person, although she had seen a few in Mexico City and on the plane. She reached up and touched his face with her small hand. When his face responded with his usual warm, broad grin, the child smiled back. She said something in Mayan.

"Ain't she just cute? What's she saying?" Lee asked Adam.

Adam, also grinning, shrugged his shoulders.

"She's saying you're a kind man and she likes you very much, Uncle Lee," explained Pepe.

"So, you speak Mayan too, young man?"

"No. Well, kind of, I guess." Pepe appeared pensive, perhaps trying to work how it was that he understood Bella. The girl said something else to Lee, and Pepe laughed.

"Spill it, Pepe," Lee said.

"She wants to know if you sing like Mama!"

"Like a frog, tell her!"

"Photographs! Uncle Lee takes photos," Pepe explained to Bella. He took the girl's passport from her and pointed to the photo, then Lee. "Photos!" he repeated.

"Ah! Photos!" echoed the girl. She then beamed and looked upwards, as if posing for a beauty queen contest. Lee patted her head.

"Geeze, man, I'm gonna have to capture that smile of hers. And those eyes! Wait till Chloe sees this little girl's eyes."

"Where is Aunt Chloe?" Pepe asked.

"Thought you'd know without me telling you!" Lee replied. "She's away, Pepe. Got a call from a lady she's been trying to get in touch with for weeks. Works for a Native American Agency, and your aunt needed to interview her about Native peoples' response to global warming. Seems like some of the old ways could be about to make a comeback, and soon, Pepe. Respect for Mother Earth!"

Adam frowned. He was eager to talk to his sister and introduce her to Bella. There had to be a lot more to the child than he knew. Only Chloe could help him.

"Where *is* Chloe, now?"

"Phoenix," Lee replied. "I had to stay behind. So much editing to do. But I've got a friend there who'll help her with the shoots."

María revealed the truth:

"I told him I'd be just fine on my own now, but he wouldn't listen. Said he'd promised you he'd keep an eye on me. Honestly, I do not know what came over me that night."

"I do," said Adam. "And it's all gonna be okay, I swear it. But where are—?"

"Carla and the twins? Dropped them off at Jorge's and Anna's on the way to the airport. Otherwise it would've been a squeeze in the car. Anna will be over the moon to see Bella." Adam hoped that the girl's ancient Mayan would be understood by the woman from the Chiapas jungle. So far, María had avoided asking Bella about her remembered past or anything to do with her torment in Xibalba, even though the girl's presence would be a constant reminder of her own death. But the woman seemed only too happy to have another child in the family.

How come she survived a return to Earth without experiencing a re-wind of time like María? Is it because of who she is? Will Chloe have an answer? Adam wondered.

Pepe chattered away in English to Bella in the back of the car as Lee drove them home, all the time teaching the girl new words:

"'Highway', 'church', 'truck... vroom vroom!'" After which, Bella call every truck a 'truck... vroom vroom'.

"You could *not* have left her behind," María said, resting her hand on Adam's. "You just couldn't. She's such a cutie! A real little angel."

Angel? Art and Jeannie? Earth Child too?

"Pepe's idea. He insisted. He said—" Adam went silent.

"He said what, honey?"

"No matter. They seem to be made for each other. That's all."

He said he loved the child before he'd even met her. What did he mean?

"That boy sure won't need to go a-courtin' in the streets when he's older, like other kids his age," Lee suggested with a half-turn of his head, flashing a grin.

Back home, they collected Carla and the twins from a friendly neighbour, and in no time the five children were playing happily in the yard as if the addition of Bella was the most normal thing in the world.

"Adam, what did Pepe say about Earth Child?"

This was the first time María used the name of the girl who had drawn them into an ancient Native prophecy with such far-reaching consequences. The children, now hungry, had stopped their play. Unseen by his parents,

Pepe stood with Bella in the doorway. He looked at Adam as if to await his father's answer.

"Papa?"

"Later, darling," Adam said to María.

"Darling?" Bella queried.

Pepe giggled.

"Darling—kiss—*moi!*" he told her, pointing to his parents. Bella immediately kissed him on the cheek. Pepe put his hand there, blushed pink but said nothing. He was given a plate of cookies and, with Bella, ran off to rejoin the play in the yard.

Bella's lessons from Pepe, in English, on American culture as it affects US middle grade children, continued well after sunset. They finally got off to bed only after Carla had shown Bella anything and everything that came into her excited little mind: books, toys, games and pretty much all her clothes as well as Pepe's drawings and paintings, Pepe's toys—and then only after she'd sung her favourite songs from her mother's latest album.

"I think my brother's gonna fall in love with you," Carla said to Bella in a matter-of-fact sort of a way when Pepe was out of earshot.

"Fall?" Bella looked frightened. "Like fall off bridge?" she asked.

"Oh no!" exclaimed Carla. "It's not like falling off a bridge." Carla knotted her eyebrows. She did that when she thought things over. "I don't think it is, anyways. I wouldn't really know, actually."

"What is love?" asked Bella who stood stroking the hair of the Barbie doll Carla had given her. She and Carla now shared a room whilst Pepe, to his absolute delight, was to sleep on the floor of Chloe's and Lee's room.

"It's like Mama and Papa and Pepe—and strawberries—and Uncle Lee and Aunt Chloe—and fajitas and swimming and playing games and Mama singing, and it's all kinda rolled into one. And helping people too. That's what love is."

Bella looked rather puzzled.

"Love," she repeated to herself, staring at the doll in her hand. "Love... love."

With all the children in bed, and Lee ensconced in front of the computer, trawling through shots for his documentary, Adam took María by the hand out into the yard. They sat on the chair swing and for a while neither spoke. The sun was sinking into golden, summer glory beyond the trees, and Adam thought how like jewels on a backcloth of gold the gaps between the leaves were. They watched in silence as the jewels faded and turned to shadows.

Life fading to death? Adam wondered.

"Remember how we watched ourselves sitting on this very same bench before going on to Xibalba?" Adam asked, breaking the silence.

"Sure," María replied. She gave his hand a gentle squeeze.

"And you found out the names of our children?"

"I *decided* on the names of our children."

"I went there again. With Pepe." María said nothing. "To see The Old Woman of the Hills."

"I know that."

"She said I'd have to go back there. To Xibalba. Pepe insisted on coming with me and — well I could never have succeeded without him. What he said at the airport about 'killing them off' was true. María." He looked at her. She was staring blankly ahead. If only he could read her mind like Chloe or Pepe might have done. "María, it was either One Death or Seven Death who killed Coyote Spirit in the end. Masquerading as Art. So... not Art protecting you! The Death Lords wanted to have you. For themselves, and forever. They'd fallen in love with you like everyone else does, honey. They knew you'd kill yourself rather than kill little Pepe when you thought that Coyote Spirit was his father. Then—" María, motionless, seemed detached from what Adam was telling her. "I had to go back. To finish it and destroy them. Otherwise you would never ever have been safe. And the Old Woman of the Hills was right. I needed Pepe with me. But I'm so sorry I had to drag him into all of this."

He looked at his wife again. She turned to face him. Tears streaked her cheeks.

"No, *I'm* sorry, Adam. Just the thought that it wasn't the real you, wondering how I would ever know who Pepe's father really was. Then when he said about being—"

"María, I saw it all. Like watching a movie, only it was really happening. With the Old Woman and Pepe beside me. I came back to you just in time twelve years ago, when Chloe was in Albuquerque. A few minutes later and—well, it wouldn't have been Pepe, would it?"

María stared at her husband as if she wished to believe him but couldn't.

"We'd just been talking about our wedding. The real one, back in ancient Mexico, and the other one. Then I was called back to Chloe, in that Place of Fear..."

"Chloe?" interrupted María.

"She was lured there by Coyote Spirit. He must've known she'd search the ends of the earth to find the descendants of Eagle Foot, to feel close to Earth Child again."

"Poor Chloe!"

"Chloe—she... María, it was awful. It was like I was being pulled in half. By the two people I love the most."

"You poor darling! Anyone else would have been."

"Then I was in the car with you. You'd been to Katy Mills, or something, to look for a wedding dress. And my face felt sore—like it had just been slapped."

Maria stroked Adam's cheek with the back of her hand.

"Hope I didn't hit you too hard," she said.

"Wasn't me you hit, but, yeah, it was still pretty sore. You must have given him one hell of a wallop. Why?"

"Adam Winters, you do not want to know why!" Adam shrugged his shoulders. "I knew it couldn't be you there in the mall at Katy Mills. But back home—"

"You undressed me. Yourself," Adam continued.

"Uh-huh!" María grinned.

"I called you my princess."

"Thank God you said that. Not the other thing!" Her grin broadened.

"And we made love."

"Uh-huh!"

"And it was heaven."

"It was. Pure heaven."

"And we were lying there, and I was stroking your cheeks, and thinking, *oh boy how lovely you look*, then I remembered Chloe. I knew she was in terrible trouble, and in a flash, I returned to her. But it was so awful to have to leave you 'cause of that dark cloud there in our bedroom. I knew it was Coyote Spirit and that he might take you too, only as me."

"He didn't, darling. Only you did. Don't worry. There'll only ever be one you from now on."

"Yeah, we got rid of the bad Adam in that little cave in the Mesa Verde six hundred years or more ago. Remember?"

"A girl never forgets her first time."

"I came back to make sure. Just for a moment. I was dying. Art and Jeannie were there. Well, that's who I thought they were. Art was about to finish me off. If I hadn't got back to Xibalba in time, and to Chloe, then you'd never have seen the real me again. Or Chloe. And you might never have escaped from the Lords of Xibalba."

"That's why I insisted on leaving the old place, Adam. When I thought that Coyote Spirit had—you know—there, in our own bed. It reminded me."

"If only I'd known. Known what you've been through all these years. You thinking that you'd given birth to Coyote Spirit's son."

"It was the nightmares that were the worst thing. Every night, night after night. Sometimes several times in one night. Art—"

"But it wasn't him. He's your guardian angel."

"I thought it was. It looked like him. Spoke like him. And always telling me to destroy Pepe before it was too late. Told me I loved him only because he was half me. But—"

"But?" A shadow of doubt darkened Adam's face.

"But the thing is, a lot of what Art, or whoever that was, said, came true. Pepe's genius, him always wanting to be the leader, his amazing paintings and his special gifts."

"Like Chloe?"

"That's what I kept telling myself over and over. Just like Chloe, I said. From my Adam's genes. But then if he was using your body? Adam, I just didn't know what to think. Only that I could never hurt little Pepe."

"And they knew that too. Jesus, María, I came so very close to losing you."

"But you didn't. And you never will." María snuggled up against Adam and he so wanted to make love to her again, there and then.

"She comes from Xibalba, then."

"You guessed?"

"Adam, I may not have a brain like yours or Pepe's, but I'm not stupid. You don't go to Mexico to see the Old Woman of the Hills and come back with an orphan girl the spitting image of Earth Child unless something mighty strange has happened."

"It was Pepe who insisted. The poor child died after an earthquake. In another life. Quite when, I can't figure out, but before the Spanish came to Mexico, anyways. Her parents died immediately, but she, poor little mite, she lived on, trapped in her broken body for two days, all alone until she found herself in Xibalba."

"How did you discover her?"

"Pepe heard her crying. He said he already loved her. I heard nothing, but he did. Through a thick wall in the underground tunnel. You never saw those tunnels. People trapped down there in perpetual fear of the ball game spectators, of Zotz, the Snake Goddess, and—" Adam paused. "I met her again."

"The giant spider? Yuk!"

"Yeah! Yuk! Well, she kind of lost her head this time. And Zotz ain't gonna bother no one no more. But those red rubber monsters, the Lords of Xibalba, they were something else!"

"Adam, you don't have to tell me any more."

"But I took a risk, María. And put you at risk."

"You had to do it."

"Only way was to lure them onto that bridge. Let them think that through me coming back here they could get to you."

"Adam—"

"The knife the Old Woman gave me, it—"

"Adam, stop! I do not need to hear any more."

"But the Old Woman — Pepe called her the—"

"Adam! No more!"

"Sorry!"

Both fell silent apart from the sound of kissing as they came together on a chair swing that a boy and a dead girl had stared at all those years back.

Chapter 24: Two Churches

"So, Tezcatlipoca is no longer a threat, the Death Lords are gone and the child has returned. The world is ready!"

The old antiques dealer hadn't felt such happiness since helping a boy from Houston prevent his Mexican girlfriend from dying a second time in a rewind following a lethal spider bite.

"You're forgetting one thing," said the scientist.

"Money?" suggested the girl's grandfather.

"Pff!" exclaimed the man of God. "We can do without Mammon, thank you very much! I told you we didn't need him here."

"We need him. His genes are inside his granddaughter," explained the scientist.

"Who or what else do we need?" asked the man who had once presided over a special wedding in ancient Mexico. "What else can we now do to prevent it from happening?"

"Mankind," replied the scientist. They all looked at her. "Only Mankind can answer that question," she explained.

***

Adam was awoken by excited whispers. He felt a pressure on his feet, and it moved up over his legs and onto his chest. He opened one eye.

"Wake up Mama and Papa!" shouted Pepe and Bella in unison, bouncing up and down on the bed.

"Good Morning to you. God Bless America!" Bella added.

Adam laughed.

"You don't need to say that every day, Bella."

Bella looked for approval from Pepe. He gave it. She grinned.

"Breakfast give Mama and Papa we!" she said proudly.

"We give Mama and Papa breakfast, Bella," corrected Pepe in a whisper.

"We Mama and Papa give breakfast."

"Hey, cool, Bella!" exclaimed María.

"Cool!" repeated the child, giggling.

"You do it," Pepe whispered.

The children climbed down, and, after further whispering, waitress Bella came forwards with a tray bearing two cups of coffee and two bowls of cereal.

"We Mama and Papa give breakfast," she repeated.

María nudged Adam who smiled sleepily at the child. He took the tray from the girl and María opened her arms wide.

"Come here, Bella. Let me give you a kiss."

Bella looked at Pepe then ran around to María's side of the bed into her new mama's arms.

"I feel I just wanna hug you the whole time, sweetheart!" María said.

She held Bella at arm's length then stroked the tears of happiness that trickled down the girl's cheeks.

"God sure has blessed you, honey. Go play with Carla and Pepe now."

Pepe took Bella off to the playroom, chattering non-stop.

"It's amazing how quickly that girl's learning English," María said.

"Uh-huh!" Adam was sitting up and tucking into his cereal.

"And her eyes. There's just something about them. Something so awesome. Something—I don't know what exactly—something special, I guess. I was that cut up about Coyote Spirit the last time I didn't see it."

Someone special? And how often did I hear that about you, Honey? Adam had gotten so used to hearing the word being used to describe María, it did seem strange in the context of a child they'd only known for a short while seven hundred years back.

"Pepe's not gonna have to go far to find his soulmate," he said.

María prodded Adam in the side.

"Neither did you, Mr Adam Winters."

"Seemed like I travelled through the history of our planet to get you, Señora López."

"No, you didn't. You got me the first time I saw you at middle school."

"Wonder what happened to Spike."

"I never fancied him! I told you. Just used the poor guy to get to you. Make you jealous."

"You succeeded in that all right! And what about the real Art and Jeannie? We seemed to lose touch after they moved."

"They called."

"What?"

"Forgot to tell you, Darling. What with you trying to explain what happened – and Bella and everything else. They called and I put them onto Chloe."

Adam looked troubled.

"Chloe gets back tomorrow, right?"

"Uh-huh!"

"I'll give her a call."

"Honey, it's six in the morning. Poor woman will be exhausted with all that rushing around."

But Adam was already out of bed, searching for the phone which he'd forgotten to put back in its charger the previous night.

"Adam?"

He ran downstairs. He looked in the play room, interrupting Pepe and Bella in their play, the kitchen, the bathroom. Finally, thank God, he saw it. On the floor, beside the settee. He snatched it up and dialled Chloe's cell phone number...

"I'm sorry, the number you are calling is unobtainable. Please try later."

***

279

Chloe awoke with a start when her alarm went off. Still half-asleep, she reached out and fumbled with the clock before managing to switch it off. Yawning, she rolled out of bed. Six o'clock! Thank God, she'd put the alarm on. Normally, like Pepe, she was up and about well before six, but having worked until two in the morning, she'd needed the extra hour or so. Plus, this was the big day. The day she was to meet up with the woman who would give meaning to their latest documentary. The shoot was to be done in the historic Heritage Square, in Phoenix, where the Victorian buildings seemed to symbolise White Man's victory over the Red Man's struggle to hold on to the old ways.

Ever since travelling back to the ancient mesas with Adam and María, and making friends with Earth Child and her family, Chloe had felt there had to be something indestructible about the Native American soul. She'd seen first-hand how the Anasazi had survived the evil from the south brought to them by Coyote Spirit, and she had read about White Man's repeated attempts to destroy the Native American soul through countless wars, massacres, starvation in reservations, alcohol and assimilation into his alien European culture. In the last century, they had fought back, not with arrows and guns, but with civil disobedience: the civil rights movements, the curious takeover of Alcatraz, claiming a right to the land as White Man had done along the length of the Americas. Chloe had worried that White Man had finally won when she heard how well some tribes were doing financially with gambling dens and casinos, but she knew Aunt Jac had done her own fighting for traditionalists eager to preserve the old ways. Nevertheless, Chloe had not accounted for the Native American's cunning and adaptability. Long before White Man appeared, he had survived the harshest of landscapes and climates by blending with the land. Perhaps White Man was yet another trial of nature to be endured.

Chloe was beginning to think like this. After her disastrous search for the descendants of Eagle Foot, she had, through Aunt Jac, met and known so many Native Americans from different tribes, and often she'd found that same depth of spirit and oneness with the Universe from which, she and Lee were convinced, not only could White Man learn from the Red People, but, somehow, he would have to for the world to survive. In some ways, her quest to be reunited with her friend, Earth Child, had fired her determination to bring Native spirituality back into focus in the land of their ancestors. Their documentary was all about tackling global warming by not only having respect for the land but having a belief in its forces and becoming part of the land, as the First Americans always considered themselves to be.

Chloe had no time for breakfast. She was to meet the woman, together with Lee's photojournalist friend, in the park at eight o'clock. With Art and Jeannie too. What a coincidence that they should be there in Phoenix! But why? Art never said when he called her. What an odd couple they were. The *real* Art and Jeannie, that is. And why should he, owner of a haulage business, be the slightest bit interested in a documentary about global warming? He'd made himself a fortune by contributing to it.

She shrugged her shoulders and picked up her phone. Damn it, she thought when she saw the battery was flat. She'd been so tired the previous night she'd forgotten to recharge it. Poor Lee! He didn't even know the name or phone number of the hotel.

Later, she humped her bag of filming equipment downstairs, and asked, when checking out, whether she could use the hotel phone.

"Sorry, lady. Comp'ny policy. There's a public call phone two blocks down."

Serves me right for checking into the cheapest bloody hotel in town, she thought to herself. She looked at her watch. Seven-thirty. The Native American woman had said she didn't have a lot of time. Didn't seem, over the phone, she was the type who'd hang around if Chloe were to turn up late. Besides, the taxi was outside, waiting. But not to call Lee, to hear his voice, to know the twins were okay, it would ruin her day. She closed her eyes and tried to reach Pepe, but she couldn't. He must have been totally absorbed in whatever he was doing.

"Got a cell phone I could borrow?" she asked the taxi-driver straightaway.

"Sorry, lady. Can't do."

"Couple of blocks down. There's a public phone. Could you stop there for just a minute or two? So, I can call my husband?"

"No sweat, lady!"

The taxi pulled in, its hazard lights winking, and Chloe leapt out, only to discover that the phone had been vandalised.

"Okay, Heritage Square then," she said with resignation after she got back into the taxi. Lee's friend was bound to have a cell phone.

***

"Why does this thing about Art still upset you so much, Adam? I'm sorry I put him through to Chloe, but he said it was important. I just assumed it was to do with the global warming documentary."

María was truly apologetic, but at the same time she couldn't understand why Adam was so desperate to get in touch with his sister.

Why is the real Art so important?

"Art and global warming? He's a great guy, María, but I hardly think he cares a damn about global warming."

"You never know!"

Adam could not risk upsetting María with the truth all over again. She'd already suffered too much over her worries about Pepe. He asked Lee to contact his photographer friend in Phoenix, get the guy to have Chloe

282

call him immediately, but, as luck would have it, the man's goddmamn cell phone was turned off.

"Come to church with us," María said, sensing her husband's mounting anxiety. "Pepe wants to bring Bella. He told her this is how we thank the Great Spirit here in Houston."

"Sure thing," Adam replied, "but can I just borrow Pepe for a minute?"

María frowned.

"Borrow him?"

"Well, just in case—"

"Adam, don't you think the child's been through enough already?"

Adam looked over María's shoulder at Pepe, Bella and Carla happily playing as young children do. It all seemed so natural. Maybe he was being stupid about Art wanting to contact Chloe. After all, he'd seen and heard One Death and Seven Death fall to oblivion from the Bridge to Xibalba. There really was no way that this could have been anyone other than the real Art. Stupid to imagine otherwise, and anyway Chloe hated being interrupted when she was in the middle of a shoot. Just like when she was painting as a child.

"You're right, Honey," he said. "Perhaps Art is reforming. Did say he was gonna sell his business, anyways. And Pepe would be sure to know if Chloe was in real danger."

At church, Bella watched Pepe all the time and copied everything he did. When he crossed himself, she did the same; if he stood, she stood, and she copied the movements of his mouth and sang and prayed silently whenever he sang or prayed.

During mass, folk turned to shake hands and greet one another. They saw Bella's eyes. Word spread around, and other church-goers came up to see the child with the 'amazing' eyes. Bella clung to Pepe, not wanting to be 'special', and uncertain about all the attention.

In the car on the way home, Bella spoke in Mayan to Pepe. Although the words meant nothing to Adam, Pepe seemed to understand perfectly, and he would speak back in English. Strangely, she always understood his English, though often looked blank when others spoke to her.

"What's she saying, Pepe?" Adam asked.

"Wants to know why we have to go into a special house to speak with the Great Spirit."

"Well, that is some question, son."

"Last time she was here, before the earthquake, she and her family would go outside to be close to the Great Spirit. And they had to stay quiet to feel the Silence."

Adam glanced sideways at María. She was frowning. He knew how important it was for her that Bella should feel not only a part of the family but also be in tune with their beliefs... their religion.

"Tell her that when White Man turned the outside into his own place and started doing bad things to it, then he had to build special houses in which to feel the Great Spirit. Tell her, Pepe, that some of these houses are very beautiful. And tell her all that singing and praying, that's to let Him know we're in those special houses. He needs to know that, see. Only then can we find that Silence with Him like she used to do."

Pepe repeated this for Bella, in English, his eyes trained upon hers all the time as she smiled her understanding.

"Love?" the child queried, her large eyes fixed on María who had turned around to look at the children. "Find love?"

"See, Honey! She's really no different from us," María said to Adam.

Adam's phone rang.

"It's Aunt Chloe," Pepe said.

"You take it, María. It's in my pocket."

"She's in trouble, Papa."

The car swerved as Adam's attention floundered.

"Darling, take care!" María warned. Her husband regained control of the vehicle whilst she fumbled in his pocket and took out the cell phone.

"Big trouble!" repeated Pepe.

"María, I'm gonna have to pull over."

"Hello, Chloe... is that you?"

***

Chloe arrived at Heritage Square just before eight. The place was strangely empty. Just right for the shoot, though. She set up her equipment in front of Rosson House, that fine old Victorian Building, a relic of White Man's final takeover of the land of Earth Mother from the Red Man.

"Chloe?"

She spun around on hearing her name. It was Jake, Lee's friend.

"Hey, how ya doing?" the man asked.

They embraced. She quickly showed him the equipment, made sure he was familiar with the camera controls, and he did a practice shoot on Chloe. She kept glancing at her watch, anxious to start filming before tourists arrived in full force. It irritated her how the public always tried to get into the frame to mouth words and wave. It was always intensely distracting, and this was to be such an important interview. She had to persuade people that the Native culture and beliefs in the spirituality of the land, of Earth, were still there, submerged, and Rose Barefoot was the person to do that. The interview was to be the climax of the whole documentary. Chloe was so fired up she entirely forgot to ask Jake if she could borrow his cell phone to call Lee.

The woman appeared fifteen minutes late. Her features were indeed Native American, although her clothes were those of any stylish businesswoman: dark grey trouser suit, smart blue blouse, discrete pendant and earrings. Her hair was short. Chloe was most disappointed about the woman's hair. She knew long hair was of

285

importance to the Red People, and it somehow seemed wrong that Rose Barefoot had short hair. Still, it was what the woman would say that mattered, and, with the correct angle and lighting, Jake could bring out the woman's Native features with close-up shots. Chloe's questions were all there, on her clip board, waiting to be asked, although she was a little thrown when Rose said she preferred to do it 'off-the-cuff and unrehearsed'.

"Get it from the heart, then, not the brain?"

Chloe did not feel herself warm to the woman as she'd hoped, something that often cramped her interview technique. She could only truly feel a rapport with people she warmed to, but they had been over it all on the phone (funny, but she liked the woman over the phone) and it should, she reckoned, be very straightforward. Then, damn it, she remembered she had forgotten all about Lee.

Too late! After the shoot, maybe?

Chloe checked out her hair with her pocketbook mirror and added last-minute touches of make-up. Jake began filming and she did the talking:

"We're standing here in front of Rosson House, in Historic Heritage Square, Phoenix, Arizona, where the Victorian Buildings remind us of the beginning of the final phase in the Native American's struggle to keep his identity in the face of the relentless march of European domination across the continent of North America, from the southernmost region of Guatamala to the far reaches of Alaska. Hundreds of years of Indian Wars, countless treaties, all broken by White Man, with terrible massacres on both sides, came to an end. Yet still the Red People were regarded as savages unless Europeanised, but no one listened to the wisdom of their chiefs and their shamans. Treated worse than animals, at times, they were herded into reservations in territories which are often little more than deserts and where life is unsustainable. Any attempt by them to rebel was met with harsh punishment, but they survived, and their survival is a testimony of human endurance. Of course, bravery and survival were attributes revered by the Native American, over and above power and wealth, for here, away from the might of the empire-seeking civilisations of the south, there was no wealth greater than freedom to live in harmony with Nature. No possessions, no greed. But now, with the future survival of our planet in question, people are at last opening their eyes to the old ways of the Red People. Folk are listening to the wisdom of their culture and are beginning to wonder whether the answers to some of our questions have been here, all along, in North America. Staring us in the face... in the traditional beliefs of the Native American.

Rose Barefoot, director of NARF, the Native American Revival Foundation, has joined me here to answer some of the questions I'll be putting to her. Questions relating to traditional Native beliefs in a changing world."

Rose smiled at the camera.

"Thank you, Chloe," she said.

"Rose, could I first ask you—" She was interrupted by shouting. "Damn!" she muttered, turning to see who it was. "Cut, Jake!"

A large red-bearded man with wild eyes came towards her. His right hand was tucked into his pocket.

"Art!" Chloe called out. "We've just started the shoot. D'you mind hanging in there a short while? Won't be long. Don't want tourists messing this up."

But Art carried on walking. Chloe saw Jeannie, holding back outside the entrance. There was something about the look in Art's eyes that worried Chloe.

"Art?"

Art came on towards her, but he was looking beyond her — at Rose.

"Art, what's up? What the heck?"

Art pushed Chloe aside, pulled out a gun and fired three shots at Rose Barefoot, two into the chest, and the third bang in the centre of the woman's forehead, before she crumpled to the ground.

Chapter 25: Evil Drips Through Generations

As they looked at the scientist, each wondered, in his own way, what she meant.

"Mankind must save itself through believing in Him. As simple as that," affirmed the priest.

"Hmm! You destroyed our gods and now you people talk so freely about Mankind destroying itself," said the girl's grandfather, once a successful businessman in Mexico.

The old antiques dealer, however, winked at the scientist. He knew what she meant. Mankind had to stop the world from dying if it were save itself. Now he knew why the son of the girl and the Golden Jaguar had sought out and rescued the child of Earth Mother. Now it was all beginning to make sense.

***

Chloe screamed and ran to hide behind Jake. She really thought it was the end and that in a few moments she'd be dead and, worst of all, that she'd never see Lee and the twins again. She trembled, gripping Jake's arm, as Art turned to face them.

"Hurry!" the big man yelled. "Car's just around the corner. I'll take the camera, Jake."

"But what about—?" Chloe began, staring at the corpse of the woman. Her words were cut short by what she saw happening on the ground in front of the Victorian building. The corpse was changing, shrinking. The face of the dead woman was elongating, the short black hair thinning and turning into grey fur. The ears became pointed, the hands, paws. The muzzle was that of a coyote. A dead coyote.

"Quick," urged Art, taking the camera from Jake as bystanders screamed. "Questions later. Only just in time—again! What is it with your family?"

They ran to join Jeannie, then on to a parking lot. All four leapt into the red Austin-Healey and Art drove off as

fast he could in the centre of Phoenix until he was sure
they were far enough away from the scene not to arouse
suspicion from the police. Chloe was still shaking when Art
finally spoke:

"The Coyote! The Great Trickster, huh?"

"But I thought he was—" Chloe felt totally confused.

"You thought Coyote Spirit was dead? Killed by One
Death and Seven Death? Sure, he was."

"Then… who was that? One of the Death Lords?"

"One of the Lords of Xibalba? No way! Your brother
took care of them. Your brother changed Xibalba for
eternity. No! But this is how the Great Trickster works.
Nothing's what it seems. Coyote Spirit's both dead and
alive. Like Schrödinger's cat."

"Whose cat?"

"Quantum realities. Never you mind. Let's just get
away from here."

"Where are you taking us, Art?" Chloe really didn't
know whether to trust Art and Jeannie, particularly after
the man's referral to 'nothing is what it seems'.

"Your hotel first, then the airport."

A police car sped past in the opposite direction with its
light flashing and siren blaring.

"That should keep 'em amused, huh? A dead coyote in
drag."

"Art, I've seen some pretty weird things, particularly
in that godawful place, Xibalba, but would you mind
explaining exactly what's happening?"

"Jeannie?"

Jeannie turned around and smiled at Chloe.

"You'll be okay now. And she'll be okay, too. Those
bullets. Made from the same kind of gold as your granny's
locket. And the Golden Jaguar, he'll not need to return.
Not now. And not here. His genes are passed on."

"So, it was Coyote Spirit?"

"Chloe, back in the mesas he had another child. Not by
Swimming Beaver. When the tribe left the Mesa Verde,

they first built a pueblo by the Rio Grande. Eagle Foot was an old man, still mourning the loss of Earth Child all those years before. Swimming Beaver's boy was chief, and he was a good spiritual leader. The cliff people lived again in harmony with Earth Mother, and the River Spirit provided them with plenty. But the chief's half-brother, Coyote Paw, a man made in the image of his father, challenged him. He was the older of the two. He told the tribe that Coyote Spirit had been their rightful leader anyhow, and that the prophecy had been false. There was a battle. All Coyote Paw's warriors were killed, and the man himself narrowly escaped death. With half a dozen arrows sticking out of his back, he fled into the hills. He was taken in by another tribe, married and had children. One of them was called Coyote Tooth, and so generation after generation spawned a new coyote. Like that, the spirit of evil gotten handed down, kept alive. And they all had the power of the Great Trickster himself."

"And the one in Xibalba?"

"Same spirit, another world," Jeannie explained. "Yeah, he was the guy who took María away that fateful day but, heaven be praised, never consummated the relationship."

"But there'll be another one? From what you say—"

"Last of the line, Chloe. This one was really bad," Art said. "But hadn't had any offspring yet. Was waiting for her to show up again. Each generation seemed to know all about María and who she is. Each wanted her for his seed. And the power issuing from such a union, it would have been terrible with all that evil in the Coyote. But no, Chloe, it's over. The world's gonna be a safer place now. For a while. But for our president."

"I don't get it," Chloe said. "It was María he was after. Right?"

"Yes and no. Look, you'll find out. Just now—"

"But that Rose Barefoot, she sounded so nice. I can't believe she—"

"I couldn't save her, Chloe. The real one. Goddamn shame. She was doin' such a grand job. But I came too late."

"So?"

"I think you knew deep down that this wasn't Rose Barefoot, huh?"

"She did strike me as different from the woman I'd spoken to over the phone."

"So, you're gonna have to work twice as hard now. You and Lee and Aunt Jac and all the others. That movie you're making has gotta make the world see sense, and maybe, sooner or later, those in government too. How about that, Jeannie? Folks in government seein' sense." Art gave a little chuckle. "Now that would be a first! Right, Jeannie? But no way with the goon they've put in charge!"

"Poor Rose," said Chloe, frowning. "And it was all my fault!"

"Oh, she'll be happy where she is now. See, this will help to bring the whole thing to the fore."

They stopped off at Chloe's hotel to pick up her bags. They wanted to drop Jake off at his place, but the guy had turned green after seeing 'Rose Barefoot' shot three times and transform into a dog, and just about freaked out at the conversation that went on in the Austin-Healey. It wasn't quite what he'd expected when Lee got in touch with him about a 'short shoot'. Not exactly the sort of 'short shoot' he was used to. He could barely escape quickly enough from the Austin-Healey.

"You sure?" asked Art when Jake was poised to rush off after opening the car door when the traffic lights turned red. "Ain't no sweat for us to drop you off at your place."

"Sure!" the man replied.

"Thanks, Jake!" Chloe called out before he disappeared around the corner. "Oh dear, I'll have to get Lee to call him. Must think I'm some kinda witch or something."

"An angel, Chloe. You're an angel. Just like Jeannie and me."

"Got a cell phone?" Chloe asked. "I've gotta talk to Lee."

"No phone. At the airport, Chloe. But first, just get yourself onto that next flight back to Houston."

"There's still a danger, isn't there? With Coyote Spirit, or with whatever his descendants call themselves."

Art glanced at Jeannie and shrugged his shoulders.

"Ain't ever used a golden bullet before," he replied. "And somehow the evil got stronger as it was passed from father to son. Just like it grew in Coyote Spirit himself during his life. We must get you to the airport, Chloe."

"If he can survive three golden bullets, surely a thousand miles between us won't stop him. But you say it's not María he's after, this time?"

"The Coyote Spirit who was already dead, the one from Xibalba, he was the only coyote ever actually knew María. His descendants only heard about her. But they knew about the other girl."

Other girl?

Chloe remained silent as they drove on to the airport. Whether through fear of slowing Art down, of not making the earlier flight, or just dumbfounded confusion about the whole goddamn story, she couldn't say. She just sat and thought about Lee and the boys, her brother and María and their children, her dead parents, and all the people she loved so much, and she thought about her documentary, what Art had said, and she even wondered why it was all so important to her. The only answer she could come up with was that it was. Vitally important. But there had always been a question at the back of her mind, something she had repeatedly tried to dismiss after ending up in Xibalba, although never succeeded in achieving this:

What happened to Earth Child?

The Austin-Healey made it in no time. She checked in on the next flight and gave Art and Jeannie each a hug.

"Who are you, really?" she questioned just before passing on through 'Departures'.

Jeannie laughed.

"Does it matter?" she asked

"Guess not," Chloe replied. "But Pepe's gonna want to know."

"Oh, he knows all right," the other woman said. "And *that's* what's important."

When Chloe turned to wave, Art and Jeannie had vanished.

She found a public phone in the Departures Lounge and dialled Adam's cell phone number.

"Hello, Chloe? Is that you?"

It was María's voice. Chloe wiped the tears from her eyes.

"Lee?" she asked. "Is Lee there?"

"We're in the car on the way home. Just been to church. Wanted to take Be—" She stopped mid-sentence when she saw Adam shake his head. "Erm... the children," she continued. "They came with us, but Lee's at home. Can I have him call you when we're back? Chloe... Chloe? You still there Chloe?"

Finally, Chloe found her voice again.

"María, are you okay? And Adam and Pepe? What happened? Are they all right? Did Adam—?" Chloe heard a scraping noise, as if the cell phone at the other end was being handed to someone else.

"Chloe? It's Adam. Just pulled in. Look, Art may not be who you think he is. He—" The phone went dead. She tried redialling, but the number was unobtainable. She phoned Lee.

"Chloe? Oh, Jesus, Chloe, thank God."

"Lee, what's happening? María, Adam... are they okay? And Pepe?"

"Chloe, where are you?"

"At the airport in Phoenix, honey. Look—"

"Police have just been on the phone, Chloe. About Rose Barefoot."

Chloe froze. Her mind jumped about and for a few moments she couldn't speak.

"Chloe, darling?"

"What about Rose Barefoot?"

"Chloe, don't you know?" Chloe said nothing. She waited for the answer to her question. "She was found dead in her apartment."

Chapter 26: Two Special Children

"But what about the coyote?" the girl's grandfather asked. *"Is he or is he not destroyed? Can no one tell me. I'm here to keep a loving eye on my granddaughter."*

"Your granddaughter came from that place beyond the white door, my friend. You seem to forget that. Her child is the child of her God and..." the antiques dealer glanced sideways at the priest. *"And his, of course. The boy, the child's father, handed on the power of your ancient gods changed by the power of her love. From the Beast known as the Golden Jaguar of the Sun. And together with Earth Child, whose mother spawned humankind, he might give those on Earth a chance to try again."*

"But what about the evil? From Coyote Spirit and his like?"

"As our scientist has told us, the evil is with Mankind. Mankind is the problem. Their problem."

"Will they succeed?" asked the other Mexican.

The antiques dealer laughed.

"You, at least, should believe in the prophecies. Why, surely—?"

"As foretold by John," interrupted the priest, *grinning. It was the first time any of the others had seen him smile.*

***

Chloe was afraid her legs would give way. She held onto the side of the public call box for support.

"Chloe? What is it, darling?" Lee's voice questioned from the phone.

"Lee, I—

"So, she never turned up, then?"

"Who?"

"Rose. Found murdered in her apartment in Los Angeles."

"Los Angeles?"

"Uh-huh! 'Course, you probably ain't seen the news yet. Her partner found her last night when he'd gotten home. That's why the police phoned. In case you had any information. Knew you'd spoken to her last night, and he'd told them she was due to take a flight to meet you in Phoenix early this morning before attending some meeting or other. They wondered whether you'd received any threats yourself."

"Los Angeles?" repeated Chloe.

"You went all that way for nothing, honey. But poor Rose. D'you think it was some kind of White Supremacist freak?"

"How? Did they say how she died?"

"Brutal. That's all they said. No specifics. Just brutal."

"Did Adam say anything about Art, Lee?"

"Surely it wasn't them? There's nothing anti-anyone about Art and Jeannie. María did say she'd gotten a call from him, though. For you." Lee paused. "Chloe, what's happening?" he asked.

"It's okay. I'm coming straight home. Just phone Jake. He'll tell you the rest. I love you, darling. And give the boys big kisses from their Mommy. My flight arrives three-thirty. Could you meet me at Houston airport? Hobby, remember, not George Bush."

"Sure thing! Love ya, baby!"

Later, Chloe peered out of the window as the plane taxied towards the runway. There, on a patch of dried-out grass, close to the runway, stood a coyote, staring up at the plane. It seemed to be looking directly at her window, and she began to doubt Art and Jeannie. Who were they? What was their real motive for the shooting? Adam hopefully knew something she didn't know.

The coyote vanished. The plane took off, and, feeling shattered, she slept for most of the flight.

The twins were over the moon to have their mommy back. When she saw their happy little faces, she began to wonder whether she and Lee shouldn't just abandon the documentary and stick to safe movies; even try a low budget feature film. If evil forces had broken out of Xibalba, far better to keep a low profile and stay alive for the kids than end up like Rose Barefoot. *But Art and Jeannie?* No way, whoever they really were. But one thing was for sure. She and Jake had come face to face with the real killer, a Rose Barefoot look-alike come coyote, that very morning. She had almost interviewed her... him... it...

Gold bullets? Why?

"Jake told me everything," whispered Lee as they got into the car. "Poor guy, I could almost hear him tremble."

"Seeing a woman get shot is one thing, but to witness her body turn into a dead coyote... what a freak-out! Look Lee, I'm no longer sure about our documentary. This whole business is kinda getting out of hand. Rose's murder, the whole coyote thing. Saw one at the airport, you know. Looking up at the plane. At me. And then there's Art. Which Art?"

"Art?"

"Adam was trying to warn me when I was at Phoenix airport, but his phone went dead. Maybe you and me ought to just get on with our own lives. Forget Old Mother Earth, huh?"

"This ain't you talking, Chloe."

"You'd have no bother getting other photographic work. I could spend more time with the boys. They deserve that. We could do a few commercials, some small TV documentaries and when the kids go to school, who knows, perhaps a feature movie or two. I was thinking about it on the plane."

"Chloe?"

"And maybe we could move to Texas. Be nearer Adam and María. And Carla and Pepe."

"And Bella."

"Who?"

"Little Bella. Didn't you know?"

"Know what?"

"That Adam adopted a Mayan girl called Bella. Well, that ain't her real name, and Pepe still calls her Mountain Flower a lot of the time."

"Lee, did I hear you right? Adam and Pepe came back from Mexico with a little Mayan girl?"

"Pepe's as happy as a lamb. They just get on so well together. Seems like they were made for each other."

"Lee, my brother has gone brain-dead crazy! Poor María's gotten enough on her plate with all her worries about Pepe. And now this?"

"María adores the child. It's strange, but she acts like the little girl's always been her daughter. Like it was perfectly natural for Adam to bring her home."

"But Lee, they can't just turn their home into an orphanage."

"And her eyes, Chloe. She'll be a real beauty when she grows up. Like María herself."

"And Mommy!" a little voice piped up.

Chloe laughed.

"See! The twins understand just about everything we say now. I must be with them some more. Give them quality time. I can't—" Chloe sighed. She felt drained by the events of the previous twenty-four hours.

"Put your own life at risk?" Lee glanced sideways at her. Chloe felt her eyes moisten. She nodded. "You know I'd be perfectly happy to move down here to Texas. Our overheads would be less, and I think we have enough contacts already. And Chloe, this Bella business, whatever you feel about it, please don't tell Adam. I know how you and he have always had this truth thing between you, but sometimes the truth, it hurts, and Bella—well, she is kind of special for them. Like I said, she and Pepe—"

"Did Adam say anything about Pepe? About Mexico? And the Old Woman of the Hills?"

"María's her old self again. Can only mean one thing. She knows Adam's the father."

"Thank God for that. No, I'll keep quiet about Bella. It's their business anyway. And I knew myself Pepe wasn't the son of Coyote Spirit. Knew all along, but knowing isn't proving, right? María needed proof."

"She's had no more of those dreams. Dreams about Art telling her to do that awful thing." Lee went silent.

"Telling her to do what thing, Daddy?" Kurt called out from the back.

"See, honey!" Chloe exclaimed. "They're growing up so fast. Even being away a couple of days, I notice the difference."

As the rusty Oldsmobile approached the last bend in the road just before the Winters' Ranch House, Chloe again promised her husband she'd not say a word about her disapproval of Adam's adoption of the little Mayan girl.

"Like I said, Lee, it's just none of my—" Chloe's sentence got cut short. Her mouth hung open in disbelief.

Three children had suddenly appeared around the bend, running towards the old car as it chugged its final few hundred yards to the house. Carla was ahead, and behind her ran Pepe holding hands with a dark-skinned girl with long black hair.

"Stop the car, Lee!" shouted Chloe.

Lee, alarmed, pulled into the side of the road. Chloe opened the door, scrambled out of the car and ran towards the children — then halted. Carla ran up to her, encircling both her legs with affectionate little arms.

"Aunt Chloe, Aunt Chloe!" the child cried out, excitedly.

But Chloe's attention was fixed on the dark-skinned girl standing hand in hand with Pepe.

"Aunt Chloe, this is my new friend, Bella. She's gonna live with us."

Chloe ignored Pepe. For a few moments, it seemed as if he, Carla, Lee and the twins simply weren't there. She was staring at the Mayan girl, looking straight into her eyes, and the girl looked back. Carla broke free from her legs, still grinning, as Chloe held her arms wide. Tears streamed her cheeks. Bella ran into those arms.

"Earth Child," Chloe whispered, as they hugged each other. "At last! At last!"

Bella whispered something in a strange language, but Chloe remembered and understood the strange words: in translation, '*Living Water*'.

"Oh, it's been so long!" Chloe said. "I never thought we'd meet up again. At the very best, perhaps a descendant of your papa, but you're here! Back with us! And even younger than before!"

Chloe held the child at arm's length to look again into her eyes, and she knew the child understood her. She could tell so much from the child's eyes, as it had been so many hundreds of years before in the canyons of the Mesa Verde.

"Bella knows you already?" Pepe asked.

"Yeah, we kinda know each other," Chloe said, smiling through her tears. With the back of her hand she lightly brushed away Bella's own tears from her little face. "We know each other very well!"

"Chloe?" Lee was standing behind her.

"Lee, this is my soulmate, Earth Child. Remember? The Mesa Verde?"

Lee, dumbfounded, looked on in silence as Chloe and Bella hugged each other again. He climbed back into the car and drove on ahead as Chloe walked back with the children, holding one of Bella's small hands whilst Pepe held the other.

"Oh, this is so weird, you still a child, even younger, and me a grown woman!"

And the small child smiled up at her.

Adam stood at the head of the drive.

"Pepe knew you were about to appear from around the bend, as always," he said, giving his sister a kiss. "Are you okay? Lee told us about that business with Rose Barefoot. And did you see Art? It has to be the real Art this time."

Chloe just shook her head. She raised Bella's hand up.

"This child changes everything, Adam. Didn't you recognise her?"

"Bella?"

Adam looked away for a moment.

"Adam, she's Earth Child. Surely you can see that?"

"Of course I can! But María and I are gonna give her a new life here. For Pepe."

"Pepe?"

"I'll tell you later, sis. Now, how about this Rose Barefoot business, huh?"

"Forget that! Her eyes, Adam. Her soul. It's Earth Child. And she recognised me straightaway. Called me 'Living Water'."

"But Art... was he there? In Phoenix?"

"Both of them. And they *were* the Hero Twins. I know it now. The real Art and Jeannie. He tried to tell me about Earth Child, but I was too uptight to pick up on the vibes. He killed the coyote, the last descendant of Coyote Spirit. The one programmed to destroy Pepe, the son of the only woman Coyote Spirit ever loved and his rival, Leaping Jaguar." Chloe paused and looked at her brother. "Or should I say, the Golden Jaguar of the Sun?"

"Just Adam Winters, please," was the man's terse reply.

"Maybe Pepe is more special than any of us can ever really know," continued Chloe. "Now, I can see what Art was trying to tell me. It was Earth Child whom this particular coyote really wanted to get to. He must have known all about her. Known how special she is, too."

Adam glanced at Pepe.

"You should have seen Papa kill that giant spider, Aunt Chloe," the boy said. "It was so cool!"

Adam laughed.

"No more giant spiders, son. Not for me, anyways."

They walked together into the house. María appeared from the kitchen and embraced Chloe.

"Thank you for taking in Earth Child," Chloe said to her sister-in-law.

"I wasn't sure whether Adam should have told you first," María said. "And Bella said nothing about knowing us. I could hardly wait for you to get back. I was so excited for you. You know, but for you two, I'd never have gotten back from the ancient mesas. And who knows what would've have happened to the history of North America under—" María glanced anxiously at her husband.

"Under King Coyote and Queen Eagle Spirit?" he suggested. She laughed nervously, and he gave her a playful slap on the bottom.

"Has Mama been naughty?" Carla asked.

"Nope! Papa was naughty for ever doubting Mama. Back then."

"Back when?" asked Carla.

"Our first time," her father replied. "Mama and me."

"There *was* one thing," Chloe cut in. "On the plane. By the runway. I saw a coyote. It was looking up at me. At least I thought it was."

Adam placed his arm affectionately around Chloe.

"Little sister, I do believe you're over-reacting! Plenty of coyotes around in Arizona. Why shouldn't one look up at a passing airplane?"

"It's just something Art said. About the golden bullets. He said—" Chloe caught sight of Bella—Earth Child—looking up at her.

"Nothing,' she added. "You're right. It was only a coyote. *Any* old coyote."

Chloe glanced at Lee.

"Well, husband, we can't stand around yakking all day! We've got a movie to get on with."

"But, Chloe, I thought you said—"

"Moving to Texas? Yeah! Sure thing. We're moving to Texas, Adam. Like as soon as we can find a house nearby."

"Hooray!" shouted Pepe.

"Build one here. On our land. Rent a place on the edge of town till it's built. With Maria's next album coming out in the fall, we could build you a palace!"

"Oh Chloe, please do!" María said. "Come and live here. The children would love it, and I'll always be around if you and Lee have to go off filming any time. I can look after the twins."

"Build a film studio, if you wish," added Adam. Chloe's eyes popped wide open.

"Can we?" she asked. Lee looked puzzled.

"But Chloe, just then, in the car, you were saying—"

"Oh, that was then. Now we've got Earth Child to help us, honey. Wow, I feel stronger already."

And the little Mayan girl never stopped smiling at Chloe.

Epilogue

"Why should anyone now fear the coyote?" asked the priest. "After all, the boy child is not his."

He turned to face the man in a suit.

"As for your granddaughter, don't worry so much. She has her guardian angels to protect her. Besides, they can reach their healing arms right back into your peoples' past."

"But not their future," the other pointed out.

"No, not anyone's future. That will be up to Him. And the daughter of Earth Mother."

"And Mankind," added the scientist.

Then they waited in that place where past, present and future spin forever like a tornado without wind...

***

Chloe walked to the top of the drive of their house. She knew the car was coming. Lee sat, working, in his study and the twins were at school. How grown up they now were, she thought. Adam's kids, as well. Pepe was almost a young man, and Bella, a beautiful young woman. They were the brightest kids the school had ever known and always seemed to come joint top of the class, but with no rivalry between them. Only love.

There was already much talk about the extraordinary son of the famous María López. The media would, sooner or later, latch onto anything out of the ordinary, and Pepe and Bella, and the love that grew from their friendship over the years, was far from ordinary. Yet still no one, not even Adam, María nor Chloe knew how far.

The backward changes in the American constitution wrought by the extremist Republican government, the crumbling structures of governments across the world and the lack of international cooperation gave Chloe's and Lee's documentary more credence. Whilst Rose Barefoot's murder had, for a while, helped the Native American cause, there was a harsh backlash from White Supremacists. This brought the spirit of the Red People into public focus at a time when the whole world was looking for answers to questions no one had dared to ask before. The world had changed, and was continuing to do so, fast... as also predicted in the ancient prophecy.

The red Austin-Healey stopped at the head of the drive. Jeannie came running up to Chloe and gave her a warm hug.

"My, you're still as pretty as ever," she said to Chloe. "And is Lee still his handsome old self too, huh?"

"Lee's just fine, Jeannie. So good to see you both again. My God, you two haven't changed one little bit."

"Change? Wouldn't know how to do that — apart from being a giant condor just once more. I did love swooping about up there in Xibalba."

"Honey, I was real proud of what you did back then. Saving his mother," said Art, also giving Chloe a hug. "And how is *she*, by the way?"

They started to walk slowly towards the house.

"*She's* quite a young lady, now."

"You think she and Pepe will — you know, when the time comes?"

"Sure of it, Art!"

"And Adam and María?"

"Couldn't be happier. Thanks to you two!"

"Remember, it's us who have to thank them. If it wasn't for their love, the Golden Jaguar would still be roaming the *Forest Without Time*, terrorising humans in parallel worlds when called to those temples of death. You know, it was Earth Mother who told me about that love of theirs, and the power of that love, after Adam turned up in Tenochtitlan searching for María. She always knew how special that sister-in-law of yours was. In providing a son who would someday give her own daughter on Earth a child. A very special child."

Art looked at the golden locket around Chloe's neck. Chloe touched the locket, peering at it.

"I still wear it all the time," she said. "It really belongs to Earth Mother's child now. I gave it to her, but Bella says I can carry on wearing it for the time being. 'Just in case', she says. But I'll give it back to her when she and Pepe get married. I think that would be the right thing to do, don't you?"

Art laughed.

"You asking me the right thing to do? Ain't no need for that. Guess you knew all along, huh? About the rest of the prophecy?"

"Only knew there was more to it. You see, Earth Child told me about us meeting up again one day — that's what made me so determined with all that searching when I made poor Lee sick with worry."

"So, it was her you were seeking all that time, not her father's descendants?"

Chloe nodded.

"Yeah, it was Earth Child. Deep down I knew."

"And you knew María was still in the rest of the prophecy."

"Sure, I knew that too."

"And her son? Pepe?"

Chloe went quiet.

"He doesn't know. Not in that way. He knows he'll become a leader, of course, and not a political leader as María once feared."

"Has Earth Child taken on their religion?"

Chloe nodded again.

"Like it was foretold, then," said Art. "And she'll know all about it from that book María keeps readin'. The Holy Bible?"

"The Book of Revelation?"

"Well, she'll know all of that, won't she? And through Bella, he'll know all about the old prophecies of the Red Man and about the peoples of the world coming together?

Through love, huh? To save Earth Mother's domain from annihilation?"

"We don't talk about it."

"No need to do that, Chloe. It's not the talkin' that matters. But just one more thing. Does María know?"

"Again, we never speak of it. But every mother knows her own son. Right?"

Art laughed.

"Of course! You'd know that without askin' her. So, from Beast to God, ay?"

"What do you mean?"

"Because of your sister-in-law, I and the beast I created for Tezcatlipoca not only changed, but through your nephew and the girl he rescued, another being will become God again."

"When?"

"See who's still in charge of your blessed country? Has to be soon. As soon as the child is old enough."

The Author

After Oliver Eade woke up one night with a ghost story in his head, he took to writing short stories, several winning prizes. During a visit to his Chinese wife's mother country in 2006, he became interested in Chinese mythology, thus inspiring his first middle grade readers' novel, *Moon Rabbit*. A winner of the Writers' and Artists' 2007 New Novel Competition and long-listed for the Waterstone's Children's Book Prize, 2008, this was followed by its sequel, *Monkey King's Revenge*, a People's Book Prize finalist, plus eight other novels, three of which are also for young adults and two for adults. One of these, *A Single Petal*, is set in ancient China and won the 2012 Local Legend Spiritual Writing Competition. A collection of adult short stories, *Lost Whispers and Other Stories*, was also published in 2012.

Although not constrained by any particular genre or style, Oliver feels most comfortable in that magical space between reality and fantasy; the space into and out of which children slip so easily in their play; the place of dreams, myths and legends and deeply ingrained in diverse cultures across the globe; the magical realism of Latin American writers like Gabriel García Márquez and Isabel Allende in her young adult novels.

The *Beast to God Trilogy* was inspired by Native North American and Mesoamerican beliefs. Oliver lived and worked as a doctor for a year in Vermont, USA, and his son and two half-Spanish eldest granddaughters now live in Houston, Texas where the trilogy is set.

Website: *www.olivereadebooks.org*
Blogs:
http://olivereade.blogspot.co.uk/
http://runawaywheeliebin.blogspot.co.uk/
http://childrenaswriters.blogspot.co.uk/

Contact: *olivereade@googlemail.com*

Novels by Oliver Eade, most also available as e-books:

For middle grade readers:
Moon Rabbit: Stevie Scott from Peebles, Scotland befriends Maisie Wu, a new classmate from China, when she when she gets teased for being different. Early one morning, he takes her to the river to see some ducklings, she falls into the water, can't swim and he dives in to rescue her. They emerge in mythological China and must undertake a perilous mission before they can get back Peebles. A fun introduction to mythical Chinese beasts and legends.
Monkey King's Revenge: Sequel to *Moon Rabbit* (available as print book only). Stevie and friends from Peebles High School must get back to mythological China to rescue Maisie from the Monkey King after he kidnaps her out of revenge.
Northwards: a brave young girl from Texas is called by Earth Mother to the High Arctic to save the world from a terrible evil.
The Rainbow Animal: Rachel takes her pet hamster for a birthday ride on a strange-looking animal at a local Texan mall carousel only to end up embroiled in a paint war between the funny little Colorwallies and Dullabillies.

For young adults:
The Terminus: Oliver's debut young adult novel, returns to the city in which he was brought up; a city now changed beyond recognition from the drab post-Word War II era and which, in a post-apocalyptic world, gives Mankind a second chance.

The Kelpie's Eyes: Scottish Borders sisters, Caitlin and Rhona, are transported, through a famous waterfall taken over by a kelpie, The Grey Mare's Tail, to a fairy-tale land consumed by evil, and to the backstreets of Victorian Glasgow, in a tale of sisterly love and rivalry. Won first prize in 2018 Words for the Wounded Young Adult Novel Competition.

Golden Jaguar of the Sun: First novel of *From Beast to God* Trilogy. Spanning the USA and Mexico, from an ancient Aztec sacrificial temple via modern drug cartels to the Mayan Place of the Dead, Xibalba, this is a story of cross-cultural first love and its dangers.

The Merging: Second novel of *From Beast to God Trilogy*. Transported to the Anasazi communities of ancient Colorado, the young Texan learns who his greatest enemy really is but gets no closer to discovering why his Mexican girlfriend is so special. A continuing story of young love with its challenges and uncertainties against a backdrop of merging cultures and beliefs.

For adults:

A Single Petal: A widowed village teacher in Tang Dynasty China links the death of his merchant friend with the disappearances of local Miao girls, endangering himself and his daughter as he digs more deeply into the mystery. Winner of Local Legend 2012 Spiritual Writing Competition

Voices: A story of murder, family love and turmoil set in London.

The Parth Path: In a post-apocalyptic Scotland, run by women, for women, a young man escapes with a beautiful 'clonie', unaware that this has all been planned as part of the parthenogenesis programme.

Walls of Words: A collection of short stories inspired by travels across the globe.

Stories for Children Ages 7 to 77: Collection of fun stories appropriate for all ages, illustrated by the writer's nine-year-old granddaughter.

Plays:

The Gap: Staged in Scotland 2012, a one act surreal comedy about a dysfunctional Peacehaven family split apart when the earth divides into two along the Greenwich Meridian. Short-listed for the Rowan Tree One Act Play competition, 2009.

Pool Britannia: Full-length farce about British ex-pats sharing a condominium pool with locals in Turkey. Short-listed for the Sussex Playwrights' 80th Anniversary Competition, 2014.

Give the Dog a Bone & The Other Nathan: One act black comedies, both long-listed for the British Theatre Challenge, 2015.

The Other Cat: Surreal black comedy take on the physics of quantum realities: was she or was she not killed? Winner of the 2018 Segora International One Act Play Competition.

For other Silver Quill Publishing books for young adults, adults and young readers, visit:
www.silverquillpublishing.com